SAFE HOUSE

Safe House

CHRIS EWAN

faber and faber

First published in this edition in 2012
by Faber and Faber Limited
Bloomsbury House
74–77 Great Russell Street
London WC1B 3DA

Typeset by Faber and Faber Ltd.
Printed and bound by CPI Group (UK) Ltd, Croydon, CR0 4YY

A CIP record for this book
is available from the British Library

ISBN 978–0–571–29063–5

FSC
www.fsc.org
MIX
Paper from
responsible sources
FSC® C101712

This book would not exist without the support and advice of my brilliant agent, Vivien Green, my wonderful editors, Katherine Armstrong and Hope Dellon, and my beautiful wife, Jo, who lured me to the Isle of Man with wild claims about sunshine, and who I love all the more through the wind, rain, fog and snow.

A Note on the Isle of Man

The Isle of Man is located in the middle of the Irish Sea, roughly halfway between the Lake District and Northern Ireland. The island is self-governing, with its own parliament and laws, and an independent police force.

For a fortnight every late May into early June, the Isle of Man stages the TT (Tourist Trophy) motorbike time-trial races. Run on public roads, the 37.7 mile track makes for one of the most spectacular and perilous motorcycle races in the world, with leading competitors recording top speeds of over 200 mph and average lap speeds in excess of 131 mph.

The island is thirty-two miles long and fourteen miles wide and has a population of eighty thousand people, none of whom form the basis for any of the characters in this book.

I don't remember much about the accident. It happened too fast. Motorbike crashes usually do. Most of what I can remember is noise. A loud pop followed by a judder. The thud of the front forks collapsing. The squeal of the engine as the rear wheel kicked up and pitched me over the bars.

And I remember Lena's scream. The way her hands pinched my waist before slipping away. The crunch of our helmets colliding.

Or at least, I think I do . . .

Part One

Chapter One

The doctor was young. Too young. She looked pale and frazzled, as if really she was the one in need of hospital rest. The skin beneath her eyes was tinged purple and she gripped my chart with unsteady hands, studying it like the script of a play she was aiming to memorise. Her lips moved as she traced the words.

'You were in a motorbike accident.' She glanced up, her spectacle lenses magnifying her bloodshot eyes.

I pulled the oxygen mask away from my mouth. 'No kidding.'

'You suffered a loss of consciousness.'

I swallowed. My throat felt raw and bloated, as if something had been shoved down there while I was asleep – a breathing tube, maybe. 'How long?'

She glanced at a clock on the wall in the corner of the room. Made a note on my file. 'You were out for almost seven hours. Before you came round the first time.'

Seven hours. It must have been some shunt. Not my only one, by any means, but probably my biggest.

'The first time?' I asked.

'You don't remember?'

I eased my head from side to side on my pillow.

'That's OK. It's perfectly normal. I'm Dr Gaskell. We met ninety minutes ago. You were only awake for a brief spell.'

I racked my brain but nothing came up. My vision was

blurred, as if someone had smeared Vaseline on my eyeballs. I blinked and the room tilted to the right.

'Don't worry, I'm not offended. Short-term memory loss is pretty common with a traumatic head injury.'

'Traumatic?'

'Try to relax, Mr Hale. Sleep if you need to. There's plenty of time for you to discuss all this with the specialist in the morning.'

'Tell me now. Please.'

She frowned. Pushed her spectacles up on her nose.

'What's the problem?' I asked. 'Afraid I'll forget?'

She chewed her lip, like she was running through a debate with herself, but then she moved around the bed and freed the oxygen mask from my hands, settling it against my face. She plucked a penlight from the pocket of her white lab coat and shone it into my eyes.

'Is that uncomfortable?' she asked.

'Hurts.' My voice was muffled. My breath condensed on the inside of the mask.

'Your speech is a little slurred. Any dizziness? Blurred vision? Nausea?'

'All of those.'

She nodded. 'You'll be in hospital for a few days, at least. You've already had a CT scan but you may need an MRI, too. We have to watch for any secondary swelling. But that's OK. It gives us time to treat your other injuries.'

The dimly lit room was growing dark from behind her, shadows bleeding in from the corners of my vision. I tried pushing myself up in bed, but someone stabbed me in the back and I groaned and crumpled.

'Careful. Your left scapula is fractured.' She placed her hands on my arm to stop me moving again. 'Not a serious break. Barely a hairline crack. But it'll take some healing. A nurse will be in soon to put your arm in a sling.'

I rolled my head to the side and saw the bandages that had been wrapped around my chest, under my armpit and over my collarbone. A fractured shoulder. It could be weeks until I had full movement. Months before I'd be able to lift heavy objects again. I was afraid of what that might mean for my business. There aren't many one-armed heating engineers around. The impact on my road-racing season was likely to be much worse. Chances were, it was over before it had begun.

'You've also bruised a couple of ribs,' she said. 'But other than that, you've been fortunate. You have some minor abrasions on your left side and bruising on your leg, but your pelvis, knees, ankles and feet are intact. And no broken fingers, miraculously. I've seen worse.'

I wasn't sure I believed her. My face must have given me away.

'I might be a junior doctor, Mr Hale, but this is the Isle of Man. I've had to treat more than my fair share of motorbike accidents, trust me.'

There was disapproval in her tone, but she was too young for it to carry much impact. Especially with a guy who was just barely awake.

'And Lena?' I asked. 'How's she doing?'

Dr Gaskell's eyebrows forked above her spectacles. She squinted, as if she didn't trust her hearing.

And I thought *I* was the one with the brain injury.

'Lena,' I said. 'My friend. She was in the first ambulance.'

7

That was something I could definitely remember. Hard not to, really. Splayed on the side of the road, my head propped against the grass bank running alongside the cold, damp tarmac, my left arm bent awkwardly beneath me. I didn't know how long I'd been out, but I'd come round to a sideways view of the pitted blacktop and the wet, gloomy clouds pressing down from above.

A paramedic in a green jumpsuit appeared. He crouched and flipped up what remained of my helmet visor.

I struggled to move, but my arms and legs were numb. I told myself not to panic. That it was only the shock.

'You'll be OK,' the paramedic said. He had close-cropped hair and a fuzzy soul-patch beneath his lower lip. The facial hair didn't suit him but I wasn't about to say as much. 'There's another ambulance on the way. But the girl is hurt worse. We have to take her first. Understand?'

I wheezed back at him. Trying to say that was fine. That it was the right thing to do. But I couldn't speak.

The paramedic squeezed my gloved hand and something snagged against the skin of my wrist. He paced away. I heard a door close. Then I glimpsed a blur of white as the ambulance sped off up the road, abandoning me to a sickly silence that faded to grey, then black.

Next thing I knew, I was talking with Dr Gaskell. She looked troubled now. She bit down on her lip. Glanced over her shoulder towards the door.

'Let me find out for you,' she said.

I watched her go, a hard lump forming in my chest. Dead, I thought. Please, don't let her be dead.

It was typical. Just when I wanted it to, the blackness wouldn't come. I was groggy but awake. And scared half out of my mind.

Lena.

My friend, I'd called her. But was she even that? She was more than a customer, I supposed. Someone I'd liked? Without question. But how long had I really known her? An hour? Two? Long enough to know there was an attraction, at least.

And what did that make it when I'd taken her out on my bike? A first date?

She'd seemed so animated when we'd ridden along the dirt track that led away from the cottage. So alive. Slapping me on the back and giggling as I accelerated beneath the rain-drenched trees. As if it was more than a trip for her. Like it was an escape, maybe.

The door to my hospital room swung open and a lanky doctor hurried inside, the tails of his white coat flapping behind him. Dr Gaskell was struggling to keep up, looking paler and more lost than ever.

'Mr Hale, I'm Dr Stanley.'

He clicked on a penlight and pointed the beam into my eyes. It seemed a popular thing to do. I tried to snatch my head away but he had a firm grip of my eyelid with his thumb. He didn't let go until he'd exhaled stale coffee across my face.

'You've suffered a traumatic brain injury.' He straightened and scratched at the stubble on his jaw. 'Blunt trauma to the frontal lobe.'

I pulled my mask free. 'So I've been told.'

'You can expect any number of side effects. Headaches. Dizziness. Nausea.'

'We've been through this already.'

'And confused thinking, Mr Hale. Cognitive disruption.'

He stared at me, as if his words should penetrate in a particular way. As if there was a secret message lurking behind them.

'I get it,' I said. 'There are consequences. But what about Lena? She's not dead, is she?'

Somehow, I managed to get the question out. I could feel more than just the soreness in the back of my throat.

'This Lena. You say she was on the motorbike with you? That she was involved in the accident?'

'She was in the first ambulance. But it's OK – I know her injuries were more serious. The paramedic told me.'

Dr Stanley let go of a long breath. His shoulders sagged. 'But that's exactly my point, Mr Hale. The fact is there was no other ambulance. You were the only one found at the scene of the crash.'

Chapter Two

My parents were sitting with me when the police arrived the following day.

I'd spent most of the morning with Dad's palm clamped over my lower leg and with Mum gripping my hand. It was good of them to come but I wished more than anything that I wasn't putting them through this right now. The past few weeks had been rough on all of us and I knew they could have done without the added worry. It wasn't as if they'd been getting their lives back together – in truth, I doubted they'd ever be capable of that – but I'd begun to sense a fragile new balance emerging. A way forward for us all, maybe. And now I'd gone and upset whatever shaky foundations we'd started to lay.

Family friends had told me how well my parents were doing. That time would heal. Things would improve. But I saw it differently. It was obvious to me that a light had gone out of them. They bore the loss in their eyes most of all, and when they met my gaze straight on, which wasn't often any more, it was like looking at precious stones that had been worn down until there was no glimmer left. Their pupils were dull and flat. Letting nothing inside.

Maybe the change wouldn't have been so hard to take if their spark hadn't been so bright before. Cheesy as it sounds, my parents were a living, breathing romance novel. Mum, the vibrant, red-haired Scouse girl, who'd ignored her father's wishes at the age of nineteen to take up with a strange Manxman on a windswept rock in the middle of the Irish Sea. And not just any strange Manxman, but one with a death wish – a daredevil motorbike racer who'd won the Senior TT two years on the bounce. A guy who liked a drink. Liked a girl. Who lived his life at speed. Or at least, he did until he fell headlong in love with the woman he'd now been married to for the best part of forty years.

Grandpa had disowned my parents in the early stages of their marriage. Nowadays, he lived with them in Snaefell View, the residential care home they own and manage, and he couldn't have a kinder word to say about my father if you handed him a thesaurus and a magnifying glass. I live there too, in a converted barn out back, with a garage on the side where Dad and I can strip down and rebuild my racing bikes. Amazing, really, that we'd become this perfect, *Waltons*-style unit. Maybe that was why we'd suffered so much just recently. Cosmic payback.

The police entered my room shortly before noon. There were two of them, a man and a woman, both wearing dark suits.

The man had an engorged head that was shaped like a pumpkin, a swollen, ruddy face and a generous belly. His grey hair was grown long over his ears and at the back of his wide neck. A navy-blue tie was knotted carelessly around his collar, like he resented it being there.

The woman was younger, mid-to-late forties, with fine black hair cut short in a boyish style, no make-up, and a biro stain on the front of her faded blue blouse. Lean and angular, her movements had a gawky, abrupt quality. She carried a can of diet coke in one hand, a black raincoat folded over her arm.

Dad knew them, of course. He knows everyone on the island.

Or everyone knows him. I'm never sure which way round it should be. But the last time they'd spoken hadn't been at some friendly get-together in a local pub, or at a Rotary dinner, and it showed. My father was slow in standing to accept the hand the man offered him, as if touching it might come at a price.

'Jimmy.' The man used the sombre tone of voice people had chosen to adopt with Dad just recently. 'Sorry to see you back here.' He spoke in a calm, measured way, like so many Manxmen of his generation. It was an easy quirk to misinterpret. Slow words for a slow thinker, you might imagine. And more often than not, you'd be wrong.

He snuck a look at me. His crimson cheeks were puffed up, reducing his deep-set eyes to slits. It made it hard to read his expression. But there was something accusing back there.

'Mick.' Dad accepted his palm, pressing his free hand over the top, like a politician. 'And Jackie.' He stretched over my bed to pull the same move with the woman.

'Mr Hale.' She dropped Dad's hand like a contagious disease. 'And Mrs Hale. How are you?'

I swear I could almost see the shutters flip closed across Mum's eyes.

'I'm fine,' she replied, tight-lipped. 'Thank you for asking, Detective Sergeant Teare.' She found her feet now, but she was sluggish. Even standing up, she looked as if she was slowly deflating. 'And Detective Inspector Shimmin. How's Jude?'

'Fine, fine,' Pumpkin-head said, but he was watching me the entire time. 'Took a fair old bump on the skull there, hey Robbie?'

Talking like we'd met before. Like we were old friends.

'Need to speak with you about this accident of yours. Now a good time?'

As if I had any choice in the matter.

'We'll stay too,' Dad said, clenching my foot through the bed covers.

Pumpkin-head sucked air through his teeth and rose up on his toes, like a mechanic about to deliver unwanted news about a cooked engine. 'Afraid we're going to need to speak with the boy alone, Jimmy.'

The boy. Like I was some kind of troublesome teen all set for a dressing-down.

'But if it's just a chat, Mick.' Dad tilted his head to one side. 'No harm us staying, is there?'

Shimmin was easily a foot taller than my father, and this time, when he drew a sharp breath through his teeth, he rocked back on his heels, as if he was afraid of accidentally inhaling him. I'm tall myself, six feet two in my socks, so I understand the feeling of authority a little extra height can give a man. And Dad was shorter than he should have been, the result of the metal plates and pins that had once been used to knit the shattered bones of his lower legs back together. His racing career had been ended by a horrific crash along the Mountain section of the TT course, when he was cruising at well over 100 mph. He was lucky the incident hadn't claimed his life.

'No can do, Jimmy. Procedure, see?' Shimmin shook his bloated head, as if he was powerless to concede the point, even to a man as remarkable as my father. 'How about you take Tess downstairs for one of those fancy coffees? We'll come and find you when we're finished. Won't be long.'

Dad was all set to try again. I could feel it in the tightening

14

of his fingers on my toes. He was used to getting special treatment on the island. The best table in a restaurant. A handsome discount in a shop. A forgiving smile when he parked on double yellow lines. It was the outcome of a combination of factors. His reputation as a local sporting legend. The swagger that came from riding away from certain death. And I don't suppose it hurt that he was handsome. Square jaw. High forehead. Unruly, tousled hair. A powerful, muscular physique, gone a little soft in later years.

'It's OK, Dad,' I said. 'It's not as if I have anything to hide.'

My father looked at me then, a broken expression on his slackened face. Mum reached for his arm. The ghost of a smile I hadn't seen in a long time tugged at her lips.

'Come on, Jim. Let them ask their questions. Rob will still be here when we get back. Right love?'

'Yeah, Mum. I'll be here.'

But it still scared me that she'd felt the need to ask.

*

'Now then Robbie, why don't you tell us about this mystery blonde of yours?'

Pumpkin-head had taken my father's seat. He was reclined with his hands behind his fat neck and his crossed heels resting on the end of my bed.

'It's Robert,' I said.

'Eh?'

'Or Rob. Not Robbie. I might be Jimmy Hale's son, but I have my own identity. Some people respect that.'

Shimmin let go of a low whistle and glanced over his

shoulder towards his colleague. Teare had taken up a position with her back against the wall, one leg bent at the knee, the sole of her shoe marking the beige paint. She took a long pull on her Coke, tapping an unpainted nail on the aluminium casing.

'Chip on the shoulder there, young Robbie?' Shimmin asked.

I rocked my head to the right, feeling the pull of the foam sling that had been wrapped around my neck and left wrist. There was a small porthole of glass in the door to my room, but all I could see on the other side was more beige.

'Hey fella, come on. I'm a friend of your father's, see?'

They were all friends of my father. Or so they told themselves.

'And I know you and he are different.' Shimmin snapped his fingers and I turned to find a dark shimmering in the pouched slits where his eyes lurked. 'Anyone who's watched you race these past three years can tell that easily enough, eh? Guess the acorn fell further from the tree than maybe you'd like to believe, young Robbie. Or maybe you remember it differently. Something else caused by that crack on your noggin.'

The blow to my head was something the neurologist had already discussed with me. I'd been fortunate, apparently. Early tests indicated there was no secondary swelling and the chances of it developing were said to be slim. I'd need to undergo more tests in a week or so, and watch for anything out of the ordinary – mood swings, difficulty keeping my balance, a change in my sleep patterns. I also had to take care to avoid any follow-up blows until the bruising had healed. But all things considered, it could have been worse.

'So come on, lad.' Shimmin tugged the knot of his tie away

from his yellowing collar. 'Tell us what you told the good doctors.'

Chapter Three

When I'd first picked the message up on my answer-machine, I'd wondered if it could be a hoax. It wasn't every day I was called to a job in the middle of a plantation, and the customer hadn't left a number. Then I'd spoken to Dad and he'd told me there used to be a Forestry Board cottage in the woods. Rumour was it had been sold to a private buyer a decade or so ago. I guessed that had to be the foreign-sounding man who'd phoned me, and since I could use the distraction, I decided to check it out.

A closed wooden gate blocked the entrance to the woods, beside a sign that read Arrasey Plantation. The gate was secured with a rusted metal chain and a shiny combination lock. The locked gate didn't strike me as unusual. Access is restricted to a lot of the island's plantations to prevent people tearing through them on off-road bikes. There are ways around that, of course, but none of them apply when you're driving a panel van.

I climbed down out of my van into the falling rain, leaving my dog, Rocky, to watch me from the warmth of the front bench. I dialled in the combination the customer had left on my machine and the lock came free in my hands. I wrapped the chain around the gate post, taking a moment to clear the beads of water from a laminated flyer that had been nailed to it.

Please help us to find Chester. Missing 5 April in this plantation.

There was a telephone number to call and a photograph of a scrawny-looking terrier with a blue collar. The dog's pink tongue was hanging out the side of his mouth, eyes squinting against bright sunshine. I hated seeing posters like this. Fifth April. Almost a month had passed but I couldn't help peering out the misted windows of the van, hoping for some glimpse of poor Chester as we drove slowly up the rutted track.

If he was out here somewhere, the weather wasn't being kind to him. A chill, grey fog was hanging low over the tops of the spruce, larch and pine trees, and the rain was faint but persistent. The narrow path curved steeply to the right and the van wheels slipped on greasy stones and mud. A smell of wet, rotting vegetation came in through the crack in my window, and as the trees pressed in around us, branches scratching along the sides of the van, Rocky turned to me with a doleful look in his nut-brown eyes that seemed to ask just what crazy adventure I'd taken us on this time.

Rocky is a pedigree golden retriever. He weighs somewhere between thirty and thirty-five kilograms, depending on which phase of his diet cycle we're currently disagreeing on, and I'm yet to find anything besides asparagus that he isn't prepared to eat. And that includes furniture, soft furnishings and van interiors. The passenger bench he was squatting on was a case in point. The vinyl upholstery had passed through his digestive system some months back now, and I didn't doubt that he had plans to chow down on the yellow foam in the not too distant future. Rocky didn't just eat me out of house and home. He ate *through* my home. But I loved him more than most things in life, and he loved me back with a force and loyalty that was beyond anything I could readily explain.

'What?' I asked him. 'You don't think this is a good idea?'

Rocky threw his head back and considered me with plaintive eyes that seemed to expect something more. I ruffled the hairs of his neck.

'They might have cake, right? Wouldn't that make this worthwhile?'

He blinked at me and parted his jaws in what I like to call his toothy-smile. It's one of his key moves. Believe me, it always slays the ladies.

We were up on a rise by now, the ground falling away sharply on our left. I looked down over the sodden gorse and treetops at a scattering of fields that sloped towards a valley stream, a collection of ramshackle farm buildings and the ruins of an old tin mine. In the distance, the swell of South Barrule hill was shrouded in the watery mist, the brake lights of a passing car shining like sea beacons.

The narrow track forked in three directions and I followed the middle path, plunging deeper into the tree cover. Water ticked off the pine needles, exploding against the windscreen, and the van pitched and rolled from side to side. A stringy grass had grown up in the middle of the path, leaving two thin bands of earth for me to follow.

The woods were dense all around and so black that I couldn't see into them for more than a few feet. The ground was knotted with fallen branches, brush and a thick brown carpet of dried pine needles and mulch. If little Chester had come this far on his own, he'd have scared himself half to death.

Ahead was another gate, open this time. A rectangle of glistening slate had been fixed to the post, two words etched into it in startling white. *Yn Dorraghys*. My grasp of Manx

Gaelic is only basic, but this was one phrase I recognised. *The Darkness*.

Fitting.

The track petered out after another twenty feet and I swung the van around in a boggy turning circle, beaching it alongside a bank of brambles and a red Nissan Micra. The wheel arches and side panels of the Micra were splattered with mud and I could see an Avis rental sticker in the rear window.

I dropped out of my van on to the marshy soil, closed the door on Rocky and paced through the rain with my vinyl clipboard in my hand.

The property was a tumbledown cottage with a sloping slate roof, clotted with moss. The once white walls were leaning towards shades of green, as if they were soaking the moisture out of the foliage that surrounded the place. Tufts of grass blocked the gutters and a collection of wonky shutters had been thrown back from the aged sash windows. A small lawn lay to one side. The grass was as high as my knees and knotted with thorns.

The black front door opened before I could knock and a swarthy man in light denim jeans and a green turtleneck sweater filled the void. He had lank, shoulder-length brown hair, and he was wearing wraparound sunglasses, the type with mirrored lenses. The sunglasses were an odd choice, considering the dreary conditions beneath the tall forest trees. He clutched a mobile phone.

The man leaned sideways and looked over my shoulder at the stencil work on my van. It was brief and to the point. *Manx Heating Solutions and Repairs*, followed by the numbers for my mobile and landline.

'You are heating man?' His accent was hard and clipped,

making me think he was from somewhere in northern Europe, possibly Germany. He sounded like the guy who'd left me the message, only more cautious. I get that all the time. Too many people have heard horror stories about cowboy tradesmen.

'Name's Rob.' I switched my clipboard in my hands and held my palm out to him through the rain.

He seemed not to notice. He was still looking past me, like he was trying to see inside my van.

'It's just my dog in there,' I told him. 'He's the brains of the operation.'

The man half-nodded. 'The hot water. It break.'

'So I understand.' I left my hand out for a moment longer before giving up and drying it on the backside of my work trousers. 'Where's your boiler?'

He pointed with his phone at a built-in garage to the side of the property. There was a high up-and-over door with a turn handle in the middle. It had fluted metal panels. The white paint was flaking.

'Is it open?' I asked.

The man delved inside the pocket of his jeans and threw me a key on a red plastic fob. 'I turn lights on for you.'

He stepped back, as if to shut the front door.

'Wait. Have you checked your oil?'

He just looked at me. It was hard to gauge his reaction from behind his sunglasses.

'Your oil tank,' I said. 'Is there any fuel in it?'

'I do not know. You can check this too.'

*

I grabbed my torch from the van and let Rocky out, and then the two of us ran through the slanted rain in search of the oil tank. We found it hidden in the tall grass behind the garage and I checked for fuel. By the time I'd screwed the lid back on the tank, we were both pretty wet. I ran back to the van for my tools and a towel. Then I unlocked the garage door and heaved it upright.

Mr Shades had been as good as his word. The lights were on. Two fluorescent tubes were humming and flickering above my head. Over to the far left was a plain internal door that would connect with the cottage. A pull cord was suspended from the ceiling alongside it.

I stepped inside and rubbed my hair, hands and face with the towel while Rocky shook himself dry. Normally, I'd have laid the towel down and made Rocky clean his paws, but really there was no point. The floor was bare, unpolished concrete and the walls were unfinished breezeblocks. There were no stacked boxes of belongings. No pushbikes or garden equipment. There was no sturdy workbench or pegboard of household tools or any of the customary junk you might expect to find in most garages. There was just a run of white laminate shelving units fitted against the wall on my left, all of them empty, and a combination boiler located near an immersion tank in the right-hand corner of the room.

The boiler was one hell of an old thing. I already knew it was going to be a crappy job before I removed the front panel and what I found inside didn't disappoint. It looked as if it hadn't been serviced in decades.

I ran a few basic tests, checking the thermostat and the burner, but it didn't surprise me that a simple solution was out of the question. The best outcome in a situation like this is when the home owner agrees to buy a new boiler. It'll be more reliable, and more efficient, and compared to the maintenance costs of keeping an old system running, it'll pay for itself within five years. But something told me Mr Shades wouldn't be interested in any of that. The shabby state of the cottage didn't suggest that anyone was looking to spend money on home improvements. And the rental Nissan and the man's accent had made me think he was most likely a temporary guest. So unless he told me otherwise, I was going to focus on getting the hot water running again, leaving the sales pitch for another day.

Behind me, Rocky slumped on to the cement floor and lowered his head on to his forepaws. Then he whined like he could tell this wasn't going to be one of those jobs where a quick fix was followed by a long walk through the woods.

'Sorry, pal,' I said.

Rocky closed his eyes and rolled on to his side. So this is what my business partner was contributing to the situation. *Nap time.*

*

An hour later, the rain had settled into a hard patter and I'd managed to suck most of the crud out of the boiler with my vacuum cleaner. I also seemed to be wearing a lot of grease and dust and oil. That was when the side door to the cottage opened and an angel walked in.

Sickening, I know, but trust me, compared to Mr Shades, she was a huge improvement.

Her smile hit me first, and it was so unexpected that I almost dropped the socket wrench I was holding. *Wham*. Neat white teeth, full lips. She was blonde, the kind of light blonde that only comes from years of sunshine. She was tanned, too, a soft caramel tint that was like a rebuke to the cheerless rain. She had on a pink vest top, frayed beige corduroy trousers and flipflops.

Dainty, that was the first thought that came to my mind. I won't tell you the second.

Rocky stirred and sidled over to her. He leaned into her thigh and she tickled the back of his ear in that way that drives him happily nuts. *Oh, right*, I thought. You can sleep through an hour's worth of vacuuming, no problem, but the moment a stunning blonde enters the room, you're super-attentive.

'Ooh, you are so beautiful,' she said, and I recognised traces of the same European accent I'd heard from Mr Shades. 'And your ears are so soft. What is your name, handsome one?'

Rob, I wanted to tell her. And then I wanted to roll over on my back and have her tickle my tummy.

Rocky beat me to it.

'He's called Rocky,' I said, as she knelt down and circled her palm over his abdomen. 'And I think he likes you.'

She smiled and glanced up from beneath long, curling lashes. 'Would Rocky like some water, maybe?'

I had some in the cooler in my van. I knew it and Rocky knew it, too. But he looked at me like he'd crap in my bed if I said as much.

'That'd be nice,' I said.

'And you?' Her fine blonde hair had fallen across her face. She tucked it behind her ear. 'Would you like some tea? It's been some time since I made tea for an Englishman.'

Now true, I could have told her I was Manx, but I couldn't

see the harm in letting it slide. I nodded and she gave Rocky a last pat before straightening and turning for the door.

'Come,' she said. 'And bring Rocky, yes?'

The dog was gone before I'd cleaned my hands on an old rag. I knocked the worst of the dirt from my clothes, took off my work boots (trying to ignore the way my big toe was poking out of my sock) and made my way into the kitchen.

It was a cramped, dingy room, with small windows that were positioned too low in the walls. Rainwater sluiced down the glass. A bare ceiling bulb cast a weak light across the aged pine units and cheaply tiled countertop.

Rocky had his head down at a bowl in the corner, doing a good job of spilling its contents across the linoleum floor and acting as if this was the finest tap water he'd tasted in his entire life. The blonde was standing beside the sink, filling an earthenware mug from a steaming kettle. And at a round table in the middle of the room sat Mr Shades and a second man I hadn't seen before.

I was looking at the man from behind. He was big and muscular, with a shock of peroxide blonde hair and a colourful sleeve tattoo escaping the left cuff of his khaki T-shirt. The T-shirt was so tight he might as well have been wearing body paint. I got the impression the guy lifted weights and that he liked people to know it. The muscles of his lower neck and shoulders stood out as if someone had braided thick rope beneath his skin.

A photography book was open on the table before him. His head was bowed, hands covering his ears, his thick elbows propped on the tabletop. The page he was studying featured a black-and-white photograph of a pale, emaciated girl with a crescent-shaped collection of studs above her top lip.

Mr Shades was tapping at a laptop. The laptop was placed alongside his phone. It seemed he wasn't a complete idiot, because his sunglasses were now balanced on top of his head.

Neither of the men paid me any attention. I stood awkwardly in my socks, shifting my weight between my feet.

'Here is your tea.'

The blonde handed me the mug and I nodded my thanks, then took a sip and gave her a goofy thumbs-up.

'You like?'

'It's perfect.'

She gave me the dazzling smile again. 'You want if we go back to the garage?'

'Fine by me.' I gestured with my mug at the two men. 'Wouldn't want to interrupt anything.'

I led the way, taking a moment to step back into my boots and glancing towards the rain-splattered concrete at the threshold of the garage. I set my mug down on top of the boiler, picked up my spanner and dropped to my knees on a square of foam I'd laid on the ground.

'Can you fix it?' she asked, closing the door behind Rocky.

'Think so,' I said, over my shoulder. 'But I might have to get some parts. The stuff I have in my van probably won't fit.'

'How long will this take?'

'I should be able to pick the parts up in the morning. I'll be finished a few hours after that.'

Her face sagged and her lips tangled into a pout. 'So I will have another cold bath, I am thinking.'

'And what, using the immersion goes against your religion?'

She peered hard at me, through the glossy blonde strands that were hanging in front of her eyes.

'The immersion heater,' I explained. 'Here.' I straightened and reached my hand through some pipes and flipped a switch that was hidden down behind the boiler. An amber diode glowed brightly. The immersion tank hummed and burbled.

'*No*.'

'You didn't know?'

'Three days, we have no hot water.' She threw up her hands. 'I keep telling them to call somebody. And here, you fix it already.'

'Well, the main system's still broken. And it's expensive this way. So it's better if I can get the boiler working again.'

'I am so happy right now.'

She did a pirouette to prove it. It got Rocky excited. He jumped up and placed his forepaws on her thighs, as if he planned to lead her in a waltz around the garage.

'Rocky is *so* cute.' She kissed the top of his head. 'Are you always bringing him to your work?'

'Unless a customer complains.'

'But who would do such a thing?' She lifted his dopey face and blew him kisses.

'You'd be surprised. He's not always so well behaved.'

'I do not believe it.' She eased Rocky down to the ground, then thrust her hand towards me. 'My name is Lena.'

We shook in a strangely formal way.

'Rob. You here on holiday?'

She shrugged and plunged her hands into the pockets of her trousers.

'With friends?' I asked, pointing with my spanner in the direction of the kitchen.

'You can call them this, I suppose.'

'You don't sound too sure.'

She smiled flatly.

'They didn't exactly strike me as fun-loving types,' I suggested.

'No? Then what types are they?'

I weighed the spanner in my hand, as if I was mulling over the options. 'Honestly? They looked to me like the bad guys who die early in a Bruce Willis movie.'

She laughed hard, throwing her head and her hair right back. I liked the way it made me feel. A lot.

'And you?' she asked. 'Are you a fun-loving type?'

'I guess.'

She nodded towards the rain out in the clearing. 'And what is there to do here, on this Isle of Man, to have fun?'

I got the impression she didn't believe there was likely to be anything. As if she thought of the island as the smallest, most ridiculous place you could possibly imagine. Maybe she'd heard some of the local myths. Like how you had to say hello to the fairies if you were passing over the humped bridge on the way to Ballasalla, or risk a dose of bad luck. How no Manx person would dare to say the word 'rat', referring instead to 'long tails'. How the local cats, as if to compensate, had no tails to speak of.

'Depends,' I said. 'Ever been on a motorbike?'

Her chin snapped up, as if I'd got her interest all of a sudden.

'Or heard of the TT races?'

'What is this *TT*?'

'It's a road race. Happens every June. Timed laps. Each lap is over thirty-seven miles long. If you like, I could show you?'

'You have a motorbike?'

'Several. I race.'

She glanced down at Rocky, as if seeking his approval. 'We could do this tomorrow, maybe?'

'If you like, we could go after I fix the boiler.'

She checked over her shoulder, towards the door. Chewed the inside of her mouth. Then she stepped closer to me. So close that I could feel the heat coming off her body.

'I do not think they will like it,' she whispered.

'I wasn't offering them a ride.'

'No.' She was being serious now. Holding my eyes. 'They maybe would not like it if I go.'

'Oh. Well.' I hitched my shoulders. 'If you want to leave it ...'

She turned and peered out of the garage doorway, into the beating rain, almost as if she hadn't heard me at all. 'Your van,' she said. 'Is it possible – can you bring your motorbike inside it?'

'I suppose I can. But –'

'Then this is perfect.' She twirled and placed her hands on my shoulders. Blinded me with her smile again. 'Here is what you must do.'

Chapter Four

'You're saying she asked you to back your van up to the garage?' Detective Sergeant Teare asked. 'Why would she do that?'

'So the two guys she was with wouldn't see my bike. Her idea was, we could wheel it out of my van and get everything ready inside the garage. Then, when we were geared up in leathers and helmets, we could be out of there before they realised what was happening.'

'Sounds like a lot of effort.' Teare had left the wall and taken a seat on the other side of my bed from Shimmin. Close up, she looked older. Her skin was dried. Pocked and lined. I could see the white of her scalp through her thinning hair. 'How about your dog?'

'I left Rocky at home.'

She nodded, as if that made sense. 'Didn't it make you suspicious at all, the way this Lena was talking about the two men you say that you saw?'

'I did see them.'

She waved a hand. No rings on her fingers, I noticed. 'Point is, the things she asked you to do are pretty unusual, agreed?'

'I think she just wanted to get away without any hassle. Like telling them would cause some kind of argument.'

Teare watched me closely. Truth is, I suppose I *had* been curious about why Lena had wanted everything done in secret. But not enough to turn her down.

'What happened when you left?' Teare asked. 'These men come outside?'

'I didn't see them.'

'So you made it out of the plantation like Bonnie and Clyde. And then you had this crash of yours.'

This crash. As if the fact I was lying before her in a hospital bed was some kind of elaborate smokescreen.

'Want to tell us about that?' she asked.

'I told you. I don't remember the accident.'

She made a humming noise, unconvinced. 'Know where you were when they found you?'

'I heard it was the track leading to the Sloc.' The Sloc is the A road that skirts South Barrule hill and connects the middle of the island with the southern coast. I'd been planning to follow it in the opposite direction towards the village of Foxdale. I was going to pick up the TT course at the Ballacraine crossroads, a key spectator point when the races are on.

'Quiet road,' Teare said. 'Single-lane. Not much traffic about.'

'So what are you suggesting? I just fell off?'

'It's possible.'

'All right, Detective Sergeant. That's enough for now.' It was the first time Shimmin had spoken for some minutes. He removed his feet from the end of my bed. Rearranged his weight in his chair. 'Sounds to me like you're delusional, son.'

'I'm not making this up,' I said, looking between them. 'Why would I?'

'Hard to say.'

'You should be searching for Lena. What if she's in trouble? What if something happens to her while you're just sitting here?'

Teare seemed to be as interested in Shimmin's response as I was. I sensed I'd got to her, at least.

Shimmin was different. He rolled out his bottom lip and glanced down at a stain on the fat point of his tie. 'Any road traffic incident, Control always send out a response team.' He scratched absently at the stain with his nail. 'We did that yesterday. They didn't see anyone else. Been no reports from the public.'

'But the paramedic *spoke* to me,' I said. 'He told me they'd put her in an ambulance.'

Teare opened her mouth but Shimmin cut her off before she could speak. 'Control keep a record of every emergency response that comes in. Every team that goes out.' He looked up and considered me with those dark, deep-set eyes of his. 'Only one ambulance unit responded to your accident. And the only casualty they found was you.'

'That's not possible.'

'The facts say otherwise.'

'Maybe the paramedic was off duty. Maybe he was in his uniform because he'd finished his shift. Or he was on his way to work.'

Shimmin's fat head swivelled from side to side. Slow and easy. 'Even supposing it *was* possible, he wouldn't have had an ambulance with him. Besides which, there'd be a record of your girl being checked into A&E. There's nothing. You were the only RTA brought in yesterday, apart from a pensioner whose husband ran over her foot down in Port Erin.'

'What about other hospitals?'

He looked at me as if I was brain-damaged. Which, come to think of it, was a reasonable assumption.

'Only other hospital is in Ramsey,' he said slowly. He didn't need to mention that Nobles Hospital, where I was currently based, was a good twenty minutes closer to the scene of the accident. Or that Ramsey, up in the north of the island, was only used for minor surgery and outpatient care.

'So what are you saying? You don't believe me at all?'

Teare was considering her hands now. They were resting in her lap.

'Listen,' Shimmin said, 'we have a duty to explore every possibility.' And his tone suggested the responsibility was wearing heavily on him right now.

'But you don't believe me, do you?'

He sighed. 'Don't you think it's possible that the blow to your head, combined with the stress of recent events, might just mean that your mind is playing tricks on you?'

'*No.*'

'You're saying it's not possible at all?' Shimmin pressed. 'Despite all the evidence going against the things you've told us?'

'What about the evidence going *for* the things I've told you? What about the two men in the cottage? Shouldn't you be speaking to them? Or what about my van? You'll find it up there, you know.'

'You have a contact number for these men?'

'No,' I said, teeth clenched. 'I already told you. They didn't leave one on my machine.'

'You still have the message?'

'I deleted it. When I got home after my first day up there.'

Shimmin pushed himself up from his chair, shaking his head. He smoothed his shirt down over his belly. Fastened his jacket. 'Here's what's going to happen. As a personal favour to your dad, myself and DS Teare will take a drive out to this *spooky* house of yours. If these men are there, we'll speak with them, see what we can find out. See if there's anything that can help your story make even a shred of sense.' He slid the knot of his tie up to his collar, as if the distraction from the real police work of his day was finally over. 'And in the meantime, you can rest. See if any alternative explanations start to occur to you.'

*

I must have fallen asleep because I woke to the sound of somebody clearing their throat. A man was standing at the foot of my bed. He was wearing a colourful knitted sweater and an awkward smile.

'Robert?'

I blinked a few times.

'Sorry to wake you. My name's Donald. I'm an occupational therapist here at the hospital. Dr Stanley thought it might be a good idea if I came by to say hello.'

I wiped the back of my hand across my gummy lips, careful not to catch the plastic tube connecting my cannula to my drip.

'Sorry to wake you,' he said again.

Donald was clasping his hands together, like he was planning to recite a prayer. There was something of the vicar about him. His garish sweater could have been knitted by a well-meaning parishioner and he wore his hair in a conservative side parting. No dog collar, mind.

'Do you have time for a quick chat?'

I nodded towards one of the plastic chairs. 'Take a pew.'

He gazed at me for a long moment. Then he went ahead and

arranged himself in a sitting position, with one leg crossed at the thigh.

'How are you feeling?'

'I've been better.'

'In much pain?'

'Only when I breathe.'

He smoothed a hand over his side parting. 'And what about emotionally?'

'What about it?'

'Are you feeling a tad low, for instance?'

'Low?'

'Low, yes. Or upset, perhaps?'

'Upset,' I said, as if I was scanning my mind for any trace of the emotion. 'Nope. I'm good, Donald.'

'Well, that's great.'

'Isn't it?'

His smile was uncomfortable. Forced. He slid his hand inside his trouser pocket and removed a small notebook and pen like he was going for a concealed weapon.

'Look, what's this about?' I asked him. 'Why are you really down here?'

'As I said, Dr Stanley –'

'But I've already spoken with the neurologist. It didn't seem as if there was anything to worry about.'

'Possibly so.' Donald turned to a fresh page in his pad. Clicked the end of his pen. 'Your parents were also keen for someone from occupational therapy to speak with you.'

I didn't like that. Not one bit. Donald could sense it. He raised a palm.

'Just hear me out,' he said. 'I'm here to help, OK?'

'Not OK.'

'I have experience of working with people in your situation. I think you could find talking to me useful.'

'My situation?' I looked down at myself in bed. One arm in a sling. The other connected to a saline drip. Bandages wrapped around my torso. Plastic identity tags on my wrists. 'Are you talking about bikers? People who've been in accidents?'

'I'm talking about people who are grieving. People who've experienced traumatic events.'

'*Out*,' I told him.

'Robert, please.'

'Leave. *Now.*'

Donald squirmed in his seat. He clutched the notebook to his chest. But he didn't get up from his chair.

'They told me about the girl,' he said.

I turned my head away. Muttered under my breath.

'The one you say was in the accident with you.'

'She *was* in the accident.'

He was silent for a moment. But I knew there was more to come.

'Look, did the neurologist talk to you about some of the symptoms you might experience? He probably spoke to you about memory loss. Am I right?'

I stayed silent.

'Well, what he may not have mentioned is the possibility that your brain could also *create* memories. False ones. I've read papers on this, Robert. Patients who've suffered a brain injury, through no fault of their own, sometimes they can find it almost impossible to tell the difference between those things that have really happened to them and events they may simply have imagined or even dreamed.'

'So what are you suggesting? I made Lena up?'

'I'm not suggesting anything right now. All I'm saying is that there are cases where something similar has happened. And when you factor in the high degree of strain you've been under in recent weeks. The unexpected loss ...'

He let his words trail away, as if he was unsure where exactly they might lead him.

I felt a stinging in my eyes. Now, more than anything, I didn't want the tears to come. But they started to brim over, almost like they'd never been away.

'Out,' I told him, unable to hide the crack in my voice. 'Leave me alone, can't you?'

I heard the scuff of chair legs on the floor. The soft percussion of his shoes crossing the room. The stiff door hinge. The burble of corridor noise.

'I understand your sister was blonde, too,' Donald said, almost as an afterthought. 'Her name was Laura, wasn't it? Laura. Lena. I'm just saying – these things are possible, you know?'

Chapter Five

I was discharged from hospital the following day. There'd been talk of keeping me in longer, so the doctors could watch for any complications from my head injury. Then Mum explained about her background in nursing and the qualifications of the staff at the care home, and the hospital decided they could use the extra bed.

It was Dad who collected me. Mum sent him in with a pair of jogging trousers and training shoes with Velcro straps. It made dressing easy, although Dad had to help me into my shirt and readjust my sling. I didn't have too much difficulty walking, and while I felt a pinch in my chest when I inhaled deeply, I didn't experience any of the dizziness I'd been warned to expect. We took it slow all the same, with Dad carrying my things in a plastic bag the hospital had provided. There wasn't much to carry. My leathers had been cut off me and thrown away and my bike helmet was beyond salvage – something I wasn't keen to see. That just left my wallet, phone and keys, together with the pain meds the doctors had given me. Oh, and a printed copy of the official police report of my accident, countersigned by DI Shimmin.

The report was short and circumspect. It listed the date and time of the 'incident' and stated that no other vehicles had been involved. There was no mention of anything connected to Lena. As far as the Manx police were concerned, Lena didn't exist.

Shimmin had phoned me earlier in the morning. He'd already dropped off the report with Dad, so I had a fair idea of what to expect, but that didn't make hearing it any easier.

'Listen,' he said, 'we've been up there. We've seen it with our own eyes. It's just not how you remember.'

'It has to be.'

'There's your van for one thing. You said you reversed it up to the garage, right?'

I agreed that was what I'd said. It was also what I'd done.

'Well, that's not where we found it. Not even close. It was parked down by the entrance to the plantation. You left your keys in the ignition.'

'I always leave my keys in the ignition when I'm working out of town. There's not usually any danger of my van being stolen. But they must have moved it.'

'Who?'

'The men in the cottage.'

Shimmin exhaled into the phone. 'Son, listen to me. Try to hear what I'm saying. The cottage was empty. There was nobody there.'

'Then it's obvious what's happened, isn't it? The men I saw must have been the ones who took Lena. And afterwards, they moved my van.'

'Why?'

'I don't know. To throw you lot off, I guess.'

'Listen, that cottage hasn't been lived in for a long time. We looked, OK? Teare even got a locksmith out so we could check inside. There was no furniture. No beds. Nothing.'

40

'There was a table and chairs in the kitchen.'

He paused. 'But nothing else. You told us this girl made you a cup of tea. But there were no groceries. No kettle. All the cupboards were empty.'

'They could have cleaned the place out. And they wouldn't have needed much furniture. They could have had sleeping bags. Air mattresses.'

'Son, nobody was living there. Nobody's lived there in a long time. We know. We checked.'

'Checked, how exactly?'

'Just trust me. My point is, you need to get past this. You need to think about what's causing it. Work on that.'

I said nothing.

'Teare spoke with your doctors, OK? Guy in occupational therapy. He told her what he thinks is going on.'

I closed my eyes. 'Did you talk to my father about this?'

'Eh?'

'About what the therapist said. Because he's wrong, you know. I didn't make this stuff up. I fixed their heating system for Christ's sake.'

'Nobody's saying you did it on purpose. We're not monsters. I mean, if what happened with your sister didn't mess you up a bit, well, you wouldn't be human, would you?'

I let that one drift. I didn't know what to say, where to take things next. Shimmin saved me the trouble.

'Rest up, OK? Let a week go by. Maybe two. If you still have questions, you have my number. But Rob? I really think you should let it go. If this girl existed, we'd have found her. I mean, this is the Isle of Man. People don't just vanish here.'

He cut the connection, leaving me to listen to the electric

hum of the machines in my hospital room. I lay still for a while, pressing my mobile against my lips, reflecting on what he'd said. I didn't like it. Not one bit.

I hadn't made Lena up. I knew it with the same certainty I knew I was lying in that hospital bed. No dream I'd ever had was as detailed as my memories of her. And one look at the boiler in the cottage would prove that I'd worked on it. Shimmin had to know that. He had to see there were loose ends. But he'd been determined to dismiss my story. And I couldn't think of one good reason why.

*

Snaefell View, the care home my parents own and manage, is located right on the TT course, on the way to Signpost Corner in Onchan, and it looks out across residential bungalows towards the Isle of Man's one and only mountain. It's a sprawling pebble-dashed property that's been adapted and extended over the years, and is currently big enough to accommodate eighteen residents (including my grandfather), plus three permanent staff, my parents' living quarters and my own place out back. Sounds grand, I suppose, but the bank has a sizeable share in the place and my parents have had to fight hard to keep the business going. I help out in my own way, for a cut in my rent, by tackling any maintenance and repairs that might be needed around the home.

We'd pulled into the driveway and Dad had silenced the rumbling engine on the home's minibus when I finally got up the courage to speak with him about what Shimmin had said.

'Dad,' I began, toying with the plastic bag that contained my belongings, 'there's something I need you to know.'

There was a tightness about his smile, a wariness around his eyes, as if he already regretted the need I felt to do this.

'I remember her, Dad. I do. There's no way I made this girl up.'

He rested a hand on my thigh. The skin on the back of his knuckles was dry and cracked, marked by sprigs of looped grey hairs. His nails were trimmed down, squared off, the flesh of his fingers swelling around them. Mechanic's hands. They'd got that way from the long hours he'd spent tuning my bikes, applying the know-how he'd picked up during his racing career in the quest for a fractional edge that might help me to draw the eye of a professional team.

I said, 'This isn't about Laura.'

His hand went limp. I felt its weight on my leg. Sunshine burned through the window glass, heating the air inside the minibus. He swallowed. Swallowed again.

'Why don't you go on inside?'

'Dad? We can say her name, can't we? We have to be able to do that, at least.'

He pulled his hand away and fumbled with the catch on the door. 'Get cleaned up,' he muttered. 'Then come and find me. Something I want to show you.'

He fell from the cab like a drunk stumbling out of a bar and I watched him tramp wearily across the gravel like a man floundering through quicksand.

*

It took me a long time to wash and pat myself dry, and when I emerged from my bathroom, Grandpa was sitting next to Rocky on the end of my bed. I can't tell you how many times we've spoken about this. It's become a kind of game, I suppose. It starts off with me explaining about personal boundaries and the value I place on my privacy, and then Grandpa nods along enthusiastically with a few sage asides about how he remembers feeling the same when he was my age, before forgetting it all just as soon as it suits him. I suppose I can understand where he's coming from. He spends most of his days cooped up with the other residents, and when he lets himself into my place, he acts as if he's just pulled off an audacious prison break.

'I was just checking on Rocky,' Grandpa said, before I could launch into phase one of the game.

'Uh huh.'

'Didn't want him to get lonely.'

'Even though I just got back from the hospital.'

'I didn't know about that. Your mother doesn't tell me anything.'

He might have blushed, but he seemed to have no problem with the lie. Truth was, we both knew he'd been watching me from the window of his room when I'd climbed out of the minibus. I'd even waved.

Grandpa's gnarled old hand was resting on Rocky's flank. Rocky was gazing at me watchfully, body tensed, forehead furrowed. He knew he should be in trouble, too. He wasn't normally allowed up on my bed.

So this is what two nights in hospital got me. Open rebellion.

'That bruise on your chest looks a real doozy,' Grandpa said.

'The ones on my leg aren't a lot of fun, either.'

44

I was standing before him in just my boxer shorts and a few sterile dressing pads. With Grandpa, this was relatively tame. He'd let himself in at worse times – including once when I had female company. Not that his visit had lasted long. And neither, oddly enough, had my date.

I picked my jogging trousers up off the floor and worked my way into them, using my good arm to pull them up around my waist.

'Help with my socks?'

I opened a drawer and passed a pair of black ankle socks to Grandpa, and he set about getting the first one ready with a look of grave concentration on his face. I lifted one foot on to his bony lap, then the next. Despite his quaking fingers and my suspect balance, we managed to complete the task without too much trouble.

'Want me to help with your sling?' he asked.

'No. But you can button my shirt.'

Grandpa nodded and patted Rocky's backside.

'Took your dog for a walk round the garden yesterday.'

Rocky exhaled loudly and looked at me as if this was a great injustice – as if really he'd been the one who'd exercised Grandpa.

I eased my bad arm through a striped shirt I'd removed from a hanger in my wardrobe, then carefully ducked down and fed my good arm inside. I stepped close to Grandpa and watched him lift his quivering fingers towards the button at my collar.

'Not the top one,' I said.

'Not wearing a tie?'

I looked down at the way my shirt tails were hanging over

my grey sweat pants. 'I don't think it would really go with this outfit.'

Grandpa pursed his lips and lowered his hands to focus on tackling the second button. He seemed to be having trouble with it. His fingers slipped on the little ivory disc. He didn't mention it and neither did I.

Grandpa is bald like a monk, with a ring of unruly, snow-white hair running from one ear to the other. His scalp has a smooth, leathery appearance, and he has a dark-purple birth-mark near the back of his skull, like Gorbachev.

'What happened to this blonde girl, then?' Grandpa asked.

'Where did you hear about that?'

'Your mother told me.'

I made a honking noise in the back of my throat. It was meant to sound like a television quiz buzzer when a contestant gets an answer wrong. 'Mum doesn't tell you anything. *Your words.*'

Grandpa shrugged. He'd finally managed to fasten the button and he was moving on to the next. 'Everyone's talking about it.'

'Everyone?'

'All the old folk.'

Grandpa liked to refer to his fellow residents that way. As if he was still young and staying at Snaefell View was simply a lifestyle choice he'd made. Sometimes he'd tell new residents he was the care home's handyman. Especially if they were female. I wasn't sure what that made me. His apprentice, probably.

I shouldn't have been surprised by what Grandpa had said. To most of the residents, fresh gossip was a rare and valuable currency. Once news of my accident had slipped out, it would have spread like a bout of winter flu.

'And what do they all think?'

'Well, some of them reckon you've gone potty. Like Valerie Gregg.' Valerie Gregg has dementia. She spends most of her days humming softly to herself in a corner of the television room. For many of the residents, she's become a kind of bogeyman – a living, breathing waxwork of the future they all fear. 'One or two think you killed her.' *Christ.* 'But I'm with the majority.'

'And what do the majority say?'

'They believe you.' He prodded me in the chest and I bared my teeth against the pain. 'And they think the police are up to no good.'

'Really?'

'It's like that old bossy one says.' *That old bossy one* was Mrs Rosemary Forbes, a retired school headmistress and, according to Mum at least, the one-time object of Grandpa's affections. 'The police have all kinds of places over here. Secret places. They use them for hiding people and the like.'

'Witness protection, you mean?'

'Damn thing.'

I looked down to where he'd fastened a button into the wrong hole, hitching my shirt up and leaving a gap that revealed my navel.

'It's fine.' I pushed his liver-spotted hands away. 'Thanks, Grandpa.'

He stood and smiled awkwardly, patting me on my bad shoulder. I winced at the electric charge that raced up my neck.

'Was she pretty?' He showed me his yellowing dentures. 'These foreign girls can be pretty.'

'Grandpa,' I told him, 'she was a knockout.'

Chapter Six

After Grandpa had left, I spent twenty minutes in my office, going over the police report of my accident and contacting those customers whose appointments I'd missed or would need to reschedule. Some were understanding. Some asked me to recommend other plumbers. Once I'd cleared my diary for the rest of the week, I whistled for Rocky and headed out to the yard. The barn doors to my bike workshop were open and I could hear voices from inside. Rocky padded on in ahead of me and I entered just as the conversation died.

I could see Dad at the far end of the garage and another figure crouching on the floor beside him. Three of my Yamaha race bikes were positioned in a wedge of sunlight in the middle of the room, stripped down and balanced on paddock stands, with bits of fairing, component parts and a stack of wheels arranged around them.

It stung to think I wouldn't be racing in this year's TT. The next few weeks were when twelve months of hard work had been supposed to bear fruit. My fitness regime. My race practice. The sponsorship we'd secured and the investment we'd made in new machinery. Now I'd have to watch the entire festival pass me by. A whole window of opportunity would be gone, not to mention my best hope of dragging my parents out of the pit of despair they'd fallen into.

I moved past a couple of red metal cabinets where most of

our tools are stored and stepped over a compressed-air gun. A set of race leathers were hanging from a metal hook above my head and I brushed them aside until I had a clearer view.

Dad's visitor was a woman. She had on light denim jeans and a collarless black leather jacket. The jacket was zipped to her chin and shimmered beneath the strip lights in a way that suggested it had never been subjected to fly spats and streaks of rain and muck on the back of a motorbike. Her coffee-coloured hair was pulled into a sleek ponytail and one delicate eyebrow was arched, as if she expected me to explain my presence. I'd have been happy to explain most things to her. She was spectacular. Early thirties. Slim nose. Sharp cheekbones. Very full lips. Wonderful brown eyes. Eyes I couldn't help staring at, and that I'd been staring at for a little too long.

I glanced down. A white dust sheet had been spread across the floor where she was crouching. Arranged on the sheet was a bent and buckled hunk of machinery that, I realised with a creeping sickness, looked very much like the remains of my road bike, a Yamaha R1.

'What's going on?'

'Robert.' Dad blinked and rocked on his heels. He looked from me to the woman and back again. Rocky jogged over and settled beside him, pushing his head into Dad's leg. 'This is my son,' Dad said, waving his hand at me, then dropping it on to Rocky.

The woman assessed me for a long moment, her lovely brown eyes running down from my face to the mid-point of my torso. They snagged on something and a smile flirted with her plump lips. I glanced down to where she was looking and immediately saw the gaping hole in my shirt.

'Your father tells me you cracked your shoulder blade,' she said.

I shrugged, my good shoulder carrying most of the gesture. I wasn't sure why, but she made me feel defensive. I covered the gap in my shirt with my hand.

'I've done that myself. Ski accident. Hurts, doesn't it?'

'It's not so bad,' I told her. 'Barely even a fracture. I can move a bit more than I expected. And the pain meds help.'

She watched me for a moment longer, her eyes seeming to grow and enlarge. Then she returned her attention to my bike, prodding and probing it with the end of a biro. The dinged frame was laid out on the dust sheet like a body on a mortuary slab. Dotted around it were chunks of metal, plastic fairing and machinery parts. It reminded me of the way museums arrange fossilised skeletons to explain how an extinct dinosaur used to be put together.

'When did you get this?' I asked.

'We collected it from the police this morning,' Dad said.

I assumed the *we* included the woman in the leather jacket. It hadn't escaped my notice that she hadn't been introduced to me yet.

'Why?'

Dad looked towards the woman. She pulled her attention away from the carcass of my Yamaha and found her feet. She was tall and long-limbed. Trim and athletic. Her face was only lightly made up and naturally pale. The bloodless tone of her skin contrasted with her lustrous brown hair.

'My name is Rebecca Lewis.' She frowned at a smear of grease on the heel of her hand. Ducked down and wiped it clean on the corner of the dust sheet. 'I work for a company called Wilton Associates.'

Rocky moved as if to approach her but the way she grimaced and wrinkled her nose stopped him in his tracks. He skulked back to Dad's side.

'And who are they?' I asked. 'Some kind of loss adjuster?' I thought perhaps she'd been appointed by my insurance company to verify that my bike was a write-off.

'Not a loss adjuster, no,' she said. 'We're a firm of private investigators.'

I felt the confusion twist my face. 'I don't understand.'

'Should I explain?' she asked Dad.

He looked up slackly, his gaze fixed somewhere below my jaw. 'I'm sorry, Rob. I just can't do this.'

And before I could reply, I watched my father, the great TT legend, hook his finger under Rocky's collar and lead him away into the sunlit yard.

*

Rebecca was a confident woman. She didn't speak for fully two minutes after Dad had left. She simply returned my gaze without giving anything away and then she stepped to one side as I approached what was left of my road bike.

The damage was worse than I might have expected. The front end had crumpled in on itself and the forks were rammed back against the engine and radiator. There were deep gouges along the side of the bike where it must have skidded along the tarmac, which might explain the matching bruises on my left leg. Oil and coolant had seeped out of the engine into the white cotton sheet, and the front wheel looked like someone had tried to beat it into something resembling a hexagon.

I went down on my haunches, the bruising taut across my thigh, and peeled back the shredded flaps of tyre. The rubber had split wide open, like it had been sliced in two with a rusty cheese wire.

'Blow-out,' I said, half to myself.

'How's that?'

I turned and grunted. 'Tyre must have exploded. Maybe I picked up a nail. Or a piece of glass.'

She pursed her lips. Nodded.

'Are you going to tell me what's going on?' I asked.

'Of course.'

'Am I going to like it?'

'That depends.'

'On?'

'Many things.'

She moved across to a workbench that was fitted along the far side of the room and leaned against it. Next to the workbench was a glazed cabinet. The cabinet contained the trophies, cups and medals that Dad and I had won in our respective careers. Most of my wins had come in junior races. Dad's were far more prestigious. Two replica trophies from his Senior TT victories, plus others from the Southern 100, run over a track in the south of the island, and the North West 200, held in Northern Ireland.

There were two giant posters on the wall above the cabinet. The one on the left showed me with my knee down on the Yamaha, grazing the tarmac as I rounded the Nook before joining the start/finish straight of the TT course. The one on the right, just above Rebecca's shoulder, showed Dad on his Honda, both wheels in the air as he was catapulted skywards by the humped rise of Ballaugh Bridge.

Rebecca rested her elbow on the surface-mounted vice next to her. 'My firm is based in London,' she said. 'Your parents appointed me two weeks ago.'

'To do what exactly?'

'To look into your sister's death.'

A gust of air escaped my lips. I felt a hollowness in my chest. Something hot and greasy was coiling inside my stomach. 'My sister killed herself,' I said, standing unsteadily. 'She drove off a cliff.' My tongue felt rubbery and swollen in my mouth. 'She *planned* it.'

'Was she depressed?'

'Didn't you hear what I just said? She – drove – off – a – cliff.'

Rebecca tipped her head on to her shoulder. Folded her arms across her chest. 'It's common for people who kill themselves to have a history of depression.'

'Really? Is that what they teach you at detective school?'

A hardness crept into her eyes. She reached down and toyed with the handle on the vice. Eased her slim hand inside. As if maybe she was thinking of squashing it. Or me.

'Don't do that,' she said.

'What?'

'Question my qualifications. I'm more than equipped to deal with this case.'

Her free hand gripped the vice handle, twisting it left and right. The mechanism squeaked. It needed oil.

'I don't doubt your qualifications.'

'But . . . ?'

'I do question the need for you to apply them.'

'Your parents disagree.'

'My parents are hurting.'

'You think my firm are exploiting them?'

'I think they're paying you to look for answers that none of us can provide.'

She removed her hand from the vice. Gave the handle a swing. *Squeak.*

'Let me ask you this,' she said. 'Were you satisfied with the police investigation into your sister's death?'

'There was nothing to investigate. Marine Drive is a no through road. She went up there for a reason.'

'Were you and Laura close?'

My head jerked back. Dumb move. I felt dizzy all of a sudden. 'What kind of question is that?'

Her eyes were hard brown enamel. 'The straightforward kind. The type I usually ask and people usually answer. They taught us it in detective school.'

I stood there, breathing hard, the air coming fast and warm through my nostrils. The heat churning in my stomach like a furnace. I could have done with sitting down, but I wasn't about to say so. 'I knew her as well as I could,' I said. 'As much as she'd let me.'

Rebecca hitched an eyebrow, expecting me to go on. I shook my head roughly, like I was trying to shed something sticky that was clinging to my face.

'She didn't come home from London very often,' I told her. 'We all found that hard.'

'Did she give a reason?'

'She blamed her job.'

'What did she say exactly?'

I shrugged. 'She worked in the City. As a trader or something. It was stressful. She worked long hours. Had to travel a lot. I don't think it suited her.'

There was a screwdriver on the workbench. Rebecca picked it up and turned it in her hands. She rested the point on the wood, her palm on the red plastic handle.

'How long have you been on the island?' I asked.

'I arrived last night.'

'And before that?'

'I was looking into your sister's life in London. Interviewing the people she knew.'

'So what led you over here?'

'Your father called. He mentioned your accident.'

I frowned. 'What does that have to do with anything?'

'He told me what happened. Mentioned the girl who was with you. The one you say has disappeared.'

'And?'

'And he believes you.'

I paused. My throat had closed up. It was difficult to speak. I tried all the same.

'Does he want you to look into it?'

'He asked me to.'

'But you don't see the point.'

She pouted, pressing down on the screwdriver with her palm. 'I didn't.'

'Something change your mind?'

'Your motorbike,' she said, pulling the screwdriver out of the workbench and jabbing it towards my bike. 'Because if you truly believe your tyre gave out of its own accord, I'd say you ought to sign up for a mechanic's course at night school.'

Chapter Seven

'God, your breath stinks.'

Rebecca was talking to Rocky. He was sitting in the back of her rental Fiesta, poking his face through the gap between our seats. It was a balmy day, and unusually for the island, there was hardly any breeze. We had the windows cracked but Rocky was panting. His tongue was hanging from his mouth like a strip of dry-cured meat.

Rebecca shot a look at me. 'What are you feeding this dog?'

'Ask him. Half the residents in the care home palm food his way.'

'Gross.'

Rebecca was not a dog person. This much was clear. She'd fought hard against the idea of having Rocky accompany us in the first place, but I'd told her it was non-negotiable. He needed exercise.

'How much further?' she asked.

'Fifteen minutes, maybe.'

She slapped her hand against the steering wheel and sucked clean air through the gap in her window like she was inhaling from an oxygen canister. It distracted her from the Ballacraine traffic lights ahead of us. The lights turned red and I braced my foot against the floor long before Rebecca stamped on the brake pedal.

'What are your impressions of DI Shimmin?' she asked me,

once we'd come to an abrupt stop and my seatbelt had slashed into my ailing ribs.

'Hard to tell,' I managed, and tugged some slack into my belt. 'I'm not sure if he's lazy, or incompetent, or if he's hiding something.'

The lights switched to green and Rebecca swung left. Rocky's muzzle swayed towards her. He was trying hard to win her over.

'How about you?' I asked. 'You've spoken to him, haven't you?'

'Yesterday.'

'And?'

'And he said I was wasting my time. You imagined the whole thing.'

'Charming.'

'He also promised me full co-operation.'

'And how's that panning out?'

Her mouth curled into a lopsided grin. 'I'm building a relationship with his voicemail.'

'Maybe you should try Teare.'

'Why? Because we're both women?'

I paused for a beat. 'No. Because she seemed like the type who asked questions. Or at least, she thought of some questions to ask.'

We drove on in silence, following a gentle gradient through the village of Foxdale, where terraced and whitewashed cottages lined the road, before beginning the climb around South Barrule. Dense, knotted woods flanked the hillside until we gained ground and a view opened up across rectangular fields and flowering gorse and purple heather. The end of the valley was dominated by the tree-lined slope of Slieau Whallian, known in Manx folklore as the Witches' Hill. In medieval times, suspected witches had been rolled down its steep incline inside spiked barrels. If they were killed, their death proved their innocence. If they survived, they were executed. I felt like I was in a similar lose–lose situation. Either I was imagining things and Lena had never existed, or my memories were accurate and there was a chance that Lena was in real trouble.

'Is this bringing any of it back?' Rebecca asked.

'Not yet.'

'Maybe something will filter through when we get to where the accident happened.'

We reached the scene five minutes later. The road was a narrow ribbon of tarmac, riddled with cracks and potholes and scattered with loose gravel. To the left, a low wire fence ran along the crowded treeline of the plantation. To the right, an area of scrubland close to the ruins of an old tin mine had been bulldozed into a dirt-bike track. A couple of lads in garish motocross gear were riding off-road bikes over the dusty humps and hollows. 125ccs, maybe. Engines like chainsaws.

Rebecca pulled over and stepped out of the car. I followed her as far as a series of yellow chalk marks that had been drawn on the crumbling tarmac. She knelt beside an arrow that pointed towards a wonky circle. In the middle of the circle, a thin trench had been gouged out of the road surface.

'You went down hard.' She pointed to the trench. 'Very hard. How fast do you think you were going?'

'Nothing crazy. I think I was still in first gear.'

'I'm not the police, Rob. I don't care if you were reckless.'

I shrugged. 'Forty-five. Maybe fifty miles an hour.' I knew

it didn't sound good. The road was only wide enough for one vehicle, the surface bitty.

Rebecca nodded. 'You were thrown from your bike.'

She straightened up and paced out the distance to a patch of flattened grass at the side of the track. It was marked by blue-and-white police tape stretched between two wooden pegs. A sign had been stapled to one of the pegs, asking for any witnesses to contact the police.

'Six metres, give or take.' Rebecca whistled. 'You can fly.'

'Great.'

'But you need to work on your landing.' She pointed to a sod of wet earth. 'I'd say this is where your shoulder hit the ground.'

I glanced at the spot, then looked away. I fought the temptation to cradle my damaged shoulder blade with my free hand.

'And Lena?' I asked.

Rebecca turned, hands on her hips. She surveyed the tarmac carefully. Kicked at some light grey scrapes with the toe of her shoe. 'Here, maybe.'

Something else caught her eye. She crossed over the road and negotiated her way down a drainage bank. Crouched behind an outcrop of brambles and gorse. She checked around and behind her, then straightened and peered further up the road, shading her eyes with her hand.

'Where did you come out of the plantation?'

'See the gate on that sheep field? It's just opposite.'

'Huh.' She climbed out of the trench and walked past me, beyond the Fiesta. Rocky watched through the rear window as I stumbled behind her towards a minor junction some two hundred metres back. Off to the right, an even smaller road followed the edge of the plantation towards a low valley stream. 'Interesting.'

'What?'

She ignored me and crossed the road towards the edge of the dirt track, where the two guys were tearing around on their bikes. She waited until they were thundering towards her and then she waved her arms and flagged them down. A fog of dust swirled around her and she covered her mouth with her forearm before showing the bikers some ID and conferring with them.

Five minutes later, she was back. In the time that she'd been away, the gnarly pain in my scapula seemed to have got a lot worse. I'd almost convinced myself that I could hear a crunch when I moved.

'A white van has been parked here during the past few weeks,' she said, pointing at a gravel pull-in beside the junction. 'Those bikers say they saw it at least twice. They also saw a man getting into the back of it. They reckon it looked like he'd been into the woods for a pee.'

'So?' I asked, cupping my elbow to ease the weight on my shoulder.

'The van was white, Rob.'

'And?'

She sighed. Shook her head. 'You were concussed, right? Dizzy? And you saw something that looked like an ambulance. But did you see any flashing lights? Hear any sirens?'

'You think I mistook a white van for an ambulance?'

She pointed back up the road towards the entrance to the plantation. 'If they parked it here, you wouldn't have seen it properly. Maybe they pulled out after the crash and you caught a glimpse of it then. You'd barely have been conscious.'

I didn't say anything. I wasn't sure there was anything to be said.

'And one, or maybe two of them, must have been hiding up there in that ditch, behind the hedge. They used a cable or some kind of concealed obstacle to burst your tyre and knock you from your bike.'

'You think?'

It was all sounding a bit far-fetched. I'd wanted someone to believe me. Now I was having doubts myself.

'Skidmarks,' she said.

'Sorry?'

'There aren't any. No sign that you braked. You're going fifty.' She raised an eyebrow. 'Maybe fifty-five miles an hour. If you'd spotted something, you'd have tried to avoid it, wouldn't you?'

'The back wheel kicked up.' I shuddered. 'I remember that much.'

'So it kicked up because of the obstacle your front tyre hit. Only explanation.'

'You believe me, then? About Lena?'

Her head jerked back and she gave me a curious look with her soft brown eyes. 'Why wouldn't I?'

She led me back to the Fiesta and spoke to me across the roof of the car. 'Listen, a road accident like yours. A story like yours. The police wouldn't send two senior detectives to quiz you in your hospital bed. They'd send uniform. Maybe later, if you persisted, you'd get to speak to the cheap suits. But if that happened, we're talking a worthwhile investigation. Something that digs below the surface. But Shimmin and Teare didn't do that. Whatever happened here, someone wants it to stay buried.'

She climbed inside the car. I opened my door and ducked down gingerly. Stared over at her.

'And there's something else,' she said. 'Shimmin claimed there were no witnesses. That nobody responded to their appeals for information.'

'So?'

'So it doesn't make sense. Somebody called an ambulance for you. We just don't know who it was yet.'

Chapter Eight

My van was parked by the lower gate to the plantation, just as Shimmin had said. It was tucked right in against the bushes and trees. There was no way I would have left it like that. I wouldn't have risked the sign work getting scratched by branches and thorns.

Rebecca peered in through the front passenger window, her hands cupped around her eyes.

'Spot anything out of place?' she asked me.

I opened the driver's door. It was unlocked, which didn't surprise me very much. A lot of people don't bother to lock their cars on the Isle of Man and Shimmin was obviously one of them – especially when the vehicle didn't belong to him.

'Nothing here,' I said. 'Let me look in the back.'

I threw the rear cargo doors open and scanned the stale and dusty interior. I'd lined the van with quarter-inch ply and fitted cubby-holes and shelving for my tools along one wall, opposite the sliding load door. The space in the middle was for storage and there were two wooden planks on the floor. I'd used them as a ramp when I was wheeling my bike into the garage up at the cottage. It made me remember something.

'I had a spare helmet and leather jacket,' I said to Rebecca. 'They belonged to an ex of mine. I loaned them to Lena.'

'That's good. Anything else?'

'I don't think so.'

I closed the doors as Rebecca considered the wooden gate and the rutted pathway beyond. The poster about the missing dog was still there, curling in the afternoon sun. But the rusted security chain and the combination padlock were gone.

The ground had baked dry in the days since I'd been there last. I could smell pollen and warm sap, hear the *crick* of insects from the grass at my side. A cloud of midges had settled over the Fiesta and I batted them away as I opened the door and released Rocky. He jumped out and stretched his back with a long groan of satisfaction.

Rebecca popped the boot, took a seat on the lip and began to lace up a pair of stout walking shoes. Then she grabbed a backpack from the parcel shelf. The backpack was compact and made of tough black nylon. It had padded straps and multiple compartments.

'It's really not far,' I told her. I was flexing and clenching the fingers of my bad arm as I spoke. It was good to get my blood pumping every now and again to ward off the pins and needles that had been bugging me since I'd been wearing the sling. 'You won't need supplies.'

She unzipped the main compartment and I caught a glimpse of the backpack's contents. A heavy-duty torch, a notepad and pen, and a pack of disposable plastic gloves. She burrowed deeper, checking for something, and I saw her remove a blue, elasticised plastic overshoe, the kind forensics officers wear. She dug further, until she found a matching one. Then she swung the backpack over her shoulder and locked the car.

'Let's go,' she said.

Rocky ran on ahead, squirming on his belly to force his way beneath the gate. There was a pedestrian swing-gate at the side, and he could have fitted through if he'd shown a little patience, but that wasn't his style.

Warm air shimmied above the dusty rock path. The spruce and pine trees pressed in around us, adding insulation we didn't need, and bees droned around the flowering yellow gorse.

'About your theory,' I said. 'There's something I don't get.'

'Go on.'

'The idea that someone was waiting for me on the road. That they'd planned to knock me and Lena off my bike. How would they know to do that? How would they know we'd be coming?'

'I don't know.'

'Right.' I listened to the beat of our shoes on the path. 'Isn't that a problem?'

Rebecca nodded. 'A big one.'

'So what does it mean?'

'It means we need to find some answers. They taught us that at detective school, too.' She winked at me, then rummaged around in her pocket, removing a mobile phone and holding it high above her head. 'Good,' she said, squinting at the screen. 'I still have reception.'

'You should be OK at the cottage, too. I was the other day.'

She closed the phone in her hand. 'Why don't you tell me again about the men you saw with Lena?'

We'd already been through it once, but I went through it a second time. I told her about Mr Shades – the way he wore his sunglasses when he answered the door, despite the gloom at the cottage. I mentioned his foreign accent, his prickly attitude. Then I described his companion. His peroxide hair and tattoos. His muscles.

'And when Lena invited you into the kitchen, you were only there for a couple of minutes?'

'If that. The atmosphere was pretty strained. So we went back to the garage.'

'It could be she wanted you to see them,' Rebecca said. 'You told me the guy who answered the door wasn't wearing his sunglasses when you went inside. Would you recognise him if you saw him again?'

I thought about it. Tried conjuring his image in my mind's eye. 'I think so.'

Sweat was beading on my face and neck and the air felt thick and hot when I inhaled. It might have been a warm day, but this wasn't the tropics, and the walk was hardly strenuous. It made me realise that the accident had probably taken more out of me than I might have liked to believe. Yes, my bruised leg was stiff, and my chest and shoulder sore, but my energy levels and stamina were down, too.

We climbed the rise and approached the three-way fork in the path. Rocky was waiting ahead of us, looking back.

'The middle one, Rock,' I said, and pointed. He dropped his head and trotted forwards. 'It's not far now,' I told Rebecca.

The trees closed over our heads, a green canopy stretching far above us, as if we were deep underwater. Daylight twinkled through the foliage, dancing like sunshine on the sea.

I looked towards the open gate with the slate sign on it. *Yn Dorraghys.* The darkness it referred to felt more appropriate than ever.

'Their car's gone,' I said.

Rebecca followed me to the pull-in where I'd seen the red Micra. Tyre treads were still visible where it had been parked, the muddy ground formed into ridges that were soft and spongy underfoot. She reached for her backpack, unclipped a pouch on the side and removed a small digital camera. She fired off photographs from a couple of angles while I caught my breath, the flashes throwing the tree trunks ahead of us into bright relief.

'Anything else look different?'

I circled around, searching for signs of change. There was nothing. The cottage appeared just as sad and uncared for. Maybe the tall grass was a little taller. Maybe a few more branches and pine leaves were blocking the gutters.

'I don't see anything,' I said.

Rebecca paced towards the cottage. She removed a pair of surgical gloves from her backpack and snapped them on over her wrists. She tried the door handle. Locked. She looked in through a darkened window, flattening her gloved hand on the glass. She went up on her toes to study the sash lock. Rattled the fitting.

'Wait,' I said. 'I have a key.'

'You do?'

'To the garage.' I dug my free hand into the pocket of my jogging trousers and showed her.

Rebecca stared at me. 'Why didn't you say so before? Why didn't you tell Shimmin?'

'I only just remembered.'

Rebecca stared at me a little harder.

'That's the problem with head injuries,' I told her. 'Unpredictable.'

'Uh huh. Or maybe you were planning to come back here and snoop around for yourself.'

I glanced down at my fingers poking out of my sling. I didn't confirm or deny it.

'So tell me about the key,' she said.

I did. I told her how Mr Shades had tossed it to me on that first day and how Lena had asked me to hold on to it for when I returned the following morning. I explained that I'd had the key on me while I'd worked on the boiler and when we rode away on my bike. I told her that someone at the hospital must have found it among my clothes and stored it with the rest of my things.

'So we caught a break,' I said. 'We can get inside the garage and access the cottage through the door into the kitchen.'

Rebecca plucked the key from my palm. 'Not *we*.' She shook her head. 'You might think you're pretty slick, but I'm going in alone. Your parents hired me to investigate. I'm a professional. This is what I do. And I don't want you or your dog contaminating anything.'

My dog. Now that she mentioned it, where was Rocky? I hadn't seen him since he'd run on ahead of us as we were nearing the cottage. An image of little Chester, the missing terrier, raced through my mind.

'I won't touch anything,' I said.

'That's right.' Rebecca fitted the key into the lock on the garage door. She compressed the handle and hauled the thing up. It made a loud metal screech. 'Because you're staying out here.'

She bent down and stretched the plastic bootees over her walking boots. Then she clicked on her torch and swept the room with the beam.

'The boiler?' she asked.

'Over there.' She pointed her flashlight in the direction I'd indicated. The boiler looked just as I'd left it. The front plate fitted back into position. The exterior wiped clean. 'The door to the kitchen's on your left. There's a light cord next to it.'

She reached above her head to yank the garage door closed. It was at knee height when she ducked down and peered out from below.

'I think I could have worked that one out for myself,' she said.

The door slammed with a shudder. I cradled my bad arm, grinding my heel into the dirt.

'Rocky?' I called, my ribs smarting with the effort. 'Rocky?'

I knew my dog. I knew he wouldn't come right away. This was his first adventure in days and he'd want to savour it.

I took a moment to think about where he might be. I'd watched him pass through the gate and trot towards the cottage. I hadn't kept track of him once Rebecca had started taking photographs but I'd have noticed if he'd stayed close.

I walked behind the garage to the oil tank. The grass was as high as my thighs, laden with pollen and cuckoo-spit. Full of bugs too. Mites and ticks. I couldn't remember the last time I'd treated Rocky's coat with something to repel them. Odds were, he'd have plunged right in, picking up an entire colony of new friends.

A rough path had been beaten through the grass to my right. It looked Rocky-sized and led to the back corner of the garden, where a wire fence had been pushed flat against the ground by the encroaching treeline. I waded through the grass. Stepped over the fence.

'Rocky?'

I heard a bark. Coming from ahead.

'Rocky?'

More barking.

I brushed branches and spider webs clear of my face. Brambles snagged on the legs of my trousers and the cotton material of my sling. I stepped over ditches and around briar patches, my feet sinking through layers of decaying pine needles.

Rocky's barking was louder now. I squinted through the tree trunks until I caught a blur of golden hair. He was barking with such vigour that his front paws were bouncing up off the ground.

'What is it?' I asked. 'What is it, boy?'

Rocky didn't answer. He just kept barking. Then he hunkered down and growled. Then he barked some more.

I clambered over a fallen log and seized him by his collar. He barked one final time, like the full stop on the end of a sentence, and nuzzled into my hand with a whimper.

That's when I heard the buzz for the first time. A low droning. Long and persistent. It repeated itself. Repeated again.

I gazed down and saw a bluish glow. A mobile phone. I picked it up just as the ringing stopped. A message flashed up.

64 Missed Calls.

I glanced towards the tree cover, pinpricks of light filtering down through the watery green. Then I stepped backwards and felt something crack under my heel. I raised my foot, expecting a branch. But I found something else.

A crushed pair of sunglasses with mirrored lenses.

Part Two

Chapter Nine

The boat was rolling and yawing, waves punching the hull, pitching the trawler high into the air, holding it aloft, then sending it plunging back down. Menser moaned and clutched his bald head. He wasn't a good sailor. Never had been. So he needed the medication. A double dose. But the idea of adding anything at all to his churning stomach contents was almost more than he could bear.

So he compromised. Took the pills. Passed on the water. And hoped like crazy it would help.

The cabin lurched to the right. Menser peered out through the drenched window glass at the jagged horizon. It was meant to make things better. It just made them worse.

He heard footfall – the clang of metal treads. It was Clarke, climbing the ladder that connected the wheelhouse to the warren of rooms below deck. He'd changed clothes, at last. Ditched the paramedic costume and put on cargo trousers and a fleece jacket, like he was off on a hike.

'*Whoa there!*'

Clarke thought he was hilarious. Swaying from one foot to the other, arms spread, acting as if he was being thrown around by the movement of the waves. His cheeks bulged. He covered his mouth and made a retching noise.

'Give it a rest,' Menser told him.

Clarke had been working the routine, riffing off variations

of it, since they'd first left Peel marina, on the west coast of the island. It had grown old very fast.

'I'm sorry, but this is priceless.' Clarke dropped his hands on to his thighs and stared at Menser like he was an animal in a zoo. 'IQ. *The* IQ. Outfoxed by Mother Nature. Undone by a dicey tum.' He grinned like a lunatic. Started the swaying again. 'Why didn't you take your tablets before we set off, eh? Egghead like you. Would've thought you'd have known to do that.'

The intellect thing had followed Menser throughout his career. A consequence of his premature baldness and, yes, his surname. One time, early on, Menser had told the dumb bastard who was ribbing him that his name was spelt with an *er* on the end, not an *a*. It just made it worse. As if having the capacity to think for himself was a bad thing. Which it wasn't. Menser knew that now. It was what had kept him in the job all these years. Made him useful. A capable employee. But it had also trapped him. Because he'd been expected to babysit a long list of idiots. Like the moron working the drunken sailor routine in front of him right now.

Menser glanced down at his wrists. The elasticised bracelets he was wearing were fitted with plastic buds that were meant to compress his pulse points. And do what exactly? He didn't know. Hokum, probably. Some kind of placebo effect.

Islands. They were a pain in the backside. Difficult to fly out of without leaving a paper trail or being monitored in some way. That was why they'd gone with the boat. That was why he'd been paired with Clarke. He had some kind of naval background, apparently. Could even be he was ex-SBS.

'How's it looking down there?' Menser asked.

'No problem. Big guy's still out of it. The girl looks pissed off. Says her wrist's broken.'

'And is it?'

'Seems more like a sprain. I offered to take a look. Wasn't having it.'

'Why not?'

'I might have suggested it'd help if she took her shirt off first.'

Menser shut his eyes and clamped his hand over his hairless scalp. This is what he had to deal with. What he was expected to manage. *Co-operation* – it was the key element in any hostage situation. Right now, the girl would barely talk. Wouldn't eat. Refused to drink. That was normal. A standard reaction. Changing it took trust. Or fear. In Menser's experience, trust worked better. It took longer – it was something you had to earn – but it could result in a useful bond. The one thing you didn't want to build was hate. Make them hate you, and their resistance would grow. Make them despise you enough, and they'd stay silent just to spite you. Reach that stage and it didn't matter what you did. Menser had seen all kinds of torture. Different varieties of pain. Some obvious. Some ingenious. The results, without exception, were unsatisfactory. Either the hostage died without saying anything, or the captor had to back down.

So it was better to be pleasant. Build their trust.

And then dispose of them.

It was something he could have told Clarke. A theory he could have explained. But Clarke wasn't the type to listen. Take that ridiculous patch of facial hair below his lip. Menser had told him to lose it. Warned him it was memorable. And what happened? The bumfluff remained.

Same thing when they'd snatched the girl. He'd told Clarke not to speak to the biker, but Clarke had gone ahead and done it anyway. He'd claimed the guy was concussed – like the green jumpsuit had convinced him he was a genuine medic – but Menser didn't like it. Taking chances was something you did if you wanted to get caught. And Menser didn't. Not ever. Especially not now.

He put his hand to his gut. He was going to have to get past the sickness. Go below deck and repair whatever damage Clarke had caused. Maybe he could turn it to his advantage. Make the girl see that he was the one she could deal with. A rational mind. A reasonable guy.

Someone she could trust.

Chapter Ten

Lena stared blankly at the figure in the doorway. Deep inside her gut, she experienced a flutter of relief. It was the older man. The one with no hair. He was clinging to the doorframe because the boat was tipping and swirling around. In his spare hand he carried a plastic mug. Steam was rising from it.

'I brought you some tea,' he said, and extended the mug towards her, spilling hot liquid over his knuckles as the boat pitched suddenly to the right.

She had to fight back a smile. *Tea.* Of course. This was what the English always offered you. It didn't matter that they'd imprisoned you in a ship's cabin in the middle of a storm. It made no difference that you'd been drugged and abducted against your will.

She wanted to decline. Or even better, ignore him. But she was thirsty. Her mouth was dry and she was suffering from a headache that wouldn't go away. It had been with her since she'd first come around to find herself in this . . . *cell*, she supposed she should call it.

The room had metal walls, painted white, and no window. There was a grubby linoleum floor, a metal toilet, a metal sink and two bunk beds with rusted frames. The door the man had come in by was metal, too. It had riveted panels and a sturdy lock. She'd tried opening it already. Many times. But the door had been bolted on the outside.

'Either you want it, or you don't,' the man said. 'But if I was you, I'd take it. You keep refusing and we might forget to come down here altogether.'

Her thirst was too much. Her headache too urgent.

Lena unfurled her right hand, the one that wasn't inflamed and throbbing. The man approached and placed the mug in her palm. It wasn't so bad when she finally took a sip. The tea had plenty of sugar in it. She could feel the sucrose zinging through her system, like a tiny spark of energy.

The cabin tipped and rocked. The door swung backwards and the man grabbed for it. He closed his eyes and swallowed thickly.

'Mind if I sit down?'

He stumbled across and collapsed on to the bunk that faced her own. The veins pulsed in his temples. His ears and his scalp were flushed red. Lena could see that he was wearing a pair of pale-blue wristbands.

'We need to talk,' the man said, and spread his clammy fingers, as if he was prepared to be entirely open with her.

Lena didn't reply.

'About the cottage,' the man continued. 'About what you've been doing up there. And about Melanie Fleming. Her, in particular.'

Lena said nothing. She sipped her tea. Nursed her wrist in her lap.

The man smiled glumly. Shook his bald head. 'You know what concerns me? What concerns me is that you're not concerned. Now, if it was me, and I was in your position, I'd be terrified.'

The man waited a beat. Exhaled sharply.

'Look, if you talk to me, I can help you. Maybe between us we can think of a way to make some of this go away.'

Lena slumped against the wall of the cabin.

'Listen, you know the police have been looking for you, right? Maybe not publicly. Not in a major way, at least. But in a discreet, persistent way. So don't think for a minute they won't jump at the chance to take you into custody. That's where we're heading, get it? That's where we're taking you right now. We have people waiting. It's all set up.'

Lena drank some more of the tea and closed her eyes to think. When she opened them again, the man was still there. He was crouched forwards, his elbows resting on his spread thighs, his palms pressed together, as if in prayer. He waited for a rolling swell to pass under them before speaking again.

'Look, if you're sitting there thinking there's some kind of problem with the evidence, you're wrong. The police have your fingerprints on a syringe and a glass vial they found in your underwear drawer. The vial contains cyanide. And the syringe has traces of the victim's blood.' The man tightened his hands into fists. He clenched hard, like he was squeezing lemons. 'Then there's the vodka. They tested it and found it was laced with a sedative. Same sedative as was in the bloodstream of the victim. They also found a cash receipt for the off-licence closest to your apartment. The receipt was for vodka. Same brand. Same volume. Time of purchase syncs with the estimated time of death.' He sucked a fast breath in through his teeth. 'Now, I'll be honest with you. There's a problem with the CCTV in the shop. But the guy behind the counter remembers a blonde buying the vodka. So the police showed him a headshot and he gave a statement that you're the blonde he remembers.'

Out of nowhere, a huge *boom* and the cabin plunged wildly. The man's bunk fell away and Lena was pitched up until she was towering above him. Tea sloshed around in her mug and her buttocks slipped on the scratchy blanket she'd spread beneath her. She braced her feet on the frame of the man's bunk as he smacked into the wall and flailed for a handhold. The cabin door slammed closed. All around them, the stiff metal structure creaked and groaned and trembled. Then, all too slowly, the ship heaved itself back on to its axis and the door swung open.

The man glanced at the doorway. He wiped his mouth with a trembling hand. 'Maybe you're planning to tell them you didn't have a motive,' he said, after a pause. 'But you should know they don't care very much about motives when they have hard evidence. And just think about who the dead guy was. Think of the ways he could have betrayed you. The threats he could have posed to you. And then there's the kicker.' The man pointed his finger at her. 'You ran and you hid. For two whole months.'

Lena felt no urge to protest her innocence. If the man really was in a position to help her – if he held a role with that level of power and influence – he would already know the truth. And if he knew the truth, then he wasn't on her side. She couldn't reveal anything to him. Not even how terrified she was. It was safer to act as if she didn't care.

'Oh, and one more thing,' the man said. 'Don't be sitting there thinking that Melanie Fleming is going to come good for you. She's not. You can trust me on that. So you really should be worried. And if you're not, the best thing you can do right now is tell me why.'

Lena swallowed the last of her tea and set the mug down by her side, wedged in between the mattress and the metal bunk frame. She rested her fingers on her swollen wrist and stared hard at the man. Stared through him, really. He'd given her plenty of information. Some of it confirmed what she already suspected. Some of it was new. But there was one thing she was absolutely sure of – the man had no idea about the secret she and Melanie had shared. He had no awareness of the chance, however slim, that she was clinging on to. It all came down to the plumber. Everything depended on how observant he might have been.

Chapter Eleven

I returned to the cottage with Rocky. The broken sunglasses were tucked inside my sling and I was clenching the mobile phone in my hand. The casing of the mobile was damp and coated in mud and pine needles. I was afraid it would buzz again before I got to Rebecca and I didn't know how to react if it did.

I was sure the sunglasses and the phone belonged to Mr Shades. The sunglasses were distinctive enough for me to remember and the phone looked a lot like the one I'd seen him with. It had a colour screen and a full Qwerty keypad. Laura had owned a phone just like it.

I was at the edge of the garden by now. Rocky had streaked ahead of me and around the front of the cottage, but I waded through the undergrowth towards the kitchen windows. I pressed my face to the dirt-streaked glass. Rebecca was standing on a chair, reaching up to the light-fitting in the middle of the ceiling. She had a pocket knife in her hand. She stretched high, rising up on her toes inside the blue plastic overshoes, the hem of her T-shirt hitching up. I waited until she'd pulled the knife clear and regained her balance before knocking.

She swung around sharply, then placed a gloved hand over her chest when she saw it was me. She stepped down from the chair and opened the kitchen door, and I explained about the sunglasses and the phone. Rebecca took them from me and turned them in her hands, her lips twisted in thought.

'Why didn't you come and get me?' she asked.

'I didn't want to forget where they were.'

'You touched these with your bare hands.'

It was a statement, not a question. I felt myself shrink.

She shook her head, then pressed a button with her gloved thumb, cycling through the lighted display. 'The only thing stored on this phone are the missed calls. All of them came from a withheld number.' She hummed. Smiled flatly. 'Someone's very keen to get in touch with the owner of this phone.'

'And you wouldn't leave something like that behind, right?' I said. 'And if you were heading away from this place, you wouldn't go in that direction. It just takes you deeper into the woods.'

'Maybe that's exactly what he wanted.'

I met her eyes. Blinked. I was about to say something more when Rocky flew past my legs and blitzed by Rebecca into the kitchen. She turned and yelled at him to get out. He considered her for a moment, head on an angle, then danced left, jinked right, and dashed around to the end of the table.

'Rocky,' I said. 'Come here. That's bad. You're a bad boy.'

He smiled his goofy smile. Wagged his tail.

'Well trained,' Rebecca said bitterly.

'It's not his fault.'

'No. You're right.' She glared at me, then seemed to lose interest in it. Her shoulders sagged and she pushed the door open wider. 'You might as well come in, too. I've stuck my head in every room and the place is definitely unoccupied. But there's something you should see.'

Her plastic overshoes crinkled as she led me towards the pine kitchen table. Several items were collected together on the scarred wooden surface. Electrical wires and hunks of plastic. A flexible, transparent cable with a bead of glass at one end. A tiny microphone bud. The pocket knife I'd seen her using, with one blade folded out.

'This place is bugged,' she said.

'You're kidding.'

She set the mobile phone and the sunglasses down on the table and picked up the bendy cable. 'I found this in the housing for the smoke alarm. It's a surveillance camera. The microphone was behind the clock on the wall over there.' She pointed at the clock in question. 'I think there's another behind the light fitting.'

I swallowed. Lowered my voice. 'Are we being listened to now?'

'I doubt it.'

My skull was tingling. It felt like there were eyes on me. Watching us.

'Who would have put this stuff here?' I asked.

'I don't know for sure. But they were professionals. So far, I've only checked this room and the garage and I've found at least eight devices. They're not state of the art, and judging by the dust on the wires and the cabling, I'd say they were installed a few years ago, at least. But you asked me how somebody could have known that you and Lena were leaving here on your bike.' She aimed the end of the cable towards me. 'This is how.'

I shuddered. Went to reach for the microphone bud, then

thought better of it when I remembered I wasn't wearing gloves.

'How far can these things transmit?' I was thinking about the way Mr Shades had been focused on his laptop when I'd seen him in the kitchen. Had he been watching over Lena and me in the garage? Had he been listening to our conversation? No, I realised. Because then he'd have known what we'd planned with my bike.

'The range on these things can vary,' Rebecca said. 'Maybe as far as two miles. Far enough, anyway, to reach that road at the end of the plantation.'

It took a moment for me to see where she was going with it. 'You think they were watching from the van you mentioned?'

'Watching *and* listening. You gave them time to get into position. To cause your accident and snatch Lena.'

I shook my head. 'This is crazy.'

'No. This is logical.'

'But for somebody to do this . . .' I let the words trail off, unsure what I'd been trying to say. Then a new thought occurred to me. 'People say there are safe houses over here. That the island's used for witness protection, hiding people connected to major crimes over on the mainland.'

'It's possible.'

'And the police would know, right? If that's what this place is for.'

'Makes sense. And it could explain why they sent two detectives to speak with you at the hospital. It might also explain why they haven't looked into what happened here too closely.'

'How do you mean?'

'This level of surveillance equipment.' She shrugged. 'It's a bit more advanced than your average police force might be used to. Smacks of a sensitive situation.'

'Sensitive, how?'

She smiled. 'That's what I intend to find out.'

'But you think they backed off deliberately?'

She opened her mouth to speak, but she was interrupted before she could get the words out. The mobile phone had started buzzing. It was glowing and vibrating against the tabletop. *Number Withheld.*

Chapter Twelve

Failure. It wasn't something Menser was used to, still less something he could tolerate. The frustration ate at him. Gnawed on his insides. The job had taught him patience. Control. But they were just skills. Part of his professional shell. And he could feel the shell cracking.

The girl's attitude was bothering him. The casual way she was slouched against the wall of the cabin in her red-and-white gingham blouse, her swollen wrist cradled in her lap like something only vaguely connected to her. The curled lip. The glazed eyes.

Clarke hadn't helped. He'd started things off on the wrong foot. Raised her hackles. But Menser had compensated for that. He'd shown her respect. Made her tea.

She'd smirked at the tea. He was sure of it. But she'd drunk it all the same. The first breakthrough. The one he'd planned to build from. But there'd been no progress. Not the slightest advance. Only silence. And that sneer, as if she knew something he didn't. It was getting under his skin. Itching like a rash.

In just a few hours, they'd reach their destination. He had to know what was sustaining her. Keeping her this way.

He'd read her file. Absorbed its contents. He saw an explanation in it.

Her father had spoiled her. Indulged her. Furnished her with a lifestyle that only the offspring of the elite and powerful could hope to enjoy. He'd protected her. Cocooned her. Taught her to believe that she was better than people like Menser. Better than the people Menser was delivering her to. A charmed existence. One it would be hard to believe was in jeopardy.

The cabin tipped. Lurched. Menser grabbed for the bunk he was sitting on. Closed his eyes. The hollow *boom* of the hull striking water. Bottoming out. The vessel slowly righting itself. Groaning. Creaking.

He hated this. Hated the feeling of powerlessness. Being at the mercy of something beyond his control. Tossed around.

When he looked up, she was smiling. His unease was lighting her face. Menser couldn't ignore how attractive she was. Lithe. Shapely. Young and fit.

Everything he wasn't.

'So, where do you take me?' Her voice was croaky. Dry from disuse. But he was pleased to hear it, all the same.

'You'll see soon enough.' He clenched his toes in his shoes. As if maybe he could clamp himself to the floor. Fight the swirl and the dip.

'How long do we have?'

'Not long.'

'So you will be killing Pieter soon, I am thinking.'

He held her gaze. Moderated his tone. 'What makes you say that?'

'Because you killed Lukas already. I heard the shots from inside the van.'

Menser could have told her she was wrong. That it was Clarke who'd done the shooting. That it was Clarke who'd stepped out of line.

Improvisation, Clarke had called it. As if it was something to be proud of. Compensation for the way he'd screwed up.

They'd waited four hours after the accident before returning to the cottage. The biker was gone by then – must have been spotted by a passing motorist. Only the two men remained, in the positions they'd discussed and practised many times. It made them simple to outflank. The leader, Pieter, had been quick to know he was beaten and easy to subdue. But the second man, Lukas, had panicked and fled for the woods. Menser had sent Clarke to deal with him while he focused on emptying the cottage of all their equipment and belongings. Everything ended up in the back of the van. Everything except Lukas.

Clarke swore that the man was dead. That he was well hidden in the woods. Menser wasn't comfortable with the situation, but time was running short. They left the body and headed for the trawler – Menser driving the van, Clarke in the red rental car. But with every minute that passed, he regretted the decision even more.

'He shouldn't have run,' Menser said. 'He left us no choice.'

She shook her head. Raised her knees to her chest and hugged her shins. 'It was his only choice.'

'Your friend Pieter didn't see it like that.'

'But Pieter will die, yes?'

The boat twisted and dived. Menser bounced up off his bunk. Landed on the small of his back. Swore under his breath.

'Got a minute?' The voice belonged to Clarke. He was standing in the doorway, wearing a drenched rain slicker and a yellow fisherman's hat. Water dripped on to the floor from his outerwear. He held a roll of gaffer tape in his hand.

Menser scrambled to his feet, using the wall for balance.

The girl twisted over on to her side. Stretched out along the bunk, pointing her toes inside her canvas training shoes.

'Goodbye, Pieter,' she said, in a small voice, and tucked herself into a ball.

Menser closed and bolted the door.

'Anything?' Clarke asked.

'Not yet.'

'Maybe she's just that stupid, you know?'

'I don't think so.'

'We could try their laptops again. Go back through their bags. See if we missed something.'

'They're clean.'

'Then you think maybe we should call him? Let him decide?'

Menser snatched the gaffer tape. It was light. The roll almost empty. He squeezed it in his hand. Felt his knuckles pop.

'No, I don't think so.'

'Why?'

'Because it's a bad idea.'

'And why's that?'

'Because, Clarke. Jesus. *Because.*'

Up on deck, it was so much worse. The painted metal was slick underfoot, as slippery as ice. Water had pooled and collected around the stacked lobster pots and dented oil drums, the puddles coloured with traces of diesel. A hook the size of a man's head swung wildly from a mast above them. Spray and foam pawed at the corroded railings.

Menser fed his arm through a metal stanchion on the exterior of the wheelhouse. The frigid water lashed against his bare scalp and hands. He watched the plastic patio chair skitter across the slanted deck. The noise was fast and frictionless, like stiff wire bristles on the surface of a mirror.

'See you gagged him.' Menser nodded at the swatch of tape across the man's mouth. 'He say much before you did it?'

'Lots.'

'Anything useful?'

'Nothing we didn't know already. Except for the stuff in Dutch. But I don't think that was for my benefit. I think maybe he was praying.'

Menser tipped his head on to his shoulder and considered the man.

Pieter – if that was his real name – was pleading with him. He could tell. It was in his eyes. The bulging white.

Menser shook his head. Wanting to communicate with him. Wanting to let him know that he should focus on himself now.

The man was naked, hunched forward against his restraints, his chemical-blond hair knotted wetly against his brow. His pale skin, where it wasn't covered in tattoos or coated with gaffer tape, was speckled with goose bumps and flushed red from the water and streaking wind. His muscular arms had been taped behind him, hands bound knuckle to knuckle. More tape had been wrapped around his chest and his elbows. More still had been coiled around his neck, looped beneath his chair, and up through his groin to his shoulders. His ankles had been secured to the chair legs, feet pointing outwards, suspended a few inches above the deck. He was stretching with his toes, trying to steady himself.

He couldn't reach.

Menser supposed he was meant to congratulate Clarke on

his inventiveness. A pat on the back for something that was seriously messed up.

He leaned back, feeling weak with fatigue. Rested his head against a rivet in the metal panel behind him.

There was land on the horizon. Some green fields. Some tan. The blurred outline of distant buildings.

Whitecaps rolled in. The vessel tipped. The chair skidded left.

Menser held fast to the stanchion with his elbow. Watched the chair skate towards the rear of the deck, where Clarke had slid aside the railings, leaving a gap perhaps two metres wide. The man screamed from behind his gag, nostrils flaring, until the boat levelled out. There was a pause, and then everything dipped to the right. The chair veered off and the man clattered into the lobster pots. He tried to tangle his head in the netting. Didn't work.

'Corner ball, back pocket.'

Clarke grinned as the swell pitched the nose of the vessel up and the chair edged away from the netting and careened towards the gap. It seemed, for just a moment, as if the momentum might abate. But no, a second wave rolled in and the chair slithered backwards, tipping the man called Pieter and his pleading eyes overboard.

Into the blackness beneath.

Chapter Thirteen

Lukas watched the cottage through the trees. He should have trusted his instincts. He'd had his doubts about the man. Questioned if he was really who he'd claimed to be. But he'd taken a chance. Indulged Lena. She'd wanted hot water. Demanded it. And Lukas couldn't face more of her whining and sulking. So he'd talked Pieter around. Agreed to make the call on her behalf and hire a repairman.

The dog. That was what had convinced him. If the man was a threat, Lukas couldn't see why he'd have a canine with him. And he *had* fixed the water system.

But then he'd taken Lena away on the motorbike. And afterwards the others had arrived.

Pieter had planned for something just like it. He'd schooled Lukas on how to defend the cottage. Taught him to fire a pistol against targets he'd rigged up in the trees. But the men who'd come had known what to expect. They'd anticipated Pieter's position and disabled him before Lukas could react. They should have thought of that. The man with the dog must have briefed them. Told them how many men they were facing. The layout of the cottage.

Lukas was no gunman. No hero. So he'd fled. Into the woods. Heard one of them chasing him. Turned and glimpsed the outline of the man braced against a tree, a rifle in his hands, the stock wedged into his shoulder and a telescopic sight glinting in the afternoon sun. Then something punched into his left thigh. Twirled him round. His feet tangled in undergrowth and he went down heavily.

That was when he'd lost his sunglasses. When he must have dropped his phone.

He'd waited for the man to approach. To finish him off. He'd waited with his finger curled tightly around the trigger of his pistol. Hands shaking. Wondering if he had the nerve to shoot. If his aim would be any good.

His thigh had pulsed and the pain had bloomed and that was when he'd glanced down and seen the blood for the first time. It had soaked through his jeans, dyed the denim an oily red. So much blood. Too much. Lukas had panicked. Crawled on his side away from his position. Kept crawling, even when the man didn't come. Crawled for close to an hour, maybe, until he found a place to hide. A hollow under a fallen tree deep inside the woods, where he'd removed his turtleneck sweater and used his T-shirt like a tourniquet, tightening it around his wound until he almost passed out. Darkness had come and he'd slept in fits, racked with pain and trembling with fear.

Early the next morning, he'd limped back to the cottage using a fallen branch as a crutch, his jeans stiff with dried blood. The place seemed abandoned and their rental car was nowhere to be seen. He'd entered the cottage slowly, pistol drawn, wondering if the men had left someone there for him. Wondering if Pieter was dead. But the place was empty. All their equipment gone. Every trace of them erased.

He hadn't known what to do. Whether to stay, or to try and get away. To get to a hospital, maybe. But if he sought help, they'd find him. They'd take him, too. And if he sheltered in the cottage, they might come back for him. He'd searched for his phone. Had no luck. And in his heart he knew he lacked the nerve to call Anderson anyway.

He'd stumbled along the path down through the woods. Asking himself what he should do. Where he could go. And that was when he'd seen the van. It was unlocked. The keys in the ignition.

He slid open the side cargo door and inside he'd found enough to sustain him. Water and sandwiches in a plastic cooler. A towel and a first-aid kit that he'd used to clean the wound to his leg. Pills for the pain. The damage wasn't as bad as he'd feared. The bullet had ripped clean a chunk of flesh, but it hadn't struck bone and Lukas couldn't feel anything lodged inside.

He'd secured a dressing pad with a tightly wound strip of electrician's tape, then found a change of clothes. A blue sweater and work jeans. Lukas remembered the man wearing them when he'd first approached the cottage. He must have shed them before dressing for his bike ride with Lena.

Lukas didn't understand why the van had been left behind. That was the part of the clean-up that bothered him. *Somebody* would have to come back for it. But maybe not too soon.

He knew that he should get to a phone and contact Anderson. But he also knew it would be bad for him when he did. He'd failed to protect Lena. But Pieter had failed, too. And Pieter was the professional.

What would Pieter do now, he'd wondered?

An idea formed in his mind. The men who'd come for Lena would want to remove her from the island. That much was clear. And there were only two options. Air or sea. Air was possible, he supposed. It was how he and Pieter had arrived. Lena, too. But Lena had had false papers. And she wouldn't co-operate with the men. Not willingly. So that meant a private plane. And a plane would leave a trail. Computer records, flight plans, everything.

That left the sea. Lukas knew there was a ferry service from Douglas. He'd seen where the ferry docked on the few occasions he'd been allowed to drive to the supermarket for supplies.

He'd clambered out of the rear of the van and circled around to take a look at the driver's seat. He was lucky. Luckier than he had any right to be. The van was an automatic and he was able to heave himself up and wedge his injured leg inside so that he could drive without too much discomfort.

The journey wasn't long. It passed in a blur. He parked the van outside the ferry terminal. The building was very dated. Grey, pitted concrete. Small glass windows. There was some kind of circular office space on top, shaped like a crown with a flagpole in the middle.

There was a waiting room inside. Thin carpets, back-to-back seating, a coffee shop in one corner. A colour monitor above a ticket counter listed the day's sailings to Liverpool and Heysham.

Lukas took a seat close to the public toilets. It was quiet when he arrived but the space soon filled up. Family groups and school parties and pensioners, hauling wheeled suitcases and holdalls behind them towards the check-in desk. That was when he realised his mistake. The men who'd taken Lena wouldn't come in here. Too public. They needed to be able to hide Lena. She'd be in the trunk of a car or the back of a van or concealed in some other way.

He limped outside and paced between the vehicles that had been parked in lines, waiting to be loaded on to the ferry. He realised then that it was hopeless. In his panic to flee the cottage, he hadn't got a good look at the men who'd come for them. He had no way of recognising them and no way of knowing which vehicle Lena might be in.

He circled anyway, staring in through people's windscreens, searching for a reaction. The worried looks he received unnerved him. He was drawing too much attention. Hobbling awkwardly between the rows of cars, the heavy pistol bulging in his pocket.

Should he make the phone call? He'd seen a public payphone inside the building.

Maybe not yet. He remembered what he'd told himself up at the plantation. Someone would have to return for the van. Someone would come for it.

So he would buy some food and drink from the coffee shop, drive back to the plantation and wait. Another day, at least.

He did exactly that, driving quickly for fear that he would change his mind. He retraced his route to the cottage, beached the van where he'd found it, opened the rear cargo doors and tidied away his clothes and the bloodied towel he'd used to tend to his injured leg.

Then he waited with his supplies, hidden in the woods. First, he saw the police come. Saw them poke around in the van. Saw them drive up the track to the cottage and summon some kind of lock service. Saw all of them leave.

Darkness fell. He fed himself and sheltered alongside the

van through the night. Stumbled up the track with a bottle of water and hunted through the woods by the cottage for his phone during the day.

And now the man was back, accompanied by a woman. She was wearing gloves and plastic covers over her feet. A professional. Lukas guessed they were finishing the clean-up now that the police were gone.

Lukas had watched the woman enter the cottage. He'd watched the man follow his dog into the woods and come back again. That was when the dog began to make sense. It must have been trained. It had found Lukas's phone. His sunglasses.

But it hadn't found Lukas.

And it hadn't found his gun.

Chapter Fourteen

Rebecca looked at me. I looked at Rebecca. The phone kept buzzing.

'What do we do?' I asked.

'I'm not sure.'

'Do we answer it?'

'I think so.'

'You *think* so.'

'What have we got to lose?'

Rocky looked like he wanted to intervene. He leapt up and rested his forepaws on the edge of the kitchen table, watching the phone buzz and jitter against the tabletop.

'Who does the talking?'

'You do,' Rebecca said. 'But I'll put it on speaker so we can both hear.'

'What do I say?'

'The truth. If you want to find Lena, this could be our best chance.'

She steadied the phone with one hand and pressed a button with the other. The buzzing stopped. She pressed another button and I could hear dead air and a crackle through the speaker.

I waited for our caller to talk. Seemed they were waiting for the same thing from me. I cleared my throat.

'Hello?'

Silence. A heavy one.

'Hello?' I tried again.

'Who is this?'

The man's voice was cultured, marked by the same European accent I'd heard from Mr Shades and Lena. It was obvious that English wasn't his first language. But he spoke it very well.

'My name's Rob. And you are?'

'Why are you using this phone?'

For some reason, I found myself answering his question, even though he'd chosen to ignore mine. 'I found it.'

'Found it where?'

'The woods. Near a cottage in Arrasey plantation.' I thought of his accent. 'In the Isle of Man,' I added.

There was a pause as the caller absorbed the information.

'And where are you now?'

'Same place. Inside the cottage.'

'And why are you there?'

I took a breath. Tried to think where to begin. Beside me, Rebecca was carefully reaching inside her backpack. She removed a notepad and pen. Pulled the lid off the pen soundlessly with her teeth.

'I'm looking for someone.'

Another pause. The man was being cautious.

I locked eyes with Rebecca. She circled her pen in the air, motioning for me to continue.

'Her name's Lena. She's missing.'

The silence lingered. It was getting to me. I filled it again.

'I took her for a ride on my motorbike two days ago. We crashed. I haven't seen her since. I don't know what's happened to her.'

Finally, he spoke. His voice was pinched. An octave higher.

'Who do you work for?'

'What?'

'Your employer. Tell me.'

Rebecca made a note on her pad. She wrote down the words: *Who do you work for?*

'I don't work for anyone. I'm a heating engineer. I came out here because the boiler was broken. That was three days ago. There were two men here with Lena. She said they were friends but I had my doubts about it. She asked me to take her out on my motorbike the following morning. I agreed. After that, I don't remember exactly what happened. I had a concussion. But now this cottage is empty. There's nobody here.' I looked around me, as if to confirm that was still the case. 'This phone belonged to one of the men. I saw him with it. And now you've dialled it. I can see that someone, probably you, has dialled it sixty-four times before this. So perhaps you can tell me where Lena is?' The static buzz seemed to charge the air in the room. 'Or perhaps I should call the police? Give them this phone, too?'

'Will you tell me something, Rob?' He said my name as if it sounded exotic to him. 'Why are you looking for Lena?'

And the funny thing was, when he asked me that, I didn't know what to say. I didn't know why exactly this was important to me. I could have told him that I was worried for Lena's welfare, which was true. I could have said that I wanted to prove to myself that I hadn't imagined the whole thing, which was also the case, though my need to do that had become less pressing since I'd found the phone and the sunglasses, and since Rebecca had discovered the surveillance equipment. I could even have said that it had something to do with the way

I'd been feeling since I'd lost my sister – the aimless, root-less sensation of a grief without explanation or resolution. The endless wondering if there was something more I could have done for Laura. If I might have saved her, even.

But instead all I said was, 'Because somebody should be.'

And to my surprise, it seemed to be enough. I heard him ex-hale heavily into the phone, like a man who'd just set down a heavy object he'd been carrying for longer than he could truly bear.

'Are you alone, Rob?'

I glanced at Rebecca. She nodded cautiously.

'Yes,' I said.

'Then please listen very carefully to what I am about to tell you. Lena's life may depend on it.'

Chapter Fifteen

'There are some things you must know about me,' said the voice on the end of the phone. 'The first is that my name is Erik Zeeger and I am Lena's father. The second is that I am a rich man. A very rich man. This is my privilege. It is also my curse.'

Rebecca scrawled the name *Erik Zeeger* on her pad. She added the word *Rich* and underlined it twice.

'Perhaps you understand. There are people who wish to hurt me. People who would prefer to take what I have rather than build something of their own. Can you understand this, Rob?'

I thought Rocky was capable of understanding it. 'I suppose I can,' I told him.

'But money. Wealth. It is only so much, yes? There is more to life than this. For me, I think so. I have hobbies. Passions. But more than any of this, I have my Lena. My child.'

I stared at the phone, waiting for him to go on. I was building an image of him now. I was picturing him in a well-appointed study in a remote wing of a large house, overlooking a manicured lawn. In my mind's eye, he was wearing a business suit. Red braces. His slicked grey hair was parted neatly along the middle of his scalp.

'These people, these evil, twisted people, will do anything to harm me. To ... unsettle me.'

'Are you saying they'd hurt Lena to get to you?'

'Exactly this.'

I glanced at Rebecca. 'And these people. Could they be the men I saw with her here?'

'Describe them to me.'

I did. I ran through everything I could remember about Mr Shades and his musclebound companion. I mentioned the laptop and the book on body art. I also told Erik that their accents sounded similar to his own.

'These men you describe – they work for me. Lukas and Pieter. They are loyal men. Men I trust. But they have not called me for two days now. And if what you tell me is true – that you are alone and you have found Lukas's phone – then I think this can only mean one thing.'

'And what's that?'

'They are dead, Rob. The people who took Lena. They killed them.'

I felt the room contract around me. I wasn't sure if he was being melodramatic or if he was a raving fantasist or if my bruised mind was playing tricks on me.

'Dead?' I asked, mainly because I couldn't think of what else to say. 'You really think someone would murder them?'

'Of course. It is simple.'

I raised my good hand to my forehead. Looked down at the surveillance equipment on the table. Then at the woman in latex gloves and forensic overshoes standing alongside me. Perhaps the idea of two men being killed wasn't so hard to believe, after all.

I let go of a long breath and asked the first question that occurred to me. 'Did you know that your men and Lena were on the Isle of Man?'

'Of course.'

'Did they tell you she'd gone for a motorbike ride with me?'

'No. It was forbidden for her to leave the house. They knew this. They knew I would not tolerate it.'

'Do you know where Lena might be? Who took her?'

'Rob, please, I have answered your questions, yes? I have been patient with you. A man I do not know. A man who has seen my Lena. My child. But now, I would like for you to listen to me. Can you do this, Rob?'

I glanced at Rocky, as if he might be able to help me with this one. 'Go ahead.'

'There is a man who works for me. He will want to speak with you. Myself, also. You have not asked where I am calling you from. I can tell you that I live in the Netherlands. We will come to your Isle of Man, Rob. We will arrive in –' he broke off and I heard a muffled sound, the noise of a hand being clamped over the speaker on his phone, '– exactly three hours. Will you meet with us at the airport?'

The man calling himself Erik had asked if I was by myself. Now I realised that I hadn't asked him the same question. I had no idea how many people were with him but I suspected there was at least one – the man he'd just mentioned.

I checked the time on the mobile phone. 'It's four o'clock already,' I told him. 'There are no direct flights from Holland to the Isle of Man. Even if you fly via London, you won't make the evening connection. But if you can get here tomorrow, I'll meet you then.'

He laughed. A sharp bark. It didn't sit easily with the tone of our conversation.

'Rob, please, do not worry about this. Three hours. Will you meet with us?'

'I guess,' I said, doubting it was a sensible move even as I made it. 'Should I call the police?'

'*No*. You must not speak with them. For Lena's sake, this is something you must promise me. Understand?'

I checked Rebecca's reaction. She rolled out her bottom lip. Raised her eyebrows.

'All right,' I said. 'But I may bring someone with me. A friend.'

He paused for a beat. 'You see, I did not think you were really alone, Rob. Please, do not lie to me again.'

And with that, he cut the connection and ended what was without question the strangest telephone conversation of my life.

*

The bald man had told Lena that he was concerned because she wasn't frightened. This had pleased her more than she could say. It meant the man had doubts. That he was questioning himself. That was good. It could be useful. Anything that disrupted their plans or gave her more time was helpful. And it told her something else. It suggested the evidence wasn't as solid as the man had claimed.

But more than that, she was proud of herself. Because the truth was that she really was scared. She'd been scared for as long as she could remember.

Mostly, she'd been scared of her father. She'd been scared of the man he'd revealed himself to be. Throughout her teenage years she'd felt suffocated. Until she finally rebelled. Kicked free. And then his tendencies became so much worse than she'd feared. Wherever she went in the world, whatever she did, anonymous men in suits would follow her. They'd monitor her and they'd type up their reports and they'd send them back to her father. Often her father would be concerned by the reports and he'd send more men to watch over her. Even from a distance, even without her consent, he was able to smother her.

So then she went to extremes to express her freedom. She indulged in every vice she could find. Sex. Alcohol. Drugs. Anything that would wound her father. Anything that would scare him, too. But the outcome was, she began to lose herself. She began to forget the real Lena.

Then she'd met Alex. The perfect insult. The ultimate rejection of everything her father stood for. But pretty soon Alex began to scare her, too. Not because of the threat she'd anticipated. Not because of the dangers she'd felt sure she was exposing herself to. No, what scared her with Alex was the way she began to feel. The emotions she experienced. They were more powerful and more overwhelming than anything she'd ever known before. They were *genuine*, and that was terrifying.

So she became afraid of losing Alex. Of the steps her father might take to separate them. Of the way others might seek to exploit their relationship.

And then she did lose him, and she felt herself break, and she had no idea how she could ever put herself back together again. If she'd ever feel the *urge* to rebuild her life. Hiding in the cottage had been nothing compared to that. Finding herself smothered by her father again, waiting for the police to come, asking herself how all of it might end. None of those things had come close to terrifying her in the same way.

But now, she was scared anew. Sitting in the cramped cabin,

being tossed around by the sea, in the process of being delivered to destinations and people unknown. She was scared of the young guy with the meaningful leer. She was scared of the older man with the questions and the threats. She was scared about what Lukas may have suffered and fearful for Pieter. She was scared of the police. She was scared of confronting what had been done to Alex. She was scared of what had become of Melanie Fleming. She was scared of having to call on her father's help.

But more than anything else, she was scared for the plumber. Because she realised that she didn't know what had happened to him. She'd assumed the two men had left him alone, but it had dawned on her now that they might have harmed him in some way. Or worse. And without the plumber, she really was on her own. And that was the most frightening thought of all.

Chapter Sixteen

I waited with Rocky in the kitchen while Rebecca took another quick tour through the rest of the cottage. She found evidence of more surveillance equipment in the living room and the bedrooms but she didn't bother to remove it. The haul from the kitchen and the garage had been enough to satisfy her curiosity. She stuffed the microphones and the camera cables inside her backpack and then she bolted the kitchen door and followed Rocky and me out through the garage.

Rebecca heaved the metal door closed and turned the key in the lock before dropping it into my palm. 'Will you show me where you found the phone and the sunglasses?' she asked.

I looked down at my hand. Something bothered me. I wasn't sure exactly what.

'Rob?' Rebecca was removing her plastic overshoes. She was leaning her weight against the garage door. 'Did you hear what I asked?'

I bent down to Rocky and ran my hand through his fur. There was a high bank of trees off to the right and I felt myself looking into them. Searching them.

'We don't have long,' Rebecca persisted. 'Not if we're going to meet this guy in under three hours.'

'Right,' I said. 'The phone and the sunglasses. We can try.'

Rocky led us through the overgrown garden and into the woods. He seemed to be doing a good job of retracing our footsteps, but the further we went, the less sure I became of my bearings. It took a good fifteen minutes of circling in frustration until I began to believe I was finally standing in the right spot.

I looked down at the dry, muddy ground, alongside the husky trunk of a nearby larch, the fronds of a wilting fern and a fallen branch covered in ivy and brambles. 'See that mark? That's from Rocky pawing at the ground.' I eased myself down and circled my hand over an area where the ground was darker because the subsoil had been churned up. I looked behind me. Shards of mirror glass were ground into the earth. 'This is definitely it. Look.'

Rebecca crouched alongside me, her hair falling over her face. I could smell the perfume she had on. Something with a citrus note. Her skin was soft and pale. Dusted with freckles. Not what I should have been focusing on.

She grabbed one of her gloves from her backpack, snapped it on over her right hand and prodded the shards around with her finger. Then she paused for a moment, as if deep in thought, and ran her hand along the fallen branch. She contemplated her fingertips. Showed them to me.

Blood. Dark and glistening against the white latex. Powdery in places.

I stood quickly, wiping my hand on the seat of my jogging trousers. I shuddered and lifted my shoes and scanned the area beneath them. There was no sign of any gore. But I still didn't like it.

'You think Erik was right?' I asked. 'That his men were killed out here?'

'Hard to tell. But somebody was definitely hurt.'

'Are you going to take a sample?'

She turned and squinted at me. 'You think I have a forensics lab with me?'

She rolled the bottom of the glove away from her wrist, bunched it into a ball and stuffed it inside her backpack. She straightened, hands on hips, and scrutinised the woods surrounding us.

'So what's next?' I asked.

'Next is you take your dog and your van back home. There are some things I want to look into. I'll meet you at your place for half past six. Will that give us enough time to get to the airport?'

'Should do.' I reached into my pocket for the phone Erik had called me on. 'What do I do if he rings me again?'

'Talk to him. But keep a note of what he says. And don't agree to change anything about our meeting until you speak to me first.' She smiled crookedly. 'Remember, the man you spoke to was just a voice on the end of the line. We don't know if anything he told us is true. And personally, I don't like that he asked you not to contact the police.'

'You sound worried.'

She nudged the bloody branch with the toe of her shoe. 'That's because I am, Rob. Truly.'

*

Lukas watched the man and the woman secure the cottage and follow the dog into the woods. He thought about tracking them but the dog bothered him. He hadn't bathed in two days.

He was caked in dirt. The stench of his own sweat and filth. The dog would smell him. Warn them.

The woman had the backpack with her. There was a chance she was carrying a weapon. And the man shouldn't be underestimated. His arm was in a sling, which was something Lukas couldn't readily explain, but he was tall and powerfully built.

Lukas waited until they were out of sight before limping away from his vantage point high up on the tree-covered bank. He hobbled across the rutted track, his gun gripped tightly in his hand, his makeshift crutch supporting his weight. He flattened his back against the wall of the cottage, shuffled past the front door and looked in at the sitting-room window. Nothing had altered. He worked his way around the far side of the cottage to the kitchen. Same thing. He wet his lip, stared hard into the woods, then stuffed the gun into the waistband of his trousers and stumbled away.

How many times had he followed this path now? Ten? Twenty? It was becoming no easier. The journey took him fifteen minutes, minimum, and there'd been times during the past few days when he'd had to duck into the trees because he'd heard people approaching. Hikers. Dog walkers.

There was nobody today – no one at all – and Lukas, breathless now, made it through the swinging gate without interruption. A small blue car was parked to the side of the van. He looked in through the windows and saw a covering of golden dog hairs on the rear seat. He tried the door. Locked. Tried the boot. It was shut fast. There was a sticker for a car rental company in the rear window – the same company he and Pieter had used when they'd first arrived on the island. Lukas wondered where their rental car was now. Hidden, probably. Or perhaps just returned and carefully cleaned. The right payments made to the right employee. The paperwork shredded. Records erased.

Lukas looked between the car and the van, trying to clear his mind, to think logically. The car was the vehicle they must have arrived in. It could be how they'd leave. But if they were at the cottage to clear the scene, it made sense that they'd drive the van away, too. And he knew the van. Knew of the dust sheets. The water he could drink.

Lukas hobbled across and slid open the loading door on the far side. The interior smelled of wood and diesel. Of stale air. He dropped his backside on to the plywood floor. Heaved his aching leg up and in. Then he slammed the door closed behind him, shuffled backwards and covered his body with the stained and musty sheets.

He waited.

Chapter Seventeen

Rocky slept deeply for most of the journey home. I wasn't nearly so relaxed. My van might have been an automatic, but it was tricky to drive with one arm in a sling. More to the point, I was way outside my comfort zone, unsure what I'd got myself involved in and whether I'd have cause to regret it. There was evidence to suggest that two men had been hurt, or worse, in the plantation. Lena, too, possibly. The sensible thing would have been to phone police headquarters and ask to speak with Detective Shimmin or Teare. Tell them what had happened. Wash my hands of the whole affair. Problem was, Shimmin had dismissed my story the first time around and Erik had asked me not to contact the police. True, I didn't owe him anything – I'd never even met the guy – but if Lena really was his daughter, then I felt like I should at least hear him out.

Hearing him out meant that I'd be relying entirely on Rebecca. So far, she'd struck me as capable and confident. She'd found the surveillance equipment up at the cottage and she'd developed a plausible theory about my crash. Most importantly, she'd believed what I'd told her about Lena and that had made me inclined to trust her. But I had no idea if my trust could really be justified. I didn't know how Mum and Dad had come to hire her. And I didn't know why.

I was still thinking about Rebecca as I parked my van in front of my bike workshop and led Rocky towards my front door. He staggered past me and up the stairs, primed for the second phase of his nap, and I shut him inside before heading off to find Dad.

It didn't take me long. I could hear the *chugga-chugga* of his lawnmower engine coming from around the front of the conservatory. Dad had invested in a ride-on machine two summers ago and he lavished just as much care and attention on its upkeep as he did on my bikes. The mower was painted green with a yellow stripe down the middle and it was fitted with a spring-mounted seat and a cup holder. I always suspected the cup holder had been the clincher when he'd gone to inspect the machines on offer at the local garden centre. It was perfect for cradling a can of chilled lager.

There was no lager today. I hadn't seen him touch a drop since Laura's death. The cup holder was as empty as his gaze, focused blindly on the sloping grass in front of him. This year, he'd chosen a circular design, the lawn patterned in concentric rings of dark and light green. Last year, it had been stripes.

'Dad?'

He didn't hear me because of the ear defenders he was wearing. I waited for him to turn and trundle back in my direction. He stopped alongside me, the clamorous engine forcing him to shout.

'Just getting a cut in before it rains again.' He removed the ear defenders and wrapped them around the steering wheel. 'And you know how the residents like to watch.'

He tipped his head in the direction of the conservatory. A motley audience of shrivelled old folk was arranged behind the glass in wing-back seats and wheelchairs. I waved an apology for the interruption.

'I wanted to talk to you about Rebecca,' I yelled.

'Can it wait? Be dark soon.'

'Not really.' I reached across and turned the key in the ignition. The engine spluttered, then died. The sudden silence felt weirdly charged. 'Why did you hire her, Dad?'

'You know that by now. She would have told you.' He scowled across the lawn at a rogue patch of grass the mower blades had somehow missed.

'But you never mentioned any suspicions about Laura's death to me. And why Rebecca? There must be private investigators here on the island. You probably know some of them. But you hired a complete stranger. From London.'

He sighed. It sounded more like a growl. 'It just happened like that.'

'Like what? You went on the internet and searched for private investigators and her firm came up? Or somebody recommended her? Or, what exactly?'

He put his hand on the ignition key. I seized his wrist, holding firm.

'What aren't you telling me? There's something, isn't there? Dad?'

He shook his head. Snatched his arm free and reached for his ear defenders. Then he turned the engine over and pulled away sharply.

'Ask your mother,' he called from over his shoulder. 'She's the one you need to speak to.'

*

I found Mum in the television room. She was kneeling beside

one of the newer residents, a lady in a matted wig and bunched stockings who had a vicelike grip on the remote control. The television volume was too loud, rousing those who'd been sleeping and forcing others to adjust their hearing aids. But the lady wanted it louder.

Mum was doing her best to prise the remote free without causing offence. It was a delicate procedure but she approached it with the calm assurance I've seen from her so often in the past. As I watched, the remote was liberated, the sound decreased and the elderly woman appeased with a loving squeeze of the hand and the offer of a fresh cup of tea.

'Got a minute, Mum?' I asked.

'Of course, love. Walk with me?'

She slipped the remote into the pocket of her apron and I followed her through the lounge into the small side kitchen, our movements tracked by every conscious resident in the vicinity. There was a hot-water urn on the counter and Mum popped a teabag into a metal teapot and filled it with steaming water.

'How's the head?' she asked.

'Fine.'

'You look a little peaky.' She placed a cool palm on my forehead. 'Hmm.' She reached down for the pulse point on my wrist. Consulted her watch. 'Hmm,' she said again.

'What's the verdict?'

'You should be resting. I told your father as much.'

The stern look she gave me faded into weary fatigue. I didn't know how long it had been since she'd slept properly but it might as well have been several years. Her skin was dry and powdery at her temples, a sign of her eczema flaring up, and the only way she could have been any paler was if she was haunting the place. The contrast with her curly red hair only served to make her pallid appearance even worse. She'd lost weight. Lost energy. Lost most things, I guess.

'I'm fine,' I said again. 'Shoulder's a bit sore, that's all.'

'No need for you to be on your feet, though, is there?'

She turned her back on me and fiddled with the hospital-green crockery on a shelf above the urn.

'I was talking to Dad about Rebecca,' I said.

No reaction.

'The investigator you hired, Mum. To look into Laura's death.'

Her shoulders dropped and she set a cup and saucer down with a clatter. Then she gathered herself and ducked below the counter to scoop a carton of milk out of the fridge.

'How's Rocky?' she asked. 'Glad to have you back, I shouldn't wonder. You should have seen him moping around this place while you were gone. Happy to help himself to biscuits, mind.'

'Mum.' *Still nothing.* 'Mum. We need to talk about this.'

She slapped the milk carton down. A splotch of milk shot out of the top and splashed the counter.

'Ah, hell.'

'Here.' I ran a cloth under the tap and passed it to her. 'Why did you hire her, Mum?'

'Oh, Rob.' She squeezed the cloth in her hand. So tight that it dribbled water on to the floor by her feet. 'Why don't you talk to your father about this?'

'He told me to speak to you. What's going on, Mum? I know it's awful about Laura. We don't talk about it and I get that. I understand why. But it hurts me every bit as much as it hurts you and Dad. And if there's something going on, I think it's only fair for you to tell me.'

She looked around for a moment, as if disoriented. 'You're right. You are.' She mopped up the spill. Glanced across at the stewing tea.

'That can wait,' I said.

'I should really just –'

'Tell me about Rebecca, Mum. Tell me why you hired her.'

She drew a halting breath, one that seemed to teeter on the edge of tears. But when she finally spoke, her words punched a hole clean through my heart.

'Because your sister asked me to,' she said.

*

Mum handed me a small piece of card, pale yellow in colour. Printed on the front of it in a modest black script were the words *Rebecca Lewis, Wilton Associates*. I turned it over. Rebecca's contact details were listed on the back.

'Your sister gave this to me,' Mum said. 'It was just a day before the accident.'

The accident. I had a problem with the way Mum and Dad kept calling it that. As if somehow Laura's foot had slipped off the brake and on to the accelerator. As if her hands had turned the steering wheel towards the cliff edge against her will.

'She was standing right here,' Mum said. 'Right where you are now.'

I really wished she hadn't said that. I could almost picture some ghostly outline of Laura's body occupying the same space as my own. My feet covering the same square of carpet. Lungs breathing the same air.

Mum had taken me through to her office. It was a small, brightly lit room just to the side of the home's main entrance. It was furnished with an ash-blonde desk and matching cabinets. There was no clutter. No mess. It was the first room that prospective clients – usually the middle-aged children of future residents – were shown into when they came to view the facilities.

I pressed a fingertip against the corner of the business card. The same card Laura had touched. Close to a month ago.

'What did she say exactly?'

Mum raised a hand to her chest. 'It was your sister's second day visiting. She'd spent most of the first day in bed, remember? She'd looked exhausted, poor love, and I'd told her to rest. I think she surprised herself by how much she slept.'

'She'd been working too hard.'

'That's what I told her. And the next day, she was a little dizzy. She barely ate any breakfast. Looked a little lost. I thought it was the tiredness catching up with her. She came and found me in here and I told her to go back to sleep. But she said she had to go out. There were things she had to do.'

'What things?'

'I don't know. She was being quite guarded. But then, she always was. That was just Laura.'

It used not to be. Not when we were growing up. Not when her laughter had filled our home. It was her job that had changed her. Her high-powered career. There'd been distance between us because of it. And not just because she was so committed to getting ahead – at the expense, it had seemed to me, of leaving us all behind – but also because I'd felt that she'd looked down on me for the choices I'd made. Not going to university. Learning a trade. I'd done it because I'd wanted to focus on my road racing – perhaps go professional one day – but Laura never understood that. She'd treated me as if my whole life was one huge missed opportunity.

I didn't say any of this to Mum. I never had.

'And then,' Mum said, pointing a finger at Rebecca's business card, 'she pulled that out of her pocket. I could tell she was nervous about giving it to me. She fiddled with it for a long time. But when she told me what it was . . .'

Mum gazed down at the telephone on her desk. Shook her head.

'She told you it was for a detective agency?' I asked.

'She said she knew Rebecca and that she'd trust her with her life. Those were her words, Rob. *Her life.* And I knew right then that I wouldn't want to hear any more. But she made me listen. Asked me to promise.'

'Promise what exactly?'

Mum looked up. There was a vacancy in her eyes. A loss. As if she was letting slip another small piece of her daughter that she'd been fighting hard to hold on to. 'She made me promise that if anything happened to her, I'd call Rebecca. And when I asked what she meant by that, she wouldn't say. She wouldn't explain.'

Her words rocked me. I fell silent. I was afraid that if I pushed too hard, Mum would fall apart right in front of me. That the subject would be closed off for ever.

'Did she say how they knew each other?' I asked, in a quiet voice.

'She said they trained together. At Laura's work.'

'Her work?'

'Yes, at the bank.'

I thought about that. I supposed it was possible that Rebecca had been some kind of financial investigator. Maybe later she'd branched out.

'When did you contact Rebecca?' I asked.

'Not until after the funeral.'

'And how did she react?'

'She was surprised. Confused. I had to explain who Laura was. She made me describe her.'

'Didn't that strike you as odd?'

'I almost hung up the phone. I really hadn't wanted to call that number. Your father was completely against it. I'd been putting it off for days. After what Laura had done . . .' Mum gulped air, like a diver about to swim to the very bottom of the ocean. 'I hadn't wanted to believe anything else could have happened to her. Understand? I could cope with the grief. The shame. But Rob, love, I knew I couldn't handle the hope.'

She searched out my eyes and I did my best to lock on to hers, as if somehow I could raise her up out of the darkness I'd led her to.

'But then,' she said, 'the funniest thing happened. Rebecca told me she'd take the case. She said she'd start work on it right away. And she said she wouldn't charge us, Rob. Not a single penny.'

Chapter Eighteen

Lukas had stayed hidden inside the van. He'd been lucky. It had only occurred to him halfway through the journey that he could find himself trapped if the man decided to lock the van when he arrived at his destination. Lukas had listened closely to the noise of a door opening and closing. The sound of the man talking to his dog. But there'd been no electronic *blip* from a car key. No mechanical *thunk*. Instead, he'd heard footsteps on gravel, moving away from him. Then nothing at all.

His leg was stiff, pulsing with a deep, relentless ache. He stretched. Winced. Stretched some more.

He slid on his buttocks towards the sliding door and his fingers groped for the latch. It was awkward to reach from his sitting position. He compressed it – a muffled *click* – and a blade of daylight sliced through the gloom.

Lukas pushed his face into the gap. He was in a sunny yard. A minibus was parked close by. He reached for his gun and used the barrel to ease the door aside so he could hang his head out. A large house was off to his right, three storeys in height, with a glass conservatory on the front. There were a lot of windows, but nobody appeared to be watching him. He could hear coarse engine noise – a generator, perhaps.

Lukas lowered himself to the ground, favouring his good leg. He nudged the door closed behind him and edged around the rear of the van. Another building, this one much closer. It was some kind of converted barn, timber-clad, with a set of double wooden doors right in front of him and a conventional doorway further along. The double doors were unsecured and Lukas was about to investigate when he heard footsteps on gravel, hurrying towards him.

The big man in the sling came into view. Lukas flattened himself against the van, body rigid, the gun down by his thigh, his finger tightening on the trigger.

But the man entered the building without looking in his direction.

Lukas was unsure what to do. The man was dangerous, he was certain of that. But it wasn't safe out in the open and he couldn't stay in the van. If Lena was here, he should try to find her. That was what Pieter would do.

Right now, he wished he could switch positions with Pieter. Lukas was no bodyguard. No hero. He was good with computers and gadgets. Capable of following Mr Zeeger's instructions without asking questions. Prepared to leave his home at a moment's notice and live in close proximity with Mr Zeeger's daughter for as long as necessary. Clever enough to know that the assignment he'd been given by Anderson wasn't strictly legal and that he wasn't in a position to contact the police. But that didn't mean he was equipped to handle this.

Whatever *this* was.

He limped towards the double doors. Set his ear to the wood. The timber was solid and he couldn't hear a thing. He prised an opening and inched forwards into the unknown.

A garage workshop. The concrete floor was painted a pale blue colour, the walls a glossy cream. Something touched his face and he raised his arm in defence, but it was only a set of biking leathers hanging from a rail.

A scratched wooden workbench extended to his right, covered in tools and machinery. There were colourful posters on the wall of men on motorbikes and some kind of trophy cabinet below them. Down on the floor, the component parts of a motorbike had been laid out on a canvas sheet. The bike looked as if it had been in an accident. The frame was dented and heavily scratched and the front forks and wheel were buckled and bent out of shape.

Lukas backed away and bumped into the handlebars of another motorbike. It had no wheels and was balanced on a metal frame. Two more bikes with a matching colour scheme – black, with orange flashes – were assembled towards the end of the garage, beyond a stack of spare tyres. The tyre rubber was smooth and jet-black, fresh from the production line.

Lukas hobbled towards a wooden door at the end of the room. The door gave no indication of what lay behind it. Not reassuring. But not something he could ignore.

He was going to have to open it.

*

By the time I got back to my place, Rocky could barely summon the energy to greet me. He'd conked out at the top of the stairs, his head hanging limply over the riser, and I had to step over him. Time was running short. Rebecca would arrive to collect me soon. I went into my bathroom and swallowed a couple of painkillers, then washed my face one-handed – something that was harder than I might have expected – and was just drying myself with a towel when I heard movement downstairs.

'Grandpa?'

He didn't answer me. I could have sworn someone had come in through the door.

'Grandpa, it's OK. I could use your help getting dressed.'

I listened closely, waiting for him to shuffle into view, but he didn't appear.

I kicked off my shoes, then squirmed out of my jogging trousers and went in search of a pair of beige chinos hanging at the back of my wardrobe. Getting them on wasn't easy but I managed it in the end, opting to go without a belt. I stuck with the shirt I was already wearing, then pushed my feet into some brown leather shoes that could have done with a clean but weren't going to receive it. I checked my watch. Still a few minutes. I scooped up Rocky's bed in my good arm and walked through to the lounge to nudge him on the backside with my toe.

'Come on, Rock. Sleepover time.'

He staggered to his feet and stretched his back, groaning loudly. Then he bundled down the stairs in what could have passed for a fall and sniffed hard at the base of the door leading into my bike workshop.

'Cut it out,' I told him, following a lot more steadily. He was squatting on his forepaws, pressing his nose against the gap. 'Hey. I said cut it out.' I opened the front door. 'Go on. Go find Grandpa.'

Finally, a command Rocky was happy to obey. He bolted through the yard and made his way up to Grandpa's room long before I got over there myself.

Grandpa was playing it innocent when I entered, sitting in his armchair with Rocky by his feet, acting as if he'd been labouring over one of the puzzles in his crossword book for most of the afternoon. He was holding his magnifying glass close to the page, gripping a biro between his lips. I can't tell you how many times I've seen him holding this pose. When we were kids, Laura and I used to try and help him with the clues, but our suggestions were always way off the mark. Eventually, he'd grow frustrated with us and hand the book over, telling us we could tackle one of the puzzles in the back. We'd do exactly that, filling squares with the right number of letters but completely the wrong answers, until we were forced to invent words of our own devising to get anywhere close to completing the thing. If Grandpa minded, he rarely said, and sometimes I used to picture him late at night, turning to the back of his puzzle books and chortling at the rude words and exotic phrases we'd scribbled down.

I dropped Rocky's bed on to the floor beneath the window and watched him clamber across it, pawing at the foam until he had it just how he liked. 'OK if Rocky stays with you tonight?' I asked Grandpa. 'I have to go out and I'm not sure what time I'll be back.'

Grandpa set his magnifying glass down on the crossword book. His eyes glimmered with mischief. 'That detective sure is pretty.'

'It's not like that, Grandpa.'

He winked. 'Would be if I was your age, my boy.'

I didn't doubt it.

'Make sure Rocky sleeps in his own bed this time, will you?' I said.

Even Rocky rolled his eyes at that one. I'm not sure why I

bothered. We all knew Rocky would be snoring the night away curled up on Grandpa's toes.

*

Lukas was spooked by how close he'd come to being caught. He'd barely opened the door from the garage and glimpsed the staircase on the other side when the man had called down from above. He'd jerked backwards. Lost his grip on the door handle. Watched in terror as it tapped against the frame.

He'd expected the man to investigate – to find him crouched below the porcelain sink, his ruined leg poking straight out from his hip – but nothing had happened until the furious drumming on the stair treads. Footsteps followed. Slower this time. And then there was a rasping, rustling noise at the base of the door. The dog. Sniffing the air for him.

An odd calm had crept over Lukas then. Relief at being caught. An end to his botched rescue attempt. But no, the man had addressed the dog in a sharp tone and the front door had opened and closed.

Was it a trick? Was the man still there? Lukas spent so long waiting that he was sure he'd blown whatever opportunity had come his way. But when, at last, he gathered the courage to crack open the door, he was surprised to find that the hallway was empty.

The staircase was carpeted and steep. Lukas approached it at a stoop, then dropped his backside on to a tread. He laboured up, one step at a time, the weighty handgun pointed down at the front door.

Perhaps the man in the sling really was gone. Perhaps he'd find Lena, after all.

Chapter Nineteen

Rebecca was running late. I'd been standing outside the care home for ten minutes, asking myself if meeting Erik was a good idea or a terrible mistake, when she swung the Fiesta into the driveway and slewed to a halt in front of me.

I opened the door and climbed inside. 'We're going to be cutting it fine,' I said. 'What kept you?'

She shook her head. 'Directions first. Tell me the fastest route.'

I had her turn right out of the care home and then I led her down beyond the Quarterbridge roundabout – one of the most famous points on the TT course – until she was accelerating hard along the A road heading south. If traffic was on our side, I thought we'd just about make it to the airport for 7 p.m. What I was less sure of was how I felt about the woman who happened to be driving me.

Mum had said that Rebecca had taken on the investigation into Laura's death on a cost-free basis. From what Rebecca had told me, she'd been working on the case for a fortnight already. And now she was helping me look into the situation with Lena, on what I assumed were the same terms. Why was she doing it, I wondered? What was in it for her?

I looked across, searching for clues. A pair of dark aviator sunglasses concealed her eyes and she was focusing hard through the windscreen at the road ahead. Her fingers flexed and tightened around the steering wheel. She chewed her lip and shook her head at the ponderous speed of the passenger bus in front of us, then consulted her side mirror.

'Who are you?' I asked. 'Why are you helping me?'

Her forehead creased in thought. 'I told you.' She scowled at her speedometer. Checked her rear-view mirror. 'Your parents hired me.'

'They said you're not charging them anything.'

She dropped her head to one side, lowered her chin and pulled out around the bus.

And immediately swerved back in again.

A minicab had been coming straight for us. I braced my palm on the dashboard. Gritted my teeth. I like to race motor-bikes. I enjoy the sensation of speed, the thrill I get from grazing my knee on a sweeping curve at well over 100 mph. But I didn't appreciate Rebecca's driving style. Not one bit.

'Oops,' she said.

'Are you going to answer my question?'

Rebecca adjusted her hands on the steering wheel. 'Which one? First, you wanted to know why I was late picking you up. Now you want to know why I'm doing this.'

'Both. But you can start by telling me why you agreed to look into Laura's death.'

Rebecca turned to me and I saw two shrunken versions of myself in the dark lenses of her sunglasses. It made me uncomfortable. She should have been concentrating on the road. The rear of the bus was only metres ahead.

'Call it a favour to your sister.'

'You knew her?'

'In a way.'

I felt myself sag. I wasn't sure what I'd expected her to say. Was even less sure which outcome I'd have preferred.

'Can you watch the road?'

Rebecca turned back to the windscreen and immediately veered out around the bus. This time, the road was clear. She overtook on the wrong side of a safety bollard. The bus driver wasn't impressed. He let her know it by leaning on his horn.

'You're a really awful driver,' I said.

'Just making up time.'

'Are you going to tell me about Laura?'

'Later, OK?'

'She was my sister, Rebecca.'

'I know that. And we'll talk. I promise. But we don't have a lot of time, and there are some things I need to tell you.'

'Just like that.'

She didn't say anything. I don't suppose there was much to be said.

'I'm not a robot,' I told her. 'I can't just switch off from this.'

'You can for a little while.' She glanced across at me again. 'I said I promise, OK? But this is about priorities, right now. And I need you focused when we meet Erik. Not distracted by anything I might tell you about Laura.'

I wanted to tell her my dead sister was a priority. That she was more than just an item on an agenda that we'd get to when it suited her. But I didn't. I just sat there, staring at the road ahead, the blur of hedgerows, the licence plate of a passing car.

'You asked what I'd been doing,' Rebecca said. 'Well, I took your suggestion and I went to police headquarters in Douglas to speak with DS Teare.'

'And?' I heard myself ask. 'What did she have to say?'

'Nothing.'

'Excuse me?'

'She was unavailable to speak with me.'

'Unavailable?'

'Some uniformed prick on the front desk called her internal line. He was listening for a good two minutes before he hung up and told me it was a no-go. I asked if she was sick. Apparently, that was none of my business. So I told him I was working on behalf of your family in connection with the botched investigation into your road traffic accident and the suicide of your sister. My voice must have been pretty loud, because it carried all the way upstairs. To DI Shimmin's desk.'

'He came down?'

'He did.'

'And?'

'And nothing. He told me to leave. Not asked, mind. *Told.* He even escorted me from the premises.'

'And you let him?'

'What would you have had me do?'

'I don't know. The way you were talking, about working on behalf of my family, it sounded like maybe you could have demanded to speak with Teare.'

She pursed her lips. 'I decided I didn't need to. Not yet, anyway. The fact Shimmin didn't want me to speak to her had already told me more than I was expecting. And besides, I had other things to do.'

I studied her, waiting for more. She pretended to be absorbed by the rush of tarmac ahead of us, the flickering white line vanishing beneath our front bumper like milk through a straw.

'Are you going to explain?'

'Happy to. You remember we talked about how somebody must have reported your accident? They would have called 999, right?'

'Makes sense.'

'Well, a place like the Isle of Man, you only have one emergency control centre. I did some research and I found that it's located right behind the police station. So once Shimmin had guided me out to my car, I drove around the block, and came back again. Then I hung around until I found somebody to speak to.'

'An officer?'

She shook her head. 'When you dial 999, what you're basically put through to is a call centre staffed by civilians.'

'So?'

'So I met a guy called Matt. He's a smoker. And a chatty one. Being a practical kind of girl, I took some of the expenses your family aren't exactly paying me, and I gave them to Matt. And in return, he checked some records and gave me some information.'

'Go on.'

'The caller was a man. Refused to give his name. But the system they use in the control centre has caller ID.' Rebecca reached two fingers inside the chest pocket of the leather jacket she had on. She removed a square of yellow paper. 'This is the telephone number of whoever reported your accident.'

I took the scrap of paper from her and studied the number that had been scrawled on it in black biro. It was for a mobile phone. There was no international code, but the number didn't begin with the prefix for a Manx mobile. It had to originate from the UK.

'What do we do with this?' I asked.

'It's five to seven. How far are we from the airport?'

We were approaching the outskirts of Ballasalla. Grey, pebble-dashed bungalows lined either side of the road. A Mercedes dealership was on our right, a family pub further ahead at the mini roundabout.

'Two minutes,' I said. 'Maybe less.'

'Good.' Rebecca veered across the road and swooped into the forecourt of the Mercedes garage. She yanked the hand-brake on. Cut the engine. Removed her sunglasses and folded them away. 'Then I suggest we call that number.'

'And say what exactly? We don't know who this person is. And we can't tell them how we came by their telephone number. They'd have no reason to talk to us.'

'Not us, no,' she said, and delved inside her jacket for her phone. 'But they might talk to a friend of ours.'

*

Menser was perched on a metal container stuffed with life jackets and buoyancy aids, his hands buried in his pockets, his feet planted on the greasy deck. A thick, wet rope was coiled nearby, discoloured with tar and gunge, the end formed into a gaping loop like a hangman's noose. So this was what it came down to. The end of his assignment. Toss a rope on to a quay, wait for it to be secured and tied off. Release the girl from below deck and hand her over to the men who were expecting her.

Then disappear.

The port was grey and dismal, hunkered down beneath a bank of low mauve clouds. Functional warehouses lined the harbour wall and a white-and-blue police van could be glimpsed through the vaporous mist. Four blurred figures were standing outside it. Two in trench coats. Two in navy-blue uniforms, heavy leather boots and baseball caps. One of the trench coats sparked a lighter and fired a cigarette. A movie fan. Amateur hour.

Menser heard the sudden din of a foghorn from behind him.

He jumped and turned. Clarke was grinning inanely from the wheelhouse, saluting towards the figure with the cigarette. Menser had a surer feel for his partner now. Clarke was the kind of guy who probably thought of himself as a maverick. To Menser's mind, that was code for idiot. Given the choice, he'd never work with him again. But choice was irrelevant. This was a one-time-only assignment. In all likelihood, he'd pass through the rest of his life without ever seeing or hearing from Clarke. And he'd certainly never learn the man's real name.

The girl had remained stubborn. She'd barely talked. Not to ask after Pieter. Not to beg to be released or to bargain with them. Menser was still bothered by her attitude, unbalanced by it. He'd come to think that maybe she was on something. One of those rich-girl drugs to keep reality at bay. But he wasn't sure of it. Her pupils showed no trace of any stimulants. There'd been no hint of withdrawal. No jitters. And he was haunted by the nagging fear that he was searching for an excuse. One that didn't involve a mistake.

He told himself that her attitude would change once they'd docked and the men came aboard to take her away. The berth was two hundred metres ahead, maybe less. The trawler veered sideways, charting a course between the docked fishing vessels. Menser watched the man with the cigarette adjust his stance. Saw the uniformed figures descend a flight of stone steps carved into the harbour wall.

That was when the *ping* first sounded. Hollow. Metallic. Like sonar.

The noise repeated itself. It was coming from inside the backpack slung over Menser's shoulder. He frowned. Unzipped the bag. Their operational equipment was inside, ready to be dismantled and ditched as soon as the girl was transferred. The screen on one of the phones was illuminated. Clarke's phone. He'd changed the damn ringtone.

Menser studied the number that appeared on screen. Not one of theirs. He pressed a button, killing the sonar *ping*, and raised the phone to his ear.

He could hear breathing on the other end.

'Yes,' he said.

'Good evening, sir. This is Detective Sergeant Jacqueline Teare, Isle of Man Constabulary. To whom am I speaking, please?'

'Sorry?' Menser plugged his free ear with his finger to cut out the rumble of the trawler's engine. 'Who did you say you were?'

The woman repeated herself. Asked who he was again.

'My name's Donald Fry.' The lie came easily. Straight to his lips. 'I think you have a wrong number. I'm not based in the Isle of Man.'

'Where are you based, Mr Fry?'

Menser shut his eyes. Forced himself to concentrate. 'Can I ask why you're calling me?'

'It's in connection with a motorbike accident. It occurred three days ago in the south of the Isle of Man. A man fell from his bike and suffered serious injuries.'

Menser knew all about the accident. He and Clarke had planned it. Carried it through. But they'd done it without leaving trace evidence. He was sure of it. So why was she calling Clarke's phone?

'I'm sorry, Detective, but I don't see what this has to do with me.'

'Somebody reported the incident to the emergency services. They requested an ambulance.'

Menser waited. He could feel the tension gripping hold of him. The creeping sensation of betrayal. The sickness that came with it.

'The call came from this number.'

Clarke.

When had he placed the call? Probably when Menser was dealing with the girl. Loading her into the van. Restraining her. His back had been turned. The van doors closed.

'Mr Fry?'

'That's impossible.'

'Our records are very clear, sir. But the reason I'm calling is connected to a related incident. The gentleman involved in the crash says that he had a passenger on his motorbike. A blonde woman. In her twenties. Is it possible you saw her?'

'You've made a mistake, Detective. A wrong number.'

'But I have the number right in front of me, Mr Fry. We're looking for a missing girl here. It's a serious situation and it would be helpful if we could talk to you in more detail. If you would consent to –'

Menser cut the connection. He snapped the back off the phone, freed the battery and the sim card, tossed all of it overboard with a grunt.

The trawler was pulling alongside the harbour wall. The uniformed figures were leaning outwards, gesturing for Menser to toss them a rope. He turned from them and waved his arms at Clarke. Warning him off.

It was no good. Menser cursed and hustled for the wheelhouse ladder. He hauled himself up the metal treads. Yanked open the cabin door and yelled the command.

Clarke stared at him blankly. Then he slammed the engine into reverse.

There was a bumping, scraping noise. The prow glanced off the stone steps. The uniformed figures snatched their legs clear and the trench coats advanced towards the edge of the quay, perplexed.

'Get us out of here,' Menser yelled.

'You've flipped, pal.'

'Take us away. Now.'

Menser barged out the wheelhouse, clomping down the ladder to the metal deck, ignoring the calls of the men they'd been scheduled to meet. He dug a hand inside his rucksack and removed the phone he'd been given for this assignment. He sucked in a breath and summoned up the number he needed to call. Clamped a hand over his eyes and raised the phone to his ear.

'It's Menser,' he said. 'We have a problem.'

Chapter Twenty

'He hung up.' Rebecca showed me her phone. 'Said I had a wrong number. That he has no connection at all to the Isle of Man, or to your accident.'

'Maybe he doesn't. Maybe the guy at the control centre was leading you on.'

'No. He hung up when I pressed him on Lena. He knows something.'

'So call him back.'

Rebecca shrugged and tried just that. Then she pulled the phone from her ear, a wry smile on her face. 'Switched off.'

'He's avoiding you.'

'Looks that way. He said he was called Donald Fry. Does that name mean anything to you?'

'Nothing.'

'It's probably a fake.'

'You think?'

'The man I spoke to was calm. Unusually so. If that had been a genuine mix-up, I reckon he'd have been curious to know more. And he definitely wouldn't hang up on a police officer and switch off his phone.'

'So what can we do about it?'

'We can go and meet Erik. See if he can shed any light on what might be going on.'

'Listen, are we sure about this?' I asked. 'You said yourself that we have no way of knowing if what he told us on the phone was true.'

'So let's go and find out. It's our best way of making fast progress.'

Rebecca reversed at speed and rejoined the road to the airport. The road took us over the level crossing for the vintage steam train that runs between Douglas and Port Erin, then past a gas station and a shabby collection of palm trees. Rebecca slalomed into a parking space and was already cracking her door and grabbing her backpack before the engine was dead and the handbrake was engaged.

I wasn't crazy about joining her, but I sensed she was going with or without me. Shaking my head, I heaved myself out of the car and followed her past a taxi rank and a vacant smokers' shelter, then inside through the sliding glass doors to the arrivals lounge. Erik hadn't explained how we'd recognise him but I didn't anticipate a problem. Ronaldsway Airport isn't exactly Heathrow. Even now, with the London City flight recently landed, there were only fifteen or so people standing around.

A petite young woman with a shock of white-blonde hair was one of them. She was dressed in what appeared to be a pilot's uniform. Tailored white blouse, smart blue trousers, polished black boots. The blouse had brass epaulets on the shoulders and a golden tulip embroidered over her breast pocket. She held a cardboard sign with the word *Rob* printed on it in marker pen.

She lowered the sign as we approached.

'You are Rob?' she asked, and glanced at my sling. Erik had

said that he lived in the Netherlands and the woman's English was marked with broadly the same accent.

'Yes. We're here to meet Erik Zeeger?'

She nodded. 'He waits for you. And this is your friend?' She turned her attention to Rebecca. Her expression hadn't altered, but I sensed a tension between them. 'My name is Anke. I will take you to Mr Zeeger. You will come with me please.'

We did as she asked, following her up a sweeping staircase towards Departures, skirting the buffet-style cafeteria and snaking through the crowd-control bollards set up outside airport security. I'd expected to be escorted to a waiting car or whisked away to a nearby hotel, but not this.

Anke had us show picture ID to the security official on duty and then we were invited to walk through a metal detector and wait for Rebecca's bag to emerge from a scanner.

'This way.'

Anke ushered us through a pair of double doors into the departure lounge, where a scattering of people occupied the bolted-down seats. A computer screen listed flights for Liverpool, Manchester and London Gatwick. The lounge was surrounded by double-height glass and I could see two passenger planes out on the tarmac and the lighted runway beyond. The airport was located on the very edge of the coast and the runway extended right out into the Irish Sea.

Anke passed a swipe card through a sensor on the wall and led us through a door and down a flight of metal stairs to the runway apron. We crossed the wrinkled tarmac towards a private jet. The jet was low-slung with a pointed nose cone, a cigar-tube fuselage and squat, slanted wings. There were two jet engines and a tail fin that featured the same insignia I'd noticed on Anke's blouse – a golden tulip, flower-head tilted to the right.

An entrance hatch was open towards the front of the plane and a set of cabin steps was suspended just above the ground. There was no indication of who exactly might be waiting inside. No way to gauge the dangers we might be exposing ourselves to. My stomach had turned to water. My heart rate was up. Last chance to back out, I told myself. Then Rebecca poked me in the back and I found that I was climbing the steps.

'Rob? Is that you?'

A tanned and sandy-haired man levered himself up out of a vast leather armchair on one side of the cream and walnut cabin and advanced towards me at a stoop. He was tall and wiry – too tall for the interior of the plane – and he was bent at the hip, craning his long neck to gaze up and meet my eyes as he offered me his hand.

I swallowed dryly. 'Erik?'

He nodded. Took in my sling. Smiled briefly.

He wasn't anything like I'd expected. The man in front of me now was mid-to-late forties, with a square jaw, a wide forehead and a prominently hooked nose. He wore white linen trousers, open-toed sandals over large brown feet, and a blue cotton shirt.

'This is Rebecca,' I managed, leaning to one side in the cramped space so that Erik could shake her hand. 'The friend I mentioned.'

'Actually, Mr Zeeger, I'm a private detective.'

Erik's eyebrows shot upwards to form two handsome arches.

'I was hired by Rob's family to look into an unrelated matter,'

Rebecca explained. 'Now I'm helping him to investigate your daughter's disappearance.'

Erik smiled, but the smile didn't reach his eyes. They were hard and so perfectly blue that the colour seemed artificial.

'And who is this gentleman?' Rebecca nodded towards a stocky guy who was lurking behind Erik.

'This is Mr Anderson,' Erik said. 'He is my head of security. A man I trust deeply.'

If Anderson was moved by the sentiment behind Erik's words, he didn't show it. He was a squat figure, dressed in a dark-blue suit, a sober tie and a clean white shirt. His shoulders were wide and his neck was short. He was clean-shaven, with a military-style buzz-cut, a low brow and a watchful expression. He was younger than Erik, but not by much. He looked like a man who was adept at handling himself in pretty much any situation. Definitely not the type of character to pick a fight with. Definitely not the type of character to aggravate.

'Mr Anderson, hello.' Rebecca extended her hand.

Anderson considered the move. He took his time over it. His expression remained hard. After a long pause, he reached out for a swift clench, then offered me the same greeting. His grip was like the first move in a brutal judo throw.

'I'll need to check you for wires.' He said it low-key, like it was customary, and his gaze lingered on my sling. His accent surprised me. He sounded American, with a slight southern drawl. 'You first, ma'am.'

Rebecca maintained her smile. 'We've just come through airport security, Mr Anderson.'

'I guess you have. But if you want to speak with Mr Zeeger, I need to vet you personally.'

'Strange,' Rebecca said, looking at Erik, 'I seem to recall it was Mr Zeeger who wished to speak with us.'

Nobody said a word. I felt a flutter deep in my gut. I wasn't sure why Rebecca was objecting. I couldn't believe she was wearing any recording equipment, so something else had to be going on. Some kind of power-play with Anderson.

Erik turned to Anderson. Forced a smile. 'Let them through.'

Anderson didn't move. His legs were spread, feet spaced shoulder-width apart. He locked on Rebecca with an intent gaze. 'I should check your bag, minimum.'

'*Should*. Such an ugly word, don't you think? But here, knock yourself out.'

She pressed her backpack into his chest, then moved past him and settled into a large, padded seat beside a lozenge-shaped window. She squirmed around, making herself comfortable, as if she was used to travelling in luxury jets. There was another chair alongside Rebecca's and a facing pair positioned on the other side of a lush walnut table.

'Go ahead and sit down,' Anderson growled.

I clambered into the chair alongside Rebecca's. The rich leather moulded itself to the shape of my body and I gripped the armrest with my free hand like I was bracing myself for turbulence.

Erik folded himself neatly into the seat opposite Rebecca. Anderson collapsed into the chair across from me. He opened Rebecca's bag. Fished around inside. It wasn't long before his hand emerged holding a clear plastic bag.

'These the sunglasses you found?'

'That's correct,' Rebecca said.

'They're Lukas's, all right. You say you found them in the woods?'

I nodded. 'My dog found them. His phone, too.'

I passed the mobile across, conscious of the tremor in my hand, and Anderson placed it on the table next to the sunglasses. His face was set, eyes wary. He was acting like a guy who'd laid down two playing cards in a high-stakes game he suspected us of rigging. He reached inside Rebecca's bag again, shifting the contents around. He removed her driver's licence and compared the photograph with the real thing, one eye closed in a squint.

'Lewis, huh?'

'Satisfied?' Rebecca asked.

Anderson grunted. He zipped the bag closed. Returned it to Rebecca. Then he opened his jacket and pulled out a small notebook and pen.

'We'll start with your full details,' he said. 'Shoot.'

I opened my jaw to reply but Rebecca raised her hand in front of my mouth.

'His surname is Hale,' she said. 'But that's all you're getting. For now. First, you can tell us about Lena.'

'I need details.'

'Details.' Rebecca tapped a nail against the tabletop, like she was trying to recall the meaning of the word. 'Mr Anderson, if you're as good as your employer thinks you are, you really don't.'

'My daughter is missing.' Erik propped his elbows on the table. 'Please understand this.'

'We do understand,' Rebecca said. 'We understand a girl has vanished. You claim that she's your daughter, and if that's the case then we're sorry to hear it. But you have to realise that we know nothing about you, aside from the fact you've flown here at short notice in a private jet.' She acknowledged our opulent surroundings with a heft of her chin. 'All we really know is that Rob was involved in a motorbike accident with a girl whose existence has been denied until now. Two men were with her and you've told us you think they may have been killed. You asked us not to go to the police, and we haven't, despite the personal risk that decision may involve.' She paused for a beat. Looked between Erik and Anderson. 'And until you begin to give us some kind of explanation for what's going on here, I'd say that's detail enough, wouldn't you?'

Erik flicked his eyes at me. I nodded, confirming that Rebecca spoke for both of us.

'Very well.' He pushed up from the table, standing awkwardly, his head bowed against the low, rounded ceiling. He delved inside the pocket of his trousers. Removed a leather billfold. 'Lena is my daughter. I promise you this.' He retook his seat and showed us a photograph that had been placed behind a plastic window inside the billfold. 'This picture was taken on Lena's fifteenth birthday.'

The photograph was of Erik with his long arm around a willowy blonde girl. Erik was shirtless and the girl wore a pale-pink T-shirt and a seashell necklace. A white, sandy beach stretched into the distance behind them.

'That's her,' I said to Rebecca. And with my words came an instant flush of relief and a heady sensation of buoyancy – as if a weight that had been tied to my ankles had finally been cut free. At long last, I was talking with people who knew for a fact that Lena was real.

'Go on,' Rebecca said to Erik.

'That picture was taken eight years ago. My daughter was a sweet girl. Innocent. You can see this, yes?'

'It's only a photograph, Mr Zeeger.'

He leaned back in his chair. Flipped his billfold closed and slipped it back inside his trousers. 'Maybe so, but it's true. Her mother died when she was just four years old. We were very close. Always, Lena would talk to me. Even business decisions, I would discuss with her. But when she was older, this changed.'

'Sounds like your average teenager,' I said.

'No, she was not average.' There was a wet glimmer in Erik's startling blue eyes. Raw emotion in his voice. 'Lena was extraordinary. Smart. Ambitious. She wanted to work for me. Alongside me. Running my company.'

'So what happened?'

'Love, Rob. Love happened.'

He was sincere. I could see it in the earnest cast to his eyes, the composed way he held himself. He was beginning to sound like some drippy song. A greeting-card sentiment. But if it bothered him, he didn't show it.

'She told me she was in a relationship,' he said, 'on her seventeenth birthday. I did not approve. The man she spoke with me about was much older. They had been together some months already. You can perhaps understand why I did not like this.'

'You were her father. Of course you didn't like it.'

'Lena, she did not understand.' The corners of his long mouth drooped downwards. 'I forbade her from seeing this man. I told her this was unhealthy.'

'And Lena rebelled,' Rebecca put in.

Erik lifted his hands, then seemed confused about what to

148

do with them. He dropped them back down on to his lap. 'There were parties. Drink. Drugs. I lost my Lena to it.'

'With all due respect, this doesn't sound all that unusual,' I told him. 'There are kids all over the Isle of Man doing the same thing.'

Erik smiled, as if indulging me. 'And do these children have trust funds worth many millions of euros? Are the parties they attend in Spain? Ibiza? Are they on yachts? In villas? With criminals? Drug dealers?'

I shook my head. Embarrassed by his intensity.

'It is like I tell you, I am rich.' Erik circled a finger, taking in the jet we were sitting in. 'Lena, too. This is the world she moves in. Everything, it is bigger, no? The world she has access to.'

'And the trouble she can get into,' Rebecca said, as if finishing an unspoken thought.

'Exactly this.'

'So is that how Lena came to be in the Isle of Man?'

'No.' Erik glanced at Anderson, then down at his hands. 'This is not why. Not directly.'

'So why mention it?'

He sighed. 'Eventually, the man Lena was with found another girl. Younger even than Lena had been. I was relieved. But Lena did not come home to me. She . . . blamed me. So she found somebody else. Someone she knew for sure I would hate. Again, he was older. Again, she fell in love. They became engaged.' He paused. Looked at me. Looked at Rebecca. 'Two months ago, the man my daughter planned to marry was killed.'

Silence. I decided to fill it.

'Was his death an accident?'

Erik turned to Anderson. The powerful American moved his jaw around, like he was chewing gum. 'The man we're talking about was a British national. He was found in an apartment Lena was renting in London. Area of Primrose Hill.' Anderson's bass American voice expanded, filling the cramped interior of the plane. 'Victim was poisoned. A cyanide derivative. The killer left no fingerprints. No real evidence. Got clean away.'

'Witnesses?' Rebecca asked.

'None.' He rested his squared-off fingers on the edge of the table. 'Lena was there when he died. They were drinking vodka together. But the vodka had been spiked with a sedative. Knocked them out cold.'

Rebecca shook her head. 'That still doesn't explain why Lena was in the Isle of Man, or why she's gone missing.'

'She was here for protection,' Erik said.

'From?'

'The killer. The people the killer worked for.' Erik looked pained. 'There had been . . . threats.' He turned to Anderson. I got the impression he was being cautious about the level of information he was prepared to give us.

'The threats were coded,' Anderson explained, opening his hands. 'But legitimate. We took them seriously. It was my strong belief that Lena would be at risk if she stayed in London. We figured the guy's death was a warning.'

'What about the police?' I asked.

'We couldn't trust them to protect her.'

'And how did they feel about that?'

Anderson didn't answer. Erik looked away.

'Wait.' Rebecca's head jutted forwards. 'Are you saying the police didn't know she was here?'

Erik's hands tightened into fists. 'We had to protect my daughter.'

'Did she at least talk to the police in London?'

'You must understand. I was prepared to do everything I could to keep her safe.'

'So who got to her?' I asked. 'The people who threatened to kill her?'

'We think so.' Erik's knuckles had whitened.

'Then I'm sorry.'

He tilted his head up. 'It is much worse than you know.'

'Worse, how?'

'The man who was killed was Alex Tyler. Perhaps you have heard of him?'

I shook my head.

'He was the leader of an organisation called the Green Liberation Group. They like to think of themselves as eco-activists. I call them terrorists.' Erik hesitated, waiting for the impact of his words to register on our faces. 'You begin to understand, perhaps, what this means for me. What it means for my Lena.'

*

Lena was nowhere to be seen. Lukas had checked every room. Twice. The apartment was not big. A living room with an open-plan kitchen at one end, a corner sofa and a television at the other, and a modest dining table in between. A cramped study with a desk, an office chair and a laptop. A bedroom with a double bed, a wardrobe and an en-suite bathroom.

No Lena. No sign of her.

Lukas rested, bracing his hands on the kitchen counter. His temples pounded. He was hot and sweating. He could feel a soggy film on his back and neck. He lifted his palms and saw that he'd left two wet prints on the black granite.

He was out of ideas. Out of options.

There was a telephone in the study. Lukas had seen it, next to an answer-machine. He limped slowly through the living room and dropped into the cushioned office chair. Reached for the phone. Smoothed his greasy thumb over the buttons.

He knew Anderson's number. Knew he had to make the call. But the call would mean that he'd failed. Let Mr Zeeger down.

He delayed. Asked himself if there was anything else to be done. Asked himself what Pieter might try.

Then it came to him. The man with the sling. Maybe he could find a name for him. Personal details. Enough, perhaps, for Anderson to use.

There was a grey metal filing cabinet in the corner of the room. It might contain papers – bills and bank statements and personal correspondence. But Lukas was a gadget guy, a computer fiend. So the first thing he did was to open the laptop.

The machine was heavy and cheap. It was slow. The hard drive whirred and hummed and chattered. The operating system was three years out of date.

The screen turned blue. An icon appeared in the centre. *User 1*. Lukas clicked on it with the trackpad. The screen went blank. Then a desktop image materialised. A photograph. The man in the sling and a woman. Arms around one another. Smiling. Laughing to camera.

Lukas pushed back from the desk. Raised a hand to his forehead.

A small charge detonated in his chest.

Lukas recognised the woman.

How could he not?

And the sight of her changed everything.

Chapter Twenty-one

I did understand the importance of what Erik had told us. I'd recognised the golden tulip insignia on his pilot's blouse and the tail fin of his jet. The motif is featured on gas stations throughout Europe and beyond. On oil rigs. On tankers. On lorries. On the fairing of TT bikes and Formula One cars. SuperZ Oil is one of the world's leading petrochemical companies, and from the way Erik had talked, I got the impression he was high up in its command.

'What's your role exactly?' I asked Erik.

'My role?'

'Your job. For SuperZ.'

He didn't even blink. 'I don't work *for* SuperZ, Rob. I *am* SuperZ. I own this company.'

So now I knew. Erik had told me that he was rich but the truth was he was way beyond wealthy. His company's turnover probably dwarfed the GDP of most nations.

No wonder he'd been so uncomfortable with Lena's choice of fiancé. Alex Tyler's role as a prominent green campaigner would have been a source of embarrassment for Erik. More pressing, though, must have been the fear that Tyler was only interested in Lena because he could use her to harass Erik in some way.

'Did you suspect Tyler was behind the threats to your daughter?'

'Originally, yes,' Anderson said.

'And now?'

'Now we figure we're dealing with a dissident branch of his organisation. Assuming his relationship with Lena was genuine –'

'They were getting married, right?' Rebecca put in.

Anderson paused. 'We don't think it was legitimate to begin with. The guy was no saint. But over time, we figure that changed. And we think there are members of his group who didn't like that it changed.'

'So what, they killed Tyler?'

'Maybe.'

'And now you think they have Lena?'

'It's a concern.'

Rebecca whistled. 'You called them terrorists,' she said to Erik. 'Just how radical are they?'

He closed his eyes. 'They are capable of terrible things.'

'Have they contacted you yet?'

'No. But if you are thinking these people would seek a ransom, I'm afraid you are mistaken. To them, my money is tainted. They have no interest in it. They wish only to hurt me.'

'Why hasn't this been in the press?' I asked. 'I don't remember reading anything about Tyler's death.'

Erik pursed his lips, as if I'd mentioned something distasteful. 'There were a few early reports. We could not help this. But since then, my company has worked hard to keep things discreet.'

'You mean you smothered the story,' Rebecca said.

His expression became strained. I waited for Rebecca to back down or apologise. She didn't.

'Seems to me you've asked enough questions.' Anderson shuffled forwards in his chair and gestured at me with his note-pad. 'You said you wanted to help us find her.'

I nodded. I did want to help them. Now, more than ever.

'Then you can start by explaining what in hell happened.'

I did just that, summarising as best I could the events that had led to my meeting Lena and the motorbike accident that followed. I was careful to emphasise that it was Lena who'd asked me to take her away from the cottage and that my memory of the accident was sketchy, at best.

Anderson monitored me closely. His brow was furrowed above narrowed, focused eyes. I became very aware of my words and mannerisms, as if Anderson was some kind of human lie detector. Every now and again, I'd experience a moment of res-pite as he glanced at his pad to scribble a note. But the moments were never long enough. And it was beginning to bother me.

I was in the middle of explaining how my motorbike had looked after the accident, going into detail about the ruined tyre and the collapsed front end, when my frustration finally became too much. 'Are you getting all this?' I asked.

'Sure,' he said.

I sighed, unconvinced, then felt Rebecca tap me on my shoulder. She pointed at an area of the cabin above our heads. Sunk into the cream headlining was a miniature camera lens.

'It's not something you need to worry about, Rob. Our every word and movement has been recorded since we stepped on to this plane. Correct, gentlemen?'

Erik and Anderson exchanged a fast look.

'This is my daughter,' Erik spluttered. 'The situation is –'

'We understand the situation,' Rebecca told him. 'And so far as I'm concerned, you can record what you like. As it happens, it reminds me of something we haven't told you just yet. The cottage where Lena was staying – this safe place you put her – it was bugged.'

Anderson screwed up his face, like he'd bitten into something sour.

'You heard me,' Rebecca said. 'The house was completely wired. Surveillance equipment and listening devices in every room.' She turned her gaze on Erik. 'Lena was being watched, Mr Zeeger. That's how she was snatched. Someone was monitoring her every move.'

Rebecca went on to explain about the white van the dirt bikers had seen in the weeks leading up to Lena's disappearance. She outlined her theory about how an obstacle had been used to throw us from my bike. Then she told them about the telephone number she'd obtained for the man who'd reported my accident. She freed the scrap of notepaper from the pocket of her leather jacket and laid it down on the table.

Anderson snatched up the paper. 'You called this number?'

'Twice,' Rebecca said. 'The first time around, the man who answered said I had a wrong number. Then he hung up. I called him back. His phone was switched off.'

'You blew the lead.'

'No, I worked the lead. But talking of screw-ups – how did you come to choose the Isle of Man as a safe haven for Lena? How did you select a location that was bugged?'

Anderson crumpled the piece of paper in his hand. 'That's not something we're at liberty to discuss with you.'

'Shame. I have a feeling I might have enjoyed the explanation.'

Anderson was about to respond when something stopped him. He leaned to one side and slipped his hand inside his jacket. Pulled out a phone. The screen was illuminated and the phone was buzzing softly. He peered at the display, then stood from his chair, holding up two fingers.

'Couple minutes,' he mumbled, and moved away towards the rear of the cabin, where his conversation couldn't be overheard.

'How long had Lena been on the Isle of Man, Mr Zeeger?' Rebecca asked.

Erik hesitated. He checked on Anderson's position, then seemed to decide that the question was harmless enough. 'A little under two months.'

'Two whole months in that cottage?' I said, and whistled. 'It's no surprise Lena was keen for a break.'

'We were hoping to move her soon. When it was safe.'

'Tell us about the police,' Rebecca said. 'You told us it would be dangerous for Lena if we contacted them. How so?'

Erik flattened a hand on the surface of the table. Spread his fingers. 'The police would . . . complicate matters.'

'With all due respect,' I said, 'they have resources none of us have access to. And they know the island inside out.'

'Please, you must trust me. The people we are dealing with, the people who wish to harm me, they do not concern themselves with the police.'

'Two men may have been killed,' I told him. 'I've been injured. You can't expect me to say nothing.'

The fingers of his spread hand arched and tensed. They inched, crablike, across the surface of the table. I could see the platinum band of his wristwatch glinting out from beneath the cuff of his shirt. 'I am sorry for your troubles. And as for my men, they worked for me. I do not forget it. Believe me.'

Rebecca rested a hand on my forearm. Clenched lightly. 'I think all Mr Zeeger is saying, Rob, is that he'd appreciate us keeping quiet for the time being. At least until he and his advisers have had an opportunity to see if they can assist Lena.'

Her face was plain, untroubled. I knew she was experienced in dealing with investigations and the tough decisions they had to throw up from time to time. But I didn't feel comfortable with what was being asked of me.

'If it's a matter of compensation . . .' Erik began.

'I'm not after your money,' I said. 'Christ. This is about my conscience. It's about me knowing I did the right thing.'

'The right thing.' He nodded, but his face was tangled, as if he was having difficulty understanding. 'But you must see, I do not have this luxury. I wish only for Lena to be safe.'

His striking blue eyes were fixed on me. I glanced down, then off along the aisle. Anderson was returning to us. He slipped his phone away and stroked his chin.

'We're almost done here,' he said. 'I just have a couple more questions. Tell me, did Lena say anything to you – anything at all – that you haven't told us? I'm thinking before the accident. About seeing anyone watching them. Wanting help from you. Anything like that?'

'I don't believe so,' I said.

'She didn't give you anything? A note? A message?'

'No,' I told him. 'Why do you ask?'

'Standard question. Shot in the dark. Final one.' He straightened his squat head on his shoulders. Stared hard at me like he was sizing me up for a headbutt. 'Melanie Fleming. That name mean anything to you?'

I felt myself rock backwards. I opened my mouth. Closed it again. Looked from Rebecca, to Erik, to Anderson. They were studying me. All of them. I shook my head. Blinked. 'No,' I said. 'Who is she? What's her involvement in this?'

Anderson grunted. 'That's something we'd sure like to figure out.'

*

Lena had her ear pressed hard against the cold metal door. She was straining to hear something, but all she could pick up were the vibrations of the engine, the pounding of the waves and the swirling vacuum sounds coming from her own ear.

Something had happened. She was sure of it. First there'd been the bleat of the foghorn. Then shouting – the bark of urgent voices. Then had come the low rumble of the engine straining hard down below. The deep churning of the propeller. The groaning and creaking of the hull. The lurching of the boat.

She wished she had a porthole, some way of looking outside. But all she had was this cabin. The painted metal walls. The noises she was straining to decipher. And the sense, somehow, that something had changed. That perhaps, after all, there was something to hope for.

*

'They're lying,' Anderson said, once the tall guy in the sling and the hot-ass investigator with the prissy attitude had left the aircraft. 'About Fleming. Probably about a lot of things.'

He crouched down and watched them walk away across the runway apron. The big man was shaking his head, like he had a bug in his ear. Rebecca Lewis was striding alongside him, her backpack over her shoulder.

'What makes you so sure?' Erik asked, watching them also.

'His reaction, for one thing.'

'And?'

Anderson stared at his employer. Lifted his phone into his line of sight. 'And Lukas is alive. He finally called in. Seems he's taken a tour through our Good Samaritan's home. He found an image there. This guy Rob, and Fleming. Together.'

Erik absorbed the information. Nodded sagely. 'Then do whatever it takes. I want Lena found. I won't lose her again.'

Chapter Twenty-two

We got back to the car and I dropped into my seat, legs trembling. I slammed the door behind me.

'We have to go to the police,' I said.

Rebecca held up a hand. 'Not yet.'

'What do you mean *not yet*? You expect me to just take this? To pretend I didn't see anything? That we didn't just have that conversation?'

She put her finger to her lips, turned the key in the ignition and cranked the radio on loud. An advert for a Manx bakery boomed out. She balanced her backpack on her knees, unzipped it and fished around inside. Her hand emerged with a grey hunk of plastic gripped between her finger and thumb. She made a point of showing it to me, then closed it in her fist and leaned towards my ear. 'They're listening,' she whispered.

Her breath was hot against my skin. I eased away. Stared at her. She unfurled her fingers. The device was no bigger than a ten-pence piece. Oval in shape.

I went to speak, but she covered my mouth with her finger. Lowered the volume on the radio.

'I feel like a walk,' she said, in a deliberate tone. 'Clear my head. Any ideas?' Her eyebrows hitched up, like she was prompting me.

'There's Castletown beach, I suppose.' My voice sounded

sullen and wooden. Like I was a bad actor reading over my lines for the first time.

'Perfect.' She dropped the piece of plastic into her bag. 'Tell me where to go.'

I kept my speech to a minimum, conscious of every word I was uttering. The world I lived in was becoming more peculiar by the day. Missing women. Private jets. Surveillance equipment and listening devices. I was having a hard time adjusting to it all. I can't tell you how much I wished I didn't have to.

Castletown beach was a sweeping band of wet sand and rockpools, fringed by dunes and wild grass and backing on to a coast road that ran alongside the airport runway. We parked behind a curved sea wall. Behind us, a terrace of imposing townhouses was painted in a pastel spectrum. Away to our right, above a tangle of seaside cottages and rooftops, I could see the distant stone outline of the medieval castle that had given the town its name.

Rebecca locked her bag inside the car. She showed me her empty hands, like a magician about to perform a card trick, then folded her arms across her chest and strolled down a wrinkled slipway to the beach. I followed her on to a bank of washed-up pebbles, then hauled her round by the shoulder.

'What the hell?'

'They bugged us.' She shrugged. 'Anderson planted it when he checked my bag.'

'You saw him? Why didn't you say anything?'

'I didn't want to appear rude.'

'Unbelievable.'

'Don't take it personally. Erik's desperate to find his daughter.'

I clasped my free hand to the back of my head. Kicked a pebble with my toe. 'What am I involved in here?'

'You tell me.'

I paused. Peered hard at her. I didn't know what she meant.

'Melanie Fleming,' she said.

'Huh?'

'Who is she? When Anderson mentioned her name, you practically wet yourself. And don't think he didn't notice. You weren't exactly cool.'

I bent down and picked up a stone. It was weighty. Solid. I felt the edges with my thumb. They were smooth. Worn flat. Dry against my skin.

I turned and walked towards the limp waves brushing the shore. My legs felt leaden. My movements stiff. Close in, the water was a muddy brown. Farther out, towards the horizon, it was a steely blue. The light was fading from the sky above. In an hour or so, it'd be sundown.

'Are you going to tell me?' Rebecca called from behind.

'I'll tell you,' I said. 'But it won't make any sense.'

She joined me at the shoreline. I was standing in a knot of seaweed, close to a jagged rock surrounded by flat, compacted sand. I felt the heft of the stone in my hand. Tossed it in the air and caught it again. Eyed the dirty froth on the waves rolling in. An orange buoy way beyond that.

I opened my hand. The pebble fell among the seaweed by my toe with a soggy *whump*.

'Melanie Fleming,' Rebecca said again.

I inhaled deeply. Caught the whiff of brine on the air. The putrid stench of the decaying seaweed that had collected in drifts away to our right. I crouched down. Placed my hand in the chilly shallows of a receding wave.

'I was Peter Parker,' I said.

'Excuse me?'

'Spider-Man.'

Rebecca shifted the weight between her feet. The toes of her black training shoes sank into the damp sand. '*OK.*'

'Laura was Melanie Fleming. It was a game we played when we were kids.' Another wave washed against the shore. I waggled my hand, watching the sand kick up from below and cloud the water. 'We used to investigate things around the care home. If we thought one of the residents was suspicious, say, we'd spy on them. Or we'd follow the staff. Take notes and meet up to discuss them. That kind of thing.'

I straightened. Flicked the water from my fingers. Finally got up the courage to meet Rebecca's gaze. 'Laura used to love detective shows. *Dempsey and Makepeace. Cagney and Lacey.* Sometimes I'd sleep over in her room and we'd watch them together. That's where Melanie Fleming came from. It was a character she created. For the game.'

I didn't know what reaction I'd expected from Rebecca, but whatever it was, I wasn't getting it. Her head was on an angle, waiting for more.

'It has to be a coincidence,' I said. 'That's why I didn't mention it to Anderson. So yes, the name meant something to me. But I couldn't see the point in telling them about it. What possible connection could it have?'

She clenched her bottom lip between her teeth. A strand of hair had come loose from her ponytail, curling around by her temple. It moved in the gentle sea breeze.

'You think I should have told them?' I asked.

'Irrelevant. You chose not to.'

I bowed my head. Dried my hands on my trousers.

'But hey, don't beat yourself up about it,' she said. 'They held back on us, too.'

'What makes you say that?'

She reached inside her leather jacket for her mobile. Prodded at some buttons. Then she turned it around and lifted it before my face.

'Something else I did this afternoon. Googled Erik Zeeger. Look what came up.'

The image Rebecca was showing me was a screen grab from the website of the *London Evening Post*.

POLICE HUNT FOR MURDER SUSPECT

METROPOLITAN POLICE INVESTIGATING THE SUSPICIOUS DEATH OF A MAN IN A PRIMROSE HILL APARTMENT ARE APPEALING FOR THE PUBLIC'S HELP IN LOCATING A MISSING WOMAN THEY WISH TO QUESTION. LENA ZEEGER, AGED 23, IS THE ESTRANGED DAUGHTER OF ERIK ZEEGER, DUTCH OIL BARON AND OWNER OF SUPERZ OIL. AN ARREST WARRANT HAS BEEN ISSUED FOR MS ZEEGER OVER THE DEATH OF PROMINENT ECO-CAMPAIGNER ALEX TYLER. MR TYLER IS BELIEVED TO HAVE DIED IN AN APARTMENT RENTED IN MS ZEEGER'S NAME . . .

I looked up from the screen. Shook my head. 'Are you telling me Lena's the main suspect?'

'Seems that way.' Rebecca lowered the phone. Slipped it back inside her pocket. 'Erik and Anderson must have decided it would sound better if they made her out to be a victim in all this. You'd be more likely to help them if you were sympathetic.'

'Well that explains why they didn't want me to go to the police.'

Rebecca pouted. 'I'm sure that's part of it. But at least some of what they said is still true. They hid her here to protect her.'

'Yeah, so she couldn't be convicted.'

Rebecca shook her head. 'Not necessarily. Somebody's still taken her. And they don't know who exactly. Or at least, if they do, they're not telling us.'

'They mentioned this green organisation. The campaign group.'

'It's possible.' She nodded. 'They could have the resources. The motivation, too. But there is another angle.'

'There is?'

'Melanie Fleming.'

I went to speak, to dismiss what she was saying, but she placed her hand on my good shoulder and held me firm.

'The name meant something to them. Anderson wouldn't have mentioned it otherwise. And he had reason to suspect a connection to you.'

'But I already told you my connection. It's nothing.'

Rebecca searched deep in my eyes. Then she said something that shook me so hard my bones jangled. 'Remember that I told you I knew your sister? Well, Melanie Fleming was the name I knew her by.'

Chapter Twenty-three

Anderson had told Lukas to look around and see what else he could find. Lukas found plenty. The man was called Rob Hale. According to the contents of the filing cabinet in the corner of the room, he ran a legitimate plumbing business. There were customer receipts and records going back three years. There were orders for heating systems and spare parts and the ownership records for his work van. There were tax returns and VAT forms and insurance documents.

The bottom drawer was different. It related to motorbikes. Warranty documents for several machines. Glossy bike magazines and clippings from local newspapers. The extracts told him the man raced road bikes in the Isle of Man and Northern Ireland. He'd enjoyed moderate success. A series of top-twenty finishes. Nothing spectacular.

He returned to the laptop. Took a tour through the man's email correspondence. The email was mostly work-related, customer communications and testimonials. Lukas reviewed the man's web history. A lot of what he found concerned motorbikes. Parts suppliers, specialist bike magazines and blogs about road racing. Then he accessed the laptop's file directory. The man's document management was a mess. Most of the documents were scattered across the desktop screen or accumulated in a trash file that hadn't been deleted. There were word-processing files, PDFs and JPEG images.

Lukas checked the time on the clock in the bottom right-hand corner of the screen. Twenty-five minutes since he'd spoken with Anderson. He crossed to the window and peeked outside. Nobody there. He pressed a button on the answer-machine. No messages.

Lukas allowed himself three minutes more and began to cycle through the documents on the man's desktop. He found business invoices. He found personal correspondence to the man's bank, his mobile-phone provider and the electricity board. He found something that caught his breath in his throat and made him crouch closer to the laptop screen.

It was a plain document with a photographic image centred on the middle of the opening page. The image was a headshot of a young blonde woman smiling to camera. Her head was on an angle, her hand in her hair. The photograph had been cropped into an oval shape, the edges blurred. There was text above and below.

Lukas recognised the woman. Melanie Fleming. The same Melanie Fleming he'd seen on the desktop image with the man called Rob Hale. But she wasn't called Melanie Fleming in the document he'd just opened. She was called Laura Hale. And according to the text set out below her image, she'd died almost a month ago.

*

The man Menser had telephoned was angry. But he was good. He ran the contingencies. Developed a plan. Called back inside ten minutes.

The first decision had to do with Clarke. They still needed

two men, on account of the girl. Menser was the clean-up guy. He was responsible. But Clarke was part of the deal. Part of the clean-up.

They followed the coast south. The coastline was low and flat. Lush and green. Outside the port, population was minimal. Houses scarce. They could follow the coast for an hour and see no one at all. No boats in the water. No fishermen on the shore. Jets passed by overhead, red tail beacons glowing against the twilit sky.

The beach, when they found it, was sheltered and mostly pebbled. A narrow track led down to it. There was a turning circle and a white-washed hut at the end of the track. Menser trained his binoculars on the hut. It was canted to one side, the wall bulging in the middle. Plywood sheets had been hammered across the window and door.

The beach looked OK. The beach would work. Menser called it in, then ducked below deck while Clarke prepped the dinghy.

The girl was sitting on her bunk, knees tucked up by her chest, chin on her knees. Her bad arm rested on the bunk, palm up, beside a bag of half-eaten potato crisps. The skin of her wrist was swollen and mottled green and mauve. He could see fluid gathered there.

She didn't look up at him. Didn't ask him what he wanted. He thought about saying something. But an explanation implied something. Undermined him. So he showed her the gun and told her to stand. Had her walk out of the cabin in front of him and made her climb the ladder while he trained the gun on her. The ladder wasn't easy. She had to climb with her good hand, her injured wrist tucked against her chest. He watched her grasping for the next rung, snatching a step up, repeating the process.

She waited for him at the top, resentful but obedient.

The dinghy was in the water and Clarke was in the dinghy. A rusted metal ladder was bolted to the hull of the trawler. Clarke had a rope wrapped around a low tread, close to the surface. The dinghy was bobbing on the rolling swell, bumping against the hull.

Clarke called up to the girl. Her lip curled, and for a moment, Menser thought she might spit.

He jabbed her forwards with his gun. She grasped the ladder, then cast an accusing look at him.

'Down,' he said.

'My hand.' She showed it to him. Gnarled and warped on the end of her arm. It sickened him. The idea of her trying to grip with it. The snag of bone against skin.

'You climbed up,' he told her. 'Now you can climb down.'

He raised the gun. Pointed it at her forehead. Held it there for the count of two until she began to descend. She struggled down three steps before Clarke was able to reach up and pluck her feet from the treads. She shrieked and fell into his arms and wriggled and bucked. Clarke held her tight for a moment too long, a wide grin slashing his face, before swinging her round and settling her on her backside in the bottom of the boat.

Menser slung his backpack over his shoulder and climbed down the ladder, his gun still gripped in his hand. The treads were slick beneath his feet. He could feel crusted salt under his fingers. A wave rolled in, sea spray wetting his bare scalp. He held fast, the inflatable floating up towards him, then dropping away. His backpack fell from his shoulder and hung from his elbow. He lowered a foot, treading air until the boat pitched up and his toes brushed rubber. Clarke grabbed him by the belt and hauled him inside.

The dinghy made things awkward. The confinement. The silence. Menser had told Clarke the change of plan and Clarke had absorbed it without comment. But he had to know there would be consequences. Repercussions.

And then there was the girl. Watching him with a neutral stare, her deformed wrist cradled in her lap. She was assessing him. Reading the change in her predicament. The change between him and Clarke.

A slow, sickly smile crept across her mouth. Teeth filmed with saliva. White gunk in the corners of her lips. Her unwashed hair greasy against her brow. Her eyes engorged in her gaunt face, like the eyes of an addict. But the light of triumph glimmered deep within them. A victory. Just a small one. She was radiant with it.

Chapter Twenty-four

'Come back with me to the car,' Rebecca said. 'I think you should sit down.'

I didn't argue. I wasn't feeling good. I was groggy and there was a flat droning in my ears. I was trying to think straight, to understand what Rebecca had said to me. Her words kept repeating in my mind. They didn't make sense. They couldn't.

My sister. Laura. With a different name?

I stumbled sideways. Staggered clumsily across the scree of pebbles and driftwood that had collected near the slipway. The sounds of the beach – the breeze through the sand, the waves collapsing against the shore, a seagull's squawk – were distorted and perverse.

'Here.' Rebecca opened my door and guided me into my seat. 'Head between your knees.' She gripped me by the back of my neck and pushed my head forwards. I could feel my sweat beneath her fingertips. Hot blood swirled around inside my skull with a violent centrifugal force.

Rebecca reached into the rear of the car for her backpack. I stayed down, snatching shallow breaths.

'Have some of this.' Rebecca was offering me a bottle of cranberry juice. I sipped the juice while she fumbled inside her backpack until she found the grey plastic bug. 'Back in a minute,' she said.

She walked to the edge of the pavement and dropped the

bug inside a storm drain. Then she closed my door and walked around and climbed in beneath the steering wheel. She turned the ignition key a quarter-circle and powered down my window.

'Better?'

I nodded.

'A shock?'

I took another sip of the cranberry juice. Wiped my lips with the back of my hand.

'You could say.'

'Ready for more?'

I nodded again. Stared out through the windscreen at the darkening sea. The crested waves. The sun was beginning to wane. The sky was blooming a pale violet.

'Laura didn't work in the City, Rob. At least, not in the way you think she did. She was an officer for British Intelligence. We both were.'

I closed my eyes. Swallowed. Listened to the pop and crackle in my ears. 'How long?'

'She joined after me. I left within a year of her being there. That was four years ago. My guess is she was still working in intelligence when she died.'

I released a long breath. Looked some more at the churning sea. What I was hearing seemed impossible to me. The story of another sister. Another life.

But it could also explain why Laura had been so distant in the past few years. Her reluctance to share all but the most basic information about her life.

'Are you saying my sister was a spy?'

'Put simply.'

'So why the false name?'

'Protection. Self-preservation.'

'But what if she met someone who knew her? Wouldn't it blow her cover?' Even as I said the words, they felt ridiculous in my mouth. How much of what you hear about intelligence work was pure fantasy? I couldn't see Laura carrying a gun, seducing foreign agents, operating behind enemy lines.

'Not everyone would do it,' Rebecca said. 'But it wasn't a big risk for your sister. She'd spent most of her life on this island, remember.'

'Not her university years.'

'True. But you have to learn to compartmentalise.'

I swivelled my head. Looked at her flatly. 'Isn't that just a fancy word for shutting yourself off?'

'You sacrifice yourself to the work. That's what it takes.'

And, by the sounds of it, Laura had sacrificed her identity, too. The thought connected to something in my mind.

'Mum said when she called you, she got the impression you didn't know who Laura was.'

Rebecca paused. Her eyelids fluttered. 'That's because to me, she was Melanie Fleming.'

'Then how did you work out who Mum was talking about?'

'For starters, it's not every day someone phones me the way your mum did. Telling me that in the days before she died, Laura asked for me to be contacted if anything happened to her.'

'It's still a leap.'

Rebecca took the cranberry juice from me. Screwed the lid back on. Tapped it with her nail. 'Her middle name.'

'Hendon?'

Rebecca nodded. 'When I was hedging with your mum, she repeated Laura's name – only this time, she said all of it.

Hendon's not exactly common. I remembered it was Melanie's middle name, too. Then everything else started to fit. Her age. Her description. The Isle of Man.'

Hendon was Grandpa's surname. Mum's maiden name. Mum had been an only child and she'd wanted to keep the name alive in some way. So her first child had been christened Laura Hendon Hale. If there'd been a hyphen in it, it might have sounded posh, but not quite so unusual. Melanie Hendon Fleming didn't sound any better.

'So why you?' I asked. 'If you didn't work with Laura for long, why did she want Mum to contact you in particular?'

'I've wondered that myself.'

'And?'

Rebecca made a humming noise, as if what she was about to tell me was a little shaky. 'We worked an assignment together when she first started. I wouldn't say we were close, but I gave her some responsibility and I think she appreciated it. It's never easy when you join. Especially as a woman.'

'That's it?'

'No. That's not it. There was one time in particular. We had a conversation. Admitted to each other we were scared. It's not something I'd have ever said to a male colleague. But I could say it to Laura. I trusted her. Looks like she trusted me, too.'

A man in a hooded coat was approaching. He was walking a dog. Some kind of boxer. The dog had a tennis ball in its mouth and when he unhooked its lead it went tearing off along the slipway to the beach. I thought of Rocky and of how much I'd have preferred to be walking him right now.

'So why did Anderson mention Melanie Fleming to me?' I asked. 'How would he know that I was related to her?'

'I don't know.'

'Did he mention her because there's some kind of a connection between my sister and Lena?'

'I don't know that, either.'

'You don't know a lot.'

'You're angry with me.' Rebecca circled her finger around the top of the juice bottle. Considered the view of the ocean through the windscreen. 'But look at it from my point of view. You're hurt, yes? You feel deceived, maybe. I suppose I didn't see any reason to expose you or your parents to that unless it became necessary.'

I stayed silent.

'I'm sorry,' she said. 'Truly.'

I could feel a stinging in my eyes. Tears pricking the surface. I clenched my jaw.

'Tell me your best guess,' I managed. 'My sister. Lena. Is there a link?'

'It makes sense.'

'How?'

'The cottage. I found wires, yes? Surveillance equipment. But the gear wasn't new. It had been there five, maybe ten years. My guess is that cottage was some kind of safe house. Probably established and wired by British Intelligence. But not used recently. So not completely abandoned, but at least halfway forgotten.' She swirled the juice around. 'A place like that – in Laura's backyard – I reckon she'd know about it.'

'Suppose you're right,' I said. 'Does that mean she was over here spying on Lena?'

Rebecca shook her head. 'I think maybe she was helping to *hide* Lena. Think about it. The Isle of Man. Why would it occur

177

to Erik to put Lena here of all places? Unless, maybe, your sister was involved in the decision.'

A memory flashed through my mind. My first meeting with Lena, in the garage. The way she'd talked about the island. The scornful tone in her voice when she'd asked me what there was to do here to have fun. As if it was somewhere she couldn't quite believe in. As if it was nowhere.

'So the British intelligence services were helping to hide Lena,' I said, like I was fitting it all together in my mind. 'Working with Anderson and Erik. And that's how they knew my sister.'

'Maybe. It would certainly help to explain something else. Erik told us he worked to smother media coverage of Lena's disappearance from London, and from the few scraps I could find on the web, I'd say the strategy was pretty successful. But I doubt he was capable of it alone. The Met are still looking to arrest Lena. They would have needed help from the press. So stopping the story from running would take more than just cash.'

'What would it take?'

'Influence. Power. The sort of influence and power that British Intelligence possess.'

'*OK*,' I said, trying to gather my thoughts. 'But we still don't know why Anderson mentioned the name Melanie Fleming to me.' A burst of movement captured my attention. The boxer dog was streaking across the beach towards the sea. He plunged into the surf with a reckless leap. 'Could the situation with Lena have had something to do with Laura's death?'

'Almost certainly.'

I drew a halting breath. Closed my hand and pressed my nails into my palm. 'Is it possible she didn't kill herself?'

'That's what I plan to find out.'

Chapter Twenty-five

The dinghy's engine was coarse and stank of petrol. A gassy plume hovered above the indigo water, curling in the chilly breeze.

Ten long minutes, then the crunch of loose stones beneath the hull. Lena watched the younger man vault over the side. The water was up to his thighs, soaking his cargo pants. He waded forwards, dragging the boat behind him. The bald man waited until the dinghy was beached, then stepped cautiously into the foam of a fading wave. He turned to Lena and beckoned at her with the gun. She levered herself up from the floor and followed mutely.

They lurked in silence in the cramped, dilapidated hut for what felt like half an hour, until the car arrived. Lena was careful to note that it was a blue Vauxhall Insignia with a UK number plate. Functional in design. No metallic paint or alloy wheels or tinted glass. The younger man pushed her forwards with one hand in her hair, pressing her head down, until she was forced into the rear.

The man behind the wheel was as unremarkable as his car. Medium height, medium build. Short dark hair. A blue Oxford shirt over grey casual trousers.

He drove in silence with the radio on low. Talk radio. The talk was about football.

The older man was watching her from the corner of his eye.

Looking for some form of engagement. She buried her fear deep inside herself and gave him nothing. She was sitting on the back seat between her two captors, peering hard through the windscreen, searching for markers she might remember. The gun was pressed into her side.

It was warm in the car. The bald man sipped from a bottle of water. He offered some to Lena. She accepted and drank the whole thing. Tipped her head right back and held her mouth open beneath the bottle to catch the very last drop. Feeling pleased with herself, she gazed ahead through the glass at the two-lane road they were cruising along. The cars they were passing. The lighted road signs.

Time passed. Then the car began to slow and veer off into a lay-by that was shielded by a copse of trees. Another Vauxhall Insignia. Another faceless man. He was leaning against the rear of the car, legs concealing the number plate. He moved aside as they pulled close and the boot lid popped up.

A lamp blinked on. Lena could see a duvet. The cover was bright pink.

She stiffened and leaned forwards, pressing her face between the front seats. Her shirt rode up at the base of her spine and she felt hands on her skin. The younger guy punched something sharp into her side. Lena gasped and turned to scratch at him. The man caught her by the wrist and started to count down from ten, that stupid leering grin fixed on to his face.

Lena was out cold before he reached seven.

*

Lukas tucked the laptop under his sweater and hobbled away from the man's home into the gathering dusk. The gravel beneath his feet sounded too loud to his ears. His movement was laboured and he was afraid of being challenged. He kept his head down and shied away from the big house to his side. He could feel eyes on him. Watching him. But he muttered encouragement to himself and shuffled on. The exit lurched closer with each awkward step. And then, almost before he knew it, the exit was behind him and he was hobbling away along a residential street.

Lukas didn't know where he was. He didn't know how long it would take him to reach the hotel Anderson had mentioned, or even if he was heading in the right direction. There was a bus stop farther along the road, beneath a yellow street light, but Lukas had no cash in his wallet. He realised now that he should have searched the man's home for money. Not that it helped. He couldn't go back. He would have to go on.

The walking wasn't easy. His leg wound burned and itched beneath his makeshift dressing. His muscles were weak, his balance unsteady, and he hadn't eaten a solid meal in days. He slowed and tried to control his palsied movements. Considered his reflection in the tinted glass of the bus shelter. A man with long hair, in need of a cut, grubby and unwashed, sheened in sweat. Dirt-smeared jeans and a worn sweatshirt. The bulge in his clothes from where he cradled the laptop. He looked like a tramp and he'd be certain to draw attention. Couldn't avoid it. But he was lucky with the time. Mid-evening, when traffic was quiet.

He followed the curving road downwards for half a mile. The neighbourhood was up on a rise and he could see the sea far below, stretching away from him like a vast, dark pool. He limped between the splashes of light from the street lamps, counting them off one after the other. A car passed. He imagined that he heard the driver slow, his passengers watching him closely. But the car didn't stop. Nobody approached.

He walked until the road opened up on his left. Some kind of shopping precinct. A lot of concrete and bricks and rusted metal bollards. Multiple parking spaces, most of them empty. There was a supermarket, too, lit brightly from within.

A taxi was parked outside, close to a cash machine. It was a white Japanese minivan and the driver was a middle-aged woman. She was reading a tabloid newspaper. Lukas lowered his head and approached the cash machine. He withdrew a wad of notes and made his way inside the supermarket for a snack bar and water. When he came out, the taxi was still there. Lukas tapped on the window and waited for it to slide down. He said the name of the hotel he needed, pronouncing it like a question, and the woman backed off for a moment, as if doubtful, before nodding reluctantly and folding her newspaper away.

Chapter Twenty-six

Rebecca turned sideways in her car seat and scrutinised me. Her dark-brown hair coiled around her neck and over her shoulder. Her neck was delicate. The skin lightly freckled.

She asked, 'How far do you want to go with this?'

'I want to get to the truth.'

'About Laura's death?'

'About everything.'

She nodded, as if she'd expected me to say that. 'And if I told you that you might not like what you hear?'

'I already don't like what I know. How much worse can it get?'

She waited a beat, searching for something in my face. It didn't take her long to find it. She reached inside her jacket for her mobile and tapped the keys with her thumb.

'We should speak to Teare,' she said, nodding to herself like she was agreeing with her own decision.

'Shimmin won't like that.'

'Shimmin needn't know. He told me Teare wasn't working today. So we'll go to her home.'

I thought about that for a moment. The Isle of Man was small, but it wasn't so small that I knew where everyone lived. 'You have an address?'

She shook her head. Raised her phone to her ear.

'Directory enquiries won't help,' I told her. 'She's a police officer. Probably ex-directory.'

She lifted her finger, hushing me. 'Matt?' Her face broke into a flirtatious smile. 'It's Rebecca Lewis. How would you like to make me even happier?'

*

Rebecca's contact at the control centre came up with an address in Laxey, a small seaside village on the north-east coast. It was a half-hour drive from Castletown, from the south of the island up past Douglas towards Ramsey in the north. I barely talked during the journey. I wanted to run through recent events in my mind and try to come to terms with the revelations about my sister's secret life. It was easier said than done. Understanding the path Laura had followed was going to take a lot longer than thirty minutes. Figuring out where that path had led her in the last days of her life might be even tougher.

Rebecca was quiet, too. She only talked to ask me for directions. She didn't expand on the nature of her relationship with my sister or their shared career in intelligence. She didn't throw around ideas about Lena's whereabouts, or our meeting with Erik and Anderson, or the circumstances surrounding Laura's death. I didn't doubt that she was thinking about some of those things. Maybe all of them. And it wouldn't have surprised me to learn that she had some theories about what had happened. She was a few steps ahead of me – had been all along – and I just hoped that speaking with Detective Sergeant Teare would lead us towards some kind of conclusion.

The address was for a place on Shore Road. It turned out to

be a small terraced cottage on a side street leading away from the beach. The cottage was a pale yellow and the front door was split in two horizontally, with the top half folded back like a stable door to let in the noise of the waves shuffling against the beach. Next to the door was a large window. There was a light on inside. It revealed a cramped kitchen with a circular cafe table positioned just behind the window glass. The table was big enough for two people, but only one of them would have a view towards the sea.

As a kid, I'd spent plenty of summer days on Laxey beach. It's a mixture of pebble and sand, and when the tide is out, you can walk beyond the cliffs at the end of the promenade into a separate cove filled with rock pools. Nowadays, the beach is somewhere I walk Rocky out of season. There's an ice-cream stall nearby, and the mint choc chip still tastes every bit as good as it did when I was a child.

Somehow, I didn't think we'd be enjoying an evening stroll and an ice cream with DS Teare. From the look on her face when she came to the door to answer Rebecca's knock, and her swift double-take when she first saw me, I didn't think we'd be enjoying much at all.

Teare was dressed in a long-sleeved white T-shirt over black tracksuit bottoms. The T-shirt looked old. It gaped around her neck and at the ends of her arms, and there was a faded orange stain down by her waist. The tracksuit bottoms were shapeless and too long for her, the fabric rolled up to reveal her bare feet. Her thin hair was scraped back from her forehead and held in place by a plastic hairband. She gripped a small dumbbell covered in pink neoprene in each fist – the kind some women use when they're jogging or exercising. It occurred to me that the top half of the door had probably been left open to draw a breeze inside while she worked out.

'What are you doing here?'

'We'd like to talk to you,' Rebecca said.

Teare glared at Rebecca and I got the feeling she didn't like what she saw. 'So you're Nancy Drew. Heard you came to the station. Heard Shimmin threw you out on your arse.'

'May we come in?'

'No, you may not. Now bugger off. I'm busy.'

'It's important,' I said.

'Then talk to Shimmin.'

'I don't trust him.'

She dipped her head. Showed me the whites of her eyes. 'You should. He's a big fan of your dad's.'

She went to swing the door closed. I put my hand in the way, palm flat against the varnished wood. The impact jarred my bad shoulder in a way I didn't relish.

'Please. This is about more than my bike crash now. It's about my sister's death, too. We think they may be connected.'

Teare paused. Breathed deeply. She looked like she wanted to bounce the door off my head. But I could see I'd got her interest.

'Connected how?'

'By Laura's work,' Rebecca said. 'She was an officer with British Intelligence.'

Teare smirked. Wiped the back of her hand across her nostrils. 'You're not serious?'

'Very,' Rebecca said. 'Now, may we come in?'

*

Teare led us along a short corridor to a dingy sitting room at the rear of the cottage. A black leather sofa faced a flatscreen television. The television was screening an exercise video featuring a minor soap actress chanting bouncy encouragement. Teare jabbed some buttons on a remote, killing the picture and the hum of a DVD machine. Then she kicked a thin blue exercise mat towards a pair of French doors that opened on to a scruffy patio terrace.

She left the room and returned shortly after with a fold-out wooden chair. I recognised it as one of the chairs that had been nestled beneath the table I'd seen through the kitchen window. She collapsed on to it and gestured at the sofa with a weary swing of her arm.

'Sit. Make yourselves uncomfortable.'

After a moment's thought, Rebecca selected the far end, positioning me closer to Teare. The bitter tang of her sweat was pungent in the enclosed room.

'So which one are you?' she asked me.

'Sorry?'

'The Hardy Boys. She's Nancy Drew. That makes you either Frank or Joe Hardy.'

'Please,' I said, and shuffled forwards on the sofa cushion to keep my shoulder clear of the backrest. 'We need your help.'

'So you said. I still don't see why.'

She dug a hand inside the pocket of her jogging trousers and removed a can of Diet Coke that she must have fetched from the kitchen at the same time as the chair. She tapped the lid twice, then popped the seal. She drank greedily, wiping her mouth with the sleeve of her T-shirt when she was finished.

'You asked questions,' I said. 'About my crash. When you came to speak to me at the hospital.'

'Shimmin asked questions, too.'

'No he didn't. He did everything *but* ask questions. He didn't want to know.'

Teare drained some more of her Coke. Her lips slurped noisily at the can. She was slouched in her chair, legs spread, with her bare toes clawing into the dark-green carpet. Her feet looked dry and callused. A thick pad of skin had yellowed at her heel.

'File's closed,' she said.

Rebecca nodded. 'We saw the incident report.'

'So then you know there's nothing to investigate.'

I glanced at Rebecca. It was difficult to know where to take things. Erik had asked us not to go to the police about Lena. He'd said the risk to her could be increased if we did. But Erik had lied to us. His credibility was shot.

'What about my sister's death?' I asked.

'What about it?'

'Is the file closed on that, too?'

''Course it is. She killed herself. I'm sorry, but that's how it was.'

'She was worried about something before she died.'

Teare pulled a face that seemed to say, *well, duh!*

'That's how Rebecca became involved,' I said. And then I went on to tell her what Mum had told me. About Laura's skittishness in the days before her death. How tired she'd been. Her difficulty sleeping. How she'd asked Mum to contact Rebecca if anything happened to her.

'So?' Teare asked.

'So she was afraid,' I said.

'Or she was depressed. Under stress. Something personal, maybe. It's still suicide. Reason doesn't change it.'

'If it was suicide, why would she have asked my mum to contact Rebecca?'

'I dunno. Maybe she wasn't thinking straight. Depression can do that to you. Paranoia, maybe. Could be a hundred reasons.'

Rebecca reached for my arm. Pulled me back gently, so that her view of Teare was unobstructed. 'Did you attend the scene?'

'Where she did it, you mean? No, I wasn't there.'

'Who was?'

'I don't know exactly. Shimmin. Some uniform, I guess. Some SOCO guys. And later I heard they had to get a fire crew and a hire crane out. To lift the car.'

'Why weren't you there?'

She shrugged. 'It was early in the morning. Before my shift. And Shimmin's my superior. He didn't need my help.'

'Did you offer?'

"Course I did.' She scratched absently at her gut. Her T-shirt hitched up, revealing a slab of pasty skin. The dark slot of her navel. 'No offence,' she said to me, 'but we don't get many like your sister. Pills, maybe. But a car off a cliff? I hadn't seen one of those.'

'So why did Shimmin say no?'

She sniffed her fingers. Grimaced. 'He already had it under control. And it's not like we're in some television cop show. We don't all have partners and go round investigating crimes in pairs.'

'You came to my hospital room in a pair.'

She shrugged again. 'I was the one who took the call from uniform, after your doctors phoned in to report some of the quirks in what you were saying.'

'And Shimmin?'

'He said he'd tag along. I guess he thought your old man might be there. Maybe he'd share a few stories with him about the good old days of the TT. Or maybe he reckoned I'd be too insensitive, what with the background of your sister's death, and all. I have a reputation for it.' She raised her can, as if in a silent toast.

'Did you know my sister was a spy?'

Teare fought a grin. Her teeth were crooked. Lips cracked. 'Oh, come on.'

'It's true,' Rebecca said. 'We worked together.'

'Oh, this is priceless.' She hooked a thumb at Rebecca. Hoisted her eyebrow for my benefit. 'You believe this?'

'I have reason to.'

'Yeah. What reason?'

I was silent. Thinking hard. My reason was Rebecca's sayso. It was Anderson's use of a name my sister had adopted when we'd played at being make-believe investigators as children. Nothing more than that. Nothing substantial.

'I want to go back to Rob's bike accident,' Rebecca said. 'Someone reported it to the emergency control centre. Otherwise how would an ambulance have turned up?'

Teare contemplated her Coke can. She rolled out her bottom lip. Peered inside the teardrop-shaped hole.

'That seems to me an obvious avenue to explore,' Rebecca said. 'I take it you did that.'

'I can't comment,' Teare muttered. 'Can't talk about an investigation.'

'Then it's just as well I called the witness myself, isn't it?'

Teare's head snapped round. Her eyes narrowed. Running calculations. 'How'd you get that number?'

'That's largely irrelevant. But what I think *is* interesting is that the man who answered my call claimed to have no knowledge of any accident. No link to the Isle of Man. Almost as if he'd never been contacted.'

'So you got the wrong number.'

Rebecca shook her head. 'Did you see the tyre tracks outside the cottage? They were recent. From the rental car Rob saw. And why didn't you get someone out to take a look at the heating system, to confirm one way or another whether any work had been carried out on it?'

'Now hold on –'

'Did you know a white van was spotted in the vicinity of the plantation in the weeks leading up to Rob's crash? Did you know the entire cottage was wired for surveillance? Every room? Cameras and microphones?'

That caught Teare. She wasn't trying to speak any longer. But her eyes were alive with questions.

'It seems to me,' Rebecca said, 'that you're either so incompetent you should be fired, or you deliberately chose not to investigate any of the *quirks* you mentioned. And yes, you work for a small police force on a small island, but you strike me as intelligent and motivated enough. You said yourself you'd been itching to get out and look at the aftermath of Laura's accident. But you didn't poke around Rob's incident at all.'

'She asked me questions at the hospital,' I pointed out.

Rebecca nodded. 'And then all that zest and inquisitiveness left you completely, Detective Sergeant Teare. Almost as if it evaporated. Which is odd, wouldn't you say? I mean, if a girl playing Nancy Drew can find a whole bunch of inconsistencies in a case like this, then a *seasoned* police investigator like yourself should have no problem at all doing the same thing. All of which makes me think someone told you not to ask any more questions. And since I'm only the amateur here, I'm going to guess it was DI Shimmin. But as the professional, maybe you could let me know if I'm right?'

Chapter Twenty-seven

Menser and Clarke took the first car, the one without the sedated girl in the boot. Clarke did the driving. He drove along a series of A roads to Preston, then joined the M6 and accelerated north. The journey ahead of them wasn't long and traffic was minimal. Darkness had fallen and it was warm and intimate inside the car. Too warm and intimate. The silence was pressing. It was a living thing, pulsing between them. Clarke switched the radio on, tuning into a local station, but Menser dialled it down. He wanted to think. To concentrate.

Clarke cleared his throat. 'So, I apologise,' he said.

'That's it? You apologise?'

'I made a mistake.'

Menser braced his elbow against the door panel and rested his head on his closed fist. 'You made a lot of mistakes.'

Clarke looked across at him, the glow of the instrument dials casting his face in an orange hue. That ridiculous soul-patch below his bottom lip. His pensive eyes.

'You want to know why I called an ambulance?' Clarke asked.

Menser said nothing.

Clarke spread his fingers above the steering wheel. 'First of all, it's not what you think.'

'What do I think?'

He shrugged. 'Brainy guy like you, you could come up with

a lot of ideas. And maybe one of those ideas is that I tried to sabotage the assignment in some way.'

Menser didn't reply. Sabotage had been his first thought. His second was to ask himself why.

'Well, I wouldn't do that,' Clarke said. 'What would be in it for me? Why would I suffer weeks in a surveillance van with you if I was planning to let you down? Why would I help you take the girl? Why would I leave her with those guys just now?'

Menser had asked himself the same questions already. Many times. He hadn't come up with an answer. Not a satisfactory one, anyway.

'Truth is,' Clarke said, 'I felt sorry for the biker.'

Menser stared at him, his eyes tracking the headlamps of the 4x4 that was overtaking them. 'You felt *sorry* for him?'

'He was hurt. Scared.'

'Jesus, Clarke. The girl was hurt and scared. The guy who ran from you in the woods was definitely scared. And what about his buddy? You know, the one you tied to a chair and drowned? He looked pretty scared to me.'

'That was different.'

'It was?'

Clarke nodded. 'He knew what he was getting into. What he was involved in. But not the biker. He got caught up in this thing by accident.'

'You think?'

'Don't you?'

There was an illuminated road sign ahead. It was the sign he'd been looking for. They were closing in on Lancaster.

'Take the next junction,' Menser said. He checked the time

on the dash. 'Ferry doesn't leave for nearly five hours. Look for a hotel. Nothing fancy. We'll get some sleep.'

Clarke flicked on his indicators. Moderated his speed.

'Will you talk to him for me?' Clarke asked.

Menser said nothing. He looked out his side window at the curving off-ramp.

'Will you explain for me? Tell him why I did it?'

Menser remained silent. He stayed that way as they approached a set of traffic lights, as they turned and crawled along the road, passing retail parks filled with two-storey office buildings and chain restaurants and garage concessions and out-of-town gyms, looking for the neon glow of a motorist's hotel.

And all the while, he was thinking hard. Thinking about the girl in the boot of the second car. About her behaviour. How disconnected she'd been. Asking himself if he was right to be concerned by her attitude. If she knew something he didn't. Something important.

Thinking about the detective on the phone. The loose end she represented. Thinking how he might tie it off. And not just that, but how he might use the situation. Transform it into something else entirely.

But mostly he was thinking about Clarke. Thinking about his mistake with the emergency call. Asking himself if it really could be a mistake, or if it was something else entirely. Thinking about Clarke's interaction with the girl. Thinking about his disposal of the man called Pieter. Thinking about his performance during the previous weeks. His behaviour inside the surveillance van. The reports he'd provided while Menser had been asleep.

Thinking. Always thinking.

Clarke would be pleased. *IQ*. Living up to his reputation.

Chapter Twenty-eight

I could tell that Teare didn't like the way Rebecca had questioned her. I could tell she didn't like Rebecca, full stop. But it was clear that she wanted to think about what Rebecca had said, and so she announced that she was going to make us both a mug of tea.

She was specific about it. A *mug* of tea. Like a cup would be far too genteel and fussy for someone like DS Jacqueline Teare.

I could hear the kettle coming to the boil. The vacuum-suck of a fridge door opening.

The delay was getting to me. Bothering me. I fussed with my sling. Cursed under my breath.

'Give her time,' Rebecca said.

'To do what? Come up with a story?'

'To reconcile herself to telling us the truth.'

'You think she even cares?'

'I'm sure she does.'

'How sure?'

'Look around,' Rebecca said, in a low voice. 'Does this look like a happy family home to you?'

It didn't look like anything of the sort. There were no pictures on the walls, no books or mementoes on the shelves. There was a single photograph on the mantelpiece. Teare, when she was younger, in a blue police uniform, with a bad perm. She was smiling crookedly, holding some kind of certificate in her hand.

I scanned the rest of the room. There was the single sofa we were sitting on, the television and the fold-out kitchen chair. Not a set-up for boisterous family gatherings. Not an environment for entertaining.

'I'd say her job means a lot to her,' Rebecca said.

'Maybe.'

She nodded at the photograph. 'She takes pride in it.'

'So perhaps she'll want to protect her career. Maybe she'll lie to do that.'

'Or perhaps it means more to her than that. Perhaps she views it as a calling.'

Rebecca whispered the last part because Teare was returning to the room with two steaming mugs in her hands. They were mismatched. One brown and squat, like it had come from an amateur kiln. One white and featuring the logo for a brand of coffee. A freebie.

'I can hear you gassing about me, you know. I'm not bloody deaf.'

I avoided Teare's eyes as she handed me my mug. Rebecca smiled graciously, like the tea was an exotic treat she'd heard of long ago and had always wanted to try.

'It was mostly complimentary,' she said, taking a sip.

'My arse. But it doesn't matter.' She collapsed on to her chair and fished around in her tracksuit bottoms again. She removed another can of Diet Coke, wet with condensation from the fridge. She opened it and tipped its contents into her mouth.

'So was it Shimmin who told you to drop things?' Rebecca asked.

'Yep.' She lowered the can. Balanced it on her thigh. 'But there was nothing fishy about it.'

'How so?'

Teare sneered. Shook her head. 'Way you talk. Sitting there all prim. In your pricey leather jacket and your flawless make-up.'

'Please,' I said. 'We've come to you about my sister. It's important.'

'Yeah. That's exactly my point.'

'Excuse me?'

'The importance. Your sister. I told you Shimmin had a thing for your dad. It's generational, maybe. Pretty much gender-specific. Manxies like Shimmin, they treat your dad like he's some kind of hero.'

'So?'

'So it affected the way Shimmin went about things.'

'Affected it how?' Rebecca asked.

Teare exhaled. She pressed the cool metal of the can against her cheek. There was a clammy film on her skin. It made me wonder how long she'd been exercising for.

'A suicide like Laura's. Something spectacular. Forgive me,' she said, catching my eye, 'but something as nutso as driving off Marine Drive, that would normally draw a lot of attention. A lot of gawpers and rubberneckers. Inside the force, the fire service, the ambulance crews, not to mention the public. Then factor in your sister's identity. Your dad's status on the island. I mean, we're talking about the daughter of Jimmy Hale, yes? Normally you couldn't keep a lid on something like that.'

Teare looked from me to Rebecca. She was expectant.

'What I'm saying,' she said, as if we were altogether too

slow, 'is it shows respect, right? Shimmin respects your dad for throwing himself around on a motorbike way back when. So he keeps things civilised. Keeps numbers low. It's the same with the press. Think about it. There wasn't much of a to-do, was there? But that's all it was so far as Shimmin was concerned. Respect. Nothing sinister.'

I reflected on what she'd said. I could see what she was driving at. Yes, I'd been caught up in the grief and the emotion of Laura's death, the sheer numbing horror of what she'd done to herself, but I hadn't been aware of a circus going on around us. There'd been well-wishers. Condolence cards. But the memorial service had been relatively modest. The coverage in the local paper and on the radio had been contained. People on the island would know what Laura had done. Maybe they were still talking about it. But it hadn't become the spectacle it might have been.

'So what about the cottage and the missing girl?' Rebecca asked. 'What about the way Rob's version of events was dismissed? That didn't have anything to do with respect.'

Teare sucked her lips in thought. 'I still say there was some of that. It's another reason Shimmin came to the hospital with me. Like I said, I couldn't be trusted not to offend, could I?'

'But that's not all, is it?'

'No, it's not. And the honest truth is I don't know what it was for sure. But Shimmin was quick to tell me not to dig around in that cottage. I got a locksmith out, to take a shufty, and we had a right barney about it. That's how come you're talking to me now.'

She wiggled her eyebrows.

'What do you mean?' Rebecca asked. 'Have you been suspended?'

'Like you care, princess. But no, not suspended. Right now I'm on a period of *extended leave*. Time to reflect on my attitude.'

'And how's the reflection going?' I asked.

'In terms of the attitude, not so good. But in terms of what happened up at that cottage, I've come to a few conclusions.'

'Such as?'

'Such as hidden cameras and microphones and vanishing blondes aren't something a smart copper goes sticking their nose into. That's something Shimmin knew already. And that's why he stopped me from asking questions. Not because he had anything to hide. Because he didn't want us to find answers we couldn't do anything with.'

I was still cradling my mug in my hand. It was hot against my skin. I hadn't drunk any of my tea just yet and I didn't think I was about to start any time soon. Rebecca was shifting around in her seat. It seemed like we'd got just about as much as we could have hoped for. But it still felt like a defeat.

'Does the name Melanie Fleming mean anything to you?' I asked.

'Nope. Can't say that it does.'

'Then we've taken enough of your time.' Rebecca straightened and placed her mug down on the carpet. I followed suit.

'You can see yourselves out,' Teare said. 'But take my advice. Do some reflecting of your own. Nothing good is going to come from poking around in what happened up at that cottage. Best to let sleeping dogs lie, you know?'

Lukas struggled out of the taxi and closed the door behind him. The hotel was built in a grand Victorian style, many storeys high, and located on Douglas seafront next to an ornate theatre. The ground floor featured large bay windows with curved glass and Lukas could see well-dressed people eating at circular tables covered in crisp white linens, drinking wine from sparkling glasses.

He thought of his dirty clothes. His unkempt appearance. Then he cursed himself for thinking of those things and started up the steps. He took them one at a time, heaving his bad leg behind him without bending his knee.

The foyer was impressive. High ceilings and shiny marble floors, oversized planters with colourful flower displays, uniformed staff behind a polished reception counter off to one side. There were two staff on duty, a man and a woman, and the instant they saw him they devoted all their attention to a computer screen sunk into the counter. He got the impression he was expected to leave without troubling them. He didn't have to.

Anderson emerged from a club chair hidden behind one of the planters. He was wearing a smart blue suit over a white shirt. His shirt collar was open and the suit was a size too small, emphasising his hard packed muscles.

He swept over to Lukas, buttoning his jacket on the way, then shaking his hand and patting him on the arm like a valued business companion. His eyes danced across the bulge beneath Lukas's grubby sweatshirt. He smiled, showing a lot of teeth and not a lot of eyes. Then he wrapped an arm around Lukas and led him through the foyer to a waiting elevator. Anderson pressed a button for the top floor and waited for the doors to close before spinning Lukas around and plucking the pistol from the waistband of his trousers with a fast, dextrous movement.

'What's under the sweater?' he asked, ejecting the magazine of bullets, then stuffing the pistol and magazine inside his jacket.

'His laptop.'

'And what's up with your leg?'

'I told you. I was shot.'

Anderson's face was impassive. 'Bad?'

'I think so.'

Anderson shook his head. 'You wouldn't be walking if it was. And you know we can't take you to a hospital. Not over here. But I'll give you a shot for the pain.'

Lukas gulped. 'They have Pieter.'

'Pieter let Mr Zeeger down.' Anderson placed a hand on Lukas's shoulder. 'You're a lucky guy, Lukas. You get a second chance.'

The doors parted on to a silent corridor. The dark-blue carpet was richly woven. The walls were papered in blue and cream stripes.

Anderson led Lukas as far as a lacquered wooden door. He knocked three times and waited for a muffled response before using a keycard to enter.

The suite was spacious, the lighting subdued. There was a well-appointed kitchen, a generous living area with multiple couches and armchairs, and a glass dining table.

Mr Zeeger was sitting in a wing-back chair at the far side

of the darkened room, beneath a powerful reading lamp that bleached all the colour from his fair hair and tanned skin. When he looked up from the papers he was reading, his face had the appearance of a fleshless skull.

'Sit down, Lukas,' he said. 'You don't look well.'

Lukas shuffled across to the chair facing Mr Zeeger and winced as he lowered himself into it. Mr Zeeger seemed relaxed and composed. He was dressed casually, with a cashmere jumper over a light-blue shirt.

Anderson stood a few paces away, at the blurred edge of the cone of white light from the lamp. His hands were on his hips, pushing the tails of his jacket behind him. Lukas could see the holster for his gun.

'Relax, Lukas,' Mr Zeeger told him. His piercing blue eyes blazed out of his ghostly skull-face. 'You've been very resourceful. Why don't you tell us what it is that you've found?'

Lukas swallowed hard, then pulled the laptop out from beneath his sweater and flipped back the lid. He tapped a key and asked himself where exactly he should begin.

Chapter Twenty-nine

Laxey village is arranged over two sides of a river valley and towards the back of the village is a giant red waterwheel. In the nineteenth century, it was the largest waterwheel in the world, built to pump fluids out of the mineshaft beneath. It's still claimed to hold that title. I couldn't say if the claim is true. But I did know it was a good place to talk.

I had Rebecca drive us away from the beach and alongside the river until we crossed the embedded tracks for the electric tram system that runs around the coast to the north of the island. We passed a line of brightly painted cottages called Ham and Egg Terrace, where the mine workers used to enjoy cooked breakfasts back in the day. Beyond the terrace was a tight right turn, a small humped bridge and an empty visitors' car park.

The wooden waterwheel towered above us, stationary at this time of night. A giant brick structure had been built to house it, painted a brilliant white, with a curved tower at one end that had been fitted with an external spiral staircase. There were two red Manx flags at the top of the tower, snapping in the coastal breeze. The flags featured the Triskelion, the emblem of the Isle of Man, made up of three conjoined legs. Another large Triskelion was embedded on the front of the brick structure housing the wheel.

There was a small entrance hut in front of us and a metal turnstile beside it. During the day they charge you to come in.

At nine in the evening, when it's close to fully dark, you can jump the turnstile for free.

We climbed over the barrier and strolled up the gravel path towards a fast-flowing stream close to the base of the wheel. Industrial floodlights bathed the white brickwork in a stark electric light. Midges and moths swirled in the glare. There was a wooden park bench close behind us. I took a seat and looked up at Rebecca, who was busy craning her neck and contemplating the wheel.

'So what do you think?' I asked her.

'I think it's a big wheel.'

'I meant about Teare. About her interpretation of Shimmin's motives.'

Rebecca cupped her hands around her eyes and looked beyond the wheel to the dark, clouded sky above. 'I think what she said is possible. That perhaps Shimmin tried to keep a lid on the circumstances surrounding Laura's death for the benefit of your family. Out of respect for your dad.'

'You don't sound certain.'

'Because I'm not. I'm not certain about a lot of things.'

'Such as?'

Rebecca sighed and lowered her head. 'Such as what kind of mess your sister had got herself into, exactly. You asked me why she wanted your mum to contact me in particular. I've been thinking about that.'

'And?'

'I told you I work for Wilton Associates.'

'So?'

'So it's a private firm. And it's independent. That must have appealed to your sister. I'm outside the intelligence community. Maybe that means the problem she had was *inside*.'

'What kind of a problem?'

'Hard to know. But we're assuming she was helping to hide Lena, OK? And that she was assisting Erik and Anderson to achieve that.'

'I guess.'

'And they told us Lena could have been taken by more than one group. There's this environmental campaign angle, for sure. They were worried about that. No question. But that wasn't all.'

'So?'

'So maybe they were also concerned about British Intelligence. Maybe Laura was concerned about them, too. Maybe, thinking about it, she was helping Erik to hide Lena from her own people.'

I backed away, my shoulder blade nudging the rough edge of the picnic table, making me flinch. I was having difficulty with the idea. 'Why would she do that?'

'Money? Erik has plenty of it. Or something else. Something we don't know just yet. But there's a logic to it. Think about the men in the white van. The way they tapped into the surveillance equipment up at the cottage. The way they staged your accident to get at Lena. That's not the type of thing a campaign group could comfortably pull off.'

'But a couple of spies could?'

Rebecca nodded. 'That couple of spies would be part of a larger network. They'd have resources. Support. They'd have the ability to keep Lena hidden. Maybe even transport her away from here. And they'd have the power to shut down a police investigation. Remember what Teare said? About why Shimmin swept everything away into one straightforward road-accident report?'

'Because he didn't want to find answers he couldn't do anything with.'

Rebecca smiled crookedly and slipped her hands inside the pockets of her leather jacket. She clinched her arms against her sides for warmth and tucked her chin down against her chest. She was watching me closely. Monitoring my thoughts.

'What?' I asked.

'Laura.'

'What about her?'

'Don't you see? If we assume she was working against her employer, rebelling in some way, then all those resources, that entire network, could be turned against her.'

My heart thudded in my chest. I waited for it to thud again. The waiting took a long time.

'What are you saying?' I asked. 'You think they staged her suicide? That she was murdered?'

She held up a hand. 'I'm not saying that. Not yet, anyway. But I'm starting to think it would be useful if I could see where she died.'

'You mean right now?'

She smiled. 'I don't imagine I'd be able to sleep just yet. Do you?'

*

Marine Drive is a coastal road carved into a gorse-covered headland at the southern end of Douglas Bay. It stretches between Douglas and Port Soderick, a small village roughly four miles away, but for as long as I can remember, the road has been closed at the mid-way point. It's blocked because of the deterioration of the road surface and the dangers associated with a winding ribbon of tarmac that hovers precariously at the top of two-hundred-foot sea cliffs. Even so, the road can still be accessed from either end. It's popular with dog walkers, cyclists and joggers. Parents take their kids there to teach them to drive. A lot of kids return when they've passed their test because Marine Drive is a choice make-out point. There are plenty of sweeping curves and secluded pull-ins with outstanding sea views, and it's quiet enough to hear an approaching vehicle.

The white hulls of the yachts in Douglas marina were gleaming beneath the electric street lamps that surround the quay by the time Rebecca drove us past the ferry terminal and swung left on to the narrow road climbing the side of the headland. We passed terraced houses and a small industrial yard. Then the view opened up and we could see the sweeping horseshoe curve of Douglas Bay below. The fairy lights strung across the prom glowed a soft, vibrant yellow, and hundreds of lights were on in the windows of the hotels and apartments that lined the seafront. The ferry dock was aglow beneath powerful floodlights. Up ahead, a squat block of luxury flats enjoyed the best of the view from just above the Victorian Camera Obscura.

I had Rebecca drive around to the right, where we approached a crumbling brick structure that had the appearance of a castle turret with two archways cut through it. Above the archways the words MARINE DRIVE had been painted in faded white lettering. The road was completely dark, with no white lines or street lamps, and Rebecca had to switch to full beam as we passed beneath.

We didn't have far to go. After following a bend for a few hundred metres, Rebecca's headlamps picked out a swathe of clear plastic by the side of the road. The plastic was wrapped around the dying remains of a bunch of white roses. Mum had placed the flowers there to mark the spot where Laura had pitched herself over the cliff.

I hadn't been up here since the accident, but it was pretty much how I'd expected it to be. There was an obvious gap where some of the concrete posts and wire fencing that ran along the edge of the road were missing. Of the posts that remained, one was bent at a sharp angle, half ripped out of the ground by the force of Laura's car bursting through the wires. Glassy fragments glittered in the light of our headlamps on the low gravel pavement. They looked like broken pieces of headlamp reflectors.

Rebecca stopped a short distance away. The engine idled. I powered down my window and felt the coastal wind on my face. I could hear the surf far below. The swirl and crunch of the waves striking the base of the cliffs. The cry of nesting gulls.

Rebecca cut the engine and dimmed the headlamps and stepped outside, walking through the slanted beams towards the flowers. She bent down and read the card, then straightened to peer over the cliff.

I hadn't planned on joining her and I was still inside the car when she turned and walked back to talk to me through the gap in my window.

'Can you pass me my torch?' she asked. 'It's in my bag.'

The torch was a weighty Maglite. It had a dimpled metal

shaft, cold to the touch. I powered the window right down and handed it to her. She compressed the switch with her thumb and headed back to the gap in the fence, the beam swinging from side to side. I watched her shine the flash into the darkness below. She took a series of sideways steps, like she was conducting a careful survey of the drop. I caught a blink of white in the glare. A seagull taking flight.

A few moments later, Rebecca beckoned to me with the hand holding the torch. The dazzling flare lanced into the night sky.

I thought about staying where I was. I thought about shaking my head and signalling that this wasn't something I could do. But she was insistent, as if she'd found something I really needed to see.

I shoved my door open. Stepped out of the car. My legs felt stiff, unbending, like my knees were locked in place. My shoes scuffed in the gravel at the side of the road. The air felt raw and wild up here. I could hear the caw of the gulls. The crash and shuffle of the surf. The darkness seemed to have swallowed the yellow light of the headlamps completely.

'Something to show you,' Rebecca called.

My throat was dry. I worked my cheeks. Swallowed some saliva.

'It's not so bad,' she told me.

Easy for her to say. For weeks now, I'd fought to keep the reality of this place shut off from my mind. I hadn't wanted to think about the long drop to the jagged rocks below, or to count the awful seconds Laura would have endured as her car tumbled through the air. I hadn't wanted to know how unforgiving the impact would have been. How sudden and absolute the out-come.

The grass verge was torn up where Rebecca was standing. The result of a combination of factors, I guessed. The jolt of Laura's car digging into the soft turf. The bite of her wheels in the mud. The snag of the wires holding her back for the merest fraction of a second before momentum and gravity took over and the concrete fence posts were yanked free in a spray of compacted earth. Then the stamp of the heavy machinery used by the rescue services to haul the remains of Laura's car back to the road.

'See this?' Rebecca asked.

She was aiming her flashlight over the side. I don't suffer from vertigo. Not in a big way, at least. But I was feeling un-steady. My legs had a treacherous urge. I kept picturing myself slipping. Or falling. Like invisible hands were pushing me for-wards.

I whipped my head down and snatched the briefest of looks, but the drop wasn't what I'd expected. I looked again. It was steep, no question, but it wasn't a sheer cliff. The ground sloped at an acute angle for fifty or so metres, then evened out, then plunged sharply, before ending in a shallow grassy bowl at the top of a spit of land sticking out into the sea. The powerful light of Rebecca's torch picked out whitish debris and bits of metal at the bottom of the second drop. Two rough trenches had been scored into the earth. I had no doubt that I was look-ing at the site where Laura's car had ended up.

'Now look at this,' Rebecca said.

She guided me away to the right, through the beams of the headlamps, and played her torch over the edge once again. The fence was still intact at the point she'd chosen and I rested my hand on a concrete post and teetered forwards. The drop rushed up at me out of the dark. A straight plunge to the foaming depths way below. The cliff face was rough and craggy, jammed with shards and fissures of broken rock.

Rebecca said, 'It's the same on the other side.'

'So?'

'So your sister's car went over at an interesting point. It's the only section along this stretch of road where there isn't a sheer drop.'

I backed away from the edge and looked to where Laura had driven over. 'There's still a hell of a fall.'

I waited for Rebecca to respond. She was distracted. Absorbed in thought. She walked past me, towards the flowers.

'It's not like she would have known what was on the other side,' I called after her. 'Look at the speed she must have been going to break through the fence.'

Rebecca pivoted at the waist and played her torch over the spit of land again. The halogen bleached the scraggly grass. The area of debris looked like someone had been fly-tipping.

'What's the rest of the coastline like along here?' she asked.

'The same, pretty much. We'd have to come back in the day-time. Why?'

She ignored the question. Chewed on her bottom lip.

'What?' I asked.

'You think you could get down there?' She swung the flash-light over the loose shingle at the beginning of the drop.

'Not with my arm like this,' I said, lifting my sling. 'And I wouldn't want to do it now anyway. Too dark. Too windy.'

She made a humming noise. 'Laura's crash was when? Five in the morning?'

'Just after. Mum heard her go out. She just assumed Laura was having trouble sleeping again.'

More humming. More lip chewing.

'What is it? Rebecca?'

She blinked. Like she was coming round from a daze. 'Let's get back in the car.'

She switched off her torch and turned from me, pacing around the reverse of the Fiesta, the cherry red of the brake lights colouring her jeans. I looked back through the broken fencing at the clotted blackness beyond. The concealed spit of land. The pounding of the waves. Then I followed her to the car and folded myself into the passenger seat and powered up my window as Rebecca pulled away.

She flipped her lights to high beam and crouched forwards over the steering wheel, peering hard towards the grassy fringe at the side of the road. Our route coiled around to the right and the headlamps coiled with us, illuminating a parked car. Two figures were huddled together in the front. They broke apart and I could see their faces. A young lad and a flustered girl. There was an R plate on the front of the car. You can learn to drive at the age of sixteen on the Isle of Man, but your car has to be fitted with an R plate for your first year on the road.

Rebecca dipped her lights.

'Doesn't go on much farther,' I said.

'I'll turn at the top.'

There was a gentle gradient ahead of us, climbing towards the locked gates at the crest of the rise. Farmland was on our right. A lone sheep grazed behind a barbed-wire fence.

'There's something I think you should consider,' Rebecca said. 'Something you might not have thought about just yet.'

'OK.'

'I want you to think about your own role in all this. How you came to be involved in the first place.'

'You know how. It was my bike crash. Lena's disappearance.'

Rebecca shook her head. 'Before that.'

The car's headlamps picked out the pale timber of the gate. It was closed and bolted. Alongside it was the cliff edge. In the far distance, I could see the milky ray of a southerly lighthouse sweeping the open sea.

Rebecca heaved the steering wheel to the right and turned the car around, setting off down the hill again. The glow of the instrument panel bathed her hands and her jaw in a green luminescence.

She said, 'You went out to fix the heating, correct?'

'You know I did.'

'And you were called to do that, yes? You picked up a message from one of the guys. The one called Lukas.'

'I'm pretty sure it was him.'

'And how many plumbers are there in the phone book over here?'

Her question threw me. 'I don't know. Close to a hundred, maybe.'

'Anything special about your ad?'

'I paid extra for a coloured box.'

'Other people do that too?'

'Sure.'

'How many?'

'Around half of them, I suppose.'

'Well, coincidence is one thing. And we shouldn't dismiss it completely. But seriously, what are the chances of them picking your name out of the phone book?'

She looked across at me. Reading my reaction. The sickly green light bathing her face from below.

'Don't you see?' Rebecca lifted a hand from the steering wheel. 'We're assuming Laura was connected to Lena in some way. Assisting her. And then, out of all the plumbers they could possibly have called, they called you.'

I let go of a breath. It sounded more like a sigh. 'So maybe Laura gave them my card.'

'Tell me about the fault with the boiler. What was the problem?'

'It needed a good service.' I shrugged. 'But other than that, it was nothing serious. Some wires had come loose. One connected directly to the circuit board. I didn't have the right connector plug to fix it. That's why I needed a spare.'

'And how often do you see a problem like that?'

'Couple of times a year, maybe. When the burner kicks in, if the boiler isn't grounded properly – say it's on sloping ground – it can shake. Over the course of a few years, that shaking can work a wire free.'

We eased by the parked car with the young couple in it. This time, they didn't break apart as we passed. Maybe they figured we'd come up here for the same reason.

Rebecca said, 'But isn't it also possible that if someone wanted to sabotage a system, that would be a good way to do it?'

'Why would anyone want to sabotage their own heating system?'

'Maybe so a plumber would have to come out. A particular

individual.' Rebecca emphasised her words, like she was handing them to me one by one and asking me to weigh them, feel their shape, try to fit them into the slots of a specific puzzle she'd constructed. 'I think maybe Laura gave *Lena* your card.'

'You think Lena sabotaged the boiler?'

'Absolutely.'

'For what purpose?'

'Based purely on the facts? So that you'd take her away from the cottage on your motorbike.'

'All that just for a bike ride?'

Rebecca slowed as she passed under the archway in the brick tower, then accelerated around the curve. Douglas promenade appeared from below, bright and gaudy, like Blackpool without the tower.

She shook her head. 'You're forgetting that your journey was cut short. Who knows where she wanted you to go?'

And that's when the penny finally dropped.

'I do,' I said.

Chapter Thirty

Lukas turned the laptop around so that Mr Zeeger and Anderson could see the document he'd called up on screen. It was the memorial sheet for Laura Hale's funeral – the one with the soft-focus image of Melanie Fleming on the opening page.

'That's her for sure,' Anderson said, tapping his finger against the glowing screen.

'Agreed,' Mr Zeeger said.

'So she gave us a false name. One that checked out. Which means she was smart. Question is, how smart?'

'Explain.'

'What I'm thinking,' Anderson said, 'is how can we be sure if she's really dead?'

Lukas spun the laptop back around to face him and got busy with the trackpad. It was a problem that had already occurred to him and one that he'd done his best to answer. He scrolled through his browser history and called up a page from the local newspaper.

The article was brief, but clear. It stated that Laura Hale, aged thirty-one, had been killed in a car accident on a coastal road more than three and a half weeks ago. No other vehicles were involved and police were not treating her death as suspicious. It stated that Laura, who lived in London, had been on the island visiting her parents and her brother, Rob. It also noted that her father was a one-time motorbike racer by the name of Jimmy Hale, who'd triumphed in the Isle of Man TT races on a couple of occasions back in the late 1970s.

'Doesn't prove anything,' Anderson said. He straightened and propped his knuckles on his hips.

Mr Zeeger leaned back in his chair. The light from the standing lamp blazed down on him. He contemplated Lukas. His blue eyes burned with intensity. 'When was the last time she visited the cottage?' Mr Zeeger asked.

'I don't remember for sure,' Lukas told him, aware that it didn't sound good.

'Would the dates fit?'

Lukas nodded, keeping his eyes down.

'We should have moved Lena sooner,' Anderson said. It sounded like he was repeating an argument he'd made many times before.

Zeeger waved his hand. 'I'm not interested in what we should have done. I want to know what you're going to do. How you plan to find Lena?'

Anderson was silent for a moment. Then he reached a decision. 'Melanie Fleming. Laura Hale. Whatever you want to call her, it's too much of a coincidence for her brother to be involved in this. And not just him, but a private operative, too. I don't like that. Not even a little.'

'So what do you suggest?'

'I already bugged the girl but the feedback is dead. I'm guessing she read my move. Next best thing is we watch them. See what they might be up to.' Anderson turned to Lukas. 'It's going to take two of us. Think you can find your way back to his place?'

Lukas toggled to a fresh Word document on the laptop. It

was one of the invoices from the man's plumbing business. He copied the address information over into a mapping tool and hit *Search*. He handed the laptop to Anderson before the processor had finished whirring and the graphic had appeared on screen.

Anderson nodded. 'I have a vehicle downstairs,' he said. 'I'll drive. You navigate.'

*

Anderson had asked me if Lena had given me anything when we'd met. I'd told him that she hadn't. And it was true. But it was also a lie.

Lena *had* given me something. It was just that she hadn't passed it to me directly. She hadn't taken me aside and told me what she was doing. She hadn't closed my hand around the item and explained its significance, or asked me to hang on to it for safekeeping. So when I told Anderson that Lena hadn't given me anything, it was true.

But it was also a lie.

It was a lie because Lena had given me a very simple, very modest object. So simple and so modest that it had taken me days to spot it.

When I first went up to the cottage, Lukas had tossed me a key to the garage. The key was relatively small. A touch flimsy. But it had fitted the lock on the garage door just fine and I'd been able to access the boiler.

Later that afternoon, Lena had come up with her plan for the following morning, involving my van and my motorbike.

She'd told me to take the garage key with me, so that I didn't need to ask Lukas for it when I returned.

I did as she suggested and the key had worked just as well the following day. I had it in my pocket when we rode away on my bike. It was still there after the crash, when my leathers were cut away from me and my belongings were collected together in the plastic bag that Dad had carried from the hospital.

That was how I'd been able to hand Rebecca the garage key when we'd walked up to take a look around the cottage. Just an ordinary key. Attached to a simple plastic key fob. I should have spotted it by then. I should have seen what I was looking at. But I hadn't. I hadn't because I hadn't been expecting it. Because it was so commonplace. So obvious.

There was a *second* key on the fob. I didn't even register that it was there until Rebecca had finished searching the cottage and had passed me the keys. But as I looked down at my palm, I finally understood that there were *two* keys. There'd been one originally. For the garage. And now there was another one.

The second key was a little longer. A touch sturdier. And it was distinctive because unlike the garage key it had a series of raised and lowered bits on both sides of the blade. The garage key had a simple circular bow, but the second key had a bow with an angular shape, like the top half of a hexagon. There was an embossed number on one side. I couldn't recall the number off the top of my head. But I knew there were three letters stamped on the other side, and I could remember those quite clearly.

'You're sure the key wasn't there before?' Rebecca asked me, once I'd finished explaining.

I thought back to the feel of the key in my hand when Lukas

had first thrown it to me. I conjured up the memory of fixing the key in the lock on the garage door. There hadn't been a choice to make. I hadn't tried one key, then the other. There'd only been one key.

'I'm sure,' I said.

'And you think Lena put it there?'

'She was watching me work, so she could have slipped it on to the fob when I was focused on the boiler.'

'Clever.'

'Not really. It took me a long time to notice.'

'But that's my point. She arranged it so that you took the key away and returned with it without even knowing. I think she was planning to have you take her somewhere. Somewhere specific that was connected to the key.'

'Didn't exactly work out for her, then, did it?'

'Maybe not. But whoever snatched Lena doesn't have the key. She must have known she was taking a risk by leaving the cottage. That's why she wanted you to carry it instead of her.'

We were driving along the promenade, gliding by the neon lights outside a club-bar, the glass and steel exterior of an off-shore bank headquarters, the well-lit interior of a fancy restaurant. We passed a long curving terrace of Victorian townhouses. We passed the ornate Gaiety Theatre, a Chinese restaurant, a fish-and-chip shop.

I realised I was hungry. I hadn't eaten for hours. I asked Rebecca to pull over and then I headed inside the steamy chip shop and returned a few minutes later with two paper packages and a pair of plastic forks.

'What the hell is this?' Rebecca asked, once she'd unwrapped her meal.

'Chips, cheese and gravy,' I told her. 'Local speciality.'

'*Eugh.*'

'Enjoy.'

I stabbed my fork into a knot of chips covered in thick gravy and melted cheese, then shovelled them into my mouth. Rebecca wasn't eating. She was too busy pulling a face.

'Trust me,' I said.

She curled up her nose and pricked a chip at the very corner of her tray, filmed with the barest smear of gravy. She raised it to her mouth. Hesitated. Then she popped it inside and chewed like she was experimenting with some far-flung tribal dish.

She swallowed. Shrugged. Ate some more.

'So where did Lena want you to take her?' Rebecca asked, between mouthfuls. 'You said you knew.'

'There were three letters inscribed on the key handle. *NSC.*'

'NSC?' Rebecca paused with her fork in the air. 'What's that? The manufacturer's logo?'

'I don't think so.'

'A bank? Maybe the key was to a safety deposit box. Maybe she'd stored something important. Something valuable.'

I jammed more food into my mouth. Mopped my lips with a napkin. 'It's not a bank. I can't think of a bank over here with the initials NSC. And our accident happened on a Saturday morning. Only a handful of high-street banks are open then. And none of them are the type with safety deposit boxes.'

'Then I give up. Tell me.'

'The National Sports Centre,' I said. 'I think it's a locker key.'

Chapter Thirty-one

Lena was lying on her side. One arm was behind her. Her other arm, the one with the swollen wrist, was in front of her face. Her legs were positioned as if she was running. Her right leg was fully extended and her left was bent at the hip and the knee. It wasn't her natural sleeping position. Someone had arranged her like this. They'd done it so that she wouldn't roll on to her back and swallow her tongue and choke to death because of the sedative they'd given her.

The sedative was still in her system. She was sure of that. Her head felt fuzzy, her muscles relaxed. There was a buzzing in her ears and her temples. She could feel a haziness all around her, prickling her skin like a field of static electricity. She recognised the sensation. She'd experienced it before.

Her mind was conscious long before she was able to move her body. That had happened the last time, too. Something to do with inhibitors in the nervous system. She knew that your body shut down when you went to sleep so that you couldn't physically act out your dreams. She guessed the sedative had a similar effect.

It was infuriating. Her neck ached and she wanted to relieve it. She must have drooled while she was unconscious because she could feel cold liquid pressed against her cheek. The arm that was below her was throbbing and tingling all over. The weight of her body had cut off the blood supply.

She tried to open her eyes. No luck. The muscles wouldn't respond. Her eyelids felt sticky and rimed with grit.

She listened for sounds from around her. Heard only the hissing and the pulsing of the blood in her ears.

She didn't think she was in the car any more. Whatever she was lying on was cushioned and soft. And there was no sensation of movement. No engine noise.

She strained her ears for more, and *bam*, just when she least expected it, her eyes snapped open.

She was staring at a wall. But it was no ordinary wall. It was covered in some kind of foam material that had been tacked up like tiles. The foam was dark grey and textured in a series of ridges and hollows, like the interior of an egg box.

She raised her head. Slowly. So slowly.

The bright pink duvet was beneath her. Beneath the duvet was a floor carpeted in thick rubber underlay.

She dropped her head back down. Into the pool of cold saliva. Then she summoned her strength and gritted her teeth and flung her rag-doll body around until she was lying flat on her back.

She let go of a wheezing breath. The foam tiles covered the ceiling, too. They blanketed the entire room. She knew why they were there now. It was the same with the rubber underlay. Soundproofing. In case she screamed for help.

The tingling was getting worse in her arm. It was intensifying as her blood flowed back through the arteries and flooded the tissue and swamped the nerve endings. She flexed her fingers. Electric charges streaked up her arm. Her fingers were clumsy and weak. She had no grip. No feel.

There was a single bare bulb in the middle of the ceiling. The bulb was burning brightly, surrounded by a blurred corona. Did that mean it was night-time still? The same day or the next?

She kicked her legs out straight. Stretched her toes. Her shoes were gone but she was wearing her socks and the rest of her clothes. She tucked her injured wrist in against her chest and sat upright.

The hissing in her ears and the buzzing in her temples grew worse. The room pitched and lurched in front of her, like she was still on the stupid boat. She ground the heel of her hand into her eye socket. Tried to fight the surge of nausea that washed over her. She felt drowsy as hell but she couldn't allow it to overcome her. She had to stand up.

Standing was a battle. She broke it down into stages. First, she struggled on to her knees on the ridged rubber floor. Then she crawled to the far side of the room. The crawling didn't take long. The room wasn't large. There was a window in the wall above her. She reached up and grasped the ledge with her good hand. She heaved with her arm and pushed with her legs. Her legs were feeble. They trembled and quaked. She rested her chin on the dusty ledge. Stared out at the view.

The view was dizzying. Far below her was a sprawling city vista of thousands of lights that extended for many miles towards the darkened horizon. She was up very high, in some kind of tower block. There were matching apartment blocks all around her, made of dull brown brick and powdered concrete and dirty glass. The towers looked to be around sixty storeys in height. They were shabby and uncared for. Discoloured net curtains hung in the windows. A weather-beaten English flag was stretched between two apartments. There was no way of telling which English city she was in. She could be anywhere.

Lena calculated that she was perhaps ten storeys below the top of the nearest tower block. The window in front of her was a fixed single pane of glass with no hinged openings. There was a hairline crack in the top left corner. The outside of the glass was covered in some kind of opaque film that was beginning to peel away just above the crack. She guessed the film was there to tint the glass and make it impossible for her to signal for help.

She rolled around until her buttocks were resting on the window ledge. The only things inside the room were the duvet and the light bulb and the egg-box soundproofing and the rubber underlay.

There was a door in the middle of the facing wall. It was covered in the grey foam tiles. The tiles had been cut away to fit around the circular door handle.

Lena pushed off from the windowsill and staggered across the room in her socks. She shook some feeling into her good arm. Then she reached out for the handle.

She hadn't expected it to turn. She'd assumed it would be locked. But the handle rotated freely and the door opened inwards and she stepped through into a much larger room.

'Good, you're up,' said a voice to her left. 'You like pizza?'

Chapter Thirty-two

Rebecca wanted to head to the sports centre right away, but I told her we couldn't. For one thing, the keys were back at my place. And for another, it was after 11 p.m. The sports centre would be closed. We'd have to wait until morning.

So Rebecca decided to drive me home to see the keys for herself. I wasn't sure what she hoped to find. Maybe she thought I'd overlooked something but I didn't believe that I had. The garage key was just that – a simple key. I'd told her everything I could about the key branded with the letters *NSC*. And the plastic fob was a translucent red disc. There was no way it contained anything more. Nothing special about it, whatsoever.

We were accelerating away from the seafront promenade and climbing up Summer Hill Road when Rebecca said, 'It's interesting, don't you think, that Lena entrusted the key to you?'

'I thought your theory was that Laura had given her my name. That Laura recommended me to her.'

'But remember what Erik told us? He said he'd placed Lena under the care of Lukas and Pieter. That they were looking out for her.'

'So?'

'So if that was the case, why would Lena involve you in the first place? Why wouldn't she just get Lukas or Pieter to take her to the sports centre? Or better still, why didn't she stay in the cottage while one of them went to the sports centre on her behalf?'

I thought about that. 'I'm not sure,' I said. 'But when I first went up to the cottage, I got the impression Lukas was wary of me.'

'Go on.'

'Lena told me that they'd been without hot water for days. She said she'd been practically begging Lukas and Pieter to call someone. She made a big deal out of it. Like she couldn't have called me herself.'

'And?'

'And your suggestion was that the heating system was sabotaged. By Lena. As if it was her only way of getting help. As if maybe Lukas and Pieter weren't protecting her so much as holding her against her will.'

I let the idea spin out in my mind. The first thing I recalled was Lena's attitude when we were riding my motorbike away from the cottage through the rainy tree cover. I remembered how excited she'd been. Giggling. Striking me on the back. *As if it was more than a trip for her. Like it was an escape, maybe.*

The second thing I recalled was Lena's response when I asked if the men in the cottage were her friends. *You can call them this, I suppose.* Did that mean they weren't friends? And if not, what did it make them? Enemies? It was hard to believe they were a threat to her. Lena hadn't behaved as if she was scared and I couldn't believe they'd have left me alone with her if that was the case. They'd have wanted to be sure she didn't tell me anything, that she didn't try to alert me to whatever danger she was in. So not enemies. But not friends, either. Something else entirely. Something in between. Guardians, maybe. Unwanted ones, perhaps. What was it Erik had said when we'd first spoken on the phone? I'd asked him if Pieter and Lukas had told him that Lena had gone for a motorbike ride with me, and he'd replied, *No. It was* forbidden *for her to leave the house.*

'Erik lied to us once already,' Rebecca said. 'He could easily have done it again.'

'You think everything he said was a lie?'

Rebecca twisted her lips in thought. 'Not all of it. I believe he's Lena's father. There's the photograph of him and Lena when she was younger. The jet with the SuperZ symbol. Faking that would be way too elaborate. And I buy the idea of her rebelling against him. Hence her relationship with Alex Tyler.'

'You don't think she loved Tyler?'

Rebecca was silent for a moment. 'Hey, they were planning to get married. So I'd say it's a given that they were in love. But Erik and Anderson said that they doubted Alex's motives were so noble when they first got together. That could have worked both ways. Lena would have known when she began the relationship that Erik wouldn't approve.'

'So?'

'So maybe Erik isn't so quick to forgive as he was making out. Maybe he's more interested in protecting himself than Lena.'

'Protecting himself from what?'

'I don't know just yet. That's the problem.'

I sat there in the drowsy warmth of the car, my head propped against the darkened window glass, thinking more about Erik and the things that he'd told us. I couldn't see where his truths ended and the lies began. I couldn't get a feel for his real motives. Did he want to find Lena for her sake, or his? Did it matter either way?

Rebecca slowed for the entrance to Snaefell View and trundled through the gravel to the parking area outside my place. Most of the care home was in darkness. I could see lights on behind the windows of my parents' quarters and the twilight glow from the safety bulbs in the corridors that connected the residents' rooms.

I stepped out of the car. Night chill wormed its way beneath the collar of my shirt. The air smelled like rain and when I glanced up, menacing grey clouds pressed down from above.

I heard a *clunk* and saw a flash of orange in the dark. Rebecca had locked her car. I turned and smiled at her, then rooted through my pockets for my house keys and headed towards my door. But I didn't need my keys. The door was hanging open, revealing a sliver of gloomy hallway beyond.

Chapter Thirty-three

'What is it?' Rebecca asked.

'I locked up when I went out,' I said, in a low voice.

'Could your parents have come in for something?'

'My grandpa, maybe.'

'Does he have a key?'

I nodded.

'Well, there you go.'

'But there are no lights on inside. And I left Rocky with him tonight. I can't think why he'd have come over.'

'Maybe he needed something for your dog.'

I shook my head. 'Rocky had everything he could have wanted.'

I could hear Rebecca's breathing from behind me. It was all I could hear. There was no noise from inside my apartment. No sound whatsoever. But it felt like someone was lying in wait. Lurking in the dark.

'What do you want to do?' she asked.

'Go in, I guess.'

'Well, here. Take this.'

She rooted through her backpack, then pressed something into my hand. I glanced down. She'd passed me a small plastic canister, like a travel-size deodorant.

'Pepper spray,' she explained. 'Just point and squirt.'

I swallowed.

'You want me to go first?' she whispered.

I didn't answer her. It was too tempting to say yes and I couldn't rely on myself not to do it. I lowered my head and clenched my jaw and reached out and swung the door back hard. It knocked against the wall. A sharp tap in the awful silence. I didn't mind that. If there was someone up there, I wanted them to know I was coming. I wanted to give them a chance to step out and hold up their hands or yell some kind of warning.

Amazing how alien my own home suddenly felt. The cupboard under the stairs and the door through to my workshop posed a threat I hadn't experienced before. Was someone hiding there? Would they lash out if I checked?

I flicked on the light. Squinted against the sudden glare. Held the chemical spray out in front of my face and moved for the stairs.

I was very conscious of my arm in the sling. The way it would handicap me if someone rushed me or attacked me at the top. I peered up. Nobody there. I half turned and braced my hip against the wall and used it for support as I climbed.

Rebecca was following me. Close on my heels. She flicked her wrist and I heard a sudden clatter. Now she was gripping something in her hand. The object was long and slim and made of shiny black steel. A telescopic baton. She must have been carrying it in her backpack. Her bag was on the floor at the bottom of the stairs. I guessed she didn't want it getting in her way. Or maybe the idea was to trip my intruder up if he managed to get past us.

I cleared my throat. 'Is anyone there?'

Nothing. No answer. I was beginning to relax. To think that

maybe I hadn't locked the door, after all. I remembered that I'd been carrying Rocky's bed when I'd left. I'd been in a hurry. Maybe I'd simply forgotten.

There was another light switch at the top of the stairs. I reached for it fast. My kitchen and living room emerged from the black.

Not my mistake. I hadn't overlooked the door. Someone had definitely been here.

The place wasn't a mess. It hadn't been ransacked. But there were still signs. A kitchen drawer was open close to the sink and the door to my storage cupboard was hanging ajar. No way would I have left things like that. I'm an organised person. I live in an ordered home. It bugs me if a drawer isn't shut properly. It rankles when the mess in my storage cupboard is on display. And there was no reason for Grandpa or my parents to go rooting though my kitchen.

There were giveaways in the rest of the apartment, too. My clothes had been disturbed. One of the doors on my wardrobe isn't hung quite right, and if you don't close it first, the other door overlaps without shutting flush. I never leave it like that. It'd irritate me too much. But it was like that now.

But what really gave it away was my study.

It isn't a large space. Just a box room, really. I have a filing cabinet there, and the bottom drawer was wide open. My chair had been rolled away from the desk, so that the plastic wheels weren't sitting on their usual indents in the carpet. And there was a tell-tale space in the very middle of my desk.

'My laptop's gone,' I said.

Rebecca was leaning her shoulder against the door frame, swinging the baton in her hand. It looked capable of breaking an arm or cracking a skull. I wondered if she needed some kind of licence to own it.

'Anything else?' she asked.

'I don't know. Maybe. It's difficult to tell.'

'You want to check downstairs?'

'*Want* is a strong word.'

We checked anyway. There was no evidence of disturbance. My motorbikes were all present and correct. My tools and equipment, too. Nobody was crouching beneath the work-bench or hiding in the cupboard under the stairs.

I closed the front door. Engaged the deadlock. Led Rebecca upstairs again.

I went to my fridge for two bottles of lager and fetched a bottle-opener. Then I slid the lagers and the opener across the granite surface of my breakfast bar to Rebecca. Tricky for me to pop the caps one-handed.

'Here,' she said, and returned a bottle.

The lager tasted good. Cold, with a bitter aftertaste on the back of my tongue.

'What was on your laptop?' she asked.

'Nothing.'

'Nothing?'

'Nothing anyone could want. Just business stuff. Family stuff.'

'Stuff about Laura?'

I drew on my lager as I thought about that. 'There were a few things,' I said, swallowing. 'I was helping Mum and Dad deal with her estate. Writing letters to her banks, her mortgage provider. I wrote an obit for the paper. We put together the order of service for her funeral. And there were family photographs on there, too.'

Rebecca slid on to one of the cushioned kitchen stools. She unzipped her leather jacket. She had on a baby-blue T-shirt underneath. The neck-line scooped low. She rested her elbows on the kitchen counter. Took a swig of her lager and pointed at me with a finger of the hand holding the bottle.

'This doesn't strike me as a random burglary. It's too neat for that. There's too much still here.'

'You think whoever took the laptop is looking for Lena?'

'Don't you?'

I pulled a face. Slumped back with my spine pressing against the kitchen sink. Nodded my head towards the open cupboard door. 'Is this how spies behave? I thought they might have covered their tracks a bit better. At least closed my front door.'

'They took your laptop, Rob. It's kind of a giveaway.'

'So no point concealing the break-in?'

Rebecca nodded. She used her nails to pick at the label on her bottle of lager. 'Do you want to call the police?'

'And what? Have Shimmin tell me I'm imagining things again?'

'Hard for him to do that.'

'Not so hard when he's done it before.'

I drank more lager. It felt good. Felt great, actually. I hadn't been drunk in a long time. I got the feeling it'd be easy to get that way tonight, especially with the painkillers I was on. Drink one bottle fast. Another quickly after. Let the buzz cloud my thinking. Disrupt my judgement. My inhibitions.

'What?' Rebecca asked.

'Huh?'

'You were looking at me funny.'

'Just resting my eyes.'

She smiled. Tilted her head to one side. 'Curious place to rest them.'

'I like the colour of your T-shirt.'

'The colour.'

'It's an interesting shade.'

'And the fit?'

I nodded. 'That too.'

Rebecca propped her head against her open hand. Laced her fingers through her hair. 'How's your shoulder?' she asked.

I moved my arm in my sling, resisting the urge to grimace. 'It's OK.'

'Slowing you up at all?'

'I'm good at adjusting.'

'Really.'

'I'm adaptable.'

'Huh.'

Rebecca drank some more of her beer. Held my eyes. She seemed to be deciding something for herself. Running through the variables.

'Do you want to show me that key?'

'The key.' I nodded. 'Right.'

'I'm thinking now would be a good time.'

'Now would be a great time.'

'So...'

I glanced down into my beer bottle. Made a humming noise. Looked back up again and winced. 'Here's the thing,' I said. 'It wasn't only my laptop they took.'

I watched my words register on Rebecca's face. Saw a tension creep into her features. She lowered both hands to the kitchen counter. Spread her fingers.

'They took the key?' she asked.

'Both keys.' I nodded. 'And the fob. They were on top of my laptop.'

'Are you sure? Maybe they fell to the floor?'

I gestured towards the study with my lager bottle. 'Be my guest.'

She slid off her stool. Walked slowly across the room. She had nice hips. A terrific silhouette. She was just my type. Hell, she was every guy's type. Completely breathtaking.

But she wasn't going to find any keys.

I watched her scan my desk. I watched her slide my chair aside and crouch down to check the carpet. I watched her straighten and turn in a careful circle and return to the far side of the living room, close to the corner sofa.

'I'm sorry,' I said.

Her arms hung heavily at her side. Long and lean. Fingers lightly curled. Tensing, then relaxing. 'Not your fault.'

'It could have been a useful lead.'

'Still might be. I guess we'll just have to see what tomorrow brings.'

'And meanwhile?'

She was silent for a moment. Watching me. Her face was plain. Open. She gazed down at the carpet between us. Tracked it slowly until she got as far as my feet. Her eyes crawled up my body. She smiled. A lazy grin. Then she shook her head, just barely.

'Bad idea,' she told me.

'No appeal?'

'It's not that.'

'Then what?'

'It would be a distraction. From what I'm here to do. From what your parents hired me for.'

'Distractions can be good. I was thinking we could get distracted on that sofa. Then in my bedroom. One long night of distractions.'

'And then?'

'I guess we'll just have to see what tomorrow brings.'

She showed me her teeth. Shook her head some more. 'Goodnight, Rob,' she said.

'Goodnight, Rebecca.'

And with that, she left and she didn't return.

Chapter Thirty-four

The voice that had offered Lena pizza belonged to the man she'd seen sitting on the boot of the car just before she was sedated. He looked typically English. Short brown hair, neatly styled. High forehead. Slim nose. Weak chin. He was holding a triangle of pizza up to his mouth. A paper napkin was tucked into the collar of his blue shirt. Three greasy takeaway boxes were stacked on the floor beside him.

The man was sitting in a wooden deckchair with a candy-striped canvas. There was a matching deckchair folded up and propped against the wall. The only other item in the room was a portable radio. It was tuned to a station playing classical music.

'There's lemonade,' the man said. 'I expect you're thirsty.'

Lena said nothing.

'Sit down. Relax. We're going to be here a while. No reason it can't be pleasant.' He took a mouthful of pizza. Used his fingers to pluck at a string of melted cheese that stretched between his lips and the triangular slice. 'The only rule is no screaming or shouting,' he said, chewing. 'You try anything funny and you go back in that room with the door locked.'

Still Lena refused to speak.

'It's good pizza,' the man said. 'Might as well eat it while it's hot.'

Lena felt a hollow churning in her stomach. Her mouth was starting to water. The pizza smelled very good.

'I need the bathroom,' she said.

The man smiled. As if they'd reached some kind of understanding. He pointed to a plain door on the other side of the room. 'Go ahead,' he told her. 'There's no lock. But don't worry. As long as you behave, I won't disturb you.'

The bathroom was beyond basic. Lena closed the door behind her and took a quick inventory. She saw a toilet with no seat. A wall-mounted sink with only one tap. A compact white tub, also with one tap. The tap was dripping. It had been dripping for a long time. The tub was stained because of it. The water was running away through a drainage hole with no plug attachment. There was no shower over the bath, hence no shower curtain and no shower pole. Four drill holes were visible in the wall where a cabinet or a mirror had once been positioned. There was a roll of white toilet paper on the floor but no toilet-roll holder. There was a single bar of soap on the sink, but no towel to dry her hands with and no towel rail.

Whoever had prepared the bathroom had done a thoroughly professional job. Anything that might have been made into an improvised weapon or used to aid an escape bid had been removed. The bathroom window was a thin horizontal strip of glass, fitted into the wall way above Lena's head. The outside of the glass was covered in the same opaque film as the window in the soundproofed room. Lena placed her foot on the rim of the toilet and stretched up, teetering there, to prod at the glass. It was solid. No give.

She stepped down and dropped her trousers and her underwear. She squatted over the toilet and tried to analyse her dilemma. Her thinking was laboured, dulled by the after-effects of the sedative. But she knew that her options were severely limited. Even if she assumed she was being guarded by only one man, without a weapon of some kind she had little chance of overpowering him. She was dizzy. She was thirsty and hungry. She was weak and her wrist was badly sprained.

But she did still have one weapon in her arsenal.

Lena found her feet and flushed the toilet. She would have liked a mirror. She would have welcomed the chance to check her appearance and brush her hair and tidy herself up.

No matter. If there was one thing life had taught Lena Zeeger, it was that she was desirable.

She stepped out of her trousers and kicked away her underwear and her socks. She unbuttoned her blouse with her good hand and struggled with her bra strap until she had it undone. She shook her hair. Threw back her shoulders and lifted her chin.

She opened the door. Raised one arm against the frame and bent one leg at the knee. She cleared her throat. Batted her eyelids.

The man gawped up from his pizza. A chunk of tomato adhered to his chin. Tendrils of cheese hung from his mouth. He ran his eyes up and down her body. Then he snorted and wiped his oily lips with the back of his hand.

'You Europeans have a funny way of dressing for dinner.' He chewed his food with his mouth open. 'But just so you know, I was assigned to watch you because I don't ride that particular bus. So you might want to think about putting some clothes back on.'

*

Menser clicked on his bedside lamp shortly after midnight. He hadn't slept. Hadn't really expected to. It was impossible for him to switch off when he was in the middle of an assignment. Always had been. Add to that the creeping sense that things were slipping beyond his control and you had the perfect recipe for a bout of insomnia.

He was getting old. Too old for the job.

No, that wasn't it. He was too old to *want* the job any more. Sometimes he wondered what had happened to the ambitious twenty-two-year-old who'd been so eager to serve. He marvelled at his desire to sign up for a cause, any cause, without bothering to stop and consider what the merits of that cause might be.

He knew the answer now. The weight of his actions crushed down on him. The things he'd done. The outcomes he'd set in motion. The times he'd stepped aside when he could have intervened. Lives had been lost. Others had been taken. But it wasn't until the past few months that the weight had finally become too much. He'd felt himself buckle. Knew he couldn't stand much more. And then the sick twist – the sting in the tail – the realisation that the cost of leaving would bring with it the heaviest burden of all.

But then, what had he expected? A simple retirement?

He remembered the look on his superior's face. The cool assessment of his request. The sharp nod and the collegiate pat on the shoulder and the assurance that something could be arranged. But not through the usual channels. The usual channels, his superior had assured him, were clogged with bureaucracy and budget cuts. They were overseen by pen-pushers and penny-pinchers. Not the type of people who could be relied upon. Not the right approach at all for a man who deserved to get out with ample reward for a lifetime of service.

The solution was ready and waiting. It was neatly packaged and beautifully wrapped and dropped right in Menser's lap. There would be one last job. A final assignment. And the pay-off would mean a generous retirement bonus and a speedy departure.

But of course, nobody could know the details. Nobody except Menser and his superior and a young, ambitious new recruit by the name of Clarke. A guy who was willing to serve, no questions asked, just as Menser once had.

Menser grumbled to himself. Ground the heel of his hand into his eye. The ferry sailed from Heysham docks at a quarter past two in the morning. They'd get there early. They couldn't afford another mistake. His superior had made that very clear. And if he was lucky, the docks might distract him from the broken record of regret and bitterness that kept stuttering and repeating itself inside his brain.

He reached a hand down to the floor and groped for his phone. Checked the display and saw that he had a message from one of the men his superior had found to watch the girl. The message was two words long. *No problems.*

Menser grunted. He wasn't so sure. He had a feeling the girl had concealed something from them. Something on the Isle of Man, maybe.

He gathered together his discarded clothes. Straightened out his trousers and fed his legs into them. It was time to get dressed and rouse Clarke. Time to shoulder more weight. To go and find out if his fears were justified.

I finished my lager after Rebecca had gone. Then I finished hers and washed the bottles in the sink. Ten minutes since she'd walked out my front door. Nine and a half minutes since I'd heard the noise of her car pulling away.

I listened to the silence down in my hallway. Walked through my flat one last time. I didn't think whoever had broken in would be back – they'd already got what they'd come for – but I wanted to make sure it was hard for them if they did return. I checked the locks on my windows. Closed and locked the drawers of my filing cabinet. Then I headed downstairs and locked the internal door to my workshop and stepped outside and yanked my front door shut behind me so that the snap lock engaged.

It was raining. The water was falling fast and hard, pooling in the shallow troughs Rebecca's tyres had carved into the gravel. It drummed off the metal roof of my van. Tumbled and spiralled in the gusting breeze.

I hunched my shoulders and ran across the yard and squelched through the lawn to the care home. I let myself into the unlit kitchen and stood among the hard stainless-steel surfaces and the smell of bleach that had been used to clean the floors. I shook myself dry and rubbed the rain from my hair. My shoes were wet and muddy. I stepped out of them and walked in my socks as far as the stairs.

Grandpa's room was at the end of the second floor. I could hear his snoring as I approached. A loud, phlegmy rasp. The noise amplified when I eased his door open. I whispered

Rocky's name and he dropped off the end of Grandpa's bed and slithered out to me.

I led Rocky back out through the pelting rain to my apartment, where I collapsed on to the sofa and he leapt up beside me, his coat wet and lank from the sheeting downpour. Water hammered against the skylight above us and sluiced down the blackened glass. I stayed there for a long time with Rocky's head on my lap. I stared at the wall across from me. Listened to the rain lash against the fragile glass. I was thinking hard. About everything that had happened before and everything that might happen yet. And all the while Rocky dozed beside me, my hand on his neck, my fingers teasing his downy hairs. Every time he breathed, I could hear a small tinkle. The barest tap of metal on metal. The noise of the two keys I'd clipped to his collar clicking gently against one another.

Part Three

Chapter Thirty-five

'I've found a way in at the back,' Clarke said. 'There was a security light, but I snipped the wires.'

He was standing outside the Vauxhall, crouching down to speak through the gap in Menser's window. They'd parked the car alongside the beach, near a boarded-up ice-cream hut. The seafront was deserted, but it wouldn't stay that way for long. 6.20 a.m., in a grey and sketchy light. People would be up soon. Maybe walking their dogs. Maybe jogging before work.

Menser stepped out of the car on to rain-slicked tarmac. He closed his eyes, fighting the tilting sensation inside his head. The overnight ferry crossing had been much calmer than his experience on the trawler. But the rocking of the waves had still wormed its way inside him.

He fitted his gloves over his hands. Pushed the leather down into the webbing between his fingers, then reached inside the car for his backpack.

'Show me.'

Clarke led him away from the beach towards a small dry dock, where several yachts were tilted on their keels in the mud. The street lighting was patchy and easily avoided. A faint drizzle spun in the moist grey air.

Menser followed Clarke through a foul-smelling lane bordered by timber fencing. The lane kinked right, running behind a terrace of cottages. Clarke stopped halfway along and ducked behind a slatted fence, beckoning Menser to join him.

'This it?' Menser asked. It wasn't much. A neglected back yard made up of concrete patio slabs, some out-of-control weeds and a rusted barbecue set. A narrow, squat property with a patched roof, two upstairs windows (one with the privacy glass of a bathroom), and a sliding glass door fitted downstairs. There was no sign of an alarm. A frayed wire hung loosely from a security lamp above the door.

'Simple, right?'

Menser unzipped his rucksack and removed his picking gun. He placed a hand on Clarke's shoulder, then deftly worked the latch on the garden gate and eased it open. The picking gun was mechanical, operated by a ratchet mechanism connected to a retractable trigger. It was slower than a battery version, but less intrusive, and it made fast work of the cheap lock on the sliding door.

The runners were smooth, well used, and emitted almost no sound. Menser stepped inside a cramped living room and found himself standing on a foam exercise mat. He waved for Clarke to follow and made his way into the hall. There was a door on his right, opening into a tiny kitchen, and a flight of carpeted stairs on his left.

Menser tested the treads for creaks and groans before committing his weight. In his mind, he saw an image of Detective Sergeant Jacqueline Teare lying alone in her bed. Unconscious. Unsuspecting.

Vulnerable.

*

Jackie Teare was in a bad mood. She always got in a funk when she couldn't sleep. She'd tut and curse and flail around, as if there was somebody lying alongside her, ready to ask what was wrong. But there was no one, and that was part of the problem. She knew how tough the job could be on a relationship, but she was sure it was harder being on your own. Especially when something was chewing on your conscience and you had nobody to talk to.

Laura Hale's death. The unexplained events up at the cottage in Arrasey plantation. Shimmin's handling of both incidents. She'd had doubts, plenty of them, and when she'd broached the subject with Shimmin, it had landed her in trouble. But the doubts remained, nagging at her, and now Laura's brother was poking around with that stuck-up investigator, raising awkward questions.

Exercise hadn't helped. Neither had half a bottle of white wine. And now sleep had eluded her, too.

She knew what she had to do, she just didn't know if she had the guts to do it. If Shimmin had received her message, he'd be round within a few hours. Then she'd have to make her decision. She could demand an explanation and make her own assessment of his motives. Or she could tell him that she was going to speak up, go above his head. It would mean risking her job. Her career. The only thing she'd ever truly cared about.

She groaned at her alarm clock. 6.20 a.m. She was an early riser, always had been, and she couldn't think of one good reason to stay in bed.

The bathroom was across the hall. She stumbled through and slumped on the chilly toilet seat. No need to close the door. That was one small advantage of living on her own.

The bathroom was tiny. From the toilet, she could easily reach the bath. She twirled the hot tap around and the water bathed her hand as she fitted the plug into the hole. Then she finished up on the toilet and considered her reflection in the mirror above the sink.

That was the problem. Right there. She wanted to be able to look herself in the eyes and know she'd done the right thing for the right reasons. Shimmin would tell her there were shades of grey in everything. Maybe give her that whole moral spectrum speech she'd heard around the station before. But she didn't see how that could apply to Laura Hale's accident. And there was no grey in what had occurred up at the cottage. Walking away from what she'd recognised as a series of obvious inconsistencies had been a black-and-white thing to do. And then there was the brother. He was grieving, in pain, looking for answers. Looking for the missing girl she'd tried very hard to block from her mind.

She couldn't do it any more. She knew that now.

Decision made.

The bath was filling. Steam was rising from the water, wafting across the mirror.

Then something moved in the glass. A dark blur.

She span around and that was when she saw them. Two men. One framed in the doorway, the other emerging from the top of the stairs.

The man in the doorway was short, but stocky. Rainwater had settled on his bald head and his craggy face and the shoulders of his black roll-neck sweater. There was a rucksack over his shoulder. Leather gloves on his hands.

Jackie stared at him. It seemed to take forever for her brain to send a message to her muscles. Her right hand twitched for the door and she drew a breath as if to scream.

Her breath was cut off fast. The man lashed out, slicing at her throat with a savage backhand blow. She dropped to her knees and clutched her throat. She tried to inhale. Failed. Tried again and made only a dry, croaking gasp.

The man snatched at her hair. He yanked her head back, exposing her throat, his free hand primed for a follow-up strike.

Jackie's eyes bulged. She felt the constriction in her throat. The flush of blood in her face.

Her eyes flicked sideways, towards the second man. He was young and muscular, with a puff of facial hair below his lip.

'We have questions,' said the man who'd hit her. 'The bike crash. The missing girl. You're going to tell us everything.'

It seemed to take a long time until she was able to speak. But once she started, she couldn't stop.

Chapter Thirty-six

The policewoman slumped in Menser's arms at the side of the bath. She was wet and bedraggled and only barely alive. Her eyes were glassy and roved uselessly in her head. Her lips and her nostrils were blue.

Menser was sure that she had nothing more to share. She'd told them plenty already, and he'd had no reason to doubt anything that she'd said. She wasn't the woman who'd spoken to him on Clarke's phone about the bike crash, but she thought she knew who it must have been – a private investigator by the name of Rebecca Lewis. She was working for Laura Hale's family, raising questions about her death.

By itself, that would have been enough to concern Menser. But there had been much worse still to come. The man on the bike, the plumber who'd visited the cottage, was Laura Hale's brother. And that nugget of information ignited Menser's fears.

The uneasiness he'd felt in Lena's company rushed back at him. The tingle of doubt he'd experienced, the drip-drip of apprehension, was becoming a flood. The brother's involvement had to mean something. He had to have been helping Lena in some way. That would explain her attitude on the trawler. It would explain the look on her face – the superior smile that seemed to suggest she was holding on to a precious secret that could wreck everything.

The policewoman was gazing blankly upwards, unable to

focus. She mumbled incoherently. He tightened his hand around her neck, heaved her torso over the side of the bath and submerged her face again. This time, she didn't fight or moan or buck against him. He stared at the off-white tiles on the wall and counted to thirty, then turned her face sideways. A string of bubbles floated out from her nostrils. Her eyes were open and sightless.

Menser turned from the bath, shaking water from his forearms. Clarke was leaning against the door frame, watching.

'Your turn,' Menser said. He rested his hands on his thighs, catching his breath. 'I'm getting too old for this. Lift her out of the bath. Carry her through to the landing.'

'What for?'

'I want you to throw her down the stairs. Break her neck. I want it to look like she fell.'

Doubt twisted Clarke's face. 'But you just drowned her.'

'I want to create confusion. A small island like this, with a low crime rate, they might convince themselves it was an accident.'

Clarke just looked at him.

Menser yanked the plug out of the bath. Watched the water begin to drain. The body begin to sink.

'Jesus, Clarke. You have gloves on, if that's what you're worried about.'

Still Clarke didn't move.

'Listen, don't make me call him and tell him you didn't help to clear up your own mess.'

At last, Clarke stepped away from the door. He bent over the bath and grabbed the policewoman by her armpits. Water trickled out of her hair and nostrils and mouth. It seeped from her T-shirt, leaving a soggy trail along the floor as Clarke dragged her limp body towards the top of the stairs. He grunted as he shifted her weight around and adjusted his grip and fought to raise her up to her feet. The muscles in his arms quivered. He was struggling to keep his balance.

Menser waited until he judged that Clarke was about to let go. Then he surged forwards very fast and cupped a hand under Clarke's chin and forced his head backwards until he was staring at the ceiling. He wrenched his neck hard one way, then the other. He heard the awful *crack* and whipped his neck sideways one last time, to make certain that the spinal cord was fully severed.

Clarke dropped from his hands and the woman dropped, too. The pair of them tumbled down the stairs like a couple of rag dolls, their limbs tangled, bodies knotted.

Menser stepped over them and moved through into the kitchen. There was a phone fixed to the wall, a freestanding unit below it. He opened a drawer and removed a telephone directory and began to flick through the pages. He needed to find an address for Laura Hale's brother. He needed to find out what he knew.

Chapter Thirty-seven

I woke with a start to the ringing of my doorbell. I squinted at the time on my bedside clock. Almost 9.30 a.m.

The doorbell was ringing in short, repeated bursts, like someone was banging their head against it. I put on my dressing gown, then my sling. Rocky was curled up at the foot of my bed and I shut him inside my bedroom as I staggered through my lounge, clumped down the stairs and unlocked the door to find DI Shimmin propped against the frame. He barged inside, then snatched the door from me and slammed it closed behind him.

'We need to talk.' He leaned into my face. 'But if anyone asks, this conversation never happened.'

'What conversation?'

'Follow me.' He started up my stairs, his shoes tramping last night's rainwater on my carpet and his grubby mackintosh spread around the backs of his legs like a bedraggled cape. 'Where's your coffee?' he called, from over his shoulder.

By the time I got upstairs, he was opening and closing cupboards in my kitchen. It didn't take him long to find what he was searching for. He grabbed the jar of instant granules and slammed two mugs down on to the counter.

'You can't just barge in like this,' I said. 'I think you should leave.'

He felt the side of the kettle. Snorted when he discovered it was cold. Filled it with water and clicked it on.

'You don't want me to leave.' He shook his head. 'Believe me, lad. Asking me to leave is about the worst thing you could do right now.'

There was a low grumble to his voice. A hard intensity. It threw me. I didn't know what to do with it.

'Teaspoons,' he snapped.

'What?'

'Teaspoons.' He snatched at a drawer in the island unit between us. Slammed it closed and swivelled and tried the drawer under the sink. 'Never mind,' he said, digging through the cutlery. 'Take milk?'

'What's going on?'

'No milk, then. Black's good. I need you to wake up. Need you to pay attention.'

'Detective Shimmin, I have to have an explanation for what's going on here.'

'Detective *Inspector* Shimmin. And I have to have an explanation, too. Where were you last night?'

'What?'

'Say *what* again. See where it gets you.'

He was angry now. I realised he'd been angry all along. His knuckles were bunched around the teaspoon he was holding, like he was planning to stab me with it.

'Your movements. Last night. I need to know them.'

I hesitated, wondering what exactly I should say. This couldn't be about my meeting with Erik and Anderson, I didn't think.

I knuckled my eye. Faked a yawn.

'I went to Marine Drive.'

He paused. Lightened his tone just a shade. 'Time?'

'I don't know. Around ten thirty?'

'And before that?'

Now I got it. Before that was the visit Rebecca and I had paid to Jackie Teare. How had he found out? And what did he plan to do about it? I could understand why he was angry. He thought we'd gone behind his back. That we'd questioned his professionalism. Which we had.

'Why?'

He snatched up the coffee jar. Unscrewed the lid like he was wringing my neck. 'I know where you were,' he said. 'All I need is for you to tell me.'

'But if you already know . . .'

'Teare called me,' he said. 'On my home number, after you'd left. She got my machine. Told me you'd been there. I don't care why. I care about times. What time were you there?'

I steadied myself against the back of one of the kitchen stools. I thought about asking him to wait while I got changed. His attitude told me he wouldn't be likely to entertain the request.

'I don't know exactly,' I told him. 'Around nine, I guess.'

'She called my home number at nine forty-five. That about the time you left?'

I nodded. 'I think so.'

'You go back?'

'What?'

'After you left Teare's house. Did you go back?'

'No. I went to Marine Drive. Then I came here.'

'Anyone confirm that?'

'Rebecca Lewis was with me. She was here until about midnight. Then she left.'

Shimmin watched me, as if hunting for anything that might raise a doubt, then dunked two heaped teaspoons of coffee into each mug. He grabbed for the kettle before it had finished boiling. Poured steaming water into the mugs and slid one across to me.

He delved inside the pocket of his mackintosh. Removed a mobile phone. Showed me the display.

'Ring any bells?'

It was a close-up photograph of a man. A headshot. The man was sleeping. He was rugged-looking, with close-cropped hair and a fuzz of stubble below his lower lip. I recognised him instantly. The shock of it made me take a step backwards.

'That's the paramedic,' I said. 'The one who treated me after my bike accident. The one who said Lena had to be taken in the first ambulance.'

My response didn't seem to surprise him. He didn't challenge it, either. He didn't remind me that he'd discounted my story about the first ambulance and the missing blonde long ago. I thought that was interesting. I was about to discover it was a lot more than that.

'You notice anyone outside Teare's place last night? Anyone hanging around?'

'I don't think so.'

'Anyone come to the door while you were inside?'

'There was nobody.' I scratched my lower arm through the sling. 'At least, no one that I saw.'

'Teare mention anything to you? She say anything about being watched?'

'No,' I said. 'Nothing like that. We just wanted to speak to her.'

'You and Rebecca Lewis.'

'That's right.'

Shimmin gathered up his phone and slurped his coffee while he prodded more buttons with his thumb. I felt like I needed to sit down. I chose the same stool Rebecca had been sitting on just hours before. Cupped the elbow of my dud arm in my hand. My shoulder was sore this morning. It felt like crushed glass was moving around in the joint.

'Going to show you something else,' Shimmin said. 'It's not pretty.'

He showed me. He was right. It wasn't pretty.

It was another image of the paramedic with the soul-patch. This time, the photograph had been taken from farther away, like the first image had been snapped by someone crouching low over him, and then for the second photograph they'd straightened and taken a step backwards. The expression on his face was exactly the same. But I could see now that he wasn't sleeping. He was dead.

He was lying against a dark-green carpet and a painted skirting board, and his head was tilted on a grotesque angle, pivoted backwards and side-on to his torso, as if someone had tried to pluck it clean from his shoulders. The skin of his neck was swollen and rolled up in folds, like blood and fluids had collected beneath it. It was stained a sickly greenish-mauve.

'I told you Teare left a message on my machine,' Shimmin said, his voice sounding a long way away. 'She asked me to call round this morning before work. I was there by seven fifteen. Nobody answered the door. I went around back. Her patio door was wide open. I found this guy at the bottom of the stairs. Jackie was lying right next to him. I don't reckon I'll show you a picture of her.'

I felt the strength go out of me. Felt it drain down through my body and out through my toes.

'Are you saying DS Teare is dead?'

Shimmin's deep-set eyes bored into me. 'Very.'

I swallowed. Tried to stay with it. 'Am I a suspect?'

His eyes stayed fixed on me. 'Should you be?'

'No.' My voice had gone hoarse. The word was little more than a croak. 'We just wanted to talk to her about Lena. About the investigation into Laura's death.'

Shimmin set his jaw. 'I told you to move on. To leave all that alone.'

'You knew this might happen?'

He bowed his head. Looked down into the polished granite. I could see the thinning strands of hair on his skull. The patina of blotched skin beneath. 'Nothing this bad.'

'I'm sorry,' I said.

And I meant it, too. Not just because of the horror of what had happened to Teare. But also because I feared I was culpable to some extent. I was thinking about the phone call Rebecca had made to the number she'd obtained from the emergency control centre. Her impersonation of Teare and the denials from the man on the other end of the line. His abrupt end to the call. If he was somehow involved in Lena's abduction, we'd given him Teare's name. We might have led him straight to her.

Could the man Rebecca had spoken with have been the paramedic? I thought about telling Shimmin, but I didn't think all that hard. It was obvious he'd been concealing things from me. That he'd worked to shut down the investigation into Lena's abduction just as we'd suspected.

'Did the paramedic kill Teare?'

'Too early to say. But it looks like they were engaged in a struggle of some kind. Jackie's hair and her T-shirt were damp. There was water on the bathroom floor. It could be he surprised her when she was about to take a bath. She must have gotten free and made it as far as the stairs. Looks like they fell together and the guy broke his neck. I don't suppose Jackie had any fight left by then.'

'Do you know who he was?'

'No ID on the body. But we'll find out.'

He looked like he meant it but I didn't rate his chances. I was getting a clearer idea of the types of people involved in this mess now. I didn't think they were average crooks or ordinary criminals. I thought they were trained professionals. Capable of anything. Maybe capable of having killed my sister.

'Is this connected to Laura?' I asked.

Shimmin glowered at me. He didn't answer. Didn't need to.

'That's why you're here, isn't it? Because you mishandled the investigation into her death. Because these people were involved somehow. And now you don't want me shooting my mouth off. Making life difficult for you.'

'That's not why.' His speech was deliberate. Like he was fighting to control his temper.

'Then why all this talk about you not being here? You're covering your back.'

Shimmin snatched up his coffee cup and drank greedily. He pulled a face and set it back down.

'I'm meant to be on my way to the station. I called in the

scene as soon as I found it. There's a SOCO unit there now. I have to co-ordinate the investigation. Work out where we go with this thing next.' He took a step forwards. Then he stopped himself. 'I came here to warn you, is all. To tell you to leave this thing alone. Leave it to us.'

'So you can bury it? Bury what happened to my sister?'

'I'm telling you for your own safety. There are factors at work here we can't control. People playing by their own rules.'

I paused for a moment. Absorbed his words. 'Based on what you just said, I'm assuming you know what my sister really did for a living.'

'Bare bones.'

'My parents told you?'

'Your dad.'

I drew a sharp breath and felt my ribs smart. It was something I'd been afraid of. Something I'd begun to suspect. My parents knew about Laura's real job and they hadn't told me, not even after she'd died. It was impossible for me to believe that Dad could know something like that about Laura and not share it with Mum. It explained how evasive she'd been when I'd asked her about Laura's connection to Rebecca and it also explained why Mum had hired Rebecca to look into Laura's death in the first place.

I can't pretend it didn't sting. They'd shut me out. And yes, they were probably trying to protect me. To shelter me from the questions that must have been plaguing them since Laura had died. Had her job had something to do with her death? Was her suicide all that it seemed?

I said, 'You knew what the cottage was used for in the plantation, didn't you?'

'I had a sense of what could be up there. The characters who might be involved.'

'My sister?'

'Maybe.'

'Did you have doubts about her death? That it was really a suicide?'

Shimmin pursed his lips. The muscles around his eyes tightened, shrouding them even more. 'No doubts.'

'You're sure? Rebecca had some observations.'

'What kind of observations?'

'Mostly it was about where Laura crashed. Almost the whole of Marine Drive is edged by sheer cliff. But Laura went over where there's a spit of land.'

'Still a hell of a drop. She didn't stand a chance. I'm sorry.'

'What if I asked to see the autopsy report? What if I demanded to speak to the coroner?'

He raised a hand. Patted the air. I wasn't sure if he was signalling for me to shut up or if it was just his frustration manifesting itself.

'This whole thing is complicated enough already.'

'So what are you going to do? Pretend none of it is happening again?'

'I had my reasons.'

'Tell that to Teare.'

I thought he was going to swing for me. He looked like he had it in mind. His shoulders had bunched. His right fist had tightened into a hard weight on the end of his arm. But he controlled himself. He held himself in. Then he growled in frustration and raised his eyes to the ceiling. Like he was searching for something there. Patience or forgiveness or strength of will.

He shook his head, as if whatever he'd been seeking had eluded him.

'I need to speak to Rebecca Lewis,' he said.

I didn't remind him that she'd been trying to speak with him during the past few days. I didn't mention that he'd ejected her from his own police station. I just said, 'I don't know where she is right now.'

'You didn't arrange to meet up today?'

'We hadn't made any plans.'

'So call her. Ask her what her movements are going to be.'

I climbed down off my stool and went into my bedroom to fetch my phone. When I returned to the kitchen, Shimmin had his notebook out, pen at the ready.

I dialled Rebecca's number and listened to the phone ring. It kept ringing. I raised my eyebrows at Shimmin. Let it ring some more. I held my mobile against my ear until the ringing stopped and a flat tone replaced it.

'No answer,' I said.

'Try again.'

I did as he said. I listened to the ringing. I listened to the flat tone. Same result.

Shimmin said, 'OK, give me the number.'

I called it up on screen. Passed my mobile across to him. He copied the details into his pocketbook. Then he turned to the back and removed a business card. Plain white stock. Navy-blue font. It had the crest of the Manx Constabulary on the front of it. Shimmin's contact details below. He laid the card on top of my phone and slid it across to me.

'Call me if she gets in touch.'

'OK.'

'As *soon* as she gets in touch.' He checked his watch. 'I have to go.' He seemed to hesitate, as if he was debating whether to take me with him. 'I'm going to try and keep your name out of this. At least to begin with. I don't know how that'll go. I can't tell you how long it might last. But I'm going to give it my best shot.'

'How come?'

'Because,' he said, 'your family has had enough on their plate just recently. And because, lad, I'm not the ogre you might take me for.'

He offered me his hand to shake. It was warm and cushioned. I watched him walk away down my stairs. Watched him walk out my front door. And all the time I was wondering why he'd go out on a limb for me. I was asking myself what was in it for him?

Chapter Thirty-eight

Lena lay curled on the pink duvet in the soundproofed room. Her stomach cramped and gurgled.

The pizza had been limp and greasy and barely lukewarm. But she'd been ravenous and she'd devoured it. And now her guts were squelching and squirming. Belching and burping. Perhaps it was just as well that the room was soundproofed.

Lena calculated that she'd been back inside the room for more than six hours. It was light outside but it was difficult to tell exactly how long the sun had been up because of the coloured film on the window glass. The radio news had said that it was two in the morning when the man had told her to return to the room. She could tell that he'd wanted to sleep. He needed her locked away before he could do that.

She'd tried communicating with the man over the pizza. She'd put her clothes back on, like he'd told her to, and she'd folded out the second deckchair and settled down opposite him. The man had slid a boxed pepperoni across the floor. Lena was a vegetarian, so she'd picked the slices of spicy sausage out of the cheese and tomato paste and piled them up inside the box lid.

'How long will you keep me here?' she asked.

The man didn't reply. He acted like he hadn't even heard the question.

'When will you give me to the police? When will I be arrested?'

The man said nothing. He chewed his pizza in silence. A blank expression on his face.

'Have you called my father?'

No response.

'Why did they give me to you? They were going to give me to the police, but they changed their mind. Do you work with them? Do you work with somebody else?'

Finally, the man looked at her. He frowned. Inclined his ear towards the radio. Raised a grease-slicked finger to his lips.

Save your energy, his expression seemed to say. *Don't embarrass yourself. Just eat and keep quiet.*

So she'd chewed her pizza and she'd drunk a litre bottle of lemonade and she'd settled back and listened to the orchestral music. Then the 2 a.m. news bulletin had come on. The same bulletin she'd heard an hour before. And the man had stretched and yawned and told her to get up, and then he'd locked her inside the soundproofed room.

She hadn't slept. Not for one minute. Not for one second. She still felt groggy but she'd wanted to get a head start on her thinking. She had to think very hard. She had to be focused. She had to concentrate on her situation and find a weakness to exploit. There had to be one. There always was. And she had all the motivation in the world to find it.

She was still thinking, hours later, when she heard the lock *thunk* back inside the door. Then the door opened and another man filled the doorway. She'd seen this guy before, too. He was the driver of the car that had come to pick them up from the beach hut.

He didn't look all that different from the man with the pizza. Sensible haircut. Plain, forgettable face. A white-and-brown check shirt tucked into a pair of pressed chinos.

'Bathroom break,' the man said. 'And don't bother getting naked. I've seen plenty better. Believe me.'

Chapter Thirty-nine

After swallowing a couple of pills, I went into my bedroom and put on my gym clothes – a pair of grey sweat pants, white sports socks and white trainers. Normally I would have worn an old T-shirt, too, but my shoulder injury wouldn't allow it. I settled for ducking my head under my sling, then feeding my good arm through one sleeve of a hooded top and leaving my bad arm under the sweater so that the left sleeve hung uselessly at my side.

I searched around in the bottom of my wardrobe for my blue sports holdall. My dirty football kit was inside. It smelled bluntly of dried sweat and aged mud. Rocky came over from the corner of the room to sniff it. He didn't seem impressed. I removed my kit and my spattered boots, bulking out the holdall with a couple of clean towels. Then I collected together a few other items and ducked down to Rocky. I freed the two keys from his collar and patted his head. The key marked *NSC* had a number on the reverse, just as I'd said. The number was 36.

When I stepped outside I found that Shimmin was huddled with my father on the lawn by the side of the conservatory. Shimmin's left palm was open and he was stabbing it with the fingers of his right hand. Dad was nodding along, like he was agreeing with each of Shimmin's points in turn. He didn't seem to have any points of his own to raise. He was the listener. Shimmin was the talker.

I climbed into the cab of my van and tossed my holdall on to the passenger bench. I fired the engine and drove away in the direction of Douglas with Shimmin and Dad watching me in my mirrors.

There was a lot I hadn't told Shimmin. I hadn't told him about Erik Zeeger and Anderson. About the meeting in Erik's jet and the likelihood of his men having been killed up at the plantation. About how they'd been hiding Lena and their reasons for doing so – both the ones they'd mentioned, and the ones they hadn't. About the environmental campaigner who'd been killed. About the break-in to my home. And, most important of all, about the key Lena had given me.

Shimmin had been right about one thing, at least. The situation was complicated and I didn't know who I could trust. I'd trusted my parents, but they'd shielded me from the truth about Laura's life. I'd trusted Rebecca, but I had a feeling she knew more than she was letting on and I was still a little suspicious of her reasons for helping me. That was why I'd told her about the locker key – to gauge her reaction to the news and to see how much it interested her. It was also why I'd lied about the keys having been stolen along with my laptop.

And I wasn't prepared to trust Shimmin just yet. I couldn't tell if he had any real desire to get to the bottom of things, or if he just wanted to bury the loose ends as neatly as possible. The stakes were too high. The key could have the potential to unlock the entire mystery. Lena had entrusted it to me, and my sister had entrusted me to Lena. I wasn't about to hand the key to anyone else. I wasn't about to let go of it just yet.

Menser was slouched in the front seat of his car, parked along the street from the driveway of the Hales' care home. It was a position he'd been in before, some weeks ago now, and not one he'd expected to find himself repeating. Things would have been a lot easier if he'd seen the brother back then. If only he'd known what he looked like, he would have recognised him when he appeared on the surveillance footage up at the cottage. He could have eliminated the threat before it had an opportunity to develop.

Chance. Coincidence. Menser didn't believe in either of them. The brother was involved for a reason. Same thing with the private detective. The two of them were a complication he couldn't afford. One he might have to eradicate. But not until he'd discovered what it was they were up to. Not until he understood what Laura Hale had hoped to achieve.

The windows were fully down on either side of him, letting in the damp morning air, but his eyelids flickered and his head lolled. He thought about stepping out of the car, but it was too risky. It was only an hour since he'd seen the male police detective arrive. At first he'd been alarmed, but then he'd calmed himself and considered what it could mean. It seemed to Menser that there were a couple of possibilities. One: the detective was there for a routine chat with the brother or his parents, something connected to the brother's bike accident or Laura's death. Two: the murder of the detective's colleague had been discovered and the brother was being interviewed as a possible suspect.

On balance, Menser felt that the first scenario was more

likely. It was just a few hours since the policewoman had been killed. The job had gone smoothly, with very little noise other than the sound of the woman and Clarke tumbling down the stairs together. Menser doubted it had been enough to alert a neighbour and the policewoman had told him that she was on a period of temporary leave, which meant she wouldn't have been missed at work. And besides, if the bodies had been found and the brother was a suspect, the male detective wouldn't have come on his own.

Menser relaxed, but only by a fraction. If experience had taught him anything, it was always to assume the worst. His superior was built the same way. That was why Menser had been ordered to dispose of Clarke. Odds were, Clarke was just a rookie making mistakes and bad decisions. But on an operation as sensitive as this one, mistakes couldn't be tolerated – no matter how innocent they might appear.

Menser rotated the ignition key a quarter-turn and set the fans to *Max*, directing cool air towards his face. He clicked on the radio and tuned into a local station, hoping for a news bulletin. He doubted there'd be anything on the incident in Laxey just yet. Truth was, he'd come to enjoy the local news during his time on the island. Most of it was trivial, but that was a novelty he appreciated.

This time, though, his listening was interrupted. The snub nose of a white van emerged from the end of the driveway. The brother was behind the wheel. He was alone. He turned left and sped off downhill. Menser waited for a passing bus to thunder by him before pulling out from the kerb and setting off in pursuit.

Further back along the road, Anderson watched events unfold through the tinted glass of his windscreen. He saw Rob Hale drive away in his work van. He saw the balding man in the blue saloon pull out from the kerb. Anderson waited until the saloon had disappeared around the bend before nudging Lukas awake and accelerating after them.

*

The National Sports Centre is a glass and steel complex with a curving metal roof shaped like a wave. There's a freeform swimming pool, with giant slides spiralling into the vaulted roof space above, and two lap pools with stadium seating alongside. There are a couple of sports halls, a lawn bowling complex, a squash centre and a well-equipped gym. I knew of at least three changing rooms, so there were a lot of possible locations for locker 36.

The main entrance to the sports centre has a revolving glass door and a reception area that overlooks the swimming pools on one side and a sports hall on the other. Outside the door are three car parks with spaces for a couple of hundred vehicles.

I didn't plan on using the main entrance. I hadn't spoken to Rebecca since she'd left my place the previous night and I had no idea what her movements were likely to be. But I knew how good she was. I'd seen her in action and I'd gained some insight into the way her mind worked. She believed the locker key had been stolen from my home. Chances were she'd assume that whoever had stolen it would come to the sports centre to try and access the locker. Therefore she might be watching. And if she saw me going inside, she was guaranteed to follow.

So I parked around back, in a distant car park provided for the outdoor training facilities. There was a red oval running track with painted white lines, an athletics field and a bank of tiered stadium seating. The entire area was deserted.

I carried my holdall across the running track and the grassy field. The field was damp from the rain that had fallen during the night. The ground made a boggy squelching noise as I marched over it and blades of wet grass adhered to the toes of my trainers. I crossed the far side of the running track and the rubbery surface seemed to spring and flex under my weight. It was greasy from the rain. A set of metal railings circled the outside of the track at waist height. I clambered over them and approached the rear of the sports centre.

There were several doors around the building. Most of them were fire exits. Good for getting out in an emergency. Not so good for getting in. But there was also an unmanned back entrance connecting the sports centre to the track and field facilities. A card reader was fitted to the side of the door. I pulled my wallet out of the pocket of my jogging trousers and removed my NSC membership card with my thumb. There was a magnetic strip on the back. I swiped the card through the reader and the door clunked and dropped on its hinges. I swung it back by the handle and stepped inside.

*

Menser followed the brother's van until he indicated and pulled off the road into a small car park that backed on to an athletics field. He drove on and parked in a lay-by, then hustled out of his car and paced back towards the brother's van. By the time he reached it, the brother was hurrying across the muddy field towards a large brick building with a sculpted metal roof. He had a gym holdall in his hand.

Menser waited until the brother had entered the building. Then he followed.

He didn't notice the four-wheel-drive vehicle with the darkened glass that eased into the car park behind him.

Chapter Forty

The rear entrance to the sports centre was silent. Not many people came in this way. The gym was on my right. Staff facilities on my left. Another pair of doors ahead. I passed through them and climbed a set of stairs and approached the reception counter.

The revolving doors set into the wall of glass at the front of the building were twenty feet away. If Rebecca was watching from a favourable angle, it was possible she could see me. Nothing I could do about that.

There was no queue at reception and the woman on duty barely looked at me as I handed over my membership card and asked to use the swimming pool. She didn't even query my sling.

I pushed through the metal turnstile to the side of the counter, then through a glass door with a rubber seal. The rubber was there to keep the heat trapped inside. The heat was instant. It bathed my face and swamped my lungs, like inhaling steam. I headed downstairs to the changing areas. I could smell chlorine and the cleaning fluid that had been used to mop the tiled floors and the mixed odours of countless shampoos and shower gels and deodorants. The air was humid and moist against my skin.

The changing facilities were unisex. Stilted cubicles had been installed around the perimeter of the space and in rows through the middle. Facing each row of cubicles was a row of lockers. The lockers and the cubicles were the same height. A little taller than me. They were the same shade of yellow. There were maybe eighty cubicles. There were perhaps two hundred lockers. The lockers had been designed so that there were three in each vertical drop. The top and middle lockers were the same size. The bottom locker was larger.

I walked past a bank of mirrors fitted above a long shelf that was equipped with a set of tethered hairdryers. There were communal showers on my left and a woman in a one-piece swimsuit was rinsing shampoo from her hair. I passed the first row of cubicles. Turned into the first row of lockers. I found a staff member there. A young girl with bleached blonde hair and long legs. She was wearing a bright yellow T-shirt and blue shorts, with flip-flops on her feet. She was searching the changing cubicles. Throwing back doors. Checking for lost property or abandoned towels. I waited until she was finished before I approached locker number 36.

It was a bottom-row locker. As tall as my thighs. Capable of holding a lot of things. All manner of items.

But it wasn't my locker.

There was already a key in the lock, connected to a green plastic wrist strap. The door was ajar. The locker was empty. I crouched down and checked it just to be sure. Bare metal interior.

Definitely not my locker.

I turned and walked back through the changing area. Back up the stairs. Back through the door with the rubber suction seal.

The reception area was a little busier. The woman at the counter was talking on the phone and a bald-headed man in a dark roll-neck sweater and sports jacket was standing across the way. His hands were clasped behind his back and he was reading the information that had been pinned to a notice board.

I headed down the stairs I'd originally come in by, then turned left into a long corridor with grey, hard-wearing carpet. I could see the artificial turf of the indoor bowling green at the far end. On my immediate left was the entrance to the sports hall. Just along the corridor on my right were two changing rooms. One for men. One for women. Lining the walls on either side of me were row upon row of green metal lockers.

I found locker 36. It was down by my knees again, the same set-up as before. The door was closed. No key in the lock. I set my bag on the floor and crouched alongside it. Checked both ways along the corridor. I took the key from my pocket and lined it up with the slot. It wouldn't fit. I turned it upside down. Turned it back again. No matter what I did, it wasn't the right key. It wouldn't open the lock.

Definitely not my locker.

I lifted the key before my eyes. Turned it in my hand. There was no telling how long it had been in Lena's possession. According to Erik and Anderson, Lena hadn't been outside the cottage for almost two months before she'd met me. The theory Rebecca had been developing was that Laura had given Lena the key. I could see the logic in the idea. I'd bought into it myself, not least because I knew Laura had often come to the sports centre when she was back on the island. Laura had died just over three weeks ago. So Lena must have had the key for a minimum of three weeks and a maximum of two months.

A period of between three weeks and two months was a relatively long time for a public locker to be in use. I'd seen the girl in the yellow T-shirt checking the changing cubicles in the swimming pool. Maybe they checked the lockers as well. Maybe the staff carried out an audit of all the lockers that stayed locked after closing time. Maybe if a particular locker stayed locked for too long it was opened with a master key and the contents were junked or placed in lost property and a new lock and key was fitted so that the locker could be used again.

I thought that made sense. And if so, I might really be screwed. Because I doubted the staff organised the lost property by locker number. They probably just kept it in one big pile. And since I didn't know what it was I was looking for, I couldn't just wander up and ask for the property in question to be returned to me.

I looked at the key some more. Then I sighed and picked up my holdall and retraced my steps as far as the bottom of the stairs. I walked through the door marked *Gym* and found myself in a small anteroom with a deserted wooden counter. The counter had an open appointment book laid out on it. A biro had been attached to the book with a length of string and Sellotape. I scanned the left-hand page. According to the book, there were four people inside the gym.

I passed into the corridor beyond and heard the pulse and thump of workout music. Fast. Energetic. Coming from the floor above.

I was all set to enter the male locker room when I stopped in my tracks. I was an idiot. I'd almost overlooked the most basic of things.

If Laura had given Lena the key, the chances were it wouldn't open a locker in the men's facilities. It would be next door. In the *women's* changing room.

281

Chapter Forty-one

I listened from outside the door to the women's locker room. It was hard to tell if there was anyone in there. I decided it was best to just open the door and try my luck. If there was someone inside, I could act like I'd made a mistake. It wouldn't be hard to do.

I opened the door and entered with my head down. There were no screams or squeals of complaint. I raised my eyes. Nobody there.

Part of the floor was tiled. The rest was covered in black plastic matting. There were slatted benches against the wall and clothes hooks above the benches. There were toilet and shower cubicles away to my left. A bank of lockers ahead of me. Not many. Sixty at most. There was a number 36. It was down on the floor and it was shut fast. There was no key in the lock. I dropped my holdall to the floor and went down on one knee. My key eased inside no problem at all. I turned it to the right and heard the clatter of a coin dropping inside the mechanism. I pulled on the key and the door swung back without any resistance.

There was only one item inside the locker. A computer memory stick. It was purple and about the size of a lipstick canister. There was a label stuck to one side. It had my sister's handwriting on it.

For Rob. 9A13D21A.

I looked hard at the writing. It was like a message from another lifetime. A precious artefact that might never have been discovered. I wondered how long ago Laura had written my name on the label. I wondered if she'd ever truly believed that it would find its way to me.

But the ladies' locker room was no place to linger. I needed to get to a computer and see what was on the memory stick. My laptop was gone but Mum had a desktop PC in her office. If I timed it right, I could use it without being disturbed.

I unzipped my holdall and dropped the memory stick inside and was just in the process of standing when the door to the locker room swung back.

A man filled the doorway.

He was the bald-headed gent I'd seen upstairs. He scanned the room quickly, then stopped with a jerk when he saw me. He looked from my face to the open locker to my holdall. He stared at the holdall very hard. Then he slipped a hand inside the back pocket of his grey suit trousers and showed me some kind of ID.

'Security services,' he said. 'Step away from the bag.'

I didn't move. Didn't flex a muscle.

'Security services.' He jabbed his ID at me like it was a weapon. 'Sir, I need to see what's in the bag.'

'It's nothing,' I said.

'Give it to me.' He flipped his billfold closed and stuffed it back inside his pocket.

'Who are you?' I asked.

He checked over his shoulder, then took a step inside the room. The door swung closed behind him.

'I told you. Security services.'

'British government?'

He nodded. Edged towards me, his shoes squeaking on the tiles.

'This is the Isle of Man,' I told him. 'You don't have authority here.'

'Hand me the bag.'

I flattened myself against the wall of metal lockers behind me.

'I know you,' he said. 'You're the brother. What did she give you?'

'Back up, old man.'

He paused. He was gauging the distance between us. Gauging me. He was assessing our comparative sizes. Not too difficult to spot the differences. He was giving away a few inches in height. A stone or so in weight. Maybe twenty-five years in age. Set against that was the arm I had in a sling, under my hoodie. Two arms against one could compensate for a lot of disadvantages.

Then two things happened very fast. His right arm bent at the elbow and he reached his hand inside his jacket. And I dropped the holdall and pushed off from the bank of metal lockers and launched myself across the room.

I crashed into him, jolting my ribs, and drove with my legs to push him back towards the door. The door opened inwards. No give in it now. It was as good as a wall. His head whiplashed against the wood, bending his lower spine the wrong way against the handle. My busted shoulder flared with pain.

His hand was squirming inside his jacket. He was still reaching for whatever he had in there. I pinned him with my weight. With my arm in the sling. We were both one-handed now.

I have size twelve feet. They're good and solid. I lifted my right foot in the air and stamped it down on his toe. He yelled. I held him up. Then I stomped on him again. This time, I stepped away and he buckled at the waist. His head came down. My knee came up. It hit him full in the temple.

I moved aside and let him fall. He was groaning but his hand was coming out of the jacket. Something heavy in it. Something black. The butt of a gun. It was all I needed to see. I lifted my foot and drove down on his elbow like I was aiming to stamp a spike into the ground. There was a moment of resistance, then his hand bent badly against the floor with a loud *snap* and his elbow rolled and he tumbled round after it, screaming wildly. Not good for his hand, I didn't think. Not good for his elbow.

I stepped back and fumbled in the pocket of my jogging trousers. My hand came out with the can of pepper spray Rebecca had given me. I flicked off the cap with my thumbnail and let him have it. The spray wasn't a fine mist. It was a brown liquid squirt. It spattered his forehead. His eyes. His nose.

He yowled and clasped his hand to his face. Tried to use the sleeve of his jacket to wipe the fluids away.

I stood there panting for a moment, watching him suffer. The moment was short. I didn't want to be found with a man in agony on the floor in front of me. I didn't want to be detained with the memory stick. I had no way of knowing if my attacker was working alone or if he had back-up somewhere.

I dropped the spray canister and grabbed my holdall. I hauled back the door and hurried away from the gym.

The rear exit of the sports centre looked clear. I burst through and climbed the perimeter railing and jogged across the running track and the athletics field. I checked over my shoulder. Nobody behind me. Nobody following. I was breathing hard. It was difficult to run with the holdall in my hand and my other arm in the sling. My shoulder ached. My ribs throbbed. My lungs burned. I was trembling with fear and adrenalin. My bruised leg felt numb and aimless.

I crossed the far side of the running track. Slowed as I approached my van. I staggered forwards and pointed my keys. The indicator lamps flashed. I opened the driver's door and drew back my arm to toss my holdall inside. But the holdall was snatched from me. Unseen hands seized the back of my neck and the top of my head and drove my skull into the side of the van. There was a fierce, splintering pain in my head.

Then there was nothing at all.

Chapter Forty-two

Lena had been thinking very carefully about the tinted window and the soundproofing. She'd been analysing the properties of the single pane of glass and the soft foam tiles. She'd been comparing and contrasting their weaknesses and their strengths. She'd formed the conclusion that they were just about the best combination of materials she could possibly have hoped for.

The textured foam was perfect because it did exactly what it was designed to do. It trapped noise. It literally sucked sound-waves inside its millions of tiny porous openings. It absorbed sound completely.

She could vouch for how good it was because she couldn't hear anything outside her room. No traffic noise. No aeroplane engines. No neighbourly commotion. And not the slightest peep from the man who was guarding her.

The man wasn't a fan of classical music. On her way back from the bathroom, as he handed her a plastic bottle of water and a dry croissant on a paper plate, she noticed that he'd re-tuned the radio to a sports discussion show. That made her think that the two men were minding her in shifts. Taking turns. But now that the door had been closed and locked behind her, she couldn't hear a sound from the radio or the man. Not a thing. She could have been in a cave deep underground. She could have been at the bottom of the ocean.

And it stood to reason that the effect worked both ways.

It had to. The foam tiling was there to stop her screaming for help. To swallow all kinds of noise. The type she might be expected to make. And the type she might not.

The window was different. The window was fulfilling a role it hadn't been intended to perform. It had been adapted to the requirements of the room. First, the original fixture must have been taken away. The original fixture would have been installed with hinges so that it could be opened to allow fresh air inside. That was no good. The new window had to be a solid sheet of glass. That way, whoever was inside the room at any given time couldn't drop a note to the street below, or wave an arm outside in the hope of alerting someone to their plight.

Second, before the replacement glass was installed, the exterior surface had been covered in an opaque adhesive film. This was a back-up move. It was intended to stop anybody looking inside from another tower block and seeing what the room was being used for. And it was designed to make it very hard for a prisoner to signal through the glass to the wider world. The wall switch for the electric bulb in the middle of the ceiling had been installed outside the room for the exact same reason.

Lena could see the appeal of the film. She could understand the logic behind its use.

But she could also appreciate its weaknesses.

She guessed that the film had been applied to the glass many years ago now. The window was single-glazed, and that probably made it at least fifteen years old. The film would have been pressed down tight and smoothed around very deliberately to prevent air bubbles forming. Then the whole thing had been installed in the window frame with the film on the outside so that a prisoner couldn't peel it away. It had been subjected to years of sunshine and wind. Over time, the sun and the wind would have dried the bonding agent between the film and the glass. The molecules themselves would have knitted together until it was almost impossible to tell where the glass ended and the film began.

And the film was still sticky. Yes, it had peeled away in the top left corner, but nowhere else. In fact, Lena was of the opinion that the film was probably responsible for stopping the hairline crack in the glass from spreading very far.

The sticky film and the hairline crack were going to help her. They were exactly what she needed.

Lena was finally ready to act. She'd done all the thinking she would ever need to do. She gathered up the duvet in the pink coverlet and spread it out as best she could and held it up against the window with her good hand. The duvet draped downwards over her wrist in a rough triangle. That was OK. She really only needed it to cover the middle of the glass because she figured that would be the weakest point.

She took one step backwards from the window and placed all her weight on her back leg. She turned her foot sideways on, so that it would give her a better foundation. Then she lifted her front leg in the air and practised the move. When she was satisfied with her balance and her positioning, she drew a sharp breath and clenched her teeth and lashed out fast. She kicked as high as she could. As hard as she could. She felt the glass crack right away. She felt the flex and the resistance of the film. She tottered backwards and placed a little weight on her front foot and marvelled at how well the duvet had smothered the pain in her heel and muffled the noise of the glass breaking. She was as sure as she could possibly be that the man wouldn't have heard a thing.

A starburst of splintered glass was adhering to the film, exactly as she'd planned. Not a fragment had dropped. There was no way it could have gone better. The shards were long and jagged and just waiting to be plucked free. She wrapped the duvet round her hand and set to work.

*

Menser was in severe discomfort. Unremitting agony. He'd staggered as far as a shower cubicle. Shut and bolted the door behind him. Fumbled for the cold feed and stuck his head beneath the icy flow, letting it douse his skin. The sudden cold was like a fearsome slap but warm water would be no good – he needed to close his pores, not open them.

He hugged himself tight and blinked furiously, ignoring for the moment what the brother had done to his wrist. He was blinking because he knew his tears would help to flush the chemicals from his eyes. His skin was burning very badly. It was itching intensely. That was why he was clutching himself so hard. If he let go, the temptation to scratch his face would overcome him again. He'd spread the contaminant around. Force it into his skin. Make the pain a lot worse.

So he stood there, shivering, with his arms folded across his chest, trying to calm himself despite the difficulty he was having breathing. That was the snag with chemical sprays. They inflamed everything. Your eyes. Your sinuses. Your airways. And unless you had an antacid to hand – a pack of Alka-Seltzer or some Milk of Magnesia, say – your only option was to wait the worst of the effects out. Ten minutes if you were lucky. Thirty if you weren't.

Menser guessed he was nearing the eight-minute mark. His symptoms showed no sign of abating. His eyes were stinging very badly. His nostrils were streaming. His lungs felt like someone was sitting on his chest.

His hair was thoroughly drenched now. The frigid water was streaming down his neck, soaking into his sweater. It was spattering his trousers and swamping his shoes.

He did his best to distract himself. To take his mind elsewhere. To *think*.

The pain made him think very fast. It rushed his thoughts just like it rushed his breathing. He came to three conclusions.

One: he'd underestimated the brother, and he couldn't afford to make the same mistake again.

Two: he needed to call and check on the girl. Enough had gone wrong already. He had to make certain she was secure and being properly monitored.

Three: he had to obtain whatever the brother had found. He needed to locate the brother. Force him to exchange. Make it very clear that his only option was to comply.

The only thing left to think about was the best way to make that happen.

Chapter Forty-three

My van was moving. It was shifting around beneath me. I could hear engine noise and feel coarse vibrations through the thin plywood floor. My tools were rattling in the shelves and cubbyholes I'd fitted along the sides. The rear cargo doors and sliding side door were juddering. The suspension was bouncing and creaking and banging. My bad shoulder was knocking painfully against the solid metal bulkhead that separated the load area from the passenger cab.

My head was in a bad way. There was blood in my left eye, trickling down from a wet gash somewhere above my forehead. I tested the area with my fingertip and sickened myself with the squishiness of what I found there. The inside of my head was pounding. It was pulsing hard. I kept replaying the sensation of the impact over and over in my mind. My skull felt eggshell-thin. It felt vulnerable. I remembered what I'd been told by the hospital doctors. To take care to avoid any follow-up blows. To report to A&E immediately if I experienced any symptoms of a concussion.

I didn't think I was being driven to A&E.

I had no idea where they were taking me. I had no idea who *they* were.

The back of the van was very dark. There was a shard of white light somewhere towards the top of the right-hand cargo door. The crack was perhaps a foot in length. A couple of millimetres wide. The light wasn't enough to see by. All it offered me was a chance to orientate myself.

I braced my good hand against the dusty plywood floor. Winced as gravity shifted things around inside my head. There was an urgent swelling in my ears. A lot of saliva in my mouth. I gritted my teeth. Tried to stay with it.

Then a voice spoke to me from the darkness.

The voice said, 'How badly are you hurt?'

It was female. I recognised it. But there was something different about it, too. Like it was constricted in some way. Hard to decipher.

I wasn't sure that I could trust my ears. Maybe it was a side effect of my head injury. Maybe I was hallucinating.

'Hey,' the voice said. 'Did you hear me?'

I said nothing. I was busy trying to swallow the fluids in my mouth without choking.

The van rocked beneath me. It pitched and rolled. We were going around a corner.

'Do you have your phone?' the voice asked.

I stared blindly into the darkness. It seemed to contract and expand and swirl around me. There were gaseous reds and wispy purples inside it. Like I was looking towards a far-off galaxy.

The voice repeated itself. Measuring out its words. 'Do . . . you . . . have . . . your . . . phone?'

'It's in the front,' I panted. My tongue felt swollen and clumsy. Too big for my mouth. 'In the glove box.'

I realised now what was different about the voice. It was thick. Nasal. Like she had a terrible cold.

'How long have you been here?' I asked.

'They threw me in after you. You don't remember?'

I didn't remember. Not even close.

I could hear the doctors' warnings coming back to me. The dangers of secondary swelling. Bleeding of the brain. Nausea. Dizziness. Confused thinking. Cognitive disruption. I had all of them. Maybe more besides.

I said, 'I need to get to a hospital.'

'Join the queue.'

There was a dry click. A blinding flare. Rebecca was holding a torch in her hands. It was the torch I keep handy at the back of my van. Her hands were in her lap. She was sitting with her back against the rear cargo doors, her legs splayed in front of her. Her expensive leather jacket was scuffed and coated in dirt and grime. It was fully unzipped. Her T-shirt was stained with a dark liquid that had pasted the material against her skin.

The torch was pointed up at her chin. It illuminated her face from below, as if she was planning to tell me a ghost story.

Her face was terrible. A wet, blood-caked mess. She had two black eyes. The bruises were a deep aubergine colour. The eyes were badly swollen. Closed almost to slits. Like she'd been stung ferociously. Her nose was worse. It was flattened. It was mush. I could see a sliver of bone. A lot of blood. She covered it with some kind of rag. The cloth was sodden. It was dripping.

She said, 'I'm starting to regret not staying over last night.'

'Who did this to you?'

Her head rolled loosely on her shoulders. She was perspiring heavily. Her hair was greasy and stuck to her forehead.

I scuffled along the floor on my backside. Stopped near her feet. I didn't want her to have to talk so loudly.

'Anderson,' she muttered. 'He flagged me down last night,

after I'd left your place. He must have been waiting outside. He said he had something he needed to discuss.'

She laughed faintly. There was a soggy wheezing in her breath.

'Anderson punched you?' I asked.

'No, he didn't punch me.' She paused. Gulped air. 'He's American. He used a baseball bat.'

She lowered the cloth. Her teeth were bloody. One of them was chipped.

I looked away. Couldn't help myself.

She clicked the torch off. 'Better?' she asked.

'I'm sorry.'

She wheezed some more. Her breaths were shallow. The wet rattle in her throat was becoming worse.

She said, 'He has a man with him. Kind of weedy. Long hair. I think he could be one of the two from the cottage.'

'Lukas.'

'I think so. But he's limping badly. I don't remember you mentioning that.'

'I didn't. What about the blond one?'

'No sign of him.'

'What did they want?'

'To know what we'd found out. They knew you were Laura's brother. They'd worked out that Laura and Melanie Fleming were the same person, and that Laura was dead. They made me tell them about the locker key.' She sucked down a halting breath. 'You still had it, didn't you?'

'I'm afraid so.'

'You lied to me.'

'I'm sorry,' I said. And I meant it, too. 'But I got the feeling you weren't being completely honest with me. I thought maybe you were holding something back.'

Silence. I freed the torch from her hand and pointed the beam towards the roof of the van. She nodded in the ambient light. The movement was slight, but it was clear. I got the impression it hurt.

'I have been holding something back,' she said.

'About Laura?'

'About her death.'

'What is it? Was she killed? Was Anderson involved?'

Rebecca turned her head slowly to the left. Eased it to the right.

'No,' she said. 'I've been asking myself if she might still be alive.'

Chapter Forty-four

The van was accelerating. We were moving fast. I could hear it in the droning note of the engine. I could feel it in the inertia when we turned a corner. I guessed that we'd left behind the built-up areas of Douglas and were moving beyond the outskirts of town on to quicker roads. There were a lot of directions we could be heading in. We could be going south, towards the airport. Or we could be following a different course entirely.

I was balancing on my knees, shining the torch over the rear cargo doors, looking for a safety catch. There was a catch on the sliding door at the side, but it wouldn't budge. I guessed the central locking had been engaged. I hoped the rear doors might be different, but I wasn't having much luck. Plastic mouldings covered the door mechanism. The gap was too thin for me to get my fingers inside.

I had plenty of tools with me inside the van. I went searching for a screwdriver, shining the torch over the wooden shelves and drawers, fighting to keep my balance as the van squirmed around beneath me.

'Do you want to explain what you mean about my sister?' I asked Rebecca.

I managed to pull myself up to my first stash of tools. Hammers and wrenches and spanners, mostly. But there were many screwdrivers in there, too. I grabbed one with a thick red handle and a metal shaft about as long as my forearm.

Rebecca said, 'You remember what I told you up at the cliffs?'

'I remember that you were bothered by the point where Laura's car went over.'

I passed Rebecca the torch. Adjusted her hands so that the beam was throwing light on to the area I was working on and tried not to gawp at her face. I slipped the blade of the screwdriver between the plastic mouldings. Pushed it in as far as it would go. Forced it one way. Then the other. I pulled on it with my good arm. Away from Rebecca. Then the van turned a corner and I lost my balance and thumped into the side.

There was a moment of silence. Then the bang of a fist against the bulkhead up front.

'Quit fooling around,' Anderson yelled. 'Don't make me come back there.'

I got back on to my knees. Fooled around some more.

'You were saying,' I said to Rebecca.

She gulped air and swallowed hard. 'If your sister was planning to kill herself, she'd have driven right over the cliff face into the sea.'

'You're assuming she knew what the cliff was like from inside her car.'

'I think she did know.' She paused. Gathered her breath. I was getting used to the nasal quality of her voice. It was becoming easier for me to understand what she was saying. 'I think she drove up there and found that exact spot. I think she mounted the kerb slowly. Drove forwards against the fence until it began to give. I think she got the car ready to drop and then she stepped out and clipped the fence wires and gave it a shove. I think she watched it go.'

298

'Laura was found dead in that car,' I said. 'A lot of people saw her.'

'You're sure about that?'

'Dad identified her body. There was an autopsy. Everything.'

Rebecca didn't say anything to that. She'd taken to tilting her head back in an effort to stop her nose from bleeding. I didn't think it would work. There wasn't much left of her nose, so far as I could see.

My screwdriver scraped against the plastic moulding. Bending it. Warping it. But it wouldn't splinter. It wouldn't crack.

I rested against the shelves of tools and let the screwdriver fall to the floor. I took the torch from Rebecca's hands. Used the sleeve of my hoodie to wipe the blood from above my eye. It was sticky. Beginning to clot.

'I have a first-aid kit,' I said.

'Could you find it for me?'

I shuffled back up the van on my knees in search of the kit. Usually I kept it stashed behind the end of the shelving unit. But it wasn't there. I turned, shining the light around me. I lifted the dust sheets from the floor. Checked underneath.

'I told you I worked with Laura,' Rebecca panted. 'And it's true. But it was a long time ago.' She paused for another breath. I heard a wet rattle in her throat. 'The real reason I knew who she was when your mum called me was because she approached my firm for a job six weeks or so ago. She said she wanted to join us, make a clean break. She gave us her real name, so we could run some checks. I noticed that she'd kept the middle name Hendon. I only stalled when your mum called because I wasn't sure who she might be. I was being careful.'

My torch beam caught a glimmer of bright green. The first-aid kit. I was surprised to find that it was open. Dressings and bandages were missing.

'Did you already use this?' I asked.

'Does it look like I did?'

No, it didn't look that way at all. I couldn't explain what had happened to the kit. There were still a couple of antiseptic wipes inside, along with a small bandage in paper packaging. There were pills, too. Paracetamol. I carried the collection to Rebecca and tore open an antiseptic wipe. I handed it across and watched her grimace and flinch as she touched the wipe to the area around her nose. I popped some pills out of the little foil packet and swallowed them. Popped some more and passed them to Rebecca.

'Did you offer Laura a job?' I asked.

'No.'

'Why not?'

'On paper, she was perfect. We knew she had a good reputation. Several of my colleagues were all set on the idea.' Rebecca slipped the pills in her mouth. She steeled herself to swallow them. Screwed up her battered face in pain. 'I was the one who blocked it. When Laura came to meet with us, I got the feeling she wasn't looking for a new career.'

'How do you mean?'

'I thought she was sounding us out. It seemed to me she was in trouble and needed help.'

'Wouldn't she just say so?'

'My feeling was that the trouble she was in was serious. She was scared. It was like I told you. I felt she had a problem inside her organisation. And the only place she could get help was outside.'

'But she didn't ask for help.'

'Not directly, no.' She paused for a beat and collected herself. When she started talking again, she took her time over her words, as if pronouncing each one risked a fresh stab of pain. It lent her speech a peculiar, faltering cadence. 'But she had a lot of questions about the kind of work we were involved in. And she really grilled me on our expertise when it came to missing-persons cases. She wanted to know if we helped to find people who'd disappeared. She asked me about the kind of techniques we might use to track down people who adopted new identities and moved to new countries. In hindsight, I think she was digging for data, for know-how. I think she was working on a solution to her problem. She was good, Rob. She was resourceful. I think she faked her own death.'

I clasped a hand to the wound on my head. Squeezed very gently. As if maybe I could ease the parted skin back together again. Like perhaps if I fixed my head my brain would be capable of fitting together all the information I was hearing.

The van pitched left and I stuck my bloodied hand out to stop myself from tumbling over. 'I already told you,' I said. 'She died in that crash.'

'She might have, I agree. But think about it. This island of yours is a small place. It's your sister's home. She grew up here. It's insular, by its very nature. By its geography. It's the kind of place that looks after its own. Where favours can be called in. Where people can be trusted and secrets can be kept. Your father has some influence here, agreed? And his daughter was in trouble.'

'That doesn't make any sense. Dad hired you to look into Laura's death.'

'No. Your mum hired me.'

'Because Laura asked her to. She told mum to contact you if anything happened to her.'

'Yes, but maybe not why you think. Maybe Laura wanted me hired because she knew I'd ask questions. I'd dig around in the mess she'd got herself in. I'd remember the way she'd quizzed me about how someone might vanish, and maybe I'd start to wonder if she was still alive. My involvement might even give your sister a chance to come out from hiding. Assuming I found something that could help her.'

'And have you found anything like that?'

'No. But you just did. In that locker.'

I thought about my holdall. The way it had been snatched from me.

'What did you find?' Rebecca asked.

'A computer memory stick. It had Laura's handwriting on the outside.'

'And what was on the memory stick?'

'I don't know. I was planning to drive home and take a look. Next thing I knew, they were using my head for a battering ram.'

Rebecca didn't say anything to that. She was contemplating the stained remains of the antiseptic wipe I'd given her. It looked almost as bad as her T-shirt. I dreaded to think how much blood she'd lost.

Better to think about what she'd told me about Laura instead.

'That's why you're here, isn't it?' I said. 'That's why you agreed to work for my parents for free. You sensed that Laura had come to you for help, and you didn't give it to her. You feel guilty.'

'Does it matter? Isn't it enough that I'm motivated?'

I didn't say anything to that. Perhaps she was right. Perhaps it didn't make any difference at all.

'I'm sorry I told them about the locker,' she said.

'Doesn't look like they gave you a lot of choice. And if they were watching my place, like you said, they would have followed me to the sports centre anyway. Speaking of which, someone else did.'

Rebecca looked up from the bloodied wipe. 'Who?'

'I don't know. But he said he worked for the security services.'

'Someone from the inside,' she said, and nodded to herself. 'The threat your sister was worried about.'

'I still don't believe Laura's alive,' I told her. 'What you're suggesting would involve too many people. One of them would say something.'

'Not necessarily. Who are we talking about here? A coroner? A funeral director? Someone in the police? Like Shimmin, for instance. You said yourself he wasn't willing to look into what happened with Lena up at the cottage. This could be why.'

'You're suggesting he helped Laura to disappear?'

She nodded. 'But I think it was your dad who approached him.'

I thought about that. About how Dad had wanted to stay in my room at the hospital when Shimmin and Teare had arrived to speak with me. About how Teare had said that Shimmin had insisted on coming to the hospital with her, and how he'd interrupted her line of questioning. About how Shimmin had come to my home to speak to me following Teare's death, and how I'd seen him deep in conversation with Dad before I drove to the sports centre.

'There's something I haven't told you yet,' I said to Rebecca. 'Teare was attacked after we left last night. She's dead.'

Chapter Forty-five

It was becoming hot inside the van. The midday sunshine was heating the metal and the interior was warming like an oven. Our air was getting stale. Rebecca was already having a hard time breathing and my bruised ribs didn't make life any easier for me.

'How do you know about Teare?' Rebecca asked, in her breathless, stumbling rhythm.

'Shimmin,' I said. 'He came to see me this morning. He knew we'd been to talk to her last night.'

'Is he treating you as a suspect?'

'No.'

'What about me?'

'I don't think so. But he planned to speak to you.'

Rebecca absorbed the information in a quiet way. She didn't seem altogether shocked. Maybe experience had hardened her to bad news. Maybe nothing surprised her any more.

'Did he tell you how Teare died?' she asked.

'Looks like she was attacked in her home. Shimmin found her at the bottom of her stairs, like she'd tried to break free. And he found a man there, too. Also dead. Shimmin showed me a photograph. I recognised him.'

'Who was he?'

'The paramedic. The one who talked to me after my bike accident. The one who took Lena.'

'Someone's cleaning house,' Rebecca said.

'They're making a hell of a mess while they're at it.'

'No choice. They're getting desperate.'

'About what?'

'Whatever's on that memory stick.'

The van braked hard and slowed, swinging to the right. It accelerated at a cautious pace, then maintained a low cruising speed. The tyres hummed and chattered and danced. I could hear the scrape of loose grit, the hollow *whump* of a wheel striking a pothole, the *rat-tat-tat* of a cattle grid. Then more braking, a left turn, and the van came to a halt.

I listened hard, but I couldn't hear anything over the noise of the idling engine. Rebecca cocked her ear against the cargo doors.

Footsteps. Moving away from the van. I tried the sliding door by my side. Still locked. The footsteps continued, followed by the distant sound of a door closing. Not our van. There had to be a second vehicle. Then engine noise ahead of us, followed by the creak of our brakes loosening off and the purr of the van edging forwards.

Rebecca read my face and picked up on the question in my eyes.

'Last night they were in a Land Rover Discovery with tinted windows. Anderson is driving us, so that puts Lukas in the Land Rover.'

The van lurched and pitched and rocked. Loose stones snapped and popped beneath our tyres. My tools and spare components rattled and jingled in their cubby-holes and plastic tubs. I dropped to my knees and hooked my arm around a timber upright. Rebecca's head bounced off the rear cargo doors.

'We're nearly there,' she said, the vibrations distorting her voice.

'Where?'

'Somewhere remote. Somewhere we won't be disturbed.'

The van listed hard to the left. Then righted itself. Like it had passed through a deep rut.

'But Anderson doesn't know the island,' I said.

'The kind of place they're looking for isn't hard to find. You just keep driving until the roads get small.'

'So we could be anywhere.'

'We could be. But if Lukas is leading the way, my guess is we're going somewhere he's familiar with. Somewhere we're familiar with, too.'

I finally caught up to her. 'The cottage,' I said.

'They know it's remote. It's not overlooked. Nobody will hear anything.'

I didn't like what Rebecca was saying, but I couldn't fault her logic. And I knew what it felt like to drive up the muddy track through the woods in my van. The lurching and the pitching and the rocking. The bouncing and the swaying and the rolling and the juddering.

'So what do we do?' I asked.

'We arm ourselves. What tools have you got in here?'

I had plenty of tools, many of them capable of wounding grievously. I had claw hammers and ball-peen hammers and rubber mallets. I had adjustable wrenches and heavy-duty spanners. I had tube benders, razor-sharp bandsaws and tin shears. I had callipers and vices and clamps. I had pliers and screwdrivers and a wide variety of knives and cutting tools. I had electric drills. I had a blowtorch.

I hauled myself to my feet and grabbed what I could as the van bucked and rolled beneath me. I passed Rebecca a nail gun and a knife with a retractable blade. I chose an adjustable wrench for myself, slipping it beneath my jumper and sliding it inside my sling, pressed flat against my chest. I hefted an electric drill in my right hand, then switched it for a rubber mallet. The mallet felt good at the end of my arm. The handle was maybe a foot in length, allowing for a fast swing and even better momentum. The rubber head was dry and cracked and very solid. Ideal for thumping aged copper piping into compliance. Excellent for attacking a temple, or an elbow joint, or a knee cap.

The van climbed a steep incline. Then the ground flattened out and we gathered speed and the wheels chattered and pummelled and thudded.

The van slowed to a halt, then reversed in a sweeping arc. It reversed very fast. Then there was a sudden hard impact at the back – a sharp metal *clang* and the dry *crack* of splintered light clusters. I was thrown to the floor. Rebecca ducked forwards, protecting her head. The rear cargo doors shook and shivered and trembled.

The engine died. The van settled in position. I could hear the whine of the Land Rover's power steering, the scrub and scrabble of its tyres on mud and stone. Then all was quiet. A car door opened and closed. Footsteps approached the van.

A fist thumped into the metal bulkhead that separated the cab from the loading bay.

'Listen up,' Anderson yelled. 'Here's what's going to happen. I'm going to pop the central locking and you're going to slide open the side door. But before you do, you're going to drop

308

whatever weapons you've picked up back there. My colleague is holding a Beretta M9 semi-automatic pistol. If he sees you with anything in your hands, and I mean anything at all, he's going to pull the trigger and keep pulling. Understand?'

We didn't say anything. We were too busy looking at one another.

'Drop whatever you have,' Anderson shouted. 'Don't make him shoot.'

I considered the rubber mallet in my hand, then shrugged and tossed it away. Rebecca looked longingly at the nail gun before setting it aside. She kept hold of the craft knife, tucking it under the sleeve of her leather jacket. The knife was small. Compact. The blade was housed inside a hard plastic case.

I watched her cup her hand and practise dropping the knife into her palm. Saw her thumb rest on the ridged metal lever that extended the blade. She seemed happy with the move. Content with her handling. She poked the knife up under her cuff and scrambled to her feet.

'Ready?' Anderson yelled.

'We won't try anything,' I called back.

Rebecca took a couple of strides towards me. I could hear her breathing. Slow and nasal and phlegmy. There was a moment of silence, followed by a series of rapid mechanical clunks as the door locks retracted. I pointed the torch beam at the latch on the side door. Once I had its location fixed in my mind, I dropped the torch on to the dust sheets near my feet and reached out and opened the door.

Daylight flooded the interior of the van. I blinked and shielded my eyes with my hand. We were parked in the small clearing in the woods in front of the cottage. The cottage and the overgrown garden were off to our left. I stuck my head outside. The rear of the van was pressing right up against the garage door. The fluted metal panels had creased and buckled where the van had been reversed into them. A black Land Rover Discovery was parked to our right, its nose pointed away from us in the direction of the dense tree cover.

The man called Lukas was standing ten paces away, his back to the treeline and the cooling Discovery, his legs parted, right foot slightly in front of the left, both arms raised level with his chin. He had a dirty big gun grasped in his hands. His right hand was curled around the butt, index finger hooked around the trigger. His left hand supported his right wrist.

It struck me as a competent pose, but he was having difficulty maintaining it. I don't know a whole lot about guns – I've never held one myself, let alone fired one – but any idiot could see the pistol was heavy. Lukas wasn't muscular and his arms were wavering, describing small, imperfect circles with the muzzle of the gun. He wet his lip. Rotated his head so that his lank hair brushed his shoulders. I wondered how soon he'd need to lower the gun and give his arms a rest. I asked myself how long I could stand there without moving.

Not long.

The driver's door opened and closed and Anderson hustled around the front of the van. He had a baseball bat propped on his shoulder. The bat was as long as my arm, made of pale blond wood and lacquered to a high-gloss finish. It looked solid. Hard. Uncompromising.

Anderson's face looked the same way.

He stopped maybe five paces from the sliding door. He was wearing pressed tan chinos over brown loafers. A navy polo shirt was buttoned to his chin and tucked into the waistband of the chinos. His biceps swelled against the cuffs of the shirt. He looked like he was dressed for an office barbecue.

Anderson checked on Lukas, contenting himself with the cover he was being afforded. I recognised the clothes Lukas had on. The old blue sweater and jeans were from the back of my van. One leg of the jeans was stained more than I remembered. It was dyed a dark, rusty red, and the material seemed to be clinging to his thigh.

Anderson beckoned me out of the van with a *gimme* gesture with the curled fingers of his spare hand. I stepped out on to compacted mud. Anderson pulled the baseball bat down from his shoulder and used the rounded end to lift my free arm in the air. He poked the bat between my thighs until I widened my stance.

'You understand I have to check you,' he said. 'Make sure you've complied with my instructions. It's a dangerous time, right?'

I didn't say anything.

'Not dangerous for me. I'm good. I have my friend here with a Beretta in his hand. I have my bat. But it's dangerous for you. Make no mistake. Dangerous if you decided to ignore my advice. If maybe you thought you'd arm yourself and take a swing at me when you got the chance.'

He tipped his head over on to his shoulder. Watched me as if he was greatly intrigued by my reaction.

I didn't open my mouth.

'Well, now's your big chance,' he said. 'I'm going to come over and I'm going to pat you down. I'm going to start at your feet and work my way up. You might think that maybe you should kick me when I'm crouched in front of you. Or stick me with a knife you have hidden away in your sleeve. But that would be a bad idea. It'd be dangerous. You know why?'

I kept my mouth shut.

'Tell me why,' he said.

'The gun,' I told him.

'And?'

'And your bat.'

'That's right. A bat can do a lot of damage.' He gestured towards Rebecca with the thick end. She was standing in the open doorway of the van, covering her pulped eyes from the hard sunlight. She looked beaten and dishevelled and grubby. She looked in dire need of medical care. 'But a gun?' Anderson continued. 'Why, a nine-millimetre round fired at short range is pretty much guaranteed to kill. Maybe not fast. It can be made to kill slow. But it'll still kill you in the end. Understand?'

I nodded.

'Good.' He used the bat to pat the air. 'Then don't move. Don't even breathe, OK?'

He moved as if to take a step towards me but he was interrupted by a loud clatter coming from the van. Rebecca's hands were open by her sides, her fingers spread. The craft knife bounced on the plywood floor.

'Well, looky here,' Anderson said. 'Good for you, sweetheart.'

He flashed his teeth at her. Then turned the dazzle on me.

'Anything you want to let go of, partner? What we have here is an official amnesty. Your friend dropped her blade, and I can forgive her for that. So if you have anything you want to show me, you just go ahead and throw it away into the dirt.'

I didn't speak. Didn't move. I just watched the guy, trying to ignore the tiny movements of the pistol muzzle I could glimpse out of the corner of my eye.

'Well, OK,' Anderson said. He spun the baseball bat in the air. A complete 360. Caught it cleanly in his palm. Passed it over to his left hand. 'Amnesty over. Change of plan.'

He took a series of sideways steps, crabbing over towards Lukas. He claimed the Beretta for himself and pointed it at me, holding the bat by his side.

'Go ahead and check him, Lukas.'

Lukas seemed uncertain.

'Go ahead. Get to it.'

Lukas shook some feeling back into his arms, then advanced towards me. He was favouring his right leg, as if he'd injured his left. There was a marked stiffness to his movements. I guessed that might explain the bloody stain on my jeans.

'That's right,' Anderson told him. 'I have you covered. Now, start down by his feet. Feel around his ankles. Check his socks.'

Lukas had some difficulty crouching down. He had to use his hands to extend his left leg out in front of him, with the knee joint locked straight. I could understand what Anderson had meant. It was tempting to lash out and kick him full in the face. It would have been easy enough to do. Simple to overpower him. But not with a gun being held on me by a man who seemed very comfortable with a pistol at the end of his arm.

Switching roles had been a sensible move. But there were disadvantages, too.

I stayed still as Lukas worked his way up my legs, patting my calves and my thighs through the flannel material of my jogging trousers. First one leg. Then the other. He seemed embarrassed by the task and concealed his eyes behind his long hair. His movements were jerky and inhibited. I felt sure Anderson would have been a lot more thorough.

Lukas got as far as my waist. Anderson told him to pay particular attention to the elastic of my jogging trousers. He found nothing there, and struggled up to his feet so that he could pat his hands up my torso. The wrench was still hidden inside my sling. My instinct was to clench my arm hard against my chest, but I didn't want to do anything that would give me away. Lukas worked along the sleeve of my free arm. Then he wrapped his fingers around my folded arm and pinched it, from the wrist to the elbow. His movements were delicate but probing, like a surgeon checking for breaks. I feigned a wince. He reduced the pressure he was applying, then abandoned the task altogether. He took a weighted step backwards and released a long breath, like he'd just inspected a primed bomb and had got away without being blown to pieces.

'Satisfied?' Anderson asked him.

Lukas nodded.

'Good. Then check the girl.'

Rebecca staggered out of the van and swayed woozily in the clearing. Lukas went through the same process, beginning with her ankles and working his way up her body to the ends of her arms. I noticed that he didn't meet Rebecca's blackened eyes as he checked her.

'She clear?' Anderson asked.

Lukas nodded again. Fitfully this time.

'Great. Then close up the van and come take this gun.'

Lukas slammed the sliding door shut, then limped back to Anderson and claimed the pistol. There was a soft breeze through the trees, swaying the tall pines and rustling the branches and needles. The sky above them was pale blue and near-cloudless. I could hear birdsong.

'So, well done guys.' Anderson sidestepped to my right, closer to the garage door. 'Just the knife, right? And you dropped it during the amnesty, so that means we're good. Except we're not, as it happens. Because I lied about the amnesty.'

He moved fast, whipping the bat back over his shoulder, twisting at the waist and swinging with everything he had. The bat was a swooping blur. It buzzed in the air. I saw his elbows rotate, his wrists extend at the end of the swing. Then I felt the meat of the bat bury itself in the fragile plate of my bad shoulder.

I hadn't expected it. I hadn't adjusted my stance or braced for the impact. I was wide open at my most vulnerable point.

The pain was immediate and startling. Fissures of agony exploded across my back. My muscles spasmed. My head jerked back and I screamed and fell to my knees.

There was nothing I could do to smother the pain. I couldn't clasp my hand to it. I couldn't reach. My body was canted to the left, almost as if Anderson's bat had passed right through me and taken a ragged slice of my torso with it. My left arm was dead. Completely busted. If the wrench hadn't been hidden inside my sling, it would have dropped to the ground for sure.

The pain got worse. It bloomed and mushroomed. My eyes watered. My ears hummed.

Rebecca reached down to me, but I pushed her away. I knew that if anyone touched me the pain would be terrible. I thought of her face. The puffed-up, discoloured mess the bat had made of it. I couldn't begin to imagine how bad it must have been for her.

'Get up,' Anderson barked.

But I couldn't get up. I couldn't move. I was making a lot of involuntary sounds. Panting and whimpering, drawing fast, shallow breaths.

'Get up or I'll hit you again.'

This time, Rebecca didn't take no for an answer. She ducked down and hooked a hand beneath my good arm and heaved me to my feet. I howled. She held me up. Her strength surprised me. I needed her there. My legs were jelly. I was twisted around to my side, face down, my back turned to Anderson. I must have looked like I was cowering. Maybe I was. All I knew for certain was that I couldn't straighten up for fear of passing out.

'That was for the knife,' Anderson said. 'You're a partnership, right? If one of you screws up, one of you has to suffer the consequences. Understand?'

'Enough,' Rebecca said. 'Just tell us what you want.'

'What I want? OK, I want you to get inside the house. Right now. Lukas, you have the key?'

Lukas fumbled in his pocket. His movements were rushed and anxious. I got the impression he wanted Anderson to hit us again about as much as we did. He circled the bonnet of my van, limping heavily, and approached the front door.

We didn't hesitate to follow. The last thing I wanted was to be struck again.

Anderson locked the van and then tracked us from behind. He was holding the baseball bat out in front of him like a cattle prod. It was just inches from my skin.

Lukas had some trouble fitting the key in the lock. His hand was shaking. He got it eventually and pushed the door open. Then he hobbled to one side and waved us into the hallway with the gun.

It was gloomy and there was a strong smell of damp I hadn't noticed before. The carpet was thin and threadbare underfoot. The corridor wasn't wide enough for two. I went first, at a stoop. Rebecca followed.

'Go on into the kitchen,' Anderson said.

Nothing had changed. The wooden table and chairs were still in the middle of the room. The cheaply tiled counters were still empty. The windows were still too low in the wall, and too small to let in sufficient light.

'Head through into the garage,' Anderson said.

There was a key fitted in a lock on the internal door. Rebecca turned it, then swung the door open and helped me to shuffle through.

The garage was close to pitch black. I stumbled down the step from the kitchen, wrenching my aching shoulder.

Anderson said, 'Move forwards. Into the middle.'

We did as we were told. There was a dry click and the fluorescent tubes twitched into life, bouncing light off the vast concrete floor. The garage was almost exactly the same as the last time I'd seen it. The boiler in the corner and the immersion tank alongside it and the tangle of piping surrounding them both. The empty cubicle shelving behind us. The garage door off to our right.

The garage door was the only thing that had changed. A horizontal dent ran across the central portion of it, at about waist height. The skirt of the door had been shunted back by the force of the impact from the van, lifting it an inch away from the floor and revealing a bar of daylight. Now I understood that Anderson wasn't simply a bad driver. He'd used my van to block off a potential exit.

That only left one way out, and Anderson was about to seal it.

'Sit tight awhile,' he said.

Then he yanked the kitchen door closed behind him and I heard the sound of the key turning in the lock.

Chapter Forty-six

Lukas sagged with relief as he set the gun down on the kitchen table. He hadn't liked holding it. He hadn't welcomed the sensation of having a weapon in his hand or the thought of what it made him capable of. He'd been terrified of having to shoot. First, because he didn't trust his aim or his nerve. Second, because he dreaded the reality of what shooting someone would be like. The gore. The guilt. The queasiness of it all.

The baseball bat had been bad enough. Anderson had made him watch while he beat the woman, and now the man, too. Somehow, he'd kept it together, and he was thankful they hadn't tried to fight back. He hated the idea of what Anderson would have done to them, but more than that, he feared what would have happened to him if they'd overpowered Anderson in some way. He was no fighter. He would have been at their mercy, and who knew what kind of revenge they might have taken?

He stared at the plain white door that separated him from their prisoners. The cheap key protruding from the lock. He'd spent weeks sitting in this dismal kitchen, looking at the exact same door, and now it was all that stood between him and a future he was scared to contemplate. What would Anderson do with the brother? With the female detective? Whatever it turned out to be, Lukas didn't think it would be good.

'Go get your laptop,' Anderson told him. He tossed the

baseball bat on to the kitchen table and reached a hand inside his trouser pocket. He removed the purple memory stick and held it between his finger and thumb, like it was an exotic fruit he'd just plucked. 'Bring it back in here. Let's see what's on this thing.'

Lukas turned and hobbled along the corridor and out into the clearing. The pain from his leg wasn't so bad. Anderson had given him drugs that numbed the feeling in his thigh. His leg felt dull and stiff, and he'd grown used to swinging it from his hip without flexing his knee.

It was silent in the clearing, but he couldn't ignore the urge to check over his shoulder. He didn't feel safe here. It wasn't the woods. It wasn't the isolation. It was the memory of fleeing the first time. Of the two men who'd arrived in a rush and overpowered Pieter. Of the panic and the confusion and the gunfire. It was the knowledge that if they'd done it once, they could do it again any time they liked.

He didn't see anyone, but that didn't mean they weren't there. And maybe it was better for them to come. Maybe it was better for them to overwhelm Anderson in the same way they'd crushed Pieter. That way, he wouldn't have to face up to whatever Anderson would make him do. It would be out of his hands.

Lukas limped over to the Land Rover and opened the passenger door. *Your laptop*, Anderson had said. But his computer equipment had been inside the cottage. It had been taken away by whoever had snatched Lena, along with everything else they'd had with them. The laptop he was left with was the one he'd taken from the brother's home, and it was far less powerful than he was used to. Three years old, at least, and the brother hadn't bothered to update the software or upgrade the processors. It was about as basic and slow as a modern laptop can get. *Your laptop.* It wasn't even close to the type of machine he'd choose for himself.

Lukas snatched it from the passenger seat and held it under the crook of his arm. Shuffled towards the cottage. He didn't look at the white van. He didn't want to think about the brother and the detective trapped inside the garage.

Anderson had taken a seat at the kitchen table by the time Lukas returned. He was toying with the pistol, aiming it towards the light fitting in the ceiling, squinting along his line of sight.

The memory stick was in the middle of the table, close to the handle of the baseball bat. Lukas scraped back a chair and sat down and flipped up the laptop screen. The hard drive purred and chattered. It was noisy and brash. It was painfully slow. The whirring grew louder and a pale-blue visual appeared. The blue washed across Lukas's hands in the murky kitchen as he traced his fingertip over the trackpad and clicked on the user icon. The desktop materialised. Lukas pulled the lid off the memory stick and poked it into the USB port. More purring. More chattering.

A likeness of the memory stick appeared on screen, above the letters *MF. MF* for *Melanie Fleming.* Lukas double-clicked on the icon. A dialogue box ballooned out from it.

Enter password.

Lukas grunted.

'What is it?' Anderson asked, glancing up from the gun.

'The files are encrypted. Password-protected.'

'So enter the password.' Anderson pointed with the muzzle

of the gun towards the memory stick and the sticky label that was attached to it. *For Rob. 9A13D21A.*

Lukas shrugged and his fingers danced across the keys. He typed *9A13D21A* and hit *Enter*.

The laptop processed the information. It was impossibly slow compared to the computing speed Lukas was used to. Then it delivered its verdict. A dissonant sound, followed by a line of red text at the bottom of the dialogue box.

Invalid password. Retry.

Lukas shrugged and typed in *For Rob. 9A13D21A*. Hit *Enter*.

The laptop ran through the cycle once more. It emitted the same rude buzz.

Invalid password. Retry.

'Problem?' Anderson asked. His elbow was propped on the table, the gun hanging loosely from where he'd poked a finger through the trigger guard.

'It doesn't like this password.'

'How many attempts do we have? Could it shut down on us if we keep entering the wrong code?'

Lukas pouted. He considered the garish memory stick, as if the answer might be contained on it. 'Unlikely.'

'Can you check?'

He pouted some more. 'If I had more equipment, then maybe.'

'How long to get the equipment you need?'

'I don't know. It could be difficult over here.'

'So keep trying.'

Lukas did. He entered the password as one complete word: *ForRob9A13D21A*. Didn't work. He tried the same thing again, only in lower case: *forrob9a13d21a*. Same result. He tried the man's name on its own: *Rob*. No go. He tried the man's full name: *Robert Hale*. Nothing. He tried the full name with the numbers. He tried the numbers before the name. All he got was a series of unpleasant dings and the familiar message.

Invalid password. Retry.

'Can you hack it?' Anderson asked.

'Not without my equipment.'

Anderson sighed. Exasperated. He pushed himself to his feet and circled around the table until he was hovering over Lukas's shoulder, one hand on the back of his chair, the hand with the gun braced against the table edge. He considered the dialogue box for a moment. Considered the memory stick.

'So the message is a code,' he said. 'That makes sense, right? Some kind of double protection. This first part, *For Rob*, that just tells us who the code is designed for. But the numbers and the letters, they're the code. So they mean something to the guy.'

'Like what?' Lukas asked.

'That's what I aim to ask him.'

*

I was kneeling on the concrete floor. Not the most comfortable position, but it was easier than trying to lower myself to sit on my backside. I didn't rate the idea of standing for long, and leaning against a wall was out of the question. My shoulder blade hurt like hell. It was throbbing and very hot. It took a seriously good reason for me to move, and when I did move, I tried to remain as stiff as possible, like I was wearing a neck brace. I kept picturing little bits of jagged bone swimming around beneath my skin. Not a reassuring image.

Rebecca was much more active. To begin with, she'd tried to open the garage door, only to find that it wouldn't budge. Now she was crouching near the bottom of the door, squeezing her hands through the gap that had been created by the van's impact. I couldn't see the point. She was doing a good job of scraping the skin from her knuckles but she wasn't achieving much else. If we had access to some screwdrivers, then maybe we could have dismantled the door and removed it from its hinges. But all we had was the wrench hidden in my sling.

'You should leave it,' I said. 'You're wasting energy.'

'Energy for what? We're trapped in here.'

'We have the wrench.'

'Against a baseball bat. And a gun.'

'At least it's something.'

'You can barely move. I can barely see.'

'Yeah, but think what we could achieve if we pool our talents.'

Rebecca gave me a sour look. Not easy with badly swollen eyes and a flattened nose. She twisted her body around to face me. 'I take it you get why they've brought us out here? Why we're locked up like this?'

'I'm guessing it's not good.'

'Come on.' She tugged on her T-shirt, showing me her blood. 'An isolated spot. Somewhere they think one of their men was killed and left to rot.'

'We don't know if that's what really happened.'

'Remember the blood we found in the woods? And look at that Lukas guy. The way he's limping. I reckon he knows from

personal experience that you can get hurt up here without anyone coming to help.'

'Shimmin knows about this place.'

'Yeah, and he was determined to leave it well alone. I don't
think there's much chance of the cavalry arriving.'

'People will see that I'm missing. My parents, for one.'

'It's the middle of the day, Rob. You've been out with me for
the last couple of days. They won't even begin to get worried
until later tonight at the earliest. Maybe not even then.'

She was right. It wasn't as if life was normal for any of us
right now. If I didn't get home to walk or feed Rocky, or to
sleep in my own bed, Mum and Dad would be unlikely to panic
right away. Especially if they thought I was with Rebecca.

She asked, 'Did anyone know you were going to the sports
centre this morning?'

'Nobody.'

'You didn't tell Shimmin about the locker key?'

'It was like I told you, I didn't know who to trust. I kept it to
myself.'

'Perfect.'

She straightened and considered the damage to the backs of
her hands. Sucked on one of her bloodied knuckles.

That was when I heard the scrabble of a key in a lock. Rebecca heard it, too. Her face jerked towards the door and I
shuffled round on my knees.

Anderson stepped into the garage.

He was holding his baseball bat out in front of him like a
sword. Two hands on the grip, right over left, body crouched
and wary. He relaxed when he saw that we weren't planning
to attack him, and he nodded back towards Lukas in the kit-

chen, as if confirming that everything was fine. Lukas released a breath and lowered the gun he was holding, and Anderson nudged the door closed with the end of his bat before pacing further into the room. His swagger returned and so did his grin. I got the impression he enjoyed the sensation of power he had over us. I hoped that might be a good thing. Maybe he'd want to prolong the experience.

'Still here?' he said, and showed a lot of teeth.

'What do you really want?' Rebecca asked. She lowered her knuckle from her mouth. 'You told us you were looking for Lena. But we don't know where she is and holding us here is only going to distract you from finding her.'

His grin became wider. 'We'll find her when it matters.'

'But there's something else going on, isn't there? She's not your primary concern.'

'Interesting,' he said, leaning his head on to his muscular shoulder. 'Now why would you think I'd tell you something like that?'

'Because you're arrogant. Because you want to show us how clever you are.'

'Oh, I'm arrogant,' he agreed. 'You got me. But I don't plan on telling you anything. And, by the way, Lena's really not your concern. Your concern should be how we resolve your situation here.'

'And how do we do that?' I asked.

He smiled down at me, like he was pleased by my response. He drew a small circle in the air with the bat. 'You tell me the code.'

'Excuse me?'

'The code on the flash stick. The one your sister left for you. The one you found this morning.'

'My God,' Rebecca said. 'You can't access the memory stick.' She poked her finger towards Anderson. 'It must be password-protected. And that's your concern. That's what Erik is worried about. Whatever is on that memory stick can harm him in some way.'

'Hmm,' Anderson said. 'Interesting again. Like I care.' He focused hard on me, watching me from over the end of the bat. 'Now, give me the code.'

'I don't know what you're talking about.'

'For Rob,' he said. 'Nine A one three D two one A.'

'If there's a password, that's it,' I said.

'No, that's not it. It's a code for something else. It means something to you.'

I shook my head. 'It means nothing to me.'

'You're lying. Tell me what it means.'

'I don't –'

I didn't get to finish my sentence. Anderson lunged and swung a fast backhand into the centre of my chest. The bat made a hollow *thunk* against my battered ribcage, like he'd struck a waffle ball. It felt a lot more painful. My ribs were still tender and the blow exploded through my solar plexus. I groaned and crumpled and Anderson barked with laughter, then stepped around behind me and jabbed the rounded end of the bat into my busted shoulder. I shrieked and rocked back, but there wasn't enough air in my lungs and the sound came out as a gargled croak. The pain from the two blows merged somewhere in the middle of my torso, roiling around inside.

I knew the next breath I took was going to hurt like crazy. It didn't disappoint.

So much for prolonging things. Suddenly, I wasn't half as keen on the idea.

From the corner of my eye, I saw Rebecca move towards me. Anderson warned her off with a forehand swipe of the bat. She danced backwards, sucking in her stomach, and the blow *swished* through the air.

Anderson conjured a smug smile and lifted my chin with the end of his bat. Pain rippled through the muscles of my shoulder. He leaned down to my face and pressed the bat hard against my throat, constricting my airway.

'You have ten minutes,' he said, and winked at me. 'Then I want the code. I'll break as many bones as it takes until you give me the right answer. Just ask your friend here. She can tell you how much I hate beating on people. And, hey, I really don't want to have to smash your other shoulder, right?'

He smiled like the idea couldn't have appealed to him more. Then he took a series of backwards steps, maintaining eye contact all the way to the door. He slammed it behind him and locked us alone in the garage once more.

Chapter Forty-seven

'Are you OK?' Rebecca asked.

'I'll live.'

She went to place a hand on my shoulder, then thought better of it. 'The guy's a sadist.'

'Tell me about it.'

'That's why he loves using the bat so much. He can dish out pain in instalments. Gauge its effects. It's not so easy for him to do that with the gun.'

I tried to stand but the pain from my shoulder blade was excruciating. It felt like someone had opened a zip that ran lengthways down my back, peeled apart the skin, separated the flesh, and stuck a bunch of razor blades inside. I grunted and rocked forwards on to my good arm, head down, spitting on to the concrete floor. I'd never known pain like it. Every fractional movement sent waves of agony through me.

'Do you know the code?' Rebecca asked me, lowering her voice. 'If you know it, you should tell him. Before he leaves you in pieces.'

'And then what?' I whispered. 'If I tell him what it means, we're no use to them any more.'

'So you *do* know it?'

I glanced towards the door. I was concerned that Anderson might be listening. I didn't want him to hear us. 'Maybe. I'm not sure. It'd be a guess.'

'A guess?'

'An educated one. But I can't tell him what he wants to know without getting someone else involved. And it still won't help us.'

'It might if it's all he needs. Erik has his private jet. They can leave the island whenever they choose. They might leave as soon as you give them the password.'

I shook my head. 'You said it yourself. He's a sadist. And look at Teare. Look at what happened to her.'

'That wasn't Anderson. I was with them the entire night.'

'But it shows how high the stakes are, doesn't it? The lengths people are prepared to go to. And there's something else.' I stared hard at her, breathing fast against the pain, and lowered my voice a fraction more. 'Suppose you're right. Suppose Laura really is alive. We might be the only ones who can help her. She left that code for *me*, not Anderson. She did it for a reason. It has to be important.'

Rebecca studied me for a moment. Her pupils danced behind her swollen eyes. Her skin was bunched up loosely above the bridge of her nose. I could see a pale glint of bone amid the dried blood and the yellow-green bruising.

'So what do you suggest?' she hissed.

'The boiler,' I said, and motioned to it with my eyes. 'If we take the cover off, I can undo the safety valve. That'll release some oil. We can cause an explosion.'

She backed off. 'How big an explosion?'

'Big.'

She shook her head. 'Bad idea. We're in a confined space. Nowhere to shelter. It puts us in as much danger as them.'

'We're in danger already. How much worse can it get?'

She shook her head some more. 'To even have a chance with something like that, you'd need to time it exactly. You'd need to lure Anderson in front of the thing and then ignite it. And you'd still be endangering us.'

'What other choice do we have?'

'The wrench,' Rebecca murmured. 'Give it to me.'

'Easier if you take it yourself.'

Rebecca reached down and eased a hand under my hoodie. Her forearm snaked up over my abdomen, until all I could see was her elbow.

'Careful,' I said.

'Got it.' She withdrew the wrench from my sling in one fluid movement. 'It's solid.' She slapped it against her palm.

It was one hell of an old thing, probably a tool I'd inherited from Dad. The metal was oxidised and dulled down to matt brown. It weighed a couple of kilos, at least, and most of the weight was in the U-shaped head.

'But it's short.' She rolled out her bottom lip. 'Anderson's bat makes his reach much longer.'

'So I'll surprise him. I'll stand behind the door and I'll hit him when he comes in.'

'Nuh-uh. *I'll* hit him.'

I went to argue, but Rebecca got to her feet and stepped beyond my reach. She held the wrench in her right hand, experimenting with a few practice swings.

She said, 'We get one shot at this. And we have to get it right. We have to disable him in one move. You're not up to it. You can't even stand.'

'I'll make myself.'

'And your reach is all wrong. If you hide behind the door,

you need to swing from your left side. But you can't with your arm in a sling. I don't think you could even hold this wrench, let alone hit him with it.'

'So I'll hold it in my right hand. I'll step out and I'll catch him unawares. The surprise gives me time.'

'Not enough.' She shook her head. 'And I've had training in this sort of situation. Chances are you'll want to hit him hard enough to stun him, but not so hard that you do real damage. I'm different. We can't afford to go easy on him, and I won't. Besides, I want payback.'

I considered her face, the blood and the bruising and the swelling. I ran through everything she'd just said. I would have liked to argue with her some more, but I already knew she was right. Anderson could come through the door at any moment, and I was still on my knees.

'What about Lukas? He has the gun.'

'He didn't look like he wanted to use it.'

'If it comes down to us against him, I think he will.'

'Then as soon as I've hit Anderson, I'll shut the door. We'll have a hostage. He'll have to back down.'

'You think?'

'Trust me. I know what I'm doing.'

*

Lukas wasn't making any progress. The password variations he'd tried had all resulted in the same failure. If he'd had more time, he might have downloaded a decoder engine from the web. But he doubted a simple programme would be good enough, so what was the point?

Anderson was standing next to the door into the garage, pressing his ear against the wood. He was holding the baseball bat crossways in front of him, his knuckles bunched around the shaft, twisting it between his hands like he was wringing water from a towel. The lacquered timber creaked against his palms.

'Time's nearly up,' Anderson said, stepping away from the door. 'You getting anywhere?'

'I need the code.'

'Then the guy's going to have to give it to us.'

Anderson tossed the baseball bat in the air, twirling it around a half-turn and catching it one-handed, then repeating the process. He was no majorette. The wood slapped loudly against his palm. But at least it was a world away from the noise of the bat striking the woman's face.

'Listen up,' he said. He caught the bat and extended it towards Lukas, squinting along its length like a swordsman sizing up an opponent. 'Our problem is, they're expecting me. I couldn't hear much of what they were saying, but it sounds like one of them is going to attack me from behind the door.' He lowered the bat and jerked his thumb at his chest. 'That's what I'd do if I was them.'

Lukas nodded. As if the suggestion made sense. As if that was what he'd do, too. But in his heart he knew it was a lie. Lukas wasn't the type to fight back. If he was in their shoes, he'd have given the code up by now.

'There are ways to counter the move. Best way is to come in via another route. That's not an option here. So we're going to go with the next best alternative. I'm going to unlock the door and then I'm going to kick it hard. If one of them is behind it, they'll be hurt. It could be I can keep them pressed there. If I can't, they'll be stunned and I can follow up with the bat.' He cocked his wrists and twisted at the waist, practising his swing. 'But basically, it's the same procedure as before. I want you to cover me with the gun again.'

Anderson gathered the pistol from the kitchen table. He lifted it by the barrel, holding the butt out to Lukas, the bat in his other hand. 'You're confident with how this works, right? If they come at me this time, we don't want any mistakes. You looked a little shaky before.'

He wasn't confident. Not really. 'Pieter showed me.'

'Good. I want you to stand behind me, like last time. But leave a little more room so's I can swing the bat. If they try anything, if they come at me at all, I want you to fire into the ceiling. One round. That should be enough to stop them. After that, use your judgement.'

Your judgement. Lukas didn't like the idea. He didn't want the gun in the first place. Most especially, he didn't want to find himself shooting if there was a chance he might hit Anderson.

'Why don't you take the gun?' he asked.

'Because the bat is better. I don't want them dead. Not yet. Not until they give us the code. And it's not like they have a weapon. You checked them, remember?'

Anderson narrowed his eyes. Prodded the pistol towards him. Lukas felt himself reach out and close wet fingers around the stippled grip.

'We clear?' Anderson asked.

He placed his hands on Lukas and shifted him into position once more. He had him turn sideways on, left foot in front of the right, arms in the air parallel with his chin. Exactly like Pieter had taught him.

'Relax,' Anderson said, flicking the safety off. 'You're insurance, that's all. This is gonna be easy. And once we have the code, we're golden. Mr Zeeger will be one very happy man.'

Anderson patted Lukas on the cheek, then turned and faced the door. He circled his head on his shoulders. Cleared his throat. Then he hoisted the bat in the air and reached for the key in the lock.

Chapter Forty-eight

On her way across the room, I watched Rebecca revise her plan. First, she moved to her right, ready to flatten herself against the wall on the hinge side of the door. Then she paused and pressed the tip of the wrench against her chin, and wavered for a moment considering the set-up. She turned and contemplated the wooden shelving units. The units were constructed from white laminate and they were square and empty. They ran along the entire length of the wall from the garage door to the kitchen doorway, next to where the light cord was hanging. They extended to within about a foot of the ceiling.

Rebecca stepped forwards and began scaling the shelving unit, close to the door. The shelves formed a makeshift stepladder and she climbed until her feet were on the second shelf from the top. She ducked her head and tried to hitch her left leg up and fit herself into the space beneath the ceiling. She couldn't do it. The unit was too narrow and the space was too cramped. She backed up and climbed down a little, so that her left foot was on the second highest shelf and her right foot was on the third highest. She braced her left arm on top of the unit and reached out with the wrench in her right hand. She was perfectly positioned to swing down and strike someone on the head.

Two problems with that. One, her position was precarious, and I wasn't sure how long she could hold the pose. And two, anyone coming through the door had a good chance of seeing her before she could hit them. It was a major downside, which is why I'd suggested hiding behind the door in the first place. But I could understand her concern. If Anderson was alert to the danger, he could kick the door open and crush her behind it. And anyway, Rebecca wasn't finished just yet. She reached out and carefully plucked the light cord downwards, so that the garage fell into full darkness with just the barest *click*.

At first, the blackness was absolute. All I could see was the red light on the front of the boiler and the band of daylight beneath the garage door. Then I began to make out shapes and angles. The rough outline of the shelves materialised from the gloom. Rebecca's leather jacket was a more lustrous black than the rest of the room, and it was visible as a deeper, liquid shade. And I could see her pale face, pressed against the side of the unit, and the grey patches of her hands. But the wrench was impossible to pick out.

I knew that when Anderson opened the door, there'd be some light spill from the kitchen. But I also knew from experience that the kitchen was far from bright and airy, and besides, the real purpose of the exercise was surprise. He wouldn't be expecting darkness. He wouldn't expect Rebecca to be halfway up the wall. I thought it was just about the best chance we had, short of me recovering in time to contribute something.

I couldn't see that happening. The darkness and the silence did very little to distract me from the suffering I was going through. I would have liked to duck behind the door and double up our attack, but Rebecca was right, it was beyond me.

But I still wanted to stand.

It seemed to me I had a couple of options. I could take it

slow and easy, or fast and hard. Slow and easy was no guarantee of success. And it wouldn't get me out of the firing line in a hurry if Lukas or Anderson decided to use the gun. Fast and hard was the right way to go.

I went for it on an out-breath. It wouldn't have been my normal approach. In a scenario where I could make as much noise as I liked, I'd have sucked in a deep lungful of air, gritted my teeth, and then yowled and cursed my way upright. Moving on an out-breath meant I wouldn't have so much oxygen to complain with.

Or so I hoped.

I complained in my head, believe me. I swore and I screamed and I yelled. But the only sound I made was a strained grunt. I pushed up in one fluid movement. Fast and hard. Painful as hell. I was up before the full force of the pain hit me. And then I staggered backwards and curled up and straightened instantly, and bit my tongue and stamped my foot and tried my hardest to keep things in focus.

If the room hadn't already been dark, I have a feeling it would have turned a lot blacker. I'm pretty sure I was close to passing out. But I stayed on my feet and I fixed my jaw and endured the discomfort until I realised it couldn't get any worse.

I was up. I was breathing.

All we needed now was for Anderson to make his move.

He made it right away.

I was still adjusting my feet beneath me and catching my breath when the key turned in the lock and the door handle squeaked and there was a sudden hard slam. Before I knew it the door had bounced off the wall and was starting to sway back and Anderson had surged into the room.

He did a few things wrong. First, he was anticipating that there'd be someone behind the door, so he instinctively turned his body to his left, ready to confront the threat. But the threat wasn't in front of him, it was behind him. He had to raise his arm to protect himself from the door blasting back into his face, and that cost him time and momentum. He couldn't lash out with his baseball bat while he was blocking the door. And he hadn't anticipated the darkness. His chin jutted forwards as he peered into the gloom.

The forward motion of his chin coincided with Rebecca's arm completing the fast arc it had been swinging through. The moment the door had opened, I'd seen in the ambient light from the kitchen how her arm had pivoted back behind her shoulder, how the mass of the wrench had extended her wrist, how her wrist had then absorbed the force and whipped back against it, how the sudden thrust had reversed the direction of her arm, how the wrench had swung forward like a pendulum, how her face had tightened, teeth bared, with the exertion of the move.

Then I saw the wrench make contact with the right-hand side of Anderson's lower jaw. A wild blow. A shattering impact. His jaw bone seemed to compress and explode all in the same moment. His head snapped back like he'd run into an invisible wall. He made a choked, gargled noise, and there was a loud *crack* from the shattered bone.

Momentum carried the wrench on. It completed its fast arc in a mist of blood and saliva, the velocity and the savageness almost pulling Rebecca clean off the shelving unit. Then the swing reached its peak and the pendulum effect kicked in and

I saw her wrist flex and pivot and reverse, and the wrench came flying back in a brutal backhand stroke.

The wrench struck Anderson's skull somewhere behind his right ear. The sound was sickening. A soggy *crunch*. But what sickened me more was the way the wrench stopped moving. It stopped instantly. Cutting Rebecca's mighty effort dead at the point of impact.

I know basic physics. I remember it from school. Force doesn't just disappear. It can't simply vanish. But it can be transferred. So all the force that had been in Rebecca's arm, concentrated on the wrench, was now in Anderson's head. It was thrashing around inside his skull. Bouncing off plate bone and brain matter and nerve endings. Radiating out like the percussive waves from a bomb blast.

I know about head injuries, too. Recent experience had taught me about those. I know about blunt trauma. Swelling of the brain. Secondary bruising. Unconsciousness. Coma. Death. I know the dangers. I've lived them myself. Now I was seeing them in action.

Anderson dropped. He went down heavily, straight to his knees. The baseball bat fell from his hands and bounced once on the concrete and toppled over and rolled harmlessly away. His arms hung limply by his sides. He knelt there for a moment, like a puppet on hidden strings, and then the weight of his head pitched him forwards and his upper body folded and he fell smack on his shattered jaw with a disturbing *crunch-crack*.

Rebecca's balance was gone. She was half falling, half jumping from the shelves. She was looking at Anderson, surveying the damage she'd caused, maybe asking herself if she'd killed the

340

guy. She was getting ready to nail her landing and crouch down beside him and see what could be done.

Then there was a blinding flash of light and a deafening *boom* and a hail of dust and debris rained down from the ceiling. I ducked and covered my head with my free arm as chunks of plaster and ceiling board fell around us. I raised my eyes and squinted out through fresh pain and powdery devastation and saw Lukas standing beside the kitchen table, smoke curling around his face from the pistol at the end of his arms.

He released the Beretta the moment our eyes locked. It clattered against the linoleum with just the barest *tap-tap* because of the thick swirl of noise jamming my hearing. He stumbled backwards. Lifted his hands in the air. Then his wide eyes flicked down to where Anderson lay prone on the floor and the colour left his face so completely that he looked like a figure in a waxwork museum.

Rebecca was up and moving through the haze of dry particles suspended in the air. She vaulted Anderson and lunged towards the kitchen floor and scooped up the gun with her hands all in one fluid movement. She crowded Lukas, holding the pistol in a two-handed grip, her arms sloping down from her shoulders.

'ON YOUR KNEES, ON YOUR KNEES, ON YOUR KNEES,' she screamed. 'DOWN, DOWN, DOWN. NOW. MOVE. ON YOUR KNEES.'

Lukas slumped down hard on one knee, with his bad leg stretched out in front of him, and placed his hands on the back of his neck. He lowered his face to the floor, like a penitent, and Rebecca held the muzzle of the pistol just an inch from his scalp.

341

I was on my feet, too. Moving through the falling debris towards Anderson. Human nature, I suppose. He was someone in trouble. I thought I might be able to help.

I was wrong.

Plaster and dust coated his hair but I could immediately tell that the back of his skull was mush. Blood was draining freely from the wound. And when I placed two fingers against the side of his neck, his pulse was a barely-there flutter. The tempo was irregular and feeble.

Then it stopped altogether.

Chapter Forty-nine

'Do you have any tape? Rob? Any tape or ropes in your van?'

I gazed up from Anderson's body. Rebecca was motioning towards Lukas with the gun.

'Gaffer tape,' she said. 'Anything like that. In your van.'

I nodded dumbly.

'Good.' She nudged Lukas with the toe of her shoe. 'Where are the keys?'

'He has them,' Lukas muttered.

The 'he' was Anderson. Lukas was keeping his head down, his hair shielding his face, his eyes fixed on a mid-point on the linoleum floor. I was pretty sure he'd already seen the state of his partner's head. I was pretty sure he didn't want to look at it again.

'Can you check him, Rob?'

I didn't want to, but I could, and I was going to have to do it. I remembered how Anderson had held the bat. He was right-handed. I worked my hand down his right side and into his trouser pockets. Found his wallet. Some loose change. No keys.

I moved around his other side. Moving wasn't hurting me so much just now. I guessed adrenalin must have flooded my system. It was functioning like a cortisone jab right inside the muscle and tissue surrounding my shoulder blade.

My van keys were inside Anderson's left-hand trouser pocket. I clasped them tight and shuffled past Rebecca and Lukas and along the hall like an injured man hurrying from a fire. The air outside felt sweet and good. I drank it in, brushing the plaster dust out of my hair and off my clothes, scrubbing my palm over my face. Then I unlocked my van and circled around to the sliding door, hauled it back and scrambled inside to where I keep my plumbing tape. I have all kinds. Teflon tape for sealing a leaky tap. Masking tape in case I need to drill holes. Electrical tape for wiring in boilers and thermostats. And several large rolls of gaffer tape for emergencies.

I grabbed the thickest roll and the craft knife Rebecca had dropped. The tape was grey, webbed with cotton fibres that gave it a very high tensile strength. Excellent for a quick fix when a pipe has burst. Even better for restraining a man.

I returned to the kitchen and exchanged the tape and the knife for the Beretta. The pain in my shoulder and chest might have begun to subside, but binding Lukas was a two-handed job and I wasn't qualified for it. I held the gun on him while Rebecca yanked his arms behind his back and wrapped the tape around his wrists.

I felt strangely relieved that Lukas had fired the pistol. Anderson's death didn't sit easily with my conscience, let alone the law, but the gunfire would help us to argue that we'd been acting in self-defence. I believed that to be the case. We'd both been scared, and for good reason, but there was a part of me that wondered if Rebecca had needed to go as far as she had. She'd been right in what she'd said. If our roles had been reversed, I would have looked to overpower Anderson but I wouldn't have wanted to be responsible for inflicting a serious injury, let alone a terminal one. But Rebecca hadn't shared my concerns. She'd hit him with everything she had, and everything she had was easily enough to kill a man.

Rebecca finished with Lukas's wrists. She'd looped the tape around tight enough to whiten and swell the surrounding skin. Before long, it would start to throb. In a couple of hours, it could be a problem. I wondered how much of her reaction was revenge for what Anderson and Lukas had done to her face. Quite a lot, I guessed.

She moved on to Lukas's ankles. She had him sit down on his backside and straighten both legs and then she peeled a new length of tape and got to work.

I was still pointing the gun at Lukas but my attention had been drawn to the kitchen table. My laptop was there, the one that had been taken from my home. The gaudy purple memory stick was poking out the side of it.

'You stole my laptop?' I asked him.

He nodded, but he wouldn't meet my eyes.

'Why?'

'Because of your sister,' he said.

'Did she help you to hide Lena?'

Lukas nodded. 'She came to Mr Zeeger. She wished to protect Lena. But we knew her by a different name.'

'Melanie Fleming.'

He seemed surprised by how much I knew. 'She would visit us here. Check on us. Bring us things.'

'For how long?'

He shrugged, the movement restricted because of the way Rebecca had bound his arms. 'A month, maybe. Every few days she would come. Then she stopped. We could not find her. We did not know why.'

I was a little surprised by what Lukas had said. It meant Laura had been on the island far longer than we'd realised. She'd stayed with us at the care home for two days before her death at Marine Drive. Mum had mentioned how exhausted she'd been. Perhaps now I knew why. She'd been running errands to the cottage. Maybe dividing her time between London and the plantation. All for Lena's benefit.

Lukas glanced down at his lap. 'I am sorry that she is dead.'

I didn't say anything to that. I didn't tell him that Rebecca had her doubts. That those doubts had been planted in my brain. That they'd begun to take root and to grow. That I wondered if there was a chance that the data on the memory stick would tell us where we might find my sister. That I hoped I might see her again.

'Should I tape his mouth?' Rebecca asked.

'What are we going to do with him?'

'I think we should take him with us.'

'Then tape it. We don't want him shouting from the back of the van.'

Rebecca used the knife to slice off a swatch of tape. Before applying it, she asked Lukas one final question.

'Where's Erik?'

He hesitated.

Rebecca pinched his chin between her finger and thumb and moved his head until he was forced to look at Anderson's prone body.

'Where's Erik?' she asked again.

'A hotel,' he stammered. 'In Douglas. A big one. Next to a theatre.'

'The Sefton?' I asked.

'Yes. I think so.'

'Good,' Rebecca said, and then she reached up and smoothed the strip of tape carefully over his lips, pressing it down hard as he moaned in complaint. His nostrils remained clear and he'd need to keep them that way. Rebecca had done a comprehensive job of restraining him. 'Get up.'

Lukas grunted and struggled for a moment before Rebecca heaved him to his feet. She motioned me across and I handed her the gun. Then she poked the muzzle into Lukas's side and he hopped along the corridor between us.

Once we were outside, I had him clamber inside my van on his elbows and knees and then I closed the door behind him. When I turned around, Rebecca's hands were behind her back, hitching up her jacket and slipping the Beretta into the waistband of her jeans. She tilted her face to the daylight, as if it might help her bruising to heal. She was rotating her jaw and I thought I knew why. I had the same problem. Grit between my teeth and gums from all the dust and debris.

'What now?' I asked.

'Now we go back inside for your laptop. Tidy up.'

Tidying didn't take long. I watched as Rebecca stepped over Anderson's body and grabbed him by the ankles. She ducked down and dragged him a few feet, trailing a wavering slick of blood on the floor. I thought at first she was intending to hide the body, but then I realised she was moving it just enough to be able to close the kitchen door. She dropped his legs and gathered the wrench from the floor. Then she locked the door behind us before handing the wrench to me and telling me to go and lose it somewhere in the woods.

I was as quick as I could be. The wrench wasn't something I

wanted to hold on to. The curved end was coated in blood and fluids, congealed strands of hair and fragments of skin. I held it down and away from my body, so that the blood couldn't drip on to my hand. The thing felt heavier than it had any right to.

I tramped unsteadily into the woods, the uneven ground jolting my back and shoulder, making me wince and grimace, until I could no longer see the cottage behind me. I thought about just abandoning the wrench where I stood, then I changed my mind and scanned the area around my feet. Leaves and branches and ferns and pine needles. But there was also a hollow beneath the exposed roots of a nearby tree. A warren of some kind. It was deep enough and dark enough to swallow the wrench, and I dropped it and used my foot to nudge it in as far as I could, leaving it there.

I was still wiping my palm clean against my hoodie when I got back to the cottage. The front door was closed and Rebecca was sitting in the driver's seat of my van. She had my laptop with her, propped against the steering wheel. I opened the passenger door and struggled up into the cab and studied the screen.

There was a dialogue box right in the middle. A cursor was flashing inside the box. Beside it were the words: *Enter password*.

'So,' Rebecca said, 'what's the code?'

I opened the glove box beside my knees and pulled out my mobile. I flipped up the screen and found that I had six missed calls, all from Dad. I ignored them and punched a few buttons. Then I raised the phone to my ear and listened to it ring.

Chapter Fifty

My parents' care home is wired up with six telephone lines with separate numbers, and Grandpa has one of them. He keeps his phone on the windowsill in his room, beside his armchair. It's a luxury that none of the other residents are permitted, and truth be told, it's an unnecessary one. I could count the outgoing calls Grandpa makes in the average month on the fingers of one hand, and I suspect his incoming calls are even fewer. But it's a privilege he likes to crow about, and so whenever he *does* receive a call, he makes something of a ceremony out of answering.

For starters, he never answers right away. If he did, none of the neighbouring residents would know about the phone in his room. Then, when he does answer, he likes to recite his telephone number in a strangely formal way, like an old-fashioned radio presenter.

I was treated to the same routine today. First, the delay while his phone rang on and on, then the carefully remembered and even more carefully pronounced sequence of numbers.

'Grandpa, it's Rob,' I said, when he was finally finished.

'Who?'

'Rob. Your grandson.'

'Oh. Hello my boy. Are you looking for Rocky? I could hear him barking for company, so I went and fetched him.'

I seriously doubted that. Rocky doesn't tend to bark at home, least of all when he's bored. He simply sleeps. And the only way Grandpa would have heard him was if he'd left his room and crossed the garden to my front door. It was much more likely that Grandpa had been the one wanting company. And that he'd let himself into my place to get it.

'It's OK,' I said. 'That's not why I'm calling.'

'Are you with that pretty detective?'

'Yes, Grandpa. Rebecca's here. That's why I'm on the phone. I need you to check something for me.'

'Go ahead, my boy.'

'Your crossword-puzzle book. Can you fetch it for me?'

Silence.

'Can you just take a look, Grandpa?'

He knew the book I meant. He'd been working on it since the beginning of the year, one puzzle a day. It was an annual compendium of 365 puzzles published in large print, on cheap paper. It had become a family tradition for me and Laura to buy him a new edition as a joint present every Christmas. We'd done it since we were kids.

'Have you got it?' I asked.

I heard the clatter of the telephone receiver being placed on the windowsill. Then some mumbling and grunting. When he eventually came back on the line, he was wheezing.

'Got it,' he said.

'Great. Can you turn to the puzzle on the back page?'

I heard the flutter of pages. Then a pause.

'Have you been filling in my puzzles again?'

I closed my eyes. 'Is there writing there?'

'It's all filled in already. Did you do this? I asked you not to do this any more.'

'It wasn't me, Grandpa. I think you're looking at Laura's handwriting.'

There was an audible intake of breath on the end of the line. A long silence. I could picture Grandpa tracing his fingers over the letters in the little puzzle squares, peering down at them through his magnifying glass. I didn't want to imagine what his face looked like as he did it. He'd seen Laura's handwriting on birthday cards and Christmas cards enough times to recognise it. This time would be different. This time would sting.

'I'm sorry,' I said.

More silence. I'd spoken about Laura's death with Grandpa more than with my parents. But Grandpa hadn't said a lot back. He'd listened and he'd nodded. He'd smiled and he'd cried. But it had been too much for him to share his own memories. And now I didn't doubt that some of the most powerful were flooding right back. Perhaps he was seeing Laura and me, lying on the floor of his room, crayons and pencils in our hands, giggling as we defaced his puzzle books. I was seeing those memories myself. Laura had known that I would. That was why she'd left the code for me.

'Grandpa, I need you to read out some of what's been written there. It's important. Can you do that for me?'

'I don't understand.'

'I know,' I said. 'It's a lot to take in. And I'm sorry not to be there with you, but I promise I'll explain later.'

'When did your sister do this?'

'A few weeks ago, I think. When she was staying with us.'

There was no need for me to mention that it would have been during the last few days before her death.

I glanced down at the memory stick poking out of my laptop. Checked the code. *9A13D21A*.

'I need to know three of the answers that are written in the puzzle, Grandpa. The first one is nine across. Can you tell me what it says?'

'Nine . . . across,' he said. 'Might drip. Three letters.'

'No Grandpa. Not the clue. I need the answer. The clue doesn't matter.'

'The answer must be *Tap*.'

'No, I know,' I said, trying not to sound impatient. 'But what has Laura written?'

I waited a moment. When he spoke again, he sounded confused. 'Well, that's not right.'

'What's not right, Grandpa? What did she write?'

'*The*.'

'Just *The*?'

'Yes, but that doesn't make any sense. The answer is *Tap*. I never understood why you two couldn't get the simplest of clues.'

'It's OK,' I told him, gazing out through the windscreen towards the trees on the other side of the clearing. 'I know it doesn't make sense, but this is really helpful. There's just two more to go. The next one is thirteen down.'

'And you don't want the clue?'

'No Grandpa, just the answer.'

'*Missing*.'

'*Missing*. That's what she's written?'

'*Missing*. Yes. But it doesn't match the clue.'

I shook my head. Glanced down at the memory stick. *21A*.

'Last one, Grandpa. Twenty-one across. What answer did Laura give?'

'She's written *Dog*.'

'*Dog*,' I repeated. '*The Missing Dog*. Is that it, Grandpa? Nothing else?'

'That's what it says here. But the answer isn't *Dog*. It's *Dim*.'

'I know Grandpa. It seems stupid. But you've been really helpful. I've got to go. Will you give Rocky a pat for me?'

'Not bright. Three letters. The answer is *Dim*.'

'OK Gramps. I've really got to go now.'

I cut the connection. Looked across at Rebecca. She'd already typed in the three words. *The Missing Dog*. She half smiled at me. Hit *Enter*.

The laptop made a croaking, whirring noise. Then a bum note sounded and the dialogue box redrew itself.

Invalid password. Retry.

'Crap,' Rebecca said.

'Try it without the spaces this time.'

Rebecca shrugged. She typed *themissingdog* and pressed *Enter*.

Another croak. Another whir. Another bum note.

Invalid password. Retry.

'Could your grandpa have given you the wrong answers?' she asked me.

He had. He'd done exactly that, because it was what I'd asked him for. Laura's *wrong* answers. She'd filled them in the same way as we had when we were kids. But maybe this time I needed the *right* answers. Grandpa had said the answer to the first clue should have been *Tap*. The answer to the final clue was *Dim*. In which case, I needed to ring Grandpa back and ask what the second clue had been. The one for thirteen down. It had to be a seven-letter word. Not *Missing*, but . . .

I was just flipping open my phone, about to redial Grandpa's number, when I froze and realised what I'd overlooked. I hadn't made a mistake. My first instinct had been correct. But *The Missing Dog* wasn't the password. It was another clue.

I grabbed the laptop from Rebecca and pointed through the windscreen towards the muddy track.

'Drive,' I told her.

'What?'

'Just go. I'll tell you when to stop.'

Chapter Fifty-one

Lena had been waiting a long time. Her waiting had been intense. She couldn't relax for a second. She couldn't allow her attention to slip. The door might open at any moment. She had no way of telling when it could be.

The talk-radio fan seemed much stricter than the pizza guy. He'd kept her in the soundproofed room by herself. He'd made sure the door was locked. He'd barely communicated with her at all.

The soundproofing had gone from being her biggest ally to her greatest problem. It meant she had no way of hearing the guy approach. She couldn't listen for his footfall. She couldn't feel the vibration of his steps through the rubber underlay. The only chance she had of attracting his attention was to shout and scream very loudly. But if she did that, he'd be fully on his guard when he opened the door.

Lena wanted him relaxed. She wanted him casual. She needed him that way because the damage to the window was clear and obvious. As soon as he saw the smashed glass, he'd know something was wrong. He'd react. And Lena needed to react quicker.

She was sitting with her back against the rubber tiles, right next to where the door would open. She'd started off standing but the effort had become too much. The nervous tension had caused muscle fatigue. The fatigue would cause cramp. And she couldn't afford that. So now she was alternating between standing and sitting, and she was currently in a sitting phase. The sitting didn't trouble her. She could cause just as much damage lower down as she could higher up.

She'd decided there were three key elements to what she needed to do once the guy opened the door.

Number One was speed. She needed to respond instantly. Before the guy saw the window. Before he sensed how close she was to him.

Number Two was aggression. She had to be violent. She had to be mean. She had to cause as much damage as she physically could in as short a period of time as possible.

Number Three was movement. Whatever else happened, she had to get herself between the guy and the door. She had to throw herself into the space. She had to ensure he couldn't shut the door. This was the most important element of all. If he managed to close the door, if he was able to lock it, then her one and only opportunity would be gone. She'd be stuck for good. All her planning and all her thinking would be wasted.

She'd decided all this a long time ago. Hours had passed. They'd crept slowly by. And all the while her body had been under stress. Her heart had been hammering against her ribcage. Her breathing shallow. Her nerves frayed.

She'd been clutching the jagged shard of glass in her hand for so long that it felt as if her fingers had numbed. Her fingertips were bleeding badly from where she'd sliced herself and snagged her nails while trying to prise the glass out of the window. The blood had trickled down her wrist. It had dried against her skin. It was sticking to her like a second skin. Like the opaque film on the back of the window.

She'd used the blade of glass to shred the pink duvet cover into strips. She'd applied some of the strips to clean the worst of the blood from her hands. The rest she'd wrapped around the end of the glass shard to form a tightly wadded handle, like the hilt on a dagger. It worked pretty well. She was pleased with the result. And she knew for a fact how sharp the blade was. The shard was broadly triangular and it was notched and barbed. It was approximately twenty centimetres in length. It was capable of inflicting serious harm.

Lena wasn't squeamish. She wasn't the least bit fazed by the prospect of stabbing the man. The last few months had taught her certain things. They'd taught her that her life could be snatched from her in an instant. They'd shown her that there were people in the world who were prepared to put their own interests ahead of her liberty. They'd proved to her that she had to fight hard to protect herself and that she couldn't rely on other people to do it for her.

She hadn't been able to rely on Melanie Fleming. She hadn't been able to rely on Pieter and Lukas. She hadn't been able to rely on the plumber Melanie had told her to contact if anything happened to her. And she most definitely hadn't been able to rely on her father.

Her father claimed to love her, but his love was a crushing, controlling force. She'd tried to explain this to Melanie. Tried to make her see that involving her father and his men in her safety was a terrible mistake. But Melanie had insisted, said they needed the resources, and now she knew for certain that Alex had been right all along. The important thing was to rely on yourself. Trust in yourself. Invest your faith only in those people you believed in absolutely.

357

The only person Lena had ever felt that way about was Alex. But now Alex was gone, so she was left with the next best thing. She was left with herself, and after that she was left with the people Alex had truly trusted. The ones he'd made her promise to call if ever she was in genuine peril. He'd made her memorise the telephone number. Made her recount the sequence over and over until she knew it by heart. She'd never met the man who would answer but she knew his name and she knew that she could trust him. She knew it because Alex had told her so.

The bolt shunted back in the door before she was ready for it. All the hours of waiting and she'd lost concentration just when it mattered most.

The door opened and the man took one step inside and she felt the long delay in her reaction like she was watching the scene unfold in slow motion.

She saw the man turn his head.

Saw him register the damage to the window.

Saw him frown and recoil in confusion.

Saw his hand grasp the door handle.

Saw him shift his weight and lean backwards and start to yank the door shut.

That was when she finally reacted. When she moved.

Key element Number One was over. She'd failed to show speed.

But that just made elements Numbers Two and Three doubly important.

Number Two was aggression. She had plenty of that. She screamed and twisted at the waist and wrenched the glass shard around in a mighty swing. She gave it everything she had. Gave it thrust. Gave it weight. She drove it deep inside his inner thigh.

The blade disappeared up to her fingers. She felt his torn flesh. His warm blood.

The spread of blood was immediate. It was pulsing. It squirted out of the wound and soaked into his tan chinos and pooled towards his groin.

She still had a hold of the blade. Tried to pull it out for a second stab. The glass was stuck fast.

Then the man howled and crumpled, ducking to clutch at his thigh with both hands. He slumped to the ground, wedging the door open with his back. He was taking care of element Number Three all by himself. His teeth were bared in a snarl. His gums were exposed. His eyes were squeezed tightly shut and he was yelling in a ragged baritone.

Lena pushed up from the floor. She vaulted the man and ran heavy-limbed through the apartment and scrabbled with the lock on the front door. She didn't need a key. Only the snap lock was engaged.

The door opened on to a deserted hallway. It was cold and there was a lot of bare concrete. An elevator was in front of her but the metal doors were dented and the light inside the call button didn't work and Lena wasn't prepared to trust it. She found a litter-strewn staircase at the end of the hall. Maybe fifty storeys to run down in her socks. Maybe one hundred flights of stairs. She looked back to the elevator. Back to the apartment door. She could hear the man hollering in pain.

Lena fled.

Chapter Fifty-two

There was a creaking, scraping noise as Rebecca eased the van away from the garage door, followed by the tinkle of falling plastic from the broken light clusters. I checked the view in my side mirror. White paint had been scratched and scraped clean from around the horizontal crease that had been imprinted in the door. But the door was still closed. Only the slight gap at the bottom remained. I didn't think anyone would find Anderson's body in a hurry.

Rebecca steered the van through the gateway at the entrance to the clearing. She followed the narrow track down through the woods. The van bounced and bounded over the stony ground. It rolled and rocked and teetered. My bad shoulder banged against my seat in a way that jarred and smarted.

But I didn't care.

Laura had reached out to me. She'd left the code, knowing that I was the only one who could possibly understand it. She was talking to me. Trusting me. And now I was repaying her trust. Deciphering her message.

I was sure that the solution to the code was at the end of the path. It was tacked to the gate post, hidden in plain sight. It was the laminated sign about the scrappy terrier who'd been lost in the woods.

Laura knew what I was like – how much I loved dogs. She knew that if Lena ever called me up to the cottage, I'd pay attention to the poster. She knew the plight of the missing dog would affect me. Knew it was something I'd remember.

I had Rebecca drive through the gate and come to a stop. She was irritable and frustrated, but I turned from her without explanation and hopped down from the cab. I walked back to the gate. Plucked the sign from the post. I looked at the photograph of the little terrier, its pink tongue hanging from its mouth, its head on an angle, ears raised as if it was listening to some distant command.

I read the printed message.

Please help us to find Chester. Missing 5 April in this plantation.

The message was followed by a telephone number. The number was for a Manx mobile. No area code.

Fifth April. Exactly two days before Laura's accident.

I climbed back up into the cab and hauled my door closed. Then I passed Rebecca the laptop and showed her the crinkled poster.

'Try *Chester*,' I said.

'Are you serious?'

'The missing dog. This poster has been here since I first came up to the cottage. I think Laura created it. I think she left it for me to find.'

'It's a hell of a risk. Anyone could have taken it down.'

'They could have, but they didn't. Try it. Type *Chester*.'

Rebecca sucked on her cheeks, then flipped open the laptop and typed the word *Chester* into the dialogue box that appeared on screen. Her hand hovered over the keyboard. She hit *Enter*.

The laptop croaked. It whirred. Then it emitted a sound. A new one. No bum note this time. It was a jaunty, upbeat *ding*.

The dialogue box expanded on the screen. An icon appeared.

'MPEG,' Rebecca said, as if she might have expected as much. 'A video file.'

'So what are we waiting for? Play it.'

*

The guy with the shard of glass in his leg had got a hold of himself. At first, he'd panicked. That was something he couldn't deny. The pain had been immediate and startling, and the sight of the glass poking out of him had been sickening, but it was the blood that had really scared him. The sheer volume of it. He knew there were a lot of major arteries and veins collected around the inner thigh. He knew that a severe loss of blood could cause death within minutes. So his reaction had been understandable. But he knew it wouldn't be forgiven.

The girl had got away. All he could do now was limit the fallout.

His every instinct screamed at him to remove the glass. He had to fight against it. He had to focus his energies on freeing one hand from the wound and reaching inside his pocket for his phone. Then he had to force himself not to call his colleague. He needed to contact him for help, but it couldn't be the first thing he did. His superior would check. His superior would verify the order of events in precise detail. He had to send the message before he did anything else.

His hand was coated in blood. It made his fingers slippery. And he was shaking and trembling. It made texting hard. But he was a determined guy. He was determined to send the message so that he could call his colleague straight afterwards.

The number was easy to find. He had it stored in his phone under the letters *IQ*.

The text was short. Necessarily so.

It consisted of just two words.

Girl gone.

Chapter Fifty-three

The digital video file opened in a new window on the laptop screen. A graphic in the bottom right-hand corner stated that it was seven minutes and fifty-seven seconds long. The video began playing automatically. There was no sound.

An angled, full-colour shot looking downwards from the top right-hand corner of a stylish living room. The room is dominated by an L-shaped sofa in cream leather. The sofa is sitting on stripped wooden floorboards, just behind a glass coffee table, and is overlooked by a floor-mounted lamp. There is also a wall of fitted bookshelves, a sleek stereo system, a glazed cabinet filled with drinking glasses and a comfortable armchair upholstered in blue fabric.

A Caucasian male is reclined on the sofa, his age approximately thirty. He is bare-chested, lean and straggly, with pasty skin. He wears a pair of low-slung charcoal jeans, with no socks. His beard is full and dark brown. Stringy dreadlocks hang around his bony shoulders. He is reading a paperback book.

The armchair is occupied by a young woman with short blonde hair. Her tanned legs are tucked beneath her. She wears a pink T-shirt over simple white briefs. In one hand, she holds a pot of nail varnish, and she is using a tiny brush to apply the varnish to the nails of her free hand.

'That's Lena Zeeger,' I told Rebecca.

'I assumed as much,' she said. Her tone was clipped, as if she didn't welcome the interruption.

After precisely twenty-three seconds, a third person enters the scene. Another woman. Another blonde. She has her back to camera. She is dressed in a dark-blue trouser suit, a small handbag hangs over her shoulder and she carries a white plastic shopping bag. The bag is stretched and drooping, as if it contains a heavy object.

Lena looks up at her with an expression somewhere between tedium and nonchalance. They engage in a short conversation. The woman appears tense. Her movements are sharp and abrupt. She gesticulates with her spare hand, raising her thumb, followed by two fingers, as if she's counting off three separate points she wants Lena to acknowledge. Lena shrugs and returns her attention to her nails.

The woman shakes her head, as if exasperated, and steps towards the glazed cabinet. She selects two glass tumblers. Then she removes a long-necked bottle of vodka from her shopping bag. She pauses, drawing a deep breath, then unscrews the bottle and splashes a generous measure of vodka into both glasses. She sets the bottle down on the cabinet next to the empty bag, lifts both glasses and turns sideways to hand a drink to the man on the sofa.

That was when my breath caught in my throat. When I jerked my head closer to the screen and felt everything become hyper-real. The cut of her hair. The shape of her eyes, nose, mouth. The way she held herself. The way she cocked an eyebrow at the man, like he was taking liberties.

The blonde woman was my sister, Laura. Unmistakably her. But also, unlike the Laura I knew, she appeared hard and un-compromising. Her jaw was set. Her eyes narrowed. She looked tough. Tougher than I'd known she could be.

I resisted the urge to press my fingers against the screen. I blinked tears from my eyes and tried to hold back the tide of emotions that gushed over me.

The skinny man accepts the vodka. He raises his glass in a silent, mocking toast, and takes a sip. He nods his approval and returns his attention to his book.

Laura straightens her spine and raises her eyes to the ceiling. Then she sets the second tumbler down on the floor by Lena's feet. She hovers, as if expecting some thanks, but after a few seconds more, she roughly adjusts the strap of her handbag and marches out of shot.

The time on the video file reads 1.33.

Very little happens for the next minute or so. The man on the sofa flicks a page of his book. Lena finishes painting her fingernails and blows on to them. The man on the sofa takes another sip from his vodka. Lena bends down and scoops up her own glass and does likewise.

They begin to talk. They drink some more.

Then, at close to the three-minute mark, Lena's head droops abruptly and her teeth strike the rim of her glass. She jerks her chin upright and blinks her eyes in an effort to rouse herself, like a bus passenger fighting a spell of drowsiness. She's unsuccessful. Her face sags again. She lowers her legs from her chair, as if to stand, but her legs are feeble and she crashes to the floor, dropping her glass and spilling vodka across the floorboards.

The skinny man springs to his feet, upsetting his own drink across the sofa cushions. He kneels by Lena's side, turns her face upright and lowers his cheek to her mouth. He shakes her roughly by the shoulders. Then he turns and pushes up on one leg, as if to fetch help, but his balance fails him and he lists precariously to one side like a drunk.

He strikes the ground on his hip and immediately attempts to push himself up. His movements are weak. He kicks out with his legs and thrashes with his arms like a beached fish, but his actions become vague and after a few final twitches his face slaps down against the bare floorboards.

Lena and the man lie prone and undisturbed for more than half a minute.

Then, at 4.23, the camera shakes violently and tilts a degree to the left, cutting off a portion of the top right-hand corner of the room. It's as if a sudden, localised vibration has upset the camera in its housing.

Two men wearing balaclavas burst into the scene. One advances on Lena, the other paces towards the skinny man.

The first man scoops Lena into an upright position, allowing her body to sag against the blue armchair, and checks her breathing. He is fast and powerfully built. He wears black cargo trousers with multiple pockets, a long-sleeved black T-shirt and black leather gloves. He pokes one gloved finger inside Lena's mouth and hooks her tongue forwards. Lena's head lolls to one side, her tongue hanging from her mouth.

Meanwhile, the second man lifts the bare-chested figure by his armpits and drags him towards the sofa. He heaves him on to the soft leather cushions and arranges him so that he is sprawled *against the backrest, his head pivoted towards the ceiling, his jaw gaping open and his dreadlocks spread around his shoulders.*

The second man is sturdier than his companion. He wears a grey suit over a light-blue shirt and a dark-blue tie. A black nylon backpack is fitted over his shoulders. He also wears a pair of black leather gloves. The man gathers up the spilt glass tumbler and holds it close to the skinny man's lips. Once he sees breath condense against the glass, he reaches up and removes his balaclava. The man is easily fifty years old. His scalp is hairless and his ears are flushed.

The first man follows his lead and tugs his own balaclava from his head. He is considerably younger. His hair is clipped short, like an army buzz cut, and he has a fuzz of hair below his bottom lip.

For perhaps five seconds, the first man grins inanely at his older companion. Then the older man says something to him and the first man reacts like he's been scolded before reaching into a pocket on his cargo trousers and removing a small glass vial and a hypodermic syringe. He upends the vial and pierces the seal with the needle. He withdraws the plunger and measures the dosage he requires.

At the same time, the second man gathers up Lena's tumbler. He slips his backpack from his shoulders and stuffs both tumblers inside. He fetches two fresh tumblers from the glazed cabinet, pours a shot of vodka into each glass, and spends a few moments fitting Lena's hand around one glass and the skinny man's hand around the second glass, until he is satisfied that their fingerprints have been successfully transferred.

Watched by the first man, he sets the glass bearing Lena's fingerprints down on the floor next to her, and tosses the glass branded with the skinny man's fingerprints across the already damp sofa cushions. He returns to his backpack and removes a white cotton cloth that is sealed inside a plastic ziplock bag. He uses the cloth to carefully clean the bottle of vodka. He wipes the bottle down thoroughly, then carries it across to Lena and with the help of his accomplice, takes her limp right hand and fits it around the bottle in several different ways, applying several different grips. Once the job is done, he returns the bottle to the top of the cabinet and the cloth to the little ziplock bag. He grabs the white plastic shopping bag and shakes it until a paper receipt tumbles out on to the cabinet, then stuffs the shopping bag and the ziplock bag inside his backpack.

Next, he adopts a position behind the sofa. Seizing the skinny man's gaping jaw in his gloved hands, he angles the man's head to one side, exposing his neck.

The first man steps away from Lena with the syringe and the glass vial in his right hand. He sets the vial down next to the vodka bottle on the glazed cabinet, flicks the syringe with his nail, flexes his arms and nods to his companion.

The move looks to be something they've rehearsed. It's a procedure they carry out with speed and efficiency. The younger man stabs the needle into the skinny man's neck and compresses the plunger. Then he removes the needle and they both step away.

The effects of the drug are very fast and very disturbing. The skinny man doesn't regain consciousness. His eyes don't snap open. But his body bucks and jerks, and his legs kick out, as if he's fighting something in his sleep. He arches his back and his chest heaves. He wrenches his head from side to side, his dreadlocks slashing his face. He flails once with his arm. His throat bulges and his lips peel back over his teeth. His skin reddens. Before long, he goes into *seizure, convulsing rhythmically, mouth frothing, until, when the footage reaches 7.02, he stops moving altogether.*

The two men don't concern themselves with his suffering. While the older man scans the floor space for anything they may have missed, his younger companion takes the syringe and the glass vial across to Lena. He starts with the glass vial and very carefully fits Lena's left hand around it. He lifts her index finger and rolls the glass around its pad. Then he takes her right hand and repeats the process with the syringe, being sure to press her right thumb down firmly on the plunger. Once he is satisfied, he collects together the syringe and the glass vial and carries them out of shot. He returns within twenty seconds, his hands empty.

The men check the room one last time and ensure that Lena is still breathing. Then they vacate the scene for good.

The footage continues for a further six seconds, and neither Lena nor the skinny man moves in the slightest.

I leaned away from the laptop. Blew a gust of air from my lips.

'Well,' I managed, 'I recognised everyone except the skinny guy on the sofa.'

Rebecca turned her face away from me and gazed out her side window. She raised her hand to her mouth. There was a long moment of silence.

'That was Alex Tyler,' she finally said, in a pinched voice.

I supposed it had to be. Lena's dead boyfriend. The eco-campaigner.

'Tell me I'm not going mad,' I said. 'We've just watched a murder, haven't we?'

Rebecca nodded, still peering out her window. 'Not just a

murder,' she said, absently. 'A comprehensive framing, too. Who were the men?'

'The younger one was my fake paramedic.'

'And the older one?'

'The older one is the guy who tackled me in the sports centre. The one who claimed to work for the security services.'

'So no surprise that he wanted you to hand him the memory stick.'

'None at all.'

'They worked as a team.' Rebecca seemed oddly disconnected. Almost robotic. I guess it didn't help that she was still talking in a pained, halting tempo, gasping air wetly through her mouth, her busted nose making her sound badly congested. 'They worked together to kill Alex Tyler and fit Lena up for his murder. Then they worked together to snatch Lena from this cottage.'

'And?'

'It's a pattern. And now the young one is dead. But it stands to reason that your man from the sports centre would have been involved in the mess at Teare's house.'

Rebecca turned to me. I searched for her eyes behind the swelling and the bruising. Her liquid brown irises seemed to pulsate.

'And Laura?' I asked, straining to kill the quaver in my voice.

'It looked to me as if she left the room before those men came in.'

It had looked the same way to me. 'You think they were waiting until she was gone?'

'Either that, or she signalled for them to go in.'

I tried not to flinch. I wasn't entirely successful.

'It's a possibility.' Rebecca shrugged. 'And we can't ignore it completely. But,' she added, tapping the laptop screen with her fingernail, 'this video file suggests otherwise.'

'How do you mean?'

'Those men didn't know they were being filmed. If they had, their first move would have been to disable the camera. And they wouldn't have removed their masks.'

'So?'

'So Laura *did* know. She was able to record and download the camera feed. And if she knew about it, and they didn't, I don't think they were working as a unit.' Rebecca paused. Regained her breath and turned her mouth down at the corners. 'You realise that if those two men really were acting on behalf of the security services, then Alex Tyler was killed by British Intelligence.'

'Laura's employer.'

'Yes, but remember why she wanted my help? I'm *outside* the organisation. The threat she was worried about was coming from *inside*. And she got this video file to you. She did it for a reason.'

'Then she's a whistleblower?'

'No.' Rebecca shook her head. 'This file would be with the press if that was the case. I think Laura was trying to find her own solution. She was buying time by hiding Lena here, but she needed freedom to work. So she faked her own death and she got the two of us involved.'

I tried to let Rebecca's words sink in, but they wouldn't settle. What she was suggesting seemed impossible to me. Difficult to believe in. Even harder to hope for.

'There's one more thing,' she said. 'There was a sedative in the vodka. You saw that, right?'

'It was hard to miss.'

'And the younger guy used a syringe to inject Alex with the poison that killed him. He seemed comfortable with the move. As if it was something he'd done before.'

'OK.'

'And if it was something he'd done before, it's something he could have done again.'

'What are you getting at?'

'Your crash. You said he was the guy who approached you as a paramedic. He talked to you, and then you lost consciousness.'

'Because I'd banged my head.'

'Maybe. It's highly likely, I don't deny that. But isn't it also possible that he could have stuck you with a needle?' She swallowed thickly, raising her hand for my patience until she'd cleared her airways and composed herself. 'You were unconscious for a long time. But from what your dad told me, the doctors who treated you in the hospital didn't find any real swelling to your brain. You were discharged about as quickly as you could have been.' She gripped my chin and turned my head to one side. Grimaced as she saw the bloody gash at the top of my skull. 'And now you've taken a big hit only a few days later, but you're coping OK.'

I cast my mind back to the crash itself. I'd definitely banged my head, because my helmet had been badly damaged. But I could also remember how the paramedic had crouched down next to me. He'd squeezed my gloved hand. And then . . .

something snagged against the skin of my wrist. Had that something been the point of a syringe?

'But surely my doctors would have noticed?'

'Not necessarily.' Rebecca shook her head. 'You presented with all the signs of a bad brain injury. They treated you that way once you reached ICU. And even if they carried out a tox screen, if the guy had used a drug routinely administered in A&E, it could have been overlooked. I'm thinking of a long-acting benzodiazepine such as diazepam. Given in the right dosage, it could knock you out for hours. You'd present with all the symptoms they'd be anticipating. And meantime, the guys who took Lena would know for sure that you'd be out long enough for them to get her off this rock before any kind of alarm was raised.'

'You really think so?'

'Hey, I learned a long time ago not to rule anything out. Speaking of which.' Rebecca lifted the poster for the missing dog from my lap. She scanned the printed information. Laughed faintly.

'What?' I asked.

'Do you recognise this number?'

I looked at the telephone number she was pointing to at the bottom of the poster. It wasn't familiar to me. I told her as much.

'I think you should dial it,' she said.

'Why?'

'Because I think Laura might answer.'

My heart stopped.

I felt a lump in my throat. A dryness in my mouth.

'Would you like me to do it?' Rebecca asked.

I shook my head as I fumbled with my mobile. My hands were hamfisted. I jabbed at the keypad with clumsy fingers. Raised the phone to my ear.

It rang. Then it rang some more. It kept ringing for close to a minute before it was answered.

'Hello,' said a voice I recognised.

It wasn't Laura.

It was much, much worse than that.

Chapter Fifty-four

I didn't talk with Rebecca during the drive. There wasn't much to be said. My mind was racing, but my thoughts were scrambled and incoherent. I jumped from one concern to the next. One worry to another. Pretty soon, my fears began to cancel each other out, leaving me in a state of uneasy calm, like listening to white noise for so long that it becomes possible to mistake it for silence.

The mid-afternoon suburban streets of Onchan seemed strangely unfamiliar to me. Mothers pushed babies in strollers. Pensioners queued for double-decker buses. People mowed lawns, or washed cars, or perused newspapers in sun-bathed conservatories. It was like driving through a film set. An unreal world on the other side of the windscreen. One where no one would believe that there was a man gagged and bound in the back of my van, and where nobody would understand what it was like to feel the pulse fade from the neck of a man who'd had designs on killing you.

My parents' care home looked just as it always has. Solid. Unremarkable. Calm.

We parked in the gravel yard outside my front door. There was an unfamiliar car parked there. A blue Vauxhall Insignia. It looked fairly new. A recent purchase. But it could have used a wash. There was dirt on the paintwork. Dust and grime on the windows.

Rebecca squirmed forwards in her seat. Under cover of the dashboard, she inspected the Beretta. She dropped the magazine out and counted the number of rounds that were left. Once she was satisfied, she reassembled the pistol, applied the safety and returned it to the small of her back, covering the bulge with her leather jacket.

'Ready?'

'Nope.'

She smiled, then winced. I could see that the pain from her facial injuries was very bad. Probably the skin was tightening as it healed.

I closed my hand around the purple memory stick. Squeezed hard.

'We should go in,' Rebecca said. 'Time's nearly up.'

I dropped out of the cab and approached my front door, glancing inside the Vauxhall on my way, but not seeing anything of importance. I fitted my key in the lock and passed on through. Just like normal. Just like coming home on any other day.

Except for the way my heart was punching against my chest. The way my scalp was itching and my palms were sweating.

I climbed the stairs. Fourteen of them. My legs shook like I was scaling a mountain.

Rebecca climbed behind me. I could feel her presence close by.

I turned at the top of the stairs and that was when I finally saw them. It took everything I had not to drop to my knees.

Dad was perched on one of my straight-backed dining chairs in the middle of the room. He was sitting on his hands, palms down, with his feet close together and his face bowed so that his chin brushed his chest.

'I'm sorry,' he said, in a dry voice.

'It's OK,' I told him.

It wasn't true. Things were a very long way from OK.

Dad's head was bowed because he had a pistol pressed against the back of his skull. The pistol was being held by the man with the cue-ball head who'd confronted me in the sports centre.

The man's temple was yellowed and grazed from where I'd struck him with my knee. His eyes were bloodshot, puffy and weeping, and his nostrils were red, like he was recovering from a bad cold. The after-effects of the chemical spray I'd blasted him with.

He was holding the pistol in his left hand. His right hand was hanging down by his side, bent at a sickening angle on the end of his arm. I remembered the sensation of stamping on his elbow and driving his wrist into the ground. The nauseating *crack*. He didn't seem preoccupied by the injury. He was focused on the task he was engaged in.

There was a mobile phone on the floor by Dad's feet. It was a cheap pay-as-you-go model. I was pretty sure it was the phone he'd answered my call on. It certainly wasn't his own.

He hadn't said much when he'd answered. Just a strained 'Hello' before the phone was snatched from him and another voice came on the line. Issuing an ultimatum. Telling me to return home with Rebecca in no more than thirty minutes, and to make sure I brought whatever Laura had left for me in the sports centre. He made it very clear that I shouldn't call the police or attempt to contact anyone else. He told me Dad's life depended on it.

He hadn't sounded like he was bluffing. Now I knew for sure that he wasn't.

'Did you bring it?' the man asked.

I unfurled my fingers. Showed him the memory stick.

'That's all?'

I nodded.

'Nothing else?'

I shook my head.

'Then why the holdall?'

I swallowed, but my voice was still croaky when I spoke. 'I didn't know what I might find. I thought it might be something big.'

He stared at me as he mulled over my answer. He took his time, as if there were hidden angles he wanted to consider, whole dimensions I hadn't thought of.

'What's on that thing?' he asked.

Rebecca took a step to my side. 'We don't know,' she said. 'And to be honest, we really don't care.'

The man considered her response. His eyes narrowed and he pushed the gun harder against the back of Dad's head. The muzzle twisted his unruly grey hair, like he was aiming to open Dad's skull with a corkscrew motion.

'What happened to your face?' he asked Rebecca.

'Erik Zeeger's people,' she said. 'We ran into them outside the sports centre. They wanted the memory stick, too.'

'I don't believe you.' His words were steady. Unhurried. 'You wouldn't be here if that was true.'

'We got lucky.'

Dad's eyes widened with alarm as he saw Rebecca's injuries for the first time. He probably thought her definition of 'lucky' was badly misplaced.

The man with the gun nodded towards the memory stick. 'You make a copy of that?'

'No.'

'You plan to speculate about what's on it? You plan to go to the police or the press?'

'We just want this whole situation to be over. We don't want anyone else to get hurt.'

'That's good. Because it wouldn't get you anywhere, anyway. I disappear after this. You never see or hear from me again. But the people I work for are powerful people. Highly capable people. They can hurt you, your family, in ways you can't even begin to imagine. And then there's your sister. Her memory. You don't want that sullied, correct?'

Her memory.

I no longer felt any need to question if Laura really was dead. She had to be. I knew that now. I knew Laura. I knew the good in her. And despite what Rebecca had suggested, there was no way she would have stayed in the background while this mess played out around us. Once it was clear her family were in jeopardy, she would have stepped out of the shadows.

I caught a glimpse of movement from the corner of my eye. Rebecca had inched away from me. Not by much, but by enough to give her a little more room. I didn't like it. I didn't appreciate what I guessed she was trying to do.

I thought about the Beretta nestled in the crook of her back. I thought about how she'd need to whip her hand behind her, hitch up her jacket, grab for the gun, straighten her arm, adjust her grip, line up a shot, pull the trigger. She was probably a good shot. Maybe better than good. She'd proved to me many times already how skilled she was. But the bald man had his pistol pressed against Dad's head. He had his finger on the trigger. And while the way he'd reached inside his jacket back at the sports centre had suggested he was naturally right-handed, I was pretty sure his left hand would do. There was no way Rebecca could get a shot off in time. And even if she did, there was a real danger she'd hit Dad.

I stared at her. Willing her not to try anything.

The man tracked my gaze.

'Whatever you're cooking up,' he said, 'I'd advise you to forget it.' He jabbed his pistol forwards, jamming Dad's head down towards his lap. 'Put your hands up,' he barked.

I complied right away, raising my right hand in the air. I couldn't do anything about my left, except keep it still.

Rebecca hesitated.

'Please,' I hissed.

She resisted a moment longer. Then she lifted her arms and laced her fingers together behind her neck.

'Good. Now put that computer stick down on the kitchen counter,' the man said to me.

I did as he asked.

'Now step away. Hand up high.'

I returned to Rebecca's side, my hand in the air.

'Now shuffle along,' the man said, jerking his gun in the direction he wanted us to move. 'Both of you.'

We sidestepped to our right. Moving further into the lounge. Away from the kitchen. Away from the stairs.

The man waited until we were bunched up in the corner, next to my television.

He tapped Dad on the skull with the end of the pistol. 'On your feet,' he said. 'Slowly. Hands on your head.'

Dad wasn't in a position to move fast. I had no idea how long he'd been sitting on his hands, but it was long enough for his movements to be stiff and slow. His legs get that way if he doesn't flex them every now and again – a legacy of the plates that had been used to stitch his shattered bones back together. And I imagined his hands were riddled with pins and needles. He was in no state to play the hero, even if he'd wanted to. For the first time in my life, he looked old to me.

The man positioned himself behind Dad and instructed him to take a series of steps in the direction of the kitchen counter. The two of them moved in sync across the floor. One step. Two. Three.

By the fourth step, the man was close enough to reach out and grab the memory stick. But he had a problem. His broken right hand wasn't capable of picking anything up. It was no better than the hand of a dummy. And his left hand held the gun. If he went for the memory stick with it, there'd be a split second when he'd be unable to shoot. It would give Dad an opportunity to try something.

He paused and thought about the problem. I got the impression he was a careful type who liked to think things through.

Dad raised his eyebrows at me, as if asking if now was a good time to attack.

I shook my head minutely.

Long seconds passed. Then the man arrived at a solution.

'Pick it up for me,' he told Dad, and poked the gun into

his ear, so that his head was forced down towards the kitchen counter. 'Do it slowly, with your left hand. That's right. Now, hold your arm straight out in front of you and move towards the stairs.'

Dad closed his fingers around the memory stick and did as he was told. The man shuffled behind him, keeping time with his steps.

'Wait,' I said. 'Don't take him with you. You can't.'

'It's OK, Rob,' Dad said, in a strained tone.

'No, it's not,' I told him. 'There's no need for this.'

'Don't worry,' the man said. 'Nobody gets hurt so long as you all do as I say.'

I glanced at Rebecca, wondering if she'd make some kind of move. She gave no indication that she was considering it.

The man caught me looking again. 'What is it?' he asked. 'What are you afraid of? Is there someone outside? Did you call the police?'

'No,' I said, shaking my head.

'What if we did?' Rebecca asked.

I glared at her. 'We didn't,' I told him, insistent now.

The man remained still, unsure of his next move. He was just two strides away from the top of the stairs. But once he started down them, he'd be committed.

'What do you want to happen here?' he asked, half to himself. 'Do you want me to step outside on my own? Is that why you don't want your father to come with me?'

'There's nobody there,' I said. 'We didn't call anyone.'

'Maybe *you* didn't,' Rebecca said.

I wanted to thump her. I shook my head wildly. 'She's lying,'

I told the man. 'Believe me. She didn't call anyone. Neither of us did. There's nobody down there. No one at all.'

He gazed down the stairs. Flicked his tongue across his lips. 'Is there another way out of here?'

'You don't need one. The yard is empty. There's nobody –'

I didn't get to finish my sentence.

Everything happened very fast.

There was the noise of my front door being thrown open against the wall. The drumming of feet on the stair treads. A booming, carefree voice from below.

'Hello, my boy, it's Grandpa. Just returning Rocky to you.'

He'd barely started to speak before the man with the gun pushed Dad away from him and leapt towards the top of the stairs. The hand with the gun in it came round in a long, looping arc. It passed over his head, started to dip.

Dad hit the floor, impacting hard on his knees.

I saw a streak of gold halfway up the stairs. Rocky, in full flight, racing to see me.

The man's eyes went wide. His gun came down even more. Moving with a terrible certainty.

Then I felt a dig in my side. Rebecca's elbow, striking me in the waist. She was clearing space. Yanking her hand out from behind her back. Whipping the Beretta through the air. Pointing fast. Aiming hastily. Pulling the trigger before her elbow was fully extended.

The noise was very loud. It exploded in my head like someone had stamped on my eardrum.

The man with the gun twirled at the hips. His left shoulder jerked backwards, like he'd been punched in the chest. His gun arm went high and loose. His legs tangled at the knee, undone by the speed of the brutal force that had spun his upper body around. He tripped and started to go down, falling away into the kitchen. The gun dropped from his hand. Then another huge explosion went off, and the back of the man's head opened up in a gaudy pink haze.

Chapter Fifty-five

I helped Dad through into my bedroom, where he slumped on the end of my bed. I closed the door on the gory scene in the living room and watched Dad prod warily at the back of his head. He lowered his arm and stared at his trembling hands.

Rebecca had ushered Grandpa and Rocky back to the care home to find Mum. I didn't expect her to return anytime soon. We'd managed to stop Grandpa before he'd made it to the top of the stairs but it would take a while to calm him down, and once Mum saw Rebecca's face and her blood-caked T-shirt, she'd insist on treating her injuries. Rebecca was bound to be swamped with questions and none of the answers would be simple.

Her absence gave me a chance to talk to Dad one on one, and despite what he'd just gone through, I didn't feel it was an opportunity I could pass up. There was a man dead in my kitchen – a man I knew to be a murderer, and very possibly an agent of the British government – and soon we'd need to decide what to do about it.

'Dad,' I said, and placed my hand on his knee. I was sitting cross-legged on the floor in front of him. 'I need to ask you something.'

He raised his head slowly, as if he'd forgotten I was there. His eyes were wet and red. He pinched the corners of them, near the bridge of his nose, like he was trying to clear his sinuses.

'It's about Laura,' I said.

He nodded. Like he knew this had been coming.

'Where did you get the mobile?'

'They found it in her car,' he said, his voice hoarse and scratchy. He swallowed. Thumped his chest. 'In the glove box. After the accident. Mick gave it to me.'

'You mean DI Shimmin?'

He nodded, eyes closed, as if in pain. 'Your sister had two phones when they got to her. The one you called me on was new. It had no records. No calls out. None coming in. I've been keeping it charged. Keeping it close.'

'Didn't Shimmin need it as evidence?'

'Evidence of what?'

Yes, evidence of what, I wondered, and then I posed the question I'd really wanted to ask. I told him about Rebecca's theory. I explained that we'd begun to ask ourselves if Laura could have faked her own death. If the crash up at Marine Drive had been an elaborate smokescreen, a way for her to evade some kind of danger associated with her job. I told him that I knew what her job had been, now. I told him I had a fair idea of what the danger had been, too, and that it was linked to the man who'd held a gun on him.

Dad considered my words for a long time. His face gave nothing away. Then he reached out and gently rubbed his thumb across the dried blood on my forehead, like he was trying to clear away an oil stain. He cupped the back of my neck and tipped my head forwards so that he could inspect my wound.

'Should have told you at the time,' he said, in a voice that was heavy with regret. 'Should have told you *and* your mum.

Would have caused some heartache, but it would have been better than this.'

'What is *this*?'

'It was like you said,' he told me, as if I had all the answers already. 'Your sister came to me and said she was in trouble. Said she needed to get away. Reckoned there was only one way to do it.' He almost smiled at the memory. Then his expression became glum and he let his arm fall away. 'You know how stubborn she could be. Had her mind all made up. I'd always told her that her career would be the death of her. She said now it could be – in a way that would help her to get out.'

'What happened?'

He met my eyes full on. It felt like the first time he'd done that in a while. 'She was scared, Rob. Truly scared. And she wouldn't listen to reason. She wouldn't entertain the idea of going to anyone at her work, or speaking with the police. She had it all figured out. Everything. She wanted it done over here, so we could control it.'

'Was Shimmin involved?'

'He was going to be. That was part of it.' Dad paused. 'But it was also where it came undone. Laura had been so sure that it was possible, she couldn't accept it when Mick started to poke holes in what she was suggesting.'

'He didn't like the idea?'

'He's a good man. A good friend. He wanted to help us. And if it was just down to him, he would have done, I'm sure. But he said there'd need to be other people involved. At least five. And he said that was too many. You couldn't rely on them all to keep quiet about it.'

'So Shimmin stopped the whole thing?'

'He tried to.'

'Tried to?'

Dad shook his head, exasperated. 'Laura wouldn't listen. She said it would all be fine. She had money saved. Enough to spread around. And when Mick still said no, she decided to force his hand.'

'I don't get it.'

'She called Mick in the middle of the night and told him what she was planning. She was up at Marine Drive by then. Said she was going to nudge her car off the road and climb down to it and make it look like an accident. Told him she had some kind of sedative and she was going to inject herself with it. Reckoned that unless anyone checked her closely, it'd look like she was dead. She told Mick he had to come out and find her before anyone else, or the whole thing would be ruined.'

'And did he?'

Dad sighed. 'He said he wouldn't go. He couldn't get involved. He hung up on her. Didn't answer when she called him again.' He clasped a hand to his forehead. Ran it down over his face. 'We think she lost it then. We think she began to believe she had no other way out. That's when she did it for real, Rob. That's when she drove off that cliff.'

I leaned backwards, shaking my head. 'But DS Teare told us that Shimmin was the first person to find Laura.'

'He was. He felt bad about hanging up. So he drove up to see if he could speak to her. Reason with her. But when he got there, it was already too late.'

'It doesn't make any sense,' I told him. 'She left me a trail. She wanted me to find that memory stick. She wanted me to call the mobile I spoke to you on.'

Dad glanced quickly away. 'Originally, maybe. I don't know anything about that. But she changed her mind, son. She made her choice. I wish I could go back and do things differently. I wish there'd been some way I could have convinced her otherwise. But I tried, Rob. Believe me. I really tried.'

*

Lena had taken a chance on the grubby cafe because it was empty. No customers. No staff. She'd pressed her face up against the wire-glass door. Spied six unoccupied table booths and an abandoned service counter. The doorway behind the counter was obscured by a curtain made up of long strips of colourful plastic tape.

An electronic bell had chimed as she pushed the door open. She'd started at the noise, then jumped again when a woman parted the coloured tapes with her hands and peered out at her. The woman was black-skinned and vastly overweight. Her mouth was very large, crammed with teeth and gums. The way the coloured tapes arranged themselves around her spherical head and rounded shoulders served only to emphasise her size.

The woman's easy smile died on her lips the moment she saw Lena. Her greasy, crazed hair. The dried blood on her arm and blouse. Her swollen, discoloured wrist. The dirty socks on her feet.

Lena felt herself shrink. She was used to walking into restaurants and being stared at. But normally the restaurants were fancy and the staring was of a different order.

'Lord, child, what happened to you?' the woman asked. She had an exotic accent. Jamaican, maybe.

'I need to use your phone,' Lena told her, in a voice that was shakier than she'd intended. 'I don't have any money.'

The woman raised a callused palm. 'Somebody been beating on you, child?'

'Please,' Lena said, and glanced back towards the door. 'Just one phone call.'

The woman rubbed her chin and stared at her some more. She leaned her considerable weight to one side and peered over Lena's shoulder towards the street.

'I won't stay long,' Lena told her.

'No, child, you'll stay just as long as you need to. Come on through. Phone's back here.'

The woman's name was Angela. She talked breezily and prepared food for the occasional customer while Lena waited in silence for the man she'd telephoned to arrive. Angela had helped with directions. She'd explained that they were in Manchester and she'd spoken to the man and told him how to find the cafe. She hadn't asked Lena who the man was. She hadn't tried to find out what kind of trouble she was in.

It was more than three hours before he arrived. Lena heard the brash rumble of a badly tuned engine, followed by the *bing* of the door chime. She tensed on her chair.

Angela wiped her hands on a dishcloth and parted the curtain to check on their visitor. When she finally allowed the man into the back room, she made it clear that she'd be waiting just outside the door with the phone close at hand.

He was older than Lena had expected. Mid-forties, with a short, muscular frame. He was wearing an army surplus overcoat, green cargo pants and desert boots. There was a ring in his nose and a collection of piercings in his ear.

He said, 'Give me one good reason why I shouldn't call the police.'

Lena gave him a bunch of reasons. She told him she'd hadn't killed Alex. She told him she had some idea of the people who'd been involved in his death, and that she'd just escaped from them. She explained how, with his help, she might be able to prove her innocence, if only they could get in touch with a plumber based on the Isle of Man. Then she told him what Alex had said. How Alex had made her promise to contact him if ever she was in trouble. How Alex had assured her that he was someone she could rely on.

The man toyed with one of his earrings as he turned over what he'd been told. Then he took a deep, contemplative breath, shook his head and emptied his lungs with a sigh.

'So come on outside and get in my jeep,' he told her. 'There's a group of people you really ought to meet.'

Lena hesitated. She bit hard on her lip and fixed him with a level stare. 'I want to make these people pay,' she said. 'For what they've done to me and the people who tried to help me. But most of all, for Alex.'

'I hear you,' the man said. 'Trust me, making people pay is what we're all about.'

*

We agreed to call Shimmin. Dad asked him to come round right away. He didn't explain why, just that it was urgent. Shimmin was reluctant – he was heading up the investigation into Jackie Teare's death – but when Dad pressed, he relented.

While we waited for his arrival, I went into my bathroom

and tended to the cut to my head. I ran water into the sink, wet a few wads of toilet paper and cleaned the laceration as best I could. Then I soaped my hand and washed the blood from my face. The water turned pink against the white porcelain. My sling was a mess. It was speckled with red blotches. My shoulder was aching and immobile, and I was stiff and sore all over. I felt a hundred years old. I pulled the plug and stared hard at myself in the mirror, trying to come to terms with some of the things Dad had told me about Laura. It wasn't easy. I knew there'd been more distance between us in recent years, and that we hadn't shared as much as we used to when we were growing up, but it was tough to accept that she hadn't come to me for help sooner, while she was still alive.

If she could have been with us now, I guessed she might have said that she'd been trying to limit the risks she was exposing her loved ones to. That confiding in Dad was already a step too far. But I didn't know if I could believe it.

I grabbed a towel. Dried my face. Pressed the fabric against the gash in my skull, then tossed the towel into the bath.

I felt like I'd let Laura down. I felt that way because, in my heart, I knew that I had. My sister had been in fear for her life and I hadn't noticed. The way I'd seen it, she'd made a choice. Gone to London. Put her career ahead of all of us. Only now did I understand that she'd done it for our own protection. And the hardest part of all was that I'd never have a chance to tell her so.

My one consolation was that she'd told Lena to trust me, and that she'd left the code on the memory stick for me to decipher. I guessed she'd been sharing out the dangers between me and Dad. She'd believed that I'd come through for her when it mattered, and now I was asking myself how exactly I was supposed to do that.

I had the memory stick. I had the video file it contained. But I didn't know what to do with it. Would Laura want the footage made public? Or had she resisted that move when she was alive for a reason? Did her appearance on the video point to her involvement in the murder of Alex Tyler, or did it absolve her? I couldn't tell for certain either way. I had no idea what to do.

DI Shimmin arrived before I'd reached a conclusion. I stepped out of the bathroom and found that Dad had met him at my front door. They were speaking in hushed tones. I didn't hear what was said, but I stood at the top of the stairs and watched Shimmin shoot glances my way. His expression grew darker and more sullen. His swollen eyes closed almost to slits, becoming ever more guarded.

He didn't talk to me until he'd knelt down and looked over the body. He did it brusquely, rolling the man's head to one side with the end of a biro. He grunted, then pointed the biro at the pistol.

'This the gun he was killed with?' he asked.

I shook my head. Told him the gun that had done the shooting was on my coffee table. Rebecca had dropped the magazine out and made the pistol safe before accompanying Grandpa back to his room.

Shimmin left the gun alone and went through the man's pockets. He came up with the ID the man had shown me back at the sports centre. A wallet. A mobile phone. A set of car keys. It was an easy guess that the keys fitted the Vauxhall I'd seen parked outside.

Shimmin opened the leather ID folder and scanned its contents. He looked up at me and Dad from his crouched position beside the dead man, then held the ID out to Dad.

Dad flipped it open and considered it in silence. I shuffled closer and took a look for myself. There was an imposing government crest. A portrait photograph of the dead man. And a name. John Anthony Menser.

'Name means nothing to me,' Dad said.

Shimmin hitched an eyebrow at me.

'No,' I told him.

Dad closed the ID and passed it back to Shimmin. He slapped it against his knee, deep in thought.

'Could anyone have heard the shots?'

His question surprised me. It took a moment for me to gather my thoughts. 'I doubt it,' I said. 'We're a fair distance from the care home. A lot of the residents are hard of hearing, and at this time of day, most of them would be in the television room. They have the sound up pretty loud.'

'What about staff?'

'It's possible. They might have heard from the kitchen.'

'Neighbours?'

'Maybe. Why?'

His eyes drifted to the dining chair in the middle of the room. The one Dad had been made to sit on. He straightened and took in the memory stick on the kitchen counter and the pay-as-you-go mobile on the floor.

'Sit down,' he said, and directed me to the sofa. 'You're going to run through *exactly* what's been going on.'

This time, I told him everything I could think of. Every detail I could remember. There was nothing I kept back. Nothing I held on to. I'd had enough of trying to deal with this on my own. Enough of the raw data that had been swirling endlessly around my head.

Shimmin didn't speak until I'd finished talking. Twenty minutes. Maybe more. He was sitting on the coffee table in front of me, his elbows on his knees, hands clasped together below his engorged chin. The items he'd taken from the dead man's pockets were arranged on the table beside him, next to the Beretta.

He cleared his throat. 'Jimmy,' he said, without looking at my dad. 'Why don't you go over and check on your father-in-law? I need to have a conversation with young Rob here. Alone.'

Chapter Fifty-six

Shimmin waited until he was sure that Dad had left. Then he inclined his head towards the lifeless figure on my kitchen floor.

'Your man here, you say he's in this video footage?'

I nodded.

'And the paramedic guy? The one we found at Teare's place?'

'It's definitely him.'

'And the two of them killed this eco guy and set it up as a frame job?'

'That's how it looked.'

'Show me.'

I did. I went downstairs to my van and fetched my laptop and then I called up the MPEG file. I didn't need to plug in the memory stick to access the video. Rebecca had copied the file to my laptop before we drove back to the care home. We'd lied about not making a duplicate.

Shimmin balanced the computer on his lap and viewed the video in silence. I watched from over his shoulder. When he was finished, he closed the laptop and set it down on the coffee table alongside the Beretta.

'Something to tell you,' he said, in a grudging rumble. 'Something I never told your dad.'

He looked up at me, and there was a pleading in his deep-set eyes. A moistness about his pupils.

He went to say something more, then changed his mind and found his feet. He brushed past me and walked around the far side of the kitchen island to the sink. He ran the tap. Lowered his head. Cupped water to his mouth.

'It's about Laura, isn't it?'

He turned the tap off and rubbed the last of the water around his face.

'Sit down,' he said.

I didn't move.

'Just do me a favour and sit down and listen. You can ask your questions when I'm finished. But first, let me tell you the way it happened. Let me get through this, OK?'

The pleading was still there in his eyes. And there was a brittleness in his voice. He rested his arms against the kitchen counter, elbows locked, like he was bracing for an impact.

I felt myself doing as he asked. I lowered myself on to the dining chair Dad had been made to sit on.

'Your dad said he told you about your sister. The plan she'd come up with. The way I found her at Marine Drive.'

I nodded.

'Well, it wasn't quite like that.'

I snatched a breath. Went to speak. Shimmin raised a hand.

'She was dead, all right. No question. But she wasn't alone.' He tilted his bloated head towards the dead man on the floor. 'This guy was with her. So was the guy I found at Teare's place. Your paramedic with the beard.' He tapped at the area of skin below his bottom lip, as if confirming who he was talking about.

The room shrunk around us. I felt the walls pressing in. I shook my head. Unable to talk. Unsure what to say.

'It was just getting light. Sun coming up. I saw where Laura's car had gone through the fence. Saw that she'd done what she'd threatened to do. So I pulled over and I sat there for a few seconds trying to decide what my next move should be. I didn't have a choice. I knew that by then. I couldn't just leave her down there. So I got out and I walked to the edge, ready to clamber down to her. And that was when I saw them.'

The room contracted again. It felt like a dark bubble, closing around us.

'They had the driver's door open. Your man here was leaning inside. The guy with the beard was looking over his shoulder. I thought they must have seen her car. I thought they were trying to help.'

He glanced down at his clenched fists, pressing into the granite counter. I felt my eyes go wide. As if I was looking over that cliff edge myself. As if I was standing there beside him, surveying the scene.

'I nearly turned around then. They hadn't seen me. The noise of the wind and the waves must have masked the sound of my car pulling up. But I went down to them. I got halfway before the guy with the beard realised I was coming. And that was when I knew something was wrong. Because he didn't shout at me. He didn't wave his arms and ask me to call an ambulance. He just tapped his pal on the shoulder and both of them gave me a look like they didn't want me coming any closer.'

I was shaking my head. Couldn't stop.

'I got out my ID and told them I was police. Made them step aside.' Shimmin rocked his head backwards on his shoulders. Drew a sharp breath as he raised his eyes to the ceiling. 'She was a mess, lad. Awful. There was a lot of blood. Bruising. I hadn't expected it. She'd told me she was going to push the car over, then walk down to it and get inside. She was going to drug herself. Her injuries wouldn't be on the outside, but that was OK. A lot of car accidents, people die from internal stuff. Force of gravity inside your body. She reckoned being unconscious would be enough to fool anyone who wasn't in on the scheme. But there was no way that had happened. It was obvious to me she'd been in the car when it went over the cliff. And she hadn't been wearing her seatbelt.'

Shimmin lowered his face, but his eyes were unfocused. Like he was looking through me, back to the memory he'd been shying away from.

I had a sudden urge to bolt from my chair. To lash out at him with everything I had.

'I checked for a pulse. Nothing there. Then I asked the two men what had happened. The guy on your floor took the lead. He said they'd found your sister like that. That they'd been trying to resuscitate her.'

'But you didn't believe him?'

'Why was she still in the car? They should have laid her flat on the ground. And mouth-to-mouth? Chest compressions? They take a lot of effort. Lot of energy. But these guys weren't even breathing hard. They didn't have any blood on them. And the first thing you do with CPR is you loosen the victim's clothing, clear their airways. They hadn't done that. Your sister had a coat on. It was still zipped. And her mouth was closed.'

I could feel a rage bubbling up inside me. Boiling over.

Shimmin shook his head roughly, like he was trying to rearrange his thoughts. 'I didn't like it. I knew the kind of people your sister had been afraid of. And these two guys were too calm. No way were they there by accident. But the thing that was bothering me most was what the guy had been doing inside her car. If he hadn't been trying to help your sister, he must have been doing something else. Then I looked at her face again. Really looked at it.' His voice began to trail away. 'Her nose and mouth were blue. And there were red marks on her skin. They were starting to fade, but they looked like fingermarks.'

I felt the fight go out of me then. Felt it drain clean away, leaving me suddenly feeble.

His words rebounded in my mind. Bouncing and thrashing around. They wouldn't settle. Their full impact wasn't sinking in.

He was telling me Laura had been killed.

And he'd done nothing about it.

He raised his hands, as if to fend off a blow.

'You don't know how it was,' he said. 'Let me finish. Hear me out.'

I was too numb to move. Too dumbstruck to talk.

He said, 'I told them I didn't believe them. Told them I was arresting them. I went for my phone. I was going to call for an ambulance and back-up. That's when the young guy pulled a gun on me. His partner, this Menser guy, said not to be hasty. There were things I needed to consider.'

'They scared you off,' I said, unable to conceal my disgust.

'Not the way you're thinking.'

'Then how was it? Because it must have been one hell of an explanation for you to let people believe my sister killed herself.'

'They told me who they were,' he said. 'Who they worked for. They said they'd been following your sister. Watching her.'

'Laura had already warned you about that.'

He bowed his head and contemplated his reflection in the polished granite. Rapped his knuckles against it, like he was seeking admission to some alternate dimension.

'They knew your sister had been up to the cottage. The one in the woods. They said she'd met with someone there. A girl. They said your sister told her what she wanted to do. How she planned to disappear. They said they had listening equipment in the cottage. They had recordings.'

Not of everything, I realised. They couldn't have, or they'd have known about me, and about the video file. Perhaps Laura had taken Lena for a walk in the woods. Talked to her there to make sure that Pieter and Lukas wouldn't overhear. By chance, they'd evaded the bugs in the cottage, too.

Shimmin kept his head down, shying away from me. So he had known about Lena. Known about her all along.

'They said Laura had mentioned that someone in the local police was going to help her. That they knew I'd been conspiring to fake her death.'

'What did that matter? They'd killed her for real, hadn't they?'

Finally, he looked at me.

I felt my skin crawl.

'They told me Lena was wanted on a murder charge. That your sister was involved. Something in London. They said your sister had gone rogue. The two of them had worked together to kill some guy. Your sister had done it for money. To line her own pockets.'

'And you believed them?'

'They had the cottage under surveillance, lad. Said it was an ongoing investigation with high-up approval.'

I realised then that Laura hadn't told anyone the whole truth. Not Shimmin. Not Dad. Not Rebecca, nor me. She must have decided it'd be too dangerous. And it had been. For her. For Lena.

'They said that if I tried to get in their way, there'd be a lot of heat coming down on me. They said I had two options. I could let your sister's death go down as suicide, or I could spark an investigation. But if I pursued it as a murder inquiry, they'd release the information about what she'd done in London. The girl up at the cottage would be arrested and they'd leak to the press about your sister's involvement. They'd smear her reputation. They'd release everything they had against her.'

'But they were involved themselves,' I said, through clenched teeth.

'I know that now. I didn't know it then. What they said made sense. It explained why Laura had been so fixed on disappearing. And she was dead already. I couldn't bring her back. There was nothing I could do.'

He was wrong. There'd been a lot he could have done. He could have questioned the story he'd been told. He could have sought justice for my sister. He could have looked into the circumstances surrounding my crash and Lena's disappearance instead of burying his head in the sand.

'So you lied,' I said. 'You hid the truth.'

'I was trying to protect your family.'

'You're pathetic,' I told him. 'Laura should never have come to you.'

I was just warming up but I was interrupted by noise from

403

downstairs. The sound of my front door opening. Cautious footsteps approaching.

Shimmin spoke to me in a rush. 'You're in a hole now, lad,' he said. 'A man dead in that cottage. Another one in your kitchen. And they'll come snooping around. The security services, I mean. This guy and his pal weren't acting alone. You can bet on that.'

Rebecca appeared at the top of the stairs. There was a white fabric dressing taped across her nose. Antiseptic cream smeared on her bruises. She was wearing a baggy, bright green T-shirt that Mum must have given her.

It was obvious to me that she'd heard what Shimmin had said. I saw her running calculations in her mind. She looked down at the corpse in my kitchen, then moved across to the coffee table. She opened the man's ID. Scanned the details. She made a small noise in her throat, like she wasn't entirely surprised by what she'd seen. Then she flipped the leather ID holder closed. Pressed the corner into her lip.

'So what is it you propose?' she asked Shimmin.

*

I hauled back the sliding door on my van and Lukas blinked hard against the sudden daylight. He was lying on his side with his head resting on the tangled dust sheets. The skin of his face had reddened and swollen around the swab of gaffer tape pasted across his mouth.

'Get him out of there,' Shimmin said. 'And cut that tape off him.'

I climbed inside and grabbed one of my craft knives, sawing

at his bindings with the blade. I started with his legs, then moved on to his hands. I finished by peeling the tape away from his mouth. There was some bleeding from his lips. Nothing serious.

I had him sit in the van doorway while he flexed his legs and shook some feeling into his arms. He didn't speak, not even when Shimmin wrenched his arms behind his back again and snapped a pair of handcuffs over his wrists. His skin was colourless and wrinkled from where the tape had been.

Shimmin grabbed one arm and I caught hold of the other. We walked Lukas as far as Shimmin's unmarked police car. Pushed his head down and guided him into the back. I shuffled in alongside him. Rebecca joined Shimmin in the front.

We drove down out of Onchan and along Douglas promenade in silence. Lukas stared through his window at the moving water and shifting tides, crouched forwards in his seat, his cuffed hands behind him. I tried to calm myself and prepare for what was to come. To clear my mind. I was a long way from successful.

Shimmin drove into the underground car park beneath the Sefton Hotel and reversed into a dimly lit space. He stepped out at the same time as Rebecca, then walked round to open my door. The garage was cold and smelled of petrol fumes and tyre rubber. We seized Lukas by his elbows and marched him across the echoing concrete, then through a rear entrance as far as the elevator bank. The hotel foyer was empty of guests and the reception counter pointed away from us. There was nobody to stare at the glum man in handcuffs, or the plainclothes detective with the menacing expression, or the guy with his arm in a sling, or the young woman with the battered face. We took the elevator to the top floor of the hotel and paced along the hushed corridor.

Rebecca rapped on the door to Erik's suite with her knuckle. Then she stepped aside and Shimmin shoved Lukas's face towards the peephole. A toilet flushed. Footsteps approached. There was a pause. Silence on the other side of the door. The turn of a well-greased lock.

The moment the door moved I kicked it fully open.

Erik Zeeger staggered backwards into his room. He was wearing a white linen shirt over dark jeans, and a panicked look on his face. He started to splutter. To protest.

'We need to talk,' I told him, and pointed an accusing finger.

Behind me, I heard the sound of Rebecca closing the door.

Then Shimmin snarled and flung Lukas hard across the room. Lukas's leg gave out from under him and he crashed on to the carpet.

I glared at Erik. I wanted answers. I was ready for them now.

Chapter Fifty-seven

'Where is Anderson?' Erik asked.

'He's dead,' I told him.

His reaction was controlled. Contained. There was barely any movement in his face. Just the merest tightening of the muscles around his eyes.

I realised then that I'd underestimated him. He dressed and talked like a professional. Like a lawyer or a banker on his day off. But he was tougher than that. I'd told him his top security man was dead and he'd calmly absorbed the information and run it through his brain and already asked himself what it might mean for him.

He swept the room with his arresting blue eyes. Assessing the situation. Counting the number of people involved. A minimum of two against him, possibly three, depending on Shimmin's exact role. Just one on his side. But that one was Lukas. The guy on the floor. Cowering in handcuffs.

Erik asked, 'How did he die?'

'Badly,' Rebecca said, her voice thick and nasal. 'He was trying to beat some information out of us. It didn't turn out the way he expected.'

Erik contemplated her disfigured face. The padding on her nose. 'What was the information?' he asked, his glittering eyes fixed solely on her.

'A code,' I said.

'For what?'

'A password.'

He sighed. Confronted me directly. 'And what was the password for?'

I shook my head. 'Tell me about my sister. Tell me why she was helping you to hide Lena.'

Erik smiled flatly. He inclined his head towards Shimmin. 'Who is this man?'

Shimmin folded his arms across his chest. 'Detective Inspector Shimmin,' he said, in a voice that made it clear he didn't appreciate the way Erik was trying to talk around him.

'I told you no police.'

'And we took that on board,' I told Erik. 'But the way you had us abducted and nearly killed sort of changed our mind.'

'I won't talk with him here.'

'You'll talk,' Shimmin grunted.

Erik snapped his head around. 'Let me ask you a question, Mr Policeman. Why haven't you arrested these people for the murder of my employee?'

Shimmin sucked air through his teeth. Rose up on his toes and summoned his full height. 'That's not the question you should be asking,' he said. 'The question you should be asking is: How much are you prepared to lose? How much are you willing to sacrifice?'

'You make no sense.'

'This is the Isle of Man, Mr Zeeger. We have our own police force here. Our own laws. Conspiracy to kidnap and kill are serious crimes in the eyes of the Manx judiciary. You could spend plenty of time in custody awaiting trial. And your sentence would tend to be on the heavy side.'

'Are you threatening me?'

Shimmin squinted at me. 'Was I not clear?'

'Perfectly,' I told him.

'Thought so.' He rocked on his heels. 'Mr Zeeger, you have one employee dead. You have another employee with a nasty gunshot wound to the leg.' Shimmin motioned towards Lukas. He still hadn't got up from the floor. He was looking up at us all with big, wet eyes. 'And he's not the toughest lad I've ever seen. I reckon he'd give evidence against you readily enough. I don't reckon I'd have to ask more than twice.'

'You plan to arrest me?'

'I don't plan, full stop. It's not the Manx way. We're mostly a relaxed bunch, as it goes. There's a saying here – *traa dy liooar*. It means *time enough*. It's a philosophy of wait-and-see. I'm prepared to apply it today. So you can think of me as an impartial observer.'

'And what do you expect to observe?'

'A trade,' I said, and watched Erik's eyes swing back towards me. 'You tell me the truth about my sister and I'll give you this.' I stuck my hand in the pocket of my tracksuit bottoms, removed the memory stick and held it in the air between my finger and thumb. 'It contains a video file. The footage proves that Lena didn't kill Alex Tyler. It shows the two men who really murdered him. They were British Intelligence officers. I want to know why they framed your daughter. I want to know what that had to do with my sister.'

Erik was silent. Thinking. Rethinking. Plotting a way forward in his mind. Testing it to see if there were any traps lying in wait for him.

I said, 'This is what you wanted, isn't it? Anderson asked me if Lena had given me anything. Well, she had. And you can have it. You need it. You want to clear her name, right?'

'You know about Lena?' Erik asked, his suspicions aroused.

'We knew when we met you,' Rebecca told him. 'It was in the press that a warrant had been issued for Lena's arrest. You didn't think we'd check something like that?'

'So then you know who has taken her.'

'We assume it's the British security services,' I said.

'Then your assumption is incomplete.'

He scowled at Shimmin again. He was still having trouble coming to terms with his presence.

'Can we trust this man?'

'You can trust him.'

Strange. Just an hour ago I wouldn't have vouched for Shimmin. I wouldn't have felt confident that I had even the vaguest understanding of his motives. Now all that had changed. I hated him for what he'd told me. For the ways he'd let my sister and my family down. But I trusted him, too. I trusted him because he was compromised. He stood to lose a lot from what he'd told me, not to mention the things he had and hadn't done back at my apartment. He could have played it by the book when we'd shown him the body in my kitchen. But instead he'd suggested an alternative approach. One that might allow him to make amends for what had happened up at Marine Drive and the impact it had had on my family and Jackie Teare.

Erik looked from Shimmin to Rebecca and back at me again. He was standing just inside the kitchen area of his suite and we were arranged around him in a rough semicircle. Crowding him. Penning him in.

He shot a look at Lukas. The muscles bunched in his jaw.

'Get up,' he snapped. 'Are you a dog? Get up and shut yourself in the bathroom. Turn on the taps. The shower. I don't want you to hear any of this. Understand?'

Lukas used his chin and knees to push himself to his feet. He leaned his weight on his good leg, a perplexed expression on his face.

'The bathroom,' Erik said. 'Go. Now. Lock the door behind you.'

Lukas hobbled across the vast carpet and through a door that was set into the wall behind an imposing dining table. He closed and bolted the door. A moment later, there was the squeak of a tap. The noise of running water. The hissing and creaking and banging of the pipes running through the walls in the room.

'We should sit down,' Erik said, gesturing to an extensive collection of sofas and armchairs. 'It is more civilised, yes?'

'You sit. We'll stand. I prefer it that way.'

Erik considered my words, then brushed by me and dropped heavily on to a leather couch. He propped his elbows on his knees and clutched his head in his hands, his fingers clawing into his sandy hair. The water hissed and gurgled in the room behind him.

Now I knew why he'd told Lukas to leave. He hadn't wanted his subordinate to see him like this.

'Do you know the work your sister was involved in?' Erik asked, once he'd decided where to begin.

I walked closer, until I was standing over him. Rebecca and Shimmin followed, keeping a little more distance.

'She worked for the security services,' I said.

'I mean specifically.'

I shook my head.

'She was proficient in close protection. Or so I was told. Six months ago she was assigned to protect Lena.'

'Protect her from what?'

'From threats to her life.' He cleared his long fringe from his eyes. Smoothed it back over his head. 'We were approached by representatives of British Intelligence. They told us that Lena was living in London. We knew this already, naturally. But they claimed her life was in danger.'

'From who?'

'From certain elements in Alex Tyler's campaign group. Disaffected people. People who did not approve of Tyler's relationship with my daughter. Your sister was to live with Lena on a temporary basis. Lena agreed to this. But only because she did not know I had been told.'

'But Lena's not British,' I said. 'Why was she given that level of help?'

'I told you once that I am a rich man. You remember? I said that there are people who wish to hurt me. People who would prefer to take what I have rather than build something of their own.'

'I remember.'

'This is true of governments, too. I am a powerful man.' He didn't look it right now. Slumped on the soft leather cushion. Tugging at the roots of his hair. 'I have oil. I *am* oil. This is a desirable commodity, yes? Essential to a country like the United Kingdom.'

'So what, your daughter gets protection in return for oil contracts?'

He pursed his lips. 'It is not really like this. It is more of an accommodation. An incentive. My company has a lot of oil. It sells some to the UK. They wish for us to continue to do this.'

'*OK.*'

'And so they wish to help me.'

'Right,' I said, and glanced towards Rebecca and Shimmin. Shimmin's brow was furrowed. He was concentrating hard. Rebecca was more relaxed, standing with her hands in her pockets. Like none of this was particularly new or surprising to her. 'So then what happened?'

'Two months ago, your sister contacted me. She did it directly. This was unusual. Normally, I would receive information through her superiors.' Erik clasped his hands together in front of his chest. 'She said that she'd received orders to drug Alex Tyler and my daughter. She'd been told that new threats had been made against Lena, and that Tyler was suspected of being involved. British Intelligence wished to extract Tyler to question him. Your sister was to facilitate this. But Lena and Alex were inseparable. They had not left Lena's apartment in many days. So your sister was told to drug them in order that Tyler might be extracted cleanly. Once they were sedated, she was to leave them alone in the apartment.'

Erik lowered his face. He watched his fingers knotting themselves together.

'Your sister was suspicious of this,' he said. 'She did not understand why she was supposed to leave. So once she had carried out her instructions, she pretended to walk away, but in fact she doubled back and remained close by. Because of this, she saw two men exit Lena's apartment. The men left *without* Alex Tyler. This is when she returned to the apartment and found that Tyler had been killed. She said she knew what had

413

happened. She claimed that Tyler had been murdered in such a way as to make it appear that Lena was the real killer.'

I thought of the video footage. If Laura had been suspicious, then I supposed it was possible that she'd set up a hidden camera to record events after she left the apartment. Later, when she reviewed the footage, she would have seen everything.

'Your sister believed that the men who killed Tyler worked for the security services. She could not explain this. She could not understand. But she was scared for Lena. And for herself. She decided to take Lena away, to hide her. Once they were safe, she would contact me again.'

'And when was that?'

'Three days later.'

'Long wait.'

He nodded eagerly. As if it had been much too long. 'During this time, I was contacted by somebody else. A man.'

'Who?'

'He would not give me his name. He told me that Alex Tyler's body had been found. He said that the police suspected my daughter of killing him. He said that unless I agreed to pay him twenty million euros, he would make sure that Lena was found and arrested and convicted. But he said that if I paid him, he could prove that Lena was innocent. He would show that Tyler was killed by somebody else.'

'Did he say who that somebody else was?'

'He did.' Erik pinned me with his eyes. 'Your sister.'

I felt the ground go soft beneath me. It took everything I had to stay on my feet.

'He said that she had purchased the vodka that was used to drug Lena and Alex. She paid for it in a local shop. They had

414

CCTV footage of this. They would claim that your sister had taken the tape from the shop, and that this was why it was not available right away. They said that they had records of your sister obtaining a sedative and cyanide. They also had two drinking glasses from Lena's apartment that were marked with the fingerprints of your sister, Lena and Alex. They would say that your sister abducted Lena and attempted to make it look as if Lena had killed Alex so that she could extort money from me.'

I thought I was beginning to understand what Laura had been afraid of. And why she'd come up with a solution of her own.

'Of course,' Erik said, 'I knew something this man did not. I knew what your sister had told me and that she would call me again. I knew she wanted to help us and that Lena trusted her. I told the man I would contact him once I'd had time to think.'

'And meanwhile Laura got in touch?' Rebecca asked.

'Yes.' Erik shrugged. 'Although to me she was Melanie Fleming. She called me and I told her what had happened. Anderson was on the call, too. Your sister was very clear. She said that we were being extorted by a rogue element in British Intelligence. The killing of Alex Tyler was not a government-sanctioned execution. She said that she did not know who she could trust, but she wished to help us. She wished to work with us to find out who was trying to harm my family.'

'Where did she call you from?'

'Here,' Erik said. 'This island. She told us that she had found somewhere to hide Lena. But she would need our help. We were to send two men to protect Lena when she was not there. When she was trying to find out who was attacking us.'

'So you sent Pieter and Lukas.'

Erik nodded in a half-hearted way. His skin had tightened across his face. It had taken on a waxy texture.

'Why not Anderson?'

'Because Anderson was more useful to me looking into what was happening. Trying to identify who was behind this plot to hurt us.'

'He wasn't working with Laura,' Rebecca said. 'No way would she risk that.'

'It was a parallel investigation.'

'It was a mistake,' Rebecca told him. 'I bet that's how they found out where Laura had hidden your daughter. I bet he screwed up. Pushed too far, or too fast, somewhere along the line. He wasn't nearly as good as you thought he was. I wouldn't be here if that was the case.'

'This is just speculation.'

Rebecca threw up her hand. 'Why didn't you just pay? Twenty million euros. And you're what, a billionaire? It seems to me that paying them would have been a pretty affordable way to keep your daughter out of prison.'

'I could not pay them. If I did, they would come back for more.'

'I doubt it. There weren't many people behind this thing. Three, maybe four. Two of them we know about already. They're the two who snatched Lena. And twenty million split three or four ways? That'd be more than enough for a comfortable retirement. They'd have no reason to come after you ever again. And that's not all. If you'd paid, Laura could have left this whole thing alone and got far away. She'd have made it, too.'

Erik glared at Rebecca. Then he turned slowly from her and

fixed his attention on me. 'Your sister wanted to help us. She saw that what was happening was wrong.'

I could believe that about Laura. She'd always had a strong sense of justice. Even when we were kids. She hated it if I cheated in a game we were playing. It had always been just about the surest way I knew to make her mad.

The one thing I still didn't understand was why she hadn't given Erik a copy of the memory stick long ago. My guess was that she was afraid the whole thing might be blamed on her. That Erik would be prepared to clear Lena's name at all costs. I guessed that was the reason she'd planned to fake her own death. Perhaps once she was secure in her new identity, she would have allowed the footage to be passed over.

Was I missing something else? I didn't know, and I couldn't think of any way to find out for sure. Whatever Laura's reasons might have been, I couldn't see how any of them could still apply. She was gone now. Untouchable. And so were at least two of the men who'd been part of the conspiracy. But Lena was still in danger. The risk to her had been multiplied many times over.

I closed my fist around the memory stick. Gave it a final goodbye clinch. Then I stepped forwards and passed it to Erik.

'Take it,' I said. 'Use it to get your daughter back. Do whatever you need to. The password is *Chester*.' I spelled it for him, just to be clear.

Erik nodded solemnly. I got the impression he wanted to say something, but the right words wouldn't come.

Shimmin shuffled his feet at my side. He checked his watch. Jabbed a finger towards Erik.

'All right,' he said. 'I've observed. And now I'm finished observing. And you're finished on the Isle of Man. I want you to

417

pack your things, Mr Zeeger. I want you and your boy in the bathroom to be off my island before the end of the day. And I don't want you coming back. Not with more thugs. Not with more questions. Not ever. Understand?'

'And Anderson?' Erik asked.

'Forget about Anderson. Forget you ever knew him.'

Chapter Fifty-eight

I got back to my place to find Mum and Dad huddled around the supine corpse in my kitchen. Dad was holding the man's slackened body up by his shoulders and Mum was wrapping a bandage around his head. She was wearing yellow rubber household gloves and pinching a safety pin between her lips. She mumbled a greeting to me around the pin, then used it to seal the bandage in place like she was administering first aid. The dressing was all bulked out. Another dressing was coiled around the man's left shoulder, where the first bullet had hit.

Next to them was a plastic shopping bag. The man's belongings and the Beretta had been packed inside. The bag was resting against a bucket of soapy water with a stiff-bristled brush floating in it. It dawned on me that Mum was planning to scrub the bloodstains from the walls and floors once we were gone. I didn't know what to say. I'd never expected to find my parents in my home, working together to clean up after a violent shooting.

'Hello, love,' Mum said. 'How did you get on with the Dutch gentleman?'

'Fine,' I mumbled. 'I think.'

'Take this, will you, son?' Dad passed me the shopping bag, then adjusted his grip under the man's armpits. 'Is your van open?' he asked.

I nodded, a little woozily.

'Mick still with you?'

'Yes, and he wants to talk to you.'

'Fine,' Dad said. 'Ask him to come and give me a hand lifting this guy downstairs, will you? I'll ride with him in the car. We'll follow you and Rebecca.'

*

Rebecca drove my van with exaggerated care, taking it slow and steady. She didn't want to attract unnecessary attention when we had a dead man sliding around in the back.

I was slumped against the passenger door, my head propped against the window. Traffic was light. The school run had finished half an hour ago. It was over an hour until the first office workers would conclude their day.

We were driving towards a bank of dark rain clouds sweeping in from the west of the island. The air was cooling and a stiff breeze was picking up, ruffling the red-and-white tarpaulin that had been wrapped around the heavy straw bales positioned along Peel Road in preparation for the TT. I glanced in the side mirror and caught a glimpse of the dead man's blue Vauxhall Insignia. It was impossible to tell how Dad was going to react to what Shimmin had to tell him. Even harder to know how Rebecca was going to respond to the questions I needed to ask.

'We have to talk,' I said.

Rebecca looked across at me. Above the dressing on her nose, the swelling around her eyes was beginning to dry. The blackened skin had started to crack. It looked more painful than ever.

'Sounds serious.'

Rebecca was relaxed. Composed. Like this was just an average day for her. An ordinary journey with an unremarkable cargo.

Which is exactly what was bothering me.

'You killed two men today.'

She pursed her lips. The top one was split. It was rimed in dried blood. 'And you think I should be more upset?'

'That's part of it.'

She spread her fingers on the steering wheel. 'It was them or us, Rob. When it comes down to it, I think I made the right decision.'

I shook my head. 'That's not entirely true.'

'You would have preferred it the other way around?'

'Of course not. But it wasn't like you say. Take Anderson. You broke his jaw with the first swing of that wrench. He was going down. But you swung back and thumped him a second time. And it was the second strike that killed him.'

'That's hindsight talking. I reacted on instinct. On adrenalin. And you're ignoring Lukas. If I hadn't hit Anderson the second time, he might not have flaked.'

I kept my eyes fixed on the road. A biker overtook us. He was going fast, but nowhere near racing speeds. There'd been times when I'd blitzed along this stretch of road so quick that the overhanging trees had merged into one long tunnel.

'That's what I told myself,' I said to Rebecca. 'That's how I justified it in my own mind. And maybe, as a one-off, I could have believed it.' I jerked my thumb over my shoulder, towards the rear of the van. 'But then there was this guy, too.'

'He was going to take your dad hostage. He had a gun.'

'He did. You're right. But your first shot punched through

his shoulder. The shoulder of his gun arm. That bullet would have caused lots of damage. Look at me. I barely fractured my scapula and my arm was next to useless even before Anderson whacked me. You knew what you were doing. You picked that shot. You picked it because you knew it would disable him.'

'So?'

'So it did. It disabled his left arm completely. He was a right-handed guy, but I'd already done something bad to his wrist. He was holding his gun in his left hand because of it. And when you shot him, he dropped his gun.'

'The way you tell it, I did a lot of thinking, in not very much time.'

'You did,' I said. 'You're good. Very good. I think you saw all that and more. You would have known that when he let go of his gun that was it for him. A busted right hand. A busted left shoulder. The threat was over. It was finished.'

Rebecca said nothing. She was indicating for the junction up ahead. The lights were green. She swooped left. Settled into the rhythm of the new road, climbing the gentle gradient towards Foxdale.

'The threat was over,' I said again, 'but you shot him in the back of the head. You chose your aim as carefully as you did the first time around. You made a choice. A second bullet. Just like the second swing of that wrench. You wanted them dead. Both of them. And I want to know why.'

Rebecca tipped her head from side to side, as if she was weighing my words. 'If your sister could have taken that second shot, do you think she'd have backed off?'

'Don't say that. Don't pretend you did it for Laura.'

'You're angry now?'

422

'Getting there.' And I was. I was fed up with having to battle to discover the truth. With only knowing fragments of the story. I'd found out more than I might have expected to learn about Laura. But now I wanted to know it all. Every angle. I didn't want there to be any dirty little secrets left lurking around.

Rebecca released a short, sharp breath. 'Alex Tyler,' she said, as if that was all the answer I needed.

'Go on.'

'He's my client.'

I stared at her. At her bruised and disfigured face.

She didn't look back at me. Didn't meet my gaze.

'*Was* my client, I suppose I should say. Had been for a couple of years.'

'I don't understand.'

Rebecca eased down on the brakes, slowing the van and turning on to the road that would take us up on to the hills. Past scrubland. Past woodland. Alongside the sloping expanse of spiky yellow gorse that lay ahead.

'Alex was from a wealthy family. Not in the same league as Erik Zeeger, but comfortably rich. His father was in pharmaceuticals and he liked to indulge Alex. That's how he could afford to be such an idealist. No time for a day job when you're busy saving the world.'

'And he hired you? Why?'

'Obvious reasons.' She shrugged. 'He was in a vulnerable position. Making trouble for a lot of powerful companies. Criticising governments. Working to keep the more radical elements of his organisation in check. Plus, he was dating Lena Zeeger, and he was aware that her father and some of the members of his own campaign group didn't exactly approve.'

'But why you? Why not the police?'

'Alex didn't trust the police. The way he saw it, they're a government agency. And he needed his threats monitored on a constant basis. Needed close protection every once in a while.'

Close protection. The role my sister had performed for Lena.

I finally understood how it all linked together.

'You were investigating his death,' I said. 'And you knew about my sister's involvement. That's why you were prepared to help my parents when Mum called you.'

Rebecca snatched a look at me. Gauging my mood. 'Alex called me when your sister was assigned to watch over Lena. He was worried. I vouched for her. Said she was reliable. Honest.'

'But then he was killed.'

Rebecca nodded. 'And there was no mention of your sister being involved. Only Lena. The finger was being pointed at her. I knew there was something up with that. And then when I heard your sister was dead, too . . .'

Her words trailed off, leaving me to follow my own thoughts. So that was why Rebecca had been so willing to believe me right from the beginning. It explained why she'd bought into my story about Lena's abduction. She must have suspected who the blonde girl was all along, and she'd have known to look for signs that the security services were involved. It also explained why she'd been so quick to question the idea that Laura had killed herself. To Rebecca's mind, either she was alive and hiding, or she'd been killed by the same people involved in Alex Tyler's death.

I guessed it might explain one more thing, too. Laura had

approached Rebecca's firm for a job. Rebecca had told me she thought that Laura was testing the water to see if she could ask for help. Now I realised it was more than that. She must have known that Rebecca worked for Alex. She must have been asking herself if she could tell Rebecca the truth. If, maybe, they could work together to uncover the conspiracy behind his death.

'That's why I didn't charge your parents a fee,' Rebecca said, interrupting my thoughts. 'I was already on Alex's retainer.'

'And what if my sister had been Alex's killer? What would you have done then?'

'But that was never going to happen. She was no assassin. She was naïve, maybe. But sometimes I think that's a good thing. Laura was like Alex. An idealist. A believer.'

'So you killed those men for Alex? For revenge?'

'Not Anderson.' She shook her head. 'You give me too much credit. I was scared. I overreacted.'

'And the guy in the back here? This John Menser?'

She gave me a level stare. 'I never worked alongside him, but I've heard of him. Long career. Distinguished record. And yes, I killed him. For Alex. And for your sister. I know how these things work, Rob. Your sister did, too. He was *inside* the system. He was part of some dirty little clique. The system would have protected him. This would have all been swept away and cleaned up. You might think that would be difficult but you'd be underestimating the people involved. They can't permit scandal. They've got no use for it. So justice had to come from the *outside*. From me.'

We skirted around South Barrule hill, ascending towards the tangle of dirty rain clouds, and Rebecca turned off on to the crumbling track where I'd had my bike accident. We trundled over a cattle grid. Drove past the dirt-bike track and the ruins of the old tin mines. Picked up the boundary of the wooded plantation.

I was quiet for a moment. Thinking. Then I said, 'You didn't do all this just because Alex Tyler was a client, did you? He must have meant more to you than that.'

'He did.' Rebecca swallowed. 'For a time. But the fact is he loved Lena. Truly, despite what her father might think. But I liked him, you're right. I liked him because there was a goodness inside him. Because he was a believer.' She sneaked a look at me. 'You remind me of him in that way.'

She pulled off the road on to the beginnings of the muddy track that led up to the cottage. The van rocked and rolled over the uneven ground. The gate ahead of us was closed. We stopped. The engine idled. The van shook and trembled.

A believer? Me? I couldn't see it. What had I ever believed in? Working hard? Doing a good job for my plumbing customers? Racing a motorbike as fast as I dared? Streaking along public roads at crazy speeds, trying to go faster than the next guy? Faster than my dad?

Rebecca saw the puzzle she'd carved into my face. She placed a hand on my knee.

'Your sister,' she said. 'You believed in her right from the beginning. You believed in her all the way through.'

She popped the door on the van and dropped down on to the compacted earth, leaving her words to bounce around my head. It was a kind sentiment. A touching remark. But I wasn't going to kid myself. I hadn't been that good a brother. Oh, I'd tried very hard to make up for it. I'd done all I could to make amends. But I already knew it would never be enough.

Rebecca approached the gate, hips swaying in her fitted jeans. She wedged the gate open against the tall grass to the side. Then she raised a hand to Dad and Shimmin, climbed back inside the cab and started up along the track.

It began to rain. Heavy drops struck the windscreen. They impacted on the glass and beaded and formed branching rivulets. Rebecca flicked on the wipers. They smeared the water. Blurred the trees outside. The massed clouds above.

The van bucked and pitched and yawed, the rainwater lashing the glass windows and the metal sidings like we were inside a boat on a rolling swell. We reached the familiar three-way fork in the track. Followed the middle path up over a muddy rise and deep inside the tree cover. The rain faded away, filtered out by the millions of pine needles above us. We neared the second gate. The aged slate. That name again. *Yn Dorraghys*. The murky green twilight that surrounded us was cold and damp and smothering. After today, I never wanted to come here again. I never wanted to set foot in this plantation as long as I lived.

Rebecca pulled over close to the cottage and Shimmin drew up alongside us in the dead man's car. The blue paintwork was slick with rain. He removed his handkerchief from his pocket and wiped down the car keys. He tucked the keys away behind the sun visor. Wiped down the visor and the steering wheel and anything else he might have touched. Used his handkerchief to force open his door. Hauled himself out and flipped up the collar of his mackintosh.

I looked across Rebecca's lap towards Dad. He was staring

blankly ahead, into the gloomy depths of the woods. He seemed disengaged. Unfocused. As if he'd zoned out of his surroundings altogether. I thought maybe he was picturing Laura up here. Running errands to the cottage. Checking on Lena. Trying to find a solution to a problem that was bigger than her.

His door opened. He stepped out. He straightened and gazed at Shimmin over the wet roof of the car. Then he walked around the bonnet and rested his hand on Shimmin's shoulder. Escorted him to the rear of the van, where Rebecca and I joined them.

Shimmin shook his head at me, his hands deep in the pockets of his mackintosh. He jutted his chin towards the cottage. 'Just wouldn't give it up, would you, lad?' He smiled flatly, almost in spite of himself. 'So I guess I was wrong. That acorn didn't fall so far from the tree, after all.'

'Mick filled me in,' Dad said, his words sounding gruff and hurried. 'About how you took control back in the hotel there. About how far you went for your sister.' His voice became pinched and he looked down, then cursed and blinked his eyes against tears. He stepped up to me and cupped his hand behind my neck and pulled my face to his chest. 'I'm proud of you, son,' he whispered, his breath in my ear. 'Laura would be, too. You didn't let her down.'

I didn't say anything back. I couldn't just at that moment. Instead I clinched him tight and nodded my head against his chest, and then I stepped away towards the van and opened one cargo door while Rebecca opened the other. Shimmin climbed up inside, pausing to rest a hand on my good shoulder, and then he heaved and slid the body of the man called Menser across the plywood floor. Dad grabbed the man's legs, together with the plastic shopping bag that contained his belongings, and shuffled backwards so that Shimmin could clamber down from the van, lifting the man by his forearms. His head swung loosely between Shimmin's knees.

'Wait,' Rebecca said. She delved inside the shopping bag. Removed the man's phone. 'OK,' she told them. 'You can go ahead now.'

I unlocked the front door to the cottage and stood aside as Dad and Shimmin carried the corpse along the hallway towards the kitchen. Shimmin rested while Dad opened the door into the garage. Then they grunted and heaved and I could hear the scuff of their shoes and the rasp of the man's body being dragged across the concrete floor to be laid out alongside Anderson.

'We can't just leave them here,' I said to Rebecca. 'Somebody will find them. They'll see this car. They'll poke around.'

'They won't be here long,' Rebecca replied. 'It's like I told you, the intelligence service is good at cleaning up after itself. I still have contacts there. People I can talk to. I'll tell them to come and tidy their mess. They won't waste time.'

'So this is it? This is where it ends?' And as I said it, I realised that it was finishing back where it had all started for me.

'No,' Rebecca said, in a voice that was hard with conviction. 'First, we need to be sure that Erik has secured Lena's release. Then I'm going to track her down and talk to her. We need to know what she knows.'

'And then?'

'There was somebody behind this whole thing. Someone on the inside.' She showed me the dead man's mobile phone. 'I'm going to find them. I'm going to trace everything back to the source and hold that person to account. For Alex. For Lena. And for your sister. Then I'm going to come back and tell you all about it. That's how you'll know that it's over.'

I looked at her then. Down into her damaged face. Through the savage bruising and the bloody cuts and deep inside her eyes. And I knew that in her heart she meant it. And I knew that in my heart I believed her. Believed *in* her.

And I reached for her hand and told her so.

Five weeks later

Amsterdam

Two men were sitting together in the lobby of the Hotel Pulitzer, a safe distance away from a window. The view through the window was impressive: a line of plane trees running the length of the Prinsengracht Canal; the honey-toned timber and polished brass of the hotel's personal boat, moored at the hotel's private jetty; the green enamel water, brightly lit by the early morning sun, showing a reflection of the terrace of thin brown houses with gabled roofs on the opposite side of the canal.

The two men weren't interested in the view. They were sitting on plush armchairs, facing one another across a low mahogany table. There was a glass vase on the table with a single white lily inside it. The lobby was very well appointed. It had been expensively refurbished. The floor was highly polished marble, laid in a chequerboard style. The walls were done out in half-timber cladding and sober beige wallpaper. There were multiple flower displays. Countless lamps. A lot of artwork and sculpture.

The lobby was filled with people. A concierge desk was located nearby. The reception counter beyond that. The staff on duty wore grey pinstripe suits with yellow neckerchiefs and ties. The porters and doormen were dressed in matching uniforms. There was a queue of guests waiting to check out. A family group was gathered around a city map close to the concierge. A selection of businessmen were reading complimentary newspapers.

The bustling lobby didn't concern the two men unduly. Their business was private, but most of the details had been negotiated over secured telephone lines during the preceding weeks. They kept their voices low. Their talk innocuous. Their tones civil.

The man on the left was a guest of the hotel. He was English, visiting from London, and he'd enjoyed a one-night stay in an executive room. Mid-fifties in age, he had salt-and-pepper hair clipped close to his scalp. He wore a blue Savile Row suit and black, hand-crafted Oxford brogues. His shirt was white. His tie was blue with diagonal red stripes. He had a lean, serious face. His every faculty was focused intently on his companion.

His companion was younger, taller, fitter. He was vastly more wealthy. He was wearing a pale-blue T-shirt over tan trousers. A brown linen jacket over the T-shirt. Open-toed sandals. His skin was tanned. His hair was sandy and grown longer than is customary for a respected businessman. He was Dutch. His name was Erik Zeeger.

The Englishman reached a hand inside his jacket. He removed an iPod with a set of earphones attached. The white cabling of the earphones was coiled around the iPod. The Englishman untangled it and switched the device on. The colour touchscreen lit up. He selected an audio file and slid the iPod across the table to Zeeger.

Erik held it in his hand and slipped one white earbud into his left ear. The recording was already playing. It featured two voices. His own and that of the Englishman sitting opposite him. He remembered the conversation. It was the one he'd expected to hear. It had taken place just over seven months ago.

On the recording, the Englishman was advising Erik about

434

the level of protection the British security services could offer his daughter during her time in England. The meeting had been requested by Erik. He'd been promised access to a man near the top of the organisation. Now that man – the man currently sitting opposite him – was detailing the hazards that Erik should be concerned by. He was focusing on the dangers created by Lena's association with Alex Tyler. The direct risk from Tyler himself. The threats posed by the more extreme factions of the environmental campaign group Tyler headed up.

And that was when Erik had interrupted the man. That was when the frustration of seeing Lena slip away from him over the course of her adult life had finally reached a head. He had looked the man in the eye and asked the question that he'd been whispering to himself in the small hours of the night, whenever sleep evaded him.

'Can you kill Alex Tyler?'

Five words. Five simple words with the power to change everything for him. The power to break the spell Tyler had cast over his daughter. The power to reunite him with Lena.

The Englishman had stayed calm. He'd remained silent. Then he'd nodded and begun to explain that it was possible, but that it would be expensive. And they would have to be very careful. They would need to keep the agreement to themselves. The arrangement would have no official sanction. Erik could tell no one. Not even his closest adviser or his most trusted friend.

Erik had complied. A fee had been agreed. The Englishman had amassed a team and Tyler had been killed.

But Erik had learned the hard way that those five simple words had the power to turn around and bite him.

The Englishman had duped him. He'd organised Tyler's

death, but he'd framed Lena for the crime. He'd requested more money in order to clear her name.

His plan would have succeeded but for the female operative who'd been assigned to protect Lena. Melanie Fleming (no, Laura Hale) hadn't been part of the Englishman's conspiracy. She'd worked hard to counter it. Through her efforts and those of her brother, Erik had the evidence necessary to clear Lena's name. Soon after leaving the Isle of Man, Erik made the appropriate call and a few short hours later the British police cancelled the warrant for Lena's arrest. They announced that they were investigating new and unspecified avenues.

Erik had waited two days until Lena contacted him. Her telephone call was short. She claimed to have freed herself from her captors, though he didn't believe it. She offered him no thanks, no gratitude. She simply informed him that she was staying with friends, and then she cut the connection.

And that should have been it. Stalemate. A reasonable, if imperfect, conclusion.

Until the Englishman called back and announced that he had a recording of their original meeting. Until he said that he would make it his mission to find Lena, somewhere, some time, and prove to her that her lover had been killed at her father's request. Until he suggested that they should meet in Amsterdam to negotiate a mutually satisfactory outcome.

Erik paused the recording. Plucked the earphone free. He looked across the coffee table at the Englishman. Met his cool, hard eyes. His complacent stare.

'Twenty million euros,' the Englishman said. 'That's the price we originally agreed. That's the price you'll pay me now.'

Erik nodded. Fixed a smile to his face that he didn't really feel.

'Then we must go to my bank. I will have my driver bring my car around.'

*

It shouldn't have been so easy, but it was.

Erik Zeeger's executive car pulled up outside the entrance to the hotel. It was a BMW 7 Series saloon in Titanium Silver with tinted glass and alloy wheels. The guy in the front passenger seat was a big fan of the colour. That was why he'd looked it up in the owner's manual in the hand-stitched leather folder he'd found inside the glove box. He liked the name even better. *Titanium Silver*. It sounded like a secret weapon. Or a superhero.

The guy in the front passenger seat liked pretty much everything about the car. He liked the supple leather seats. The generous leg space. The fresh, new car smell. Sure, he was an eco campaigner. An anarchist, some would argue. But now that he found himself inside the BMW, he couldn't ignore the luxury feel and the quality finish.

The driver was less impressed. He was a green activist to his core, Alex Tyler's most trusted lieutenant, but he was also nervous, and the way his partner was flicking through the owner's manual had been annoying the hell out of him. He checked his mirrors for other vehicles, but there was only a passing cyclist on an old-fashioned bicycle. No police. Nothing to suggest that Erik Zeeger's real driver had been found in the rubbish-strewn alley where they'd left him gagged and bound.

A sun-bleached red carpet led towards the front of the hotel.

A uniformed doorman stood to one side of the automatic re-volving doors, between symmetrical topiary.

If it wasn't for the BMW's tinted privacy glass, the two men might have aroused suspicion. The guy in the front passenger seat wore his hair in a long pony-tail beneath a paisley head-scarf. He had a full beard over pimpled skin. The driver had on a military-style shirt in khaki green. The sleeves had been rolled up on his swollen biceps, revealing a Celtic tattoo. His ear was pierced in seven different ways. There was a ring in his nose. Not your average BMW passengers. Not your typical em-ployees of a billionaire businessman.

Erik Zeeger must have seen his car from inside the lobby. He came out through the conventional door to the side of the revolving glass. A second man followed. The driver recog-nised him. He was the man from the photograph they'd been provided with.

Zeeger walked around the back of the car to the rear door located behind the driver. His companion approached from the passenger side. They opened their doors at the exact same moment. Dropped inside together. Hauled their doors closed.

That was when the man in the front passenger seat swivelled and pointed his gun at them. He nudged the central-locking control with his free hand. Since he'd earlier engaged the child safety locks on the rear doors, they were now impossible to open from the inside. And that, he told the driver as they glided away from the front of the hotel, was the benefit of consulting the owner's manual.

*

The place they'd rented was a houseboat – a traditional Dutch barge. It was moored on the Amstel River, six miles outside the city. Another barge was tied up nearby. It was currently unoccupied.

The houseboat had been Lena's idea. She had firsthand knowledge of how disorienting it could be to be held in the bowels of a ship. And Rebecca could appreciate the benefits. Fitted with the right locks, the cabins below deck were as good as prison cells. The boat was in an isolated spot, where screams and shouts wouldn't be heard. And then there was the river. It was deep and very dark. Perfect for hiding evidence. Ideal for submerging a body.

Rebecca waited alone in the aft lounge. She listened to the sound of movement below deck. Footsteps. Barked commands. Muted responses. The thud of doors being closed. The *snick* of locks being turned and bolts being driven home.

Then nothing at all until the two activists entered the room. The pimply one with the pony-tail came first. He was followed by the broad, muscular one in the khaki shirt with the multiple piercings. The men were carrying the belongings they'd taken from their prisoners. They set the items down on a fold-out table. Wallets and phones. A pair of highly polished brogues. A pair of sandals. One black belt. One tan. An iPod.

Rebecca sorted through the collection. She parted the wallets and checked all of the compartments. She accessed the phones and cycled through the call logs and message records. She split the phones open. Removed the batteries and snapped the sim cards in half. Stacked the weightless handsets to one side. She reached for the iPod. It contained a single audio file. Nothing else. No music or videos or photographs or games.

Rebecca plucked the earphone jack out of the iPod and connected the device to some portable speakers. She hit play on the audio file and watched the faces of the two men as they listened to the recorded conversation between the Englishman and Erik Zeeger.

The recording was less than three minutes in duration. In three minutes, Rebecca saw the long weeks of talking and planning and preparing and speculating transformed into an unavoidable outcome.

She nodded to the guy with the piercings. He fixed his eyes on her and removed the automatic pistol she'd given him from the back of his jeans. The gun was in perfect working order. Rebecca had made sure of that. She'd stripped, oiled and reassembled it personally, checking the mechanism very carefully. That was important. They didn't want any mistakes. No distractions whatsoever.

The two men left the room without another word. The guy with the pony-tail placed a reassuring hand on his companion's shoulder.

Rebecca set the iPod down on the table among the other items. She paced to the opposite side of the boat. Glanced outside through the brass porthole, checking that the canal path was deserted. She listened intently. To the creaking of the boat. The lapping of the water against the tarred hull. The sound of footfalls below deck. The *thunk* and *snick* of the bolt being withdrawn and the lock being turned. A long pause. Enough for a shred of doubt to creep in. Then a loud bang. An echoing *boom*. It started in the tiny downstairs cabin, reverberated against the metal framework, funnelled up from below deck and raced out to dissipate in the late-afternoon calm.

The Englishman was dead. Rebecca was sure of that now. One shot. One clap of fire. She asked herself if the punishment had been too lenient, and the answer was probably yes.

But then, there was balance in all things.

She reached for the baseball bat propped against the curved lounge wall. Ran her hand along the swollen shaft. The smooth, varnished timber. Once the men had returned with the gun, she'd hand the bat to the muscular activist. No point giving it to the weedy guy. Then she'd take the iPod and drive the few kilometres to her rendezvous with Lena.

This was something they'd agreed on. No way could Lena listen to her father suffer. And in truth, it wasn't something Rebecca would relish. The sound of the bat striking flesh and bone would be likely to bring back painful memories, flashes of agony that no amount of facial surgery and healing would ever be able to erase.

But also, in the end, it would bring some form of resolution. And if Erik agreed to their wishes quickly, his suffering would be short. He'd be allowed to live. He had to, if he was going to make good on the promise they'd extract from him. An endowment to environmental causes, given in the name of Alex Tyler and Laura Hale. Twenty million euros ought to be a reasonable starting point, just to begin with. It was a fee he'd grown comfortable with before.

Rebecca tightened her grip on the bat and wondered how she'd explain it all to Rob. If she ever could. But then, there was balance in all things. And she'd really like to try.

Acknowledgements

Grateful thanks to:

Adrian Cain, Debbie Cormode, Allison Ewan, Allan Guthrie, Katrina Hands, Dr Lucy Hanington, Bob Harrison, Stuart MacBride, Donna Moore, Greg Norton, Juan Norton, Gavin Quiggin, Zoë Sharp and her husband Andy, Mum and Dad, my wife, Jo, our dog, Maisie (the inspiration for Rocky), my US agent, Valerie Borchardt, and all at Sheil Land Associates, Faber and Faber and St Martin's Press.